continued . . .

Novels by Christina Dodd
Danger in a Red Dress
Thigh High
Tongue in Chic
Trouble in High Heels
In Bed with the Duke

Novels in the Darkness Chosen Series
Scent of Darkness
Touch of Darkness
Into the Shadow
Into the Flame

Novels in the Chosen Ones Series
Storm of Visions
Storm of Shadows
Chains of Ice

CHRISTINA DODD

CHAINS of FIRE

THE
CHOSEN
ONES

A SIGNET SELECT BOOK

SIGNET SELECT
Published by New American Library, a division of
Penguin Group (USA) Inc., 375 Hudson Street,
New York, New York 10014, USA
Penguin Group (Canada), 90 Eglinton Avenue East, Suite 700, Toronto,
Ontario M4P 2Y3, Canada (a division of Pearson Penguin Canada Inc.)
Penguin Books Ltd., 80 Strand, London WC2R 0RL, England
Penguin Ireland, 25 St. Stephen's Green, Dublin 2,
Ireland (a division of Penguin Books Ltd.)
Penguin Group (Australia), 250 Camberwell Road, Camberwell, Victoria 3124,
Australia (a division of Pearson Australia Group Pty. Ltd.)
Penguin Books India Pvt. Ltd., 11 Community Centre, Panchsheel Park,
New Delhi - 110 017, India
Penguin Group (NZ), 67 Apollo Drive, Rosedale, North Shore 0632,
New Zealand (a division of Pearson New Zealand Ltd.)
Penguin Books (South Africa) (Pty.) Ltd., 24 Sturdee Avenue,
Rosebank, Johannesburg 2196, South Africa

Penguin Books Ltd., Registered Offices:
80 Strand, London WC2R 0RL, England

First published by Signet, an imprint of New American Library,
a division of Penguin Group (USA) Inc.

First Printing, September 2010

Copyright © Christina Dodd, 2010
All rights reserved

SIGNET SELECT and logo are trademarks of Penguin Group (USA) Inc.

Printed in the United States of America

ISBN-13: 978-1-61664-851-0

For the inimitable Eloisa James,
who is always there with a translation,
a scandalous piece of gossip,
and in my moment of desperation,
Italian glass Christmas trees.
Thank you for your wit and charm,
and most of all,
thank you for your warm and lasting friendship.

ACKNOWLEDGMENTS

Leslie Gelbman, Kara Welsh, and Claire Zion, my appreciation for your constant support. Kerry Donovan, we're a great editing team, but we should consider going into show business. More appreciation to NAL's art department, led by Anthony Ramondo, for the bright and glorious Chosen Ones covers. Rick Pascocello, head of marketing and video brilliance, thank you! Thanks to the publicity department with my special people, Craig Burke and Jodi Rosoff. My thanks to the production department, and of course, a special thank-you to the spectacular Penguin sales department: Norman Lidofsky, Don Redpath, Sharon Gamboa, Don Rieck, Richasrd Adamonis, and Trish Weyenberg. You are the best!

THE LEGEND

"Long ago, when the world was young . . ." a gorgeous and vain woman abandoned her children, a boy and a girl—twins with hideous birthmarks—to the river and the forest to meet their deaths. Instead, they became the first of the Abandoned Ones, gifted with abilities that could save the world . . . or end it.

The boy was marked with a sinister tattoo and given the gift of fire, and he gathered others around him with similar gifts to become the Chosen Ones—seven men and women who became a powerful force of light in a dark world.

The girl had the mark of an eye on the palm of her hand and became a seer. She turned to the devil, gathering six other gifted ones to her. They became the Others, bringing darkness and death to the world.

The Chosen Ones and the Others have fought for centuries for the hearts and souls of the Abandoned Ones.

That battle goes on today . . . in New York City and around the world.

THE SEVEN CHOSEN

❖ **Jacqueline Vargha:** Gifted with the ability to see the future and an eye on her palm to prove it. With Caleb D'Angelo at her side, Jacqueline must take her adopted mother's place as chief seer to the Chosen Ones.

❖ **Aaron Eagle:** Raised by Native Americans and marked with the wings of an angel, Aaron has a talent for melting into the shadows that surround him. But he can only be truly whole once prim and proper librarian Rosamund Hall enters his life.

❖ **Charisma Fangorn:** A young Goth with tattoos on her wrists and the gift of hearing the earth song in crystals and stones.

❖ **Isabelle Mason:** One of the upper-class Boston Masons, Isabelle is a physical empath with the ability to absorb the pain of others and heal them.

❖ **Samuel Faa:** A lawyer with the ability to control minds; he has a mysterious connection to Isabelle.

❖ **Aleksandr Wilder:** Aleksandr is a college student; he has no mark, no discernible gift, and is blessed with a loving family, yet he is drafted into the Chosen Ones because of his connection to the Wilder family of Washington State (from the Darkness Chosen series).

❖ **John Powell:** Former member of Gary White's team, he is famous for the strength and power he wields . . . as well as for the dark and dreadful secret that torments him and has driven him into exile.

FRIENDS AND ENEMIES
OF THE CHOSEN ONES

- ❖ **Irving Shea:** The ninety-plus-year-old retired director of the Gypsy Travel Agency and the owner of the mansion the Chosen Ones now use as headquarters.

- ❖ **Martha:** Dedicated Gypsy servant of the Chosen Ones.

- ❖ **McKenna:** Scottish butler, chauffeur, and aide to Mr. Irving Shea.

- ❖ **Vidar Davidov:** Owner of Davidov's Pub located deep in the tunnels under New York City, where the Chosen hang out. Davidov sports an inexplicable knowledge about the Chosen Ones and their descendants.

- ❖ **Osgood:** The mastermind behind the destruction of the Gypsy Travel Agency, and the devilish director of the Others.

Chapter 1

Zurich, Switzerland

Martha's information about the security in the Swiss bank was dated. Samuel went through not two metal detectors, but five, and two full-body scans. The guards politely requested he remove his shoes, and they examined them with a machine that had so many warnings printed on its side and made such ominous noises Samuel wanted to cover his balls or step behind a lead wall or something.

He intended to have children someday.

He was contemplating the lineup of shoes from the poor schmucks who didn't get theirs returned to them when the guards very politely requested his pen, his belt, his tie clip, and his watch. They placed them in a safety-deposit box, had him lock them inside, and gave him the key.

Then they frisked him.

The Swiss took their security very, very seriously.

Don't make a joke. Don't mess up now.

He heard the woman so clearly, he turned to see where she stood.

But she wasn't here. She was in New York, in a hospital, sitting at Irving Shea's bedside, smelling of cigarettes and passing on Irving's instructions in that freaking spooky telepathic way of hers. Dina was in her sixties, short, bitter . . . and a mind-speaker, one of the most talented ever born.

She was also one of the Others. She held an old and towering grudge against Irving, and why any of them were trusting her, Samuel didn't know. Why *he* was trusting her, he didn't know. If he got caught trying to pull this off, *he'd* be the one rotting in a Swiss jail for the rest of his life.

Life's full of tough choices, isn't it? that rough female voice asked.

"Damn it!" he said.

The guards looked up inquiringly.

"Stubbed my toe," he explained.

Inside his head, Dina laughed.

He didn't react to her amusement, but only because he knew cameras followed his every move, and somewhere a computer was analyzing his features, looking for his resemblance to any known criminal.

Not that the Swiss banks didn't allow known criminals to hold accounts in their hallowed vaults, but they liked to make sure those criminals didn't have designs on other criminals' money.

He knew how this operation was supposed to work. They—the Chosen Ones, aided and abetted by Martha, their Gypsy Travel Agency adviser—had set up Samuel's schedule. He was to go into the bank, talk to the bank president (the bank president and no one else, Martha warned), and convince him to open the Gypsy Travel Agency accounts, frozen since the explosion of the headquarters almost three years before. Because with Irving in the hospital and deemed incompetent by his doctors, the Chosen Ones' funds had dried up and they were in danger of losing their shirts, not to mention Irving's mansion and their ability to perform the task for which they had been recruited—rescuing abandoned children from the Others.

Samuel couldn't carry a wire or have any mechanical way to remain in touch with the Chosen Ones, so he had memorized script after script of what to say, what to do, whom he might meet, plus the Chosen would occasionally give him a surprise setup and have him wing it. He was a natural. As a child, he'd learned to be fast on his feet—it was a matter of survival—and law school had honed his talents.

Mostly, he had been picked for this mission because he was a mind controller.

He found it a useful talent for a lawyer.

He had also used it to destroy his own happiness. Because yes, everyone knew he was blunt to the point of rudeness, abrasive, impatient with fools, and he was fine with all that.

But he was also a monumentally stupid ass.

That hadn't turned out so well for him.

When all of the Chosen Ones had been satisfied he was as prepared as he could be and he was on the way to the airport to catch his flight to Switzerland, he went to the hospital to say good-bye to Irving . . . and Dina was there.

The old man struggled to communicate in words, but he made himself clear in other ways—through Dina's interpretation, through the few instructions he could manage aloud, and with gestures that indicated approval or rejection. Irving intended that she help Samuel with little reminders.

Samuel thought it was a bad idea.

Dina thought it was a bad idea.

But for some reason, Irving was intent on getting his way. He was ninety-four. He had fallen down the stairs, broken his hip and his shoulder, started rehab, had a small stroke, spent months in the hospital . . . and he was insistent on this point.

Samuel gave in.

Because it isn't like you have a choice. If I want to talk in your head, I will. I know the way.

Knock it off. Samuel accepted his shoes back from the guard, put them on, and walked directly into the elevator. *You're a mind speaker, not a mind reader.*

She was quiet for so long, he began to relax, thinking she hadn't heard him.

Then she said, *You're a strong receptor.*

It's not like I have a choice here, he snapped back.

You're a strong sender, too, probably part of your gift.

And I don't know why, but . . . if I listen, I can hear your thoughts. Sometimes. Lately my abilities seem to have expanded.

Samuel knew what was going on, and that comprehension made him want to thump his head against the stainless-steel walls of the elevator. He would have, too, except he knew the guards who observed him on the cameras would flag that behavior and escort him back down to the lobby and out the door.

Dina was not only one of the Others, the enemy of the Chosen Ones. She also shared a past with Irving. A pretty intense past, if the way those two acted proved anything. So she might be wicked. She might be cruel. She might have been stalking every single Chosen for the past two and a half years, delivering cryptic warnings into their minds and scaring the crap out of them. But because of the prophecy that affected the Chosen Ones—when a Chosen sacrificed his or her greatest fear for true love, that love expanded his or her gifts in ways no one could have foreseen—her talents had expanded.

Not that she was Chosen. Quite the opposite. But the Chosen Ones and the Others were flip sides of the same coin. All had been abandoned as infants. All had been given gifts. Some used them for good. Some for evil.

If Samuel needed proof that Dina loved Irving, this assistance was it.

But still it didn't mean she wasn't going to betray Samuel. Women had a history of betraying him.

Or rather . . . one woman.

Never mind her, Dina said in his mind. *You can worry about her later.*

If I live through this.

There is that.

He grinned.

If Dina wasn't a lying, cheating, treacherous minion of the devil, he would almost like her.

She reminded him of himself: rude, conflicted . . . and tainted. Tainted by birth, tainted by living, tainted by dark blemishes on their souls.

No matter what they did, no matter what reparations they made, how honorably they behaved . . . they could never escape themselves.

Chapter 2

The elevator doors opened and a man stood there, six-foot-six, fit, fair and blond, with long arms, broad shoulders, and no neck. Adelbrecht Wagner, bank president, looked like a billboard advertising the Aryan Nations.

Two guards stood behind him.

Samuel didn't know what purpose they accomplished. He wasn't going to attack Wagner. The guy looked like he could crush Samuel with one fist.

Wagner extended his hand. In precise, German-accented English, he said, "Mr. Faa, how good to meet you. I'm Adelbrecht Wagner. We haven't seen anyone from the Gypsy Travel Agency for several years. In fact, we had heard reports that an explosion at their headquarters had killed everyone on their board."

Samuel shook hands, did the male dominance thing by squeezing too hard and making sure his hand remained on top, and put on his solemn face. "Did you?

The explosion was a tragedy that deeply affected our organization." It was a nonanswer, one worked out ahead of time and given Irving's nod of approval.

Samuel had learned a few things about one-upmanship, and he understood Irving's position about this operation.

Just in case he didn't remember, Dina repeated the instructions. *Say as little as possible. Don't explain yourself. Don't defend yourself. Make it clear from the beginning you are the man in charge.*

Yeah, thanks.

Samuel strode beside Wagner down the short corridor to his office and was ushered inside. The place was immense, luxurious, and windowless.

The guards took up their positions at the sides of the entrance. Wagner closed the doors, and they gave a *thunk* that all too clearly proved they were reinforced with metal.

Wagner's office was a vault, protecting the bank president, everything he represented and everything he knew.

Samuel would either succeed here or die in prison.

No pressure.

Samuel didn't even know who thought it first.

Pulling a two-by-two slip of yellow paper out of his inside pocket, he placed it on the desk in front of Wagner. "I need you to transfer control of the Gypsy Travel Agency accounts to this address."

Wagner didn't bother to glance down. "Without the necessary legal documents, I'm afraid that's impossible."

Which was exactly what Samuel expected him to say. So he removed the formidable set of papers from his manila envelope and placed them beside the slip with the address for Wagner's perusal. "The originals of the documents we sent ahead."

"Without the signatures of at least three of the Gypsy Travel Agency board members, I'm afraid this is impossible."

"As you know, the whole board is deceased. As a former board member and former CEO, Irving Shea—"

"Has been declared incompetent and is therefore not a legal signer."

Crap. Wagner knew it all.

They were getting nowhere.

So Samuel used his mind to take control of Wagner's thoughts.

To his surprise, his intention skidded off as if Wagner's mind were Teflon protected.

Crap.

What's wrong? Dina asked.

I can't reach him. In a reasonable tone of voice, Samuel said, "But surely you're not saying you intend to keep these not-inconsiderable accounts in your bank forever?" He reached out again, this time with more force.

Wagner appeared to be oblivious. "Perhaps you're not aware, but we have hundreds of unclaimed accounts which will never be opened because the owners have lost their minds, forgotten their passwords, or died. There are fortunes that haven't been touched for over a hundred years."

Samuel took a breath, looked straight into Wagner's eyes, and concentrated.

Wagner stared at him. "Will there be anything else?"

Samuel couldn't believe it. This had never happened before. He had never failed.

Dina snapped, *What is this? Mind-control dysfunction?*

Is he one of you? Samuel snapped back.

Sarcastically: *I don't know. I'm not personally acquainted with every miscreant in the organization.*

He knew it. He knew Dina would betray them.

But I don't think so. Samuel could almost hear her tapping her fingers on the table. *He could be an undiscovered talent, hired for exactly this capacity.*

"Mr. Faa?" Wagner stood. "I believe we've concluded our business."

Samuel sent another shot at Wagner's mind.

The mind was locked tight as a vacuum cylinder.

Wagner said, "In fact, I believe the Swiss police are waiting for you in the lobby below. They want to question you about your knowledge of and intentions for these particular accounts."

A cold sweat trickled down Samuel's spine.

Urgently, Dina said, *I can distract him. Touch him. Touch him!*

Samuel stood, extended his hand, and when his flesh touched Wagner's, he heard Dina's voice say, *Look out!*

Somehow the contact of their hands opened Wagner's brain to Dina, and Wagner heard her voice, too.

His surprise gave Samuel his chance.

Samuel slammed a command into Wagner's head. *Do what I tell you.*

Wagner blinked at him. "I apologize. I thought I heard a woman's voice."

"A woman?" Samuel raised his eyebrows as if amazed.

"A woman's deep voice, hoarse, a smoker's voice . . ."

"You've been working too hard," Samuel said sympathetically.

"Yes. A temporary distraction." Wagner blinked again, his defenses broken, his mind bending to Samuel's will. "What was it you wanted?"

Samuel instructed him without words. *Transfer control of the Gypsy Travel Agency funds to the account on that paper.*

"I remember. You wanted me to transfer the Gypsy Travel Agency funds to this account." Wagner indicated the yellow paper and sat down at his desk.

Samuel stood, barely breathing, as Wagner typed on his computer, checked the numbers on the paper, then pushed SEND.

Wagner looked up. "That's that. Is there anything else you require?"

"Call off the police downstairs."

Samuel heard Dina say, *It is done.*

Control of the funds had been transferred into the control of John Powell, the trustworthy leader of the Chosen Ones.

Samuel wanted to laugh in triumph. How he had enjoyed this!

Instead he spoke with cool composure. "There's nothing more I require."

Maybe a good stiff drink, Dina suggested.

"Very good. It's been a pleasure doing business with you." Wagner stood again.

Samuel walked toward the door. "It's been a pleasure doing business with you, also."

"I trust now that your business is concluded, you'll have a chance to experience our magnificent skiing. It has been a record year for snow." Wagner pressed the button on the wall. The doors swung open. "I've lived here twenty years, and I've never seen powder this deep."

They walked into the corridor and toward the elevator. The guards fell in behind them.

"Tonight I'm going to Monastère for the party benefitting the World Children's Literacy Foundation; then, alas, tomorrow I must return to New York," Samuel said.

"Probably just as well. There's a storm coming in. Just wind, they're saying, but that always makes the slopes dangerous. Avalanche weather, you know."

Samuel didn't know, but he smiled and nodded, wanting nothing more than to clear out of here before Wagner realized what had been done and why. "That's it, then."

They shook hands.

The guard punched the elevator button.

The doors opened and Samuel stepped in.

The doors started to close—and right before they snapped shut, Wagner stuck his arm in.

The doors reopened.

"We should probably clarify one matter." Wagner frowned.

Samuel's heart stopped.

Wagner asked, "Will someone else return to claim the contents of the safety-deposit box?"

Samuel stepped back out of the elevator. "The safety-deposit box?"

Chapter 3

Monastère, Switzerland

At first Isabelle Mason thought the bump from behind was an accident. The ballroom was, after all, full of guests wearing designer clothing, expensive jewelry, and subtle colognes, all ostensibly to support the World Children's Literacy Foundation.

Then a maternal hand slid its way around Isabelle's waist, and in perfectly accented French, Patricia Mason asked, "Ambassador, would you forgive me if I steal my daughter away for a moment? I need her help."

Isabelle glanced around to find her mother, thin and elegant, standing at her side, and she tried not to look surprised at the interruption. Because for all Patricia's graceful, fragile appearance, Isabelle knew her mother was perfectly capable of directing this party, auditing the charity's books, and arranging next year's vacation in Aspen all at the same time. She most certainly did not require Isabelle's help.

Michel Moreau managed to contain his skepticism, also; Patricia Mason was famed for her competence. Instead he kissed Isabelle's fingers, a lingering yet respectful kiss the French performed so expertly. He bowed to Patricia Mason. "Madam, your party is, as always, a tribute to charity and elegance." With a smile, he made his way toward the buffet, leaving Patricia and Isabelle alone in the midst of the crowd.

For all of her urgency, Patricia took a moment to stare after the balding, stylish Moreau. "Such a charming man. Such aristocratic lineage. Why couldn't you have married him?"

Isabelle did not sigh. There was no point. She'd heard it all before, and until she married the proper man, she would continue to hear it. "Because Michel is twice my age. And half my height. And he's already married."

"I suppose. But—"

"Mother, I can't believe that's why you interrupted our conversation. He was about to get out his checkbook to make a sizable donation to the foundation."

"I'm sorry, dear." Patricia patted Isabelle's hand. "You do make the gentlemen loosen their purse strings in a formidable way."

"I learned from the best. Now—what's wrong?"

Recalled to her grievance, Patricia said, "Look. There!"

Something had put an edge to her mother's voice, so Isabelle scanned the ballroom.

The Masons' nineteenth-century château had been decorated with the same subtle elegance that marked her mother as a leader of society in Europe and the States. Flowers had been flown in from the Riviera to fill tall Tiffany vases. The walls glowed with carefully restored Renaissance murals, and rich metallic gold gilded the arched ceilings. The quartet played quiet background music; in about an hour, they would strip off their coats and ties and make the move to dance music, taking the party to its next stage.

Society had traveled by plane and train, then on icy roads up to the tiny, exclusive village for the privilege of dancing, eating, and, most important, being *seen* at one of Patricia's exquisite charity events. Young women wore Kane and Zac Posen; older women wore Dior and Prada. Patricia herself wore a conservative black satin Chanel evening gown; she preached the classics.

Isabelle had learned from her mother, and wore Versace, a simple pale gold silk that clung in all the right places and gave her bosom (so the designer said) "height."

Now, with nothing visibly wrong with the flowers, the atmosphere, or the people, Isabelle said, "Mother, I really don't see—" Then the crowd parted and gave her a clear view of Senator Noah Noble. "Him? It's okay, Mother; he's merely my ex-fiancé, and since the breakup we've met amicably if not fondly."

"Not *him*. I invited *him*." Patricia's voice changed to warm interest. "Although if you haven't heard, he and his wife have just secured a divorce."

Isabelle allowed herself a single, spiteful smile. "Did they? Good. I hope she took him for everything and ruined his political career in the process."

"Hm."

"Mother, do you not remember the scene he made when he broke our engagement?"

"Yes, yes. But you were going to break the engagement yourself!"

"Proving I have good instincts about men."

"Not necessarily." Patricia used her clasp on Isabelle's arm to direct her. "What I want to know is— what is *he* doing here?"

Isabelle pretended to search with her gaze, but she had caught sight of him. Now she knew who had her mother in an uproar.

"There," Patricia said. "Speaking to Prince Saber. It's *Samuel Faa*."

"Oh. Him." Isabelle infused her voice with boredom. "I invited him."

"You? You?" Patricia hustled Isabelle toward a curtained alcove and in a hushed voice said, "But, darling—the gossip!"

"What gossip? Mother, we haven't been together for over . . . what? . . . Five years? Six years?"

"Five years, and everyone remembers."

"Few *knew*, and only you would care. Half the people in here are ex-lovers of the other half." Isabelle watched her mother struggle with the universal truth that among the wealthy, sex was entertainment.

"It's true. But I don't have to like it."

Samuel wore his tuxedo with a flair that made women turn and look, some in disdain—the outfit was so obviously not his natural state—and some in pure, absolute lust. He looked like the kind of man who could drink too much, make love all night, steal the Hope Diamond from the Smithsonian, and do it all without breaking a sweat. With his black hair and swarthy skin, he was clearly Gypsy. She would call him Romany, but there was nothing politically correct about Samuel. Ever.

Right now he was chatting up Lady Winstead, a female old enough that she shouldn't be blushing under his regard.

But she was.

Because Samuel knew the secret of charm; when he used those dark brown eyes on a woman, she had his full attention—and she knew it.

Isabelle remembered the force of his charm all too well. More than once in her life, she had been that woman, melting under his regard.

But she was wiser now. She knew what it meant when he concentrated on her. It never ended well.

The man was the kind of lawyer who gave the law profession its bad reputation. He barely acknowledged the high moral standards demanded of the Chosen Ones. He was gifted with a capital "G"—a mind controller, totally without scruples.

When they had been together, she'd heard him say, many times, that the end justified the means.

She simply hadn't realized he intended to use her for his own ends.

One of the waiters stopped and offered a tray of drinks and one of canapés.

Isabelle snagged a glass of sparkling water, took a sip, and said, "Samuel came to Geneva on business for the Gypsy Travel Agency. He is here. So are we. It's ridiculous to leave him out of the festivities."

Patricia chose a shrimp canapé and champagne, and finished the canapé rather too quickly.

"Is that all you've had to eat tonight?" Isabelle asked.

"No!"

"Because before a party, you never eat as you should." Isabelle plucked a mushroom polenta appetizer from the proffered tray and offered it to her mother.

Patricia started to argue, then gave in with a huff. "Thank you, dear. I am feeling a little empty." Patricia ate the polenta, took one of the pâté-stuffed pastries, then waved the waiter away.

Isabelle knew her mother. With a little fuel in her, she would march right back into battle.

And she did. "If Samuel acts up, your father will have to throw him out!"

"Daddy went to bed an hour ago. If Samuel acts up, you could have the butler throw him out. No, wait!" Isabelle's diamond bracelets jingled as she held up her hand in a stop signal. "The butler is Samuel's foster father."

"I wasn't going to bring that up," Patricia said primly.

"Since *when*?"

"Since you seem to be sensitive about the subject."

Somehow, in the space of a minute, mother and daughter had resorted to the snappish relationship of Isabelle's adolescence. That was odd, for in public both of them—Patricia and Isabelle—were known for their soft-spoken good sense.

But on a personal level, nothing had changed.

Everything needed to change.

Taking a breath, Isabelle settled herself back into maturity. "Samuel is quite civilized, I promise."

"Civilized?" Patricia laughed in a brief, bitter burst. "No, he is not. When I rescued him, I thought such a small child could be rehabilitated, but at the foundation of his being, he is still that little pickpocket who grabbed for everything to make his a better life." When Isabelle would have spoken, Patricia held up her hand. "Dear, I know you'll always support him, but his character is set, and he will never outgrow his desperate need to prove his worth with success and power."

"There's nothing wrong with that. Since he joined the Chosen Ones, his actions in the field have been nothing but brave and honorable." That was true, and those actions were undoubtedly the ones that weighed the most on the great cosmic scales. But on a personal level, in the mansion the Chosen Ones shared as headquarters and home, he was a jerk. Everyone thought so. Most of them said so.

Samuel never seemed to care. He smiled as if no one comprehended how much worse he could be.

But Isabelle did. She'd glimpsed the dark depths of his soul and been burned. She wouldn't do it again.

Nevertheless, fairness drove her to add, "I do know him very well. I work with him almost every day."

Her mother sighed and clutched the thick rope of pearls around her neck. "You know what I think of that."

"Yes, but we're not going to fight about it now. Not at a party." Isabelle added the clincher. "Samuel has a lot of money. You can tap him for a large donation."

"He has money now, does he? What did he do for it, I wonder?"

Isabelle turned a cool gaze on Patricia. "That's unkind, and not like you at all. He worked for his money; you know he did."

Patricia grappled with the indignity of being scolded by her daughter before collapsing into a rueful smile. "You're right, darling. But he is the butler's son!" She was joking. Feebly, but joking.

"I've been reminded of that often enough. He's been reminded enough, too. Perhaps we could talk about the fact he's now"—Isabelle almost choked on the phrase—"a respected lawyer?"

"I know, dear. University of Texas law school. Passed the bar in Texas before returning to Massachusetts to pass the bar and work for a law firm. There, one of my friends on the bench sent him down to New York to join the Gypsy Travel Agency." Patricia ticked off Samuel's credentials on each finger before turning her clear blue gaze on Isabelle. "I don't think Samuel joined because he wanted to."

No. Samuel hadn't joined because he wanted to. But Isabelle didn't have to tell her mother everything she knew. "You don't need to worry that he'll misbehave, Mother. When he wants to be, Samuel is quite civilized."

"I know that! I've always thought Sammy is a charming, deceitful beast."

Isabelle patted her mother's hand. "Then you know everything there is to know about him."

Chapter 4

———⋘≫———

Isabelle and her mother were talking about him. Samuel could tell by the way Mrs. Mason stood at a ninety-degree angle to Isabelle and spoke too quickly, indignation spilling from her, while Isabelle held that aloof smile in place like a Mardi Gras mask to cover her exasperation.

Isabelle was accomplished at using that mask. When she was around him, she wore it all the time.

It made him want to shake her, or shout at her, or kiss her until the mask shattered and she was his Isabelle once more.

Lady Frances Winstead tapped his ribs with the bent head of her cane. "Young man, you shouldn't be gabbing to an old crone like me when you could be courting that beautiful creature."

Recalled to the here and now, he refocused his attention on the spry, cheerful, bent octogenarian beside him. "One beautiful creature a night is all I can handle." He offered his arm. "They're starting to set out the buffet. May I escort you?"

"You are a sweet boy. I always thought so. I wish I could take advantage of you." She sighed with real regret. "I used to drink and dance and eat all night, but since the accident"—she glanced at her watch— "Cinderella must turn in at ten."

"Accident?" He sounded, looked relaxed. But he was anything but casual, because in his experience, very few occurrences were actually accidents.

"Last year, defective brakes on my car sent me and my poor chauffeur off a cliff in Maine into the ocean. The impact blew out the windshield. Brendan died." Her voice quavered, then strengthened. "I got out before the car sank, and I've always been a swimmer, so I made it to shore."

"You swam the Atlantic Ocean in Maine?" He felt her biceps admiringly. "If you can do that, heaven knows what you could do to little ol' me. I'll make a note to be more respectful in the future."

"You are so full of poop," Lady Winstead said forcefully. But she laughed.

"What did you do then? Climb the cliff and hitchhike home?"

"No." She still smiled, but it was a formality only. "I was pretty much done for. But that dear young lady you were leering at earlier had seen the car career off the road and she came to my rescue. If it hadn't been for Isabelle, I would have died from my injuries."

"She . . . healed you?"

"Ah, you know her secret," Lady Winstead said with deep satisfaction.

Samuel looked up from Lady Winstead to gaze at Isabelle.

As if she felt his interest, she looked back at him, her dark blue eyes cool and considering. Then she shifted her attention to Lady Winstead and smiled.

"I do like her," Lady Winstead said, "and not merely because she saved my life. Didn't you two used to date or something?"

"Or something."

"Why did you break up?" Lady Winstead frowned at him. "You're handsome. You're suave. You're one of *those*, aren't you?"

"Those?" he asked cautiously.

"An adulterer." Lady Winstead smacked his arm with her cane. "You cheated on her."

"No, I did not. We've been on-again, off-again for years, and we've both made our mistakes, but when we were together, we were *together*. There was no cheating from either of us." He spoke clearly and forcefully.

"I'm glad to hear that. I hate the underhandedness of a cheater." She rubbed his arm in apology. "You two should give it another try. Get married this time. I know it's old-fashioned, but there's something about standing in the eyes of God and making vows that binds you more tightly. Makes you work out your problems."

"She isn't interested."

"Piffle. I saw her look at you. I saw you look at her.

And I'm not so old I can't feel the heat when I'm standing by a blast furnace."

He chuckled. "No one in his right mind would ever call you old or unobservant."

"Isabelle is single. You're single. Think about it," she urged.

"I most certainly will."

"I've enjoyed our little chat." Lady Winstead was leaning heavily on her cane, her usual erect posture sagging. "But as I said, since the accident, I've not been my usual bouncy self."

"Can I take you to your car?" He offered his arm.

"That sounds lovely, but Todd said he would accompany me home."

"Todd." Unspoken was Samuel's addition of, *That insignificant little worm.*

But Lady Winstead was sharp, and she heard the reaction in his tone. "He's not worth much. I've never understood how one of my grandchildren could be satisfied doing nothing, but he is. At least he makes himself useful when I need an escort."

Samuel scanned the ballroom. Todd, of course, was nowhere to seen. One thing Samuel knew Todd could always be depended on to do was to be undependable. "Todd's a big boy."

"Forty." Lady Winstead rolled her eyes.

"He can get himself home. Why don't I tell your chauffeur to bring the car around?" She was going to resist, he could see, so he gave her mind a little push.

She wavered.

He gave another push.

She sighed and nodded. "That would be pleasant."

He gestured a server over and gave him the instructions, then turned her toward the door.

"You know," Lady Winstead said, "my family moved from Oklahoma to California during the dust bowl. We worked in the orchards and got our educations."

"I didn't know." A lie; he had heard the story more than once.

"By the time I met Lord Winstead, I owned my own flower store. All that youthful experience—I hesitate to call it hardship, although I guess it was—taught me how to work and the value of an occupation. Todd thinks I should pay for him when he flies with me to a party. First-class. On my nickel. I do so miss Lord Winstead on occasions like these." She patted Samuel's arm. "Not that you aren't an admirable substitute."

"I'm delighted to assist you." He helped her into her coat and carefully wrapped her scarf around her sagging throat. "And devastated to lose your company so soon."

Her bright blue eyes scrutinized him. "Such pretty manners. If I were fifty years younger . . ."

"You'd be too young for me." He steered her outside into the cold, windy night. "I like a little maturity in my women."

"Do you ever run out of the soft soap?"

"God forbid. I'm a lawyer."

She chortled as he helped her into the backseat of her limousine. "Next time you're in Boston, stop by for a visit. I do enjoy our conversations."

"I'm living in New York City now. . . . Let me know when you're in town and free, so I can take you to dinner and a play."

She chortled again, an old-lady snort of amusement; then he stood and waved while the chauffeur drove her away.

Sticking his hands in his pockets, he huddled his shoulders and stared out at the landscape. The scene out here resembled a bad painting; whipped by the wind, record-breaking snows grew to great drifts against every tree and hedge. Clear skies and a full moon illuminated the ragged Alpine peaks and the now-idle ski lifts.

"Even God cooperates when Patricia Mason throws a party," he muttered sourly.

Today had been a hell of a long day, the most recent in a series of hellish long days filled with grief, anguish, and worry. After the explosion that destroyed the Gypsy Travel Agency and all of the Chosen Ones except for Samuel's group of seven newbies, they had been lucky enough to find a mentor in Irving Shea. He had supported them, helped them, directed their missions. Samuel doubted that they would have survived those first two and a half years without his tutelage . . . or his fortune.

Then he tumbled down the stairs. No one expected him to live.

But he did, conscious only in brief intervals, and their difficult lives had grown impossible. Irving was still in the hospital. He refused to allow Isabelle to help him—he had some dumb-ass notion about being a willing sacrifice—and the Chosen endured anguish as they watched him suffer.

It was Irving's butler, McKenna, who first called their attention to the practicalities.

Irving's fortune had supported the Chosen Ones. Irving had handled the money, dispensing it as needed to run the household where they lived and worked, and to fund their missions to hold back evil. He had made provisions that the fortune be put in trust for the Chosen when he died.

He had not made provisions for this lingering illness.

Now the taxes on Irving's New York City mansion were due. The electric company wanted to be paid. Their cook and loyal supporter, Martha, needed money for groceries. And if the Chosen Ones didn't somehow receive an influx of cash, they would not be traveling the world to rescue children abandoned by their parents.

This was, Martha said, the traditional dilemma that stalked the Chosen Ones. If they used their gifts to help others, they starved. If they used their gifts for profit, they went to hell. The Gypsy Travel Agency had traditionally provided them with support, but now the Gypsy Travel Agency had been blasted to smithereens.

Their leader, John Powell, had a fortune he'd made by sheer intelligence and determination. Isabelle, of course, had access to her trust fund.

But . . . the Gypsy Travel Agency had been making a profit ever since Irving took over as CEO, and that money had been carefully stashed in Swiss banks. The trouble, of course, was that the people who knew how to access the accounts were gone. So after some discussion, Samuel had been sent to retrieve the fortune.

He rubbed his eyes wearily. Yes, it had been one hell of a long day.

A man's British-tinged voice spoke behind him. "Sir, it's cold out. Would you care to come back in, or should I fetch your coat?"

Samuel turned on his heel and stared at the militarily upright posture of the man in the doorway. "Dad! I didn't know you'd accompanied the Masons to Switzerland."

"Well! Son. This is a mutual surprise. I didn't know you'd come to the party." A faint disapproving note sounded plainly in Darren Owen's speech.

"Don't worry, Dad. I was invited."

"Not by Miss Isabelle, surely."

"Most definitely by Miss Isabelle."

"She and you are not—"

"No. We're not together again."

Darren's stiff form relaxed. "Thank God."

"Although they say the third time's a charm." At his father's open alarm, Samuel laughed. "I'm kidding, Dad. *I'm* here on business. *She's* here to help Mummy Dearest. This was a chance encounter which will lead the same place the other encounters led—nowhere."

"The other encounters took some ruinous detours before they got nowhere," Darren said tartly.

"But I've learned my lesson, and I daresay Isabelle has learned hers." He waited for his father to correct him, to require him to call her "Miss Mason."

But although Darren quivered at having to restrain himself, he bit his tongue, satisfied with Samuel's disavowal—which was so much crap. Given the chance, Samuel would grab her, run with her to his cave, and keep her there forever.

Yet Darren didn't have to know that.

Nor did he have to know that if Samuel tried anything the slightest bit bold, Isabelle would slap him silly.

Samuel had found that out the hard way.

The wind gusted snow into his face. He looked up at the mountains. "Adelbrecht Wagner said this was avalanche weather."

"Yes. The ski patrol will be out tomorrow, setting charges, and all the guests will be stuck inside instead of out skiing."

Samuel grinned. His father sounded disgusted, but he would be in his element, juggling meals and entertainment for a full house. "There's no one better than you to handle the situation."

"You could help," Darren said.

Samuel's smile faded. "No. I couldn't." Almost from the first moment Samuel had come into the Mason household, his father had persuasively explained that being a butler was a profitable, respectable profession for Samuel to follow. He had shown Samuel everything there was to know about being a top-end servant. He was almost medieval in his desire for Samuel to follow in his footsteps.

That, as far as Samuel was concerned, conclusively proved he was not Darren's natural son. Not that he needed proof; he'd been five when Mrs. Mason had convinced Darren and his wife to adopt a needy child, and he well remembered his new parents' fumbling attempts at dealing with a proud, headstrong son of indeterminate Gypsy heritage.

It wasn't that Samuel was ashamed of his father's profession, but . . . Samuel didn't serve. He didn't crawl. He didn't wait on anyone. Ever.

He moved toward the door.

Darren didn't budge.

"Dad," Samuel said, "it's cold out here."

"Of course." Darren moved aside, so much the proper butler he wouldn't even tell his kid to behave or get the hell out.

Samuel strode inside to the top of the stairs by the cloakroom—and paused, arrested by the sight of Isabelle as she walked across the ballroom. She moved like a model, arms gracefully curved at her sides, her long neck held proudly, the sleek, cool, gold ankle-length silk gown draping her body and framing the warmth of her skin. She had pulled her straight hair back into one of those bun things at her neck, and diamond hairpins sparkled like stars in midnight velvet. The gown was designer. He didn't know which one, but at an event like this, the Mason women always wore designer. The gown flowed around her body, swaying with every motion. The way the silk caressed her . . . he couldn't take his gaze away.

He broke into a sweat.

Did she wear any panties under that skirt? Did she wear any underwear at all?

She looked absolutely natural, absolutely beautiful, her almond-shaped eyes lifted by expertly applied makeup, her coolly golden skin flawless.

He wanted to go to her, kneel before her, bare his chest so she could put her stiletto heel over his breastbone and push him flat onto the floor. Then he would do anything she commanded. Kiss her manicured toes. Run his lips up the inside of her leg. Let her sit on his face while he licked her, sucked her until she came once, twice, so often that she forgave him everything.

Isabelle looked so serenely chic, most men couldn't imagine that Isabelle Mason would play the dominatrix.

He knew better. Only he knew that beneath the elegance a passion burned so intensely a man could die trying to contain her fire.

She joined Michel Moreau, the French ambassador.

Moreau, short, stout, middle-aged, and bald, couldn't take his eyes off her.

Which figured. What man wouldn't want her?

Not Samuel, for sure.

But then, he was crude and vulgar and unfit for a lady like Isabelle.

At least, that was the gospel according to Patricia Mason.

Too bad. Because he meant to win Isabelle once more.

Chapter 5

Samuel started down the stairs toward Isabelle. Glanced toward the side. And halted.

Todd stood there.

Todd, tall, handsome, with a haircut that cost as much as a small car and a suit that cost more than the budget of a third-world country. Todd, the wealthy. Todd, the worthless.

What burned Samuel was that, as far as Mrs. Mason was concerned, Todd would be an appropriate mate for Isabelle. Todd was heir to a fortune, but more than that, Todd had no rough edges. He was a suave, useless George Clooney, just the kind of man Patricia Mason could successfully manipulate into doing her bidding.

Now Todd stood indolently, a glass of port held between manicured fingers, surveying the ballroom from the steps leading up to the cloakroom.

Samuel joined him, alive with malice. "Lose something?"

"My grandmother. She's probably huddled in some corner, snoring with her mouth open." Todd sounded absolutely disgusted, although whether with his grandmother or with the fact that Samuel spoke to him, Samuel did not know.

"It's very late for a woman of her age." Samuel made a show of checking his watch.

"That's for sure. I don't know why she insists on coming to these functions."

"Because she likes to get out occasionally?"

"But it's not pleasant to see her." Todd spoke smoothly, warmly, as if he weren't being absolutely offensive. "She's so bent and saggy, clothes aren't attractive on her, and don't even ask about the time wasted getting her into a coat and into the car, then out of the car and out of the coat; then she's not at the party for an hour before she's whining that she's tired and wants to go home."

Samuel smiled and nodded as if he were sympathetic. He had always had a natural talent for acting. "I did see her not long ago make her way toward the library with that gentleman . . . I can't remember his name. You know, the distinguished gentleman with the gray hair, the one who romances wealthy women and marries them?"

For the first time, Todd faced Samuel. "That Czech? That phony nobleman? Count Ladislav Kucera?"

Samuel shrugged with elaborate casualness.

"That perfidious bastard." Outrage vibrated in Todd's voice. "The library, you say?"

"Well, down the corridor toward the library. They could be anywhere." Samuel spread his hands in a display of innocence. "By now, they could be in the bedrooms."

Todd took off like a shot down the stairs, across the ballroom, toward the family rooms.

Samuel watched, satisfied that Todd would not enjoy the rest of his evening. He was going to be too busy searching for Lady Winstead.

Samuel's gaze returned to Isabelle. And Ambassador Moreau.

He started down the stairs. To speak to Isabelle. To rescue her from Moreau. Before Moreau leered himself into a major ass kicking.

But before Samuel took more than two steps, a Frenchman's low, urgent voice caught his attention.

It said, "What do you mean, you had to injure *le petit garçon*?"

Someone had hurt a little boy.

"The kid wouldn't stop fighting." The voice was young, male, surly. And American. Very American.

Samuel stood absolutely still, listening, trying to pinpoint the source of the muffled voices.

"How badly did you hurt him?"

No answer.

Something thumped against the wall of the cloakroom. *"How badly?"*

"When I left, he was clutching his chest and bitching about the pain." The American sounded as if he'd been what thumped against the wall.

"*Merde*, Bull! You are the dumbest *imbécile* I ever worked with!"

Samuel eased himself closer to the open door, slid behind a ficus, and prepared to listen.

"His arm is a little broken," Bull said.

"I *told* you not to hurt the merchandise." The Frenchman sounded furious. "Do *you* want to explain to the boss why we can't collect the ransom?"

"The boss can't be that tough." Bull was cross.

The slam this time shook the wall by Samuel's head.

"The boss will dine on your beating heart."

Who are these guys?

"All right," the Frenchman said decisively. "We'll move the schedule ahead. I'll deliver the letter to his *papa* ASAP. If we can get the ransom fast enough, we can give him his kid before he dies."

Samuel barely breathed as the Frenchman—six-foot-three, two hundred and fifty pounds of pure muscle, dressed in a waiter's suit—strode past him, scowling.

Inside the cloakroom, the flunky muttered and kicked the wall. Repeatedly.

When the Frenchman disappeared from sight, Samuel stepped inside the cloakroom and softly shut the door behind him.

No wonder the Frenchman called this guy *Bull*. He looked Hawaiian and Japanese and like a young sumo wrestler on steroids. And he was fast—at the click of the latch, he turned, saw Samuel, and charged. He had the speed of a linebacker and the hostility of a young gangster who a minute ago had been chided by his superior.

But Samuel had trained for this. At the last second he stepped aside, then kicked Bull in the ass. The youth smashed into the freestanding chrome coatrack, sending it and the jackets, furs, hats, and gloves crashing against the wall. Bull's head slammed a hole through the plaster before he and all the paraphernalia toppled onto the floor.

He seemed to feel nothing. He came up in a flash and charged again, eyes gleaming with rage.

Samuel stepped on a hat, waved his arms in exaggerated dismay, fell over—and when Bull lifted his foot to smash Samuel's ribs, Samuel grabbed the guy's boot and lifted.

Bull fell. The floor quaked.

Bull shook his head, trying to recover whatever wits he possessed.

Samuel rolled behind him, grabbed a silk scarf, and wrapped the length around the sumo's stub of a neck. He twisted hard, cutting off Bull's air, making him spasm and claw at Samuel's hands.

Bull had hurt a kid, almost killed him, and the street-smart little boy Samuel had once been exalted in the guy's writhings. He wanted him to suffer. He deserved to suffer.

Samuel twisted tighter and tighter until Bull's motion ceased and his eyes rolled back in his head.

Putting his mouth by the man's ear, Samuel asked,

"Where's the child?" He loosened the scarf to allow Bull to speak.

Bull came to life like an animated corpse. Grabbing Samuel's ears, he used them like levers to pull Samuel forward.

Samuel felt his flesh rip. His head slammed into Bull's hard skull. Blood trickled down his face on both sides, and he saw stars.

Bull grabbed Samuel's hair and rolled over the top of him. "Who are you?" He slammed Samuel's head against the floor. "Who are you?" *Slam.* "Who are you?" *Slam.*

The only thing that saved Samuel's life was the fur coat underneath him, cushioning him from the impact. He groped beside him, seeking something to use as a weapon. A can! Mace! He sprayed Bull's face.

It was hair spray.

But it did the job. Bull yelped and let go to dig at his eyes.

Samuel slammed his fist into Bull's nose. The crunch was satisfying. Bull's squeal was even more satisfying. The spurting blood made Samuel almost giddy with glee, and when he wrapped the scarf around Bull's throat again, he took real pleasure in applying pressure and using expletives he hadn't used since his adoption twenty-six years ago. He didn't take a chance this time; he found a real can of Mace in one of the coats tumbled around them on the floor, sprayed Bull, choked him repeatedly, and finally loosened the scarf. "Where is the boy?" he asked again.

"Château. Schneider Road." As Bull got his breath, his hand shot up, groping toward Samuel's head. He didn't volunteer any more details.

Samuel sprayed him with the Mace again and, with a sigh, gave up trying to do this the hard way.

Because mind control always worked . . . and mind control came as easily to Samuel as breathing.

Chapter 6

Isabelle coolly ignored the waiter standing by her side. But although he was respectful, he was insistent. "Excuse me. Miss Mason?"

She swiveled gracefully to face him. *Why are you interrupting my conversation with Ambassador Moreau?* But no, she couldn't say that, nor could she allow her irritation to show. "Yes?"

"I have a message from Mr. Samuel Faa. He requests your presence at once."

"He's going to have to wait." She smiled, teeth clenched. She had been angling for that check from the ambassador for fifteen minutes, and she was not about to give up now.

The waiter offered her a slip of paper, folded in two and torn from a cheap tablet. "If you had any objections, Mr. Faa said to give you this."

She opened it. Roughly sketched on the paper was an empty cradle.

Damn Samuel. He knew how to get her attention.

A child was in danger.

She folded the paper and turned back to the ambassador. "I am so sorry. This requires my immediate attention."

The ambassador bowed and once again kissed the back of Isabelle's hand. "I am desolated. Apparently, we are not allowed a whole conversation tonight."

"No." She kissed his cheek. "Another time." Catching her gown in her fingertips, she moved toward the door without appearing to hurry, smiling and nodding at the guests, but never slowing.

She jumped when Samuel stepped out from behind a potted plant dressed in his heavy coat . . . with an amber wool scarf wrapped around his head and tied like a turban. Over the turban, he wore a dark knit cap.

She didn't laugh. Not quite. "That's quite a fashion statement."

"I'm a fashion maven." He stuffed gloves on her hands.

Samuel had never gotten over his impression that she was still a pampered little girl in need of help.

"The scarf is quite attractive on you." She fought back a smirk. "The color complements your eyes."

"It stopped the blood from leaking out of my ears, too."

She looked. Saw the crimson stains. Realized he had a bruise forming on his jaw.

He'd been fighting again. He'd been trying to get himself killed again.

She had to physically restrain herself from reaching out to him, touching him, healing him. He was Chosen; unless he desperately needed help, he would heal quickly on his own. In repressive tones, she asked, "What did you do now?"

"I got the information we need." He held out an ankle-length mink coat for her to slip into.

"That's not mine."

"Close enough." He shook the coat. "Come on; we haven't got time to waste, and it's windy and frigid out there. Like someone else I know."

"I'm not frigid"—she slid into the heavy fur—"for the right man."

"I know." Samuel held out a knit cap. "Because I am the right man."

She wasn't getting into that argument with him again. "I am *not* wearing that hat. It'll ruin my hair."

"Put it in your pocket. We'll see what you say when you step outside. Now—let's go." Taking her arm, he hurried her toward the rear of the château.

As they walked, she rearranged her fingers in the gloves. "*Where* are we going?"

"About a mile north as the crow flies, about five miles by road. The Others commandeered the De Luca château."

She led him through the darkened, vacant living rooms on their way out. "It's empty."

"They've grabbed a boy. He's hurt."

She expected the news, but her heart sank.

As they reached the back door, Samuel opened it and rushed through.

He was right. When she stepped outside, the icy air took her breath away. But she didn't put on the knit cap.

He led her to an idling four-wheel drive. He opened the door for her, and glanced down as she climbed inside. "Shit. I forgot about your stupid shoes. I should have grabbed you some boots."

"From the same shop where you got the fur?" she asked tartly, and tucked her strappy sandals under the seat.

He shoved the trailing hem of her gown inside. "Yes." He slammed the door and hurried around the car, climbed in, and had the car in motion before she'd even buckled her seat belt.

The sky was clear, the moon was bright, and the headlights skimmed over the mountainous terrain, twisting like ice dancers performing a tango. Snow blanketed the icy road, driven by the wind to pile against the trunks of the evergreens and on the banks the plows had piled on the sides of the pavement.

Samuel drove like a maniac over the snow-covered road, but she didn't care. She trusted his driving, and she felt his urgency. His tight face, his intent gaze, his taut body—he was ready to fight any way he had to, with his mind and with his fists.

"Tell me everything," she said.

He did, including the part where he probed the other

guy's mind, forced him to tell him the child's location. She didn't say a word of reproach. She saw the blood that stained the scarf on his head. She knew very well it had to be done that way to save the child.

But he said, "What!" in that voice that snapped at her composure.

"Nothing, Samuel. You did exactly right."

"All right then." He slowed, turned off the head-lights, drove using the moonlight.

"If it's bright enough to drive, they're going to see us coming whether we have the headlights on or not," she said.

"We passed the drive to the château half a mile back." He pulled over to the side of the road. "Give me thirty minutes." He pointed at the clock in the dash. "That'll make it twelve fifteen. Then drive in, head-lights off, and I'll bring the kid out."

"Why don't we go in together?"

"Right." He laid on the sarcasm. "You're going to be very helpful to me in your Parda spike-heeled strappy sandals."

"It's called Prada. And these are Jimmy Choo. What if you get done early?"

"I'll call you." He handed her his cell.

She weighed it in her hand. "What if you don't come out?"

"Call the cops. And"—he handed her a small, loaded revolver—"use this if you have to."

She clicked off the safety. "Believe me. I will."

Chapter 7

Samuel opened the car door. The wind whistled in, biting at her. At him.

"Sammy," she said.

He looked back at her.

"Be careful."

He nodded, got out, and headed back up the road.

Isabelle climbed over the console into the driver's seat. She adjusted the mirrors, eased the car around to face the right direction, removed the voluminous mink and placed it in the back for the child. She examined his phone; it was a smartphone with lots of apps. . . . She played two games of Boggle. And checked the time.

Only fifteen minutes had passed. It was midnight. She knew from experience the next fifteen minutes would drag, second by second, while she worried about Samuel. And about the child.

This was the trouble with being a physical empath. When she touched someone who was hurt, she took on his or her injury. If the injured person had a gunshot wound, she developed a gunshot wound, drawing the pain and the shattered skin, muscle, and bone into herself. Using her gift, she healed her patient—and exhausted herself.

So when she reversed the process and tried to hurt that person, she felt the injury like a shock to her system. The anguish echoed back and forth, amplified by her cruel intentions, and she had to fight her own ability to heal.

Consequently, she wasn't worth spit in a brawl.

Samuel said she had been given the directive from the Powers That Be that she should not exchange blows. The other Chosen agreed.

Even Isabelle agreed.

But she didn't have to like being left behind during a fight.

Ten minutes left.

She drove the car to the edge of the château's driveway.

Five minutes.

Samuel's phone rang.

She snatched it up.

"Come on. Come in. Door's open." His voice was gruff.

She tossed down the phone and, with meticulous care, drove up the steep, winding driveway.

Why had Samuel sounded so worried? The child wasn't dead already, was he? On those rare occasions when the Chosen Ones failed, when they lost a child to the Others, or found an infant abandoned and still, she cried. They all cried.

A light burned in a black limo parked by the door.

She whipped the four-wheeler around to face outward, ready for escape. She cut the motor, donned the fur, and slid the pistol into the capacious pocket, then stepped gingerly through the snow and ice toward the door. As Samuel promised, it was unlocked. She opened it little by little.

Deep in the dim interior, she heard Samuel's rumble, the low, warm, comforting voice he used only when he dealt with old ladies and small children, and certainly never to her. She followed the light to a main-floor bedroom.

There, in the corridor, a tall man with a big belly lay dead, shot through the heart.

Samuel had been busy.

Without concern, Isabelle stepped over the body.

Whoever he was, if he had been holding a child hostage, he deserved death and more.

Where his soul was going, she hoped he got exactly what he deserved.

Inside the bedroom, she found Samuel, coat and hat flung off, easing a thin, tense seven-year-old back on the pillows.

She would have sworn that she hadn't made a sound, but in French that sounded almost native, Samuel said, "Mathis, here's Isabelle. She's the lady I told you would come and take away the pain."

The child mewled like a hurt kitten.

Isabelle hurried to the bed and smiled down at the boy. He was so thin his bones poked at his chalky skin. He coughed, his body racked by agony, and flecks of blood gathered at the corners of his mouth.

Her gaze flicked to the wheelchair in the corner. It listed to one side; a wheel had been broken. But it bore the imprint of the child's body. The child suffered from some cruel wasting disease; she could hope to cure only the immediate damage.

Samuel carefully covered the child with the blankets.

Mathis's arm rested on the covers, his hand at an awkward angle to the upper arm; the kidnappers had twisted until they broke the radius and the ulna, those bones between the wrist and the elbow.

Her eyes filled with tears, for him and for her.

He suffered horribly now: from his arm, and from his internal injuries.

She would suffer horribly as she took the injuries into herself to heal him. That was the price she paid for her gift.

Samuel knew it, and he hated it. Hated it even as he understood it was necessary. He pulled a chair up to the bed, helped her out of her coat. He scowled heavily, but he continued his lighthearted French conversation. "Guess what. That man in the corridor? I didn't shoot him."

"You didn't?" She wasn't really listening. She was looking into the child's eyes, nodding and smiling, preparing him for the moment she would touch him.

"Mathis did it." Samuel helped her into the seat.

That got her attention. The boy was so ill, so hurt . . . yet he had killed his captor? "Really?"

"I'm not sorry, either," Mathis said defiantly.

"How brave!" She smiled at him. "How smart you are!"

"What a good shot!" Samuel heaped on the praise.

Isabelle remembered the hole in the middle of the man's chest. "A very good shot."

"Papa taught me to shoot. He said I should know because we are important people and the scum of the world . . . they would try to destroy us. Because we are wealthy. And important." Mathis half closed his eyes, breathing hard, fighting for air. Fighting the pain. "These scum . . . thought they could leave me alone with one man because they hurt me. They said I was a cripple."

"They are stupid, cruel people," Isabelle answered.

"Yes." Mathis's head fell back on the pillow. If possible, he grew even paler, and he said again, "I'm not sorry."

"Who is your papa?" Samuel asked. "Do you know his name?"

"*Papa* . . ." A tear slipped down the boy's cheek.

"I asked him once before." Samuel leaned close and spoke in her ear. "He doesn't seem to remember."

"He's in shock," Isabelle whispered back. For the first time, she touched the little boy. She flinched at the blast of pain from his arm. The tearing misery of broken bones. The bleeding in his lungs. The disease that rested in his genes and ate at his muscles.

She struggled to take control of his anguish. Yet it overwhelmed her senses, swamped her with sensation. She sagged in her chair.

Then Samuel put his hands on her shoulders.

Strength flowed into her. A trickle. A heat. And the memory of a cold day long, long ago when she had helped Samuel . . .

Mathis sighed as he felt the first modicum of relief that flowed into his wasted muscles.

Isabelle took a breath, gained control. The disease that ate at him retreated a little bit, allowing her to place her hand on his chest, to breathe for him as she took his injury and healed it.

"That's better." Mathis sighed, and relaxed. "So much better."

"Yes." As his pain eased, Isabelle's pain eased, and she laughed softly. "Look at Samuel. Doesn't he look handsome with his scarf tied rakishly around his head?"

Samuel struck a pose, hands on hips, head back. "Like a sheik," he said, and flipped the ends of the scarf over his shoulder.

"Like a sheik who lost his desert." Isabelle touched Mathis's shoulder, his upper arm.

"He does look funny," Mathis acknowledged; then his lip trembled. "But isn't that blood on the scarf?"

"You should see the other guy." Samuel took her shoulders in his hands again.

She didn't want him to help her. But he fed her strength. And she desperately needed that strength.

"Samuel is a very powerful fighter." She stroked the air above the boy's lower arm. "He'll take care of us until we get you home."

"My mother and father will be so worried." Mathis's lip trembled again; then, as Isabelle lightly stroked his skin, knitting the torn muscles, the shattered bones, his face relaxed and he gave a small sigh of relief.

"That is better. *Merci, mademoiselle.*"

"Do you remember your parents' names?" Samuel asked. "I could give them a call and let them know you're safe."

"Of course I know their names." Mathis sounded impatient and superior, as if he'd never had a lapse in memory. "They are the Moreaus of Paris."

The name fell into the room with the weight and prestige of a thousand years of French aristocracy.

Yet Isabelle covered her dismay with a casual tone. "The French ambassador to the United States? I know him. I saw him earlier tonight."

"You know my *papa*? Please call him and tell him to come and get me." The child's eyes brimmed with tears.

"It would be better if we take you to him." Isabelle signaled to Samuel. "We don't want to stay here any longer than we have to, do we?"

"No!" Mathis said.

"Your wheelchair is injured, so Samuel will carry you to the car and we'll drive as quickly as we can to your home."

"Yes, please."

"Then you can sleep in your own bed. You'd like that, wouldn't you?"

Mathis yawned.

Isabelle stood and swayed.

Samuel caught her by the waist and steadied her. "I wish you'd take an aspirin or something."

"For me, medication merely gets in the way."

"What do you get out of this?" Samuel's voice was scratchy with irritation.

She indicated the child, relaxed and no longer in pain.

"Yeah, yeah." Samuel leaned over and gathered him up. "Let's get out of here."

Chapter 8

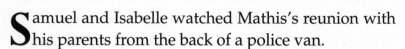

Samuel and Isabelle watched Mathis's reunion with his parents from the back of a police van.

"This is *so* touching. Do you think they'll remember us before the police put us away for three hundred years?" Samuel chafed at being treated like a criminal.

The Swiss police clearly didn't believe a word of Samuel and Isabelle's story. Officials stopped the car before they got within a mile of Moreau's château. While Mathis shrieked at the police to stop, Samuel and Isabelle were yanked out of the car, handcuffed, and stuck in the back of the van.

Then the Moreaus arrived, wild-eyed and panicked, and Mathis's shouts dissolved into the tears of a small boy who no longer had to maintain his brave facade.

"Look at them. They are so happy." Isabelle peered through the window and wiped sentimental tears onto her shoulder.

"Here." Samuel seated himself on the bench beside

her and offered his shoulder. "My coat has got to be better than that fur."

"I'm fine." She could hear the tremor in her own voice, and cursed her sentimental nature. Normally she didn't mind, but with Samuel, she hated to show a single sign of weakness. He was so quick to take advantage.

But he could be charming, too, like now, when he bumped her arm with his. "We'll be okay."

"Yes. I suppose." Although the police were pacing around the van like trainers about to transport tigers to the zoo. She watched for another minute, then voiced the thought that had occasionally bothered her in the past. "Have you ever thought about all the Chosen Ones who were out in the world when the Gypsy Travel Agency blew up?"

"I thought all the Chosen Ones were in the Gypsy Travel Agency when it went up?"

"There's no way. Some of them had to be on missions that couldn't be broken off. Some of them surely had been captured by the Others, or had drawn suspicion on themselves for the covert operations. There are parts of the world that imprison you merely for being different, and the Chosen *are* different. Somewhere, one or two or more must have been accused and imprisoned by . . . by . . ."

"The Swiss police?" The floodlights illuminated Samuel's grim expression.

"Exactly. And the usual mechanism that should rescue them—the Gypsy Travel Agency—is no longer in place, and they languish still in prison."

"Are you trying to tell me we could get put away and never see the light of day again?" He didn't wait for an answer. He stood up, slammed himself against the door, and shouted, "Moreau! Mathis! Hey, come on! We're in here!"

As he rammed the door again, one of the cops opened it.

Samuel flew headfirst out onto the road.

Twenty-five pistols pointed his way.

Isabelle shrieked, "Don't shoot!"

Moreau's head swiveled in their direction. His gaze lit on Isabelle, on Samuel. He focused. He pressed Mathis into his wife's arms, pushed them toward their limousine, and strode to the van, shouting, "Halt! Lefèvre, you've made a mistake!" He spoke to the police chief, quietly at first, then, as Lefèvre shook his head, more emphatically. Finally, Lefèvre nodded and indicated the police could unlock Samuel's handcuffs and allow him to stand.

Moreau indicated Isabelle, and the officers showed less reluctance as they released her hands and helped her out.

Samuel pried himself off the ice and rose slowly, shaking out his legs and rotating his shoulders.

Isabelle watched, holding the collar of the coat tightly under her chin, trying to stop her teeth from chattering.

It was two in the morning. The sky was clear, the wind blowing, the temperature hovering in the low teens. Cold seeped through the thin soles of her strappy heels and slid up her bare legs. Her efforts with the child had exhausted her. She had knitted Mathis's bones along with her own, and now her arm ached. When Samuel wrapped his arm around her, she held herself stiffly until he shook her. That rattled her composure, and she leaned against him.

"That's better," he said gruffly.

On two things she could always depend: If she suffered a weakness, Samuel knew it, and if he could, he would assist her—and point it out as often and as obnoxiously as he could.

Moreau was throwing his weight around. "I know these people. They are guilty of nothing except saving my child."

"That remains to be seen, Ambassador." Lefèvre was clearly irritated at the challenge to his authority. "Even if they are not guilty, they know things about this crime. They must be questioned."

"Of course, and as soon as possible." Moreau noted Isabelle's weakness, Samuel's protective stance. "We'll take them in our car to our home. You can follow and question them."

Madame Moreau joined them. She was the exact opposite of her husband: tall, thin, nervous, with a full head of curly blond hair. She exuded an authority all her own as she said, "Yes, please, Lefèvre. Let me have you and your men up to our home so I can show our appreciation for your efforts. I have refreshments waiting for you, and you can perform your interrogation in warmth and comfort."

Isabelle could see Lefèvre wanted to argue. She could also see he knew he would lose. So he pointed a black-gloved hand at her. "What about the charges of stealing Frau Reidlinger's hundred-thousand-euro mink?"

"Oh, Samuel." Dismayed, Isabelle ran her hands over the luxurious fur. "I knew it was expensive, but . . . a hundred thousand euros?"

"What can I say? I have good taste." Samuel shrugged.

"I'll handle Frau Reidlinger," Madame Moreau said. "She'll have a new coat in the morning."

Moreau winced.

She turned on him. "The kidnappers were demanding twenty million euros. Surely a coat is a small price to pay for the return of our Mathis."

"So it is." Moreau put an arm around his wife. "Now, let's go so you can put the child to bed. He's exhausted, and so are you."

She clung to him for another moment; then, with a tremulous smile, she broke away, took Isabelle's arm, and led her toward the limo. Moreau and Samuel walked behind them.

Lefèvre shouted to his men to load up and follow, and hurried to his car.

The Moreaus and Samuel and Isabelle climbed into the warmth of the car and found Mathis curled up under a throw, fast asleep.

Madame Moreau picked him up and cradled him in her arms. "He's tired, but he seems better than he has for many months."

The chauffeur drove the narrow lane to the château. The Swiss police followed closely.

Isabelle sank into the leather seat, soaking up the heat, but still she remembered her theory about the Chosen Ones, lost when the Gypsy Travel Agency was destroyed. "The police were very determined that we were guilty."

"It's easier that way," Samuel said. "Now they have an unsolved crime on their hands. Kidnappers who prey on the children of wealthy parents. Switzerland can't afford that kind of publicity, or the exodus of wealthy tourists that will ensue."

"Exactly. Lefèvre is truly suspicious of you, but I have the advantage of knowing you both since you were children." Moreau's pleasant face was grim. "What do you plan to tell Lefèvre about the rescue?"

"The truth," Samuel said. "I overheard the kidnappers at the party. I started to go to the rescue myself, and Isabelle insisted on coming, too."

"I seem to remember a note delivered to her hand," Moreau said.

"She has so many suitors."

Isabelle had to admire Samuel's capacity to dodge the question while telling the truth.

"Why didn't one of you call the police at once?" Moreau seemed to be quizzing them, giving them a chance to get their stories straight.

"I'm a grandstander," Samuel said.

Moreau turned to Isabelle. "But you are not."

"There's nowhere on this gown to carry a cell."

Isabelle gestured at herself, at the diaphanous silk she wore. "So I left without mine. Samuel is stingy with his, especially when he's, er, grandstanding."

Moreau nodded as if satisfied, then leaned over his sleeping child and kissed his hair.

"We almost lost him," Madame Moreau whispered. She looked up at Isabelle, tears in her eyes. "We couldn't have children of our own, and this child—he was abandoned as an infant on our doorstep."

"Really?" Samuel's deep, sure voice was at odds with Madame Moreau's trembling recital. "He's an abandoned child?"

"It was the hand of *le bon Dieu*, I thought, and we adopted him." With trembling fingers, Madame Moreau stroked Mathis's forehead. "For the first three years, he was so bright, so happy, so perfect. Then . . ."

Moreau put his hand over hers. "You don't have to tell them."

"Yes. I do. Listen to what I say, and you'll understand why." She turned back to Samuel and Isabelle. "He began to fail. He lost weight. He couldn't grasp things. He fell. We took him to the doctors, the best specialists in the world. They didn't know. Couldn't find the problem. Suggested many things, including that I was hurting him on purpose. Finally, they diagnosed him. A genetic disease, so rare there is no name for it. It eats at his brain, at his nervous system. They tell me he'll die. My boy. My gift from God."

"I'm so sorry." Samuel sounded as brokenhearted as Madame Moreau, and Isabelle knew, in his way, he was. No matter what else she thought of him—and she held her grudges carefully before her like a shield— she always knew he loved children. Loved them, cherished them, cared for them.

"You risked your life for him," Madame Moreau said, "and for that, I thank you. In so many ways, he is a special child. He has gifts you cannot imagine."

"Try me," Samuel said.

Isabelle dug her elbow into his side. "We have some experience with gifts such as Mathis's."

Madame Moreau looked directly at her. "I think you do. For he told me he was hurt, badly hurt, and you . . . you cured him."

That was always a problem. Discretion was *not* a child's gift.

Isabelle dropped her gaze and looked at her fingers, laced together in her lap. "He exaggerates."

"He is not a foolish child. He sees the face of death every day. His disease has made him mature beyond his years. He says you healed his broken arm. Healed his chest." Reaching out, Madame Moreau grabbed Isabelle's arm. "You healed my child."

Isabelle looked up into Madame Moreau's eyes. "I cannot . . . cannot do that. Cannot fix such an affliction. I'm sorry."

"It would kill her," Samuel said bluntly.

"He's better. I feel it," Madame Moreau insisted.

Isabelle didn't know what to say.

But when she would have tried, Madame Moreau waved her to silence. "No. Wait. You'll see I'm right."

The limo slowed as they approached the Moreau château, where every light burned and servants lined the steps.

Turning to Moreau, Madame Moreau said, "As soon as Mathis is up to it, we're going home to Paris."

"Yes. Our security is tight there, and I swear to you"—Moreau took her hand and kissed it—"this will never happen again."

The chauffeur brought them to a halt.

The servants swarmed the car.

The police pulled up in front and back, as if halting an escape attempt.

Moreau hit the privacy locks. He turned to Samuel and Isabelle, and his usually suave sophistication transformed itself into stern resolve. "If there is ever anything I can do for you, no matter how big, no matter how small, let me know. I owe you everything. *Everything*. And I will repay my debt."

Chapter 9

————⟡————

Chilled and exhausted, Isabelle fastened her seat belt, huddled into her coat, closed her eyes, and let herself drift.

The road was winding, swaying her back and forth as Samuel drove its length, taking her back to her mother's house. Although it was three in the morning, she knew her mother would be awake, ostensibly supervising the cleanup, while in reality, she'd be waiting . . . for Isabelle to return with Samuel.

Isabelle had had so much experience with this situation, she knew everything that would happen.

Patricia would look them over, her eyes sharp, silently demanding an explanation.

Isabelle would give her one. *Mother, we had a job to do.*

Patricia wouldn't like that. But once she ascertained that they betrayed no undue fondness for each other, showed no signs of lovemaking, she would invite Samuel to stay the night.

Isabelle would insist he do so.

He would agree.

Patricia would assign him a room so far away from Isabelle's he might as well be in Italy.

Isabelle smiled painfully. As if that would matter to Samuel. If she gave him the slightest encouragement, he would swim Lake Geneva and scale the Matterhorn to reach her. To sleep with her. To shake her world.

She turned her head to gaze at his warrior's profile, his chin shadowy with stubble, his dark gaze fixed intently on the road.

God, how she loved him. Most of the time, she could dismiss the knowledge that for as long as they both lived, she would love only him. But when she was tired, when her guard was down . . .

Then she remembered the good times between them. So many good times, filled with laughter and tenderness, lust and glory. She had believed they were soul mates. Sometimes she still dreamed of what it would be like to live with him forever.

But no. No matter how much her body yearned, she wasn't going to give in to him again. She wouldn't allow him to destroy her once more.

The tires skidded on the pavement. The vehicle slipped toward the edge of the road.

She straightened in her seat and looked around. Moonlight sprawled over the vast, snowy expanse of meadow that stretched to the right, over the dark silhouette of the medieval castle turned dark and empty ski lodge snuggled against the sleek groomed slopes of the mountain, over the lifts and trams, over the parking lot waiting for tomorrow's influx of skiers. The narrow ribbon of road before them was shiny-slick with ice. On their left, the land fell away and only a snowdrift stopped them from falling into the dark precipice.

They were moving too fast, taking too many chances in these conditions—and for all that Samuel loved speed, she had never felt endangered by his carelessness.

"Samuel? What's wrong?"

"Sh." He didn't lift his gaze from the road, but something about the way he held himself made her look again across the meadow and above.

The mountains rose abruptly toward the deep black velvet sky, blocking the stars, challenging the moon. In the daytime, their beauty lifted Isabelle's heart. Right now, she remembered how cruel they could be. . . . "Samuel, *what's wrong?*"

He slammed on his brakes, skidding again.

Her breath caught in her throat.

Yet he corrected so expertly the car slid around sideways, slowed. Then he accelerated around the next corner.

In the headlights, she saw evergreen branches spread across the road and a huge trunk in their midst. The wind had caught the ancient evergreen and blown it over.

Except . . . the stump was cut. The tree had been deliberately used to block the road.

Samuel eased the car to a halt.

Now she knew why he acted so out of character. Somehow, he'd caught the scent of danger.

This was a trap.

With a low curse, he put the vehicle in reverse, flung his arm over her seat, and, with his body arched and his gaze fixed behind them, he backed up as fast as he could. At the driveway leading to the ski lodge, he slammed on the brakes, skidded back, then forward, then accelerated into the parking lot. In a low, terse voice he said, "Emergency kit is behind my seat. Get back there. Get it. Stay there and jump out as I stop." He put the car into a skid and they skated sideways toward the lodge.

The mountains, their peaks softened by huge mounds of snow, loomed menacingly in the windshield.

With a swift economy of movement, she unsnapped her seat belt and climbed between the seats. She grabbed the black nylon bag, heavy with the gear the Chosen carried when they could—flashlight, flare, first-aid kit, matches—and as the vehicle slid up over the curb and eased toward the ski lodge, she unlocked her door. As soon as they settled to a stop, she was out.

He was out.

They ran toward the ski lodge.

Her heels sank into the snow. Snow sifted through into her strappy sandals, freezing her toes. A minor annoyance.

High above, she heard a deep, menacing boom.

She jerked her head toward the mountain and saw the snow lift off the slope like a cashmere blanket being fluffed by a giant hand. She stopped and stood transfixed as it settled back, slid toward them, gathering speed as it moved. . . .

She prided herself on her cool good sense. She was known for her serenity. But she screamed now. "Samuel! Avalanche!"

He leaned over, slammed his shoulder into her gut, lifted her, and ran.

She gasped, the air knocked out of her, draped over him like a sandbag and bouncing until she was almost sick.

"Hang on to the bag," he shouted.

She'd never heard Samuel sound like that before: desperate, afraid.

She heard the rumbling, too, and as Samuel slammed against the building, she heard another one of those deep, menacing booms far above.

Someone was setting off dynamite charges, creating avalanches that catapulted toward them under the influence of steep slopes and the weight of the snow.

And Samuel had known this was coming. Somehow, Samuel had known.

He set her on her feet.

The ground shook beneath her as the massive wall of snow thundered toward them.

The ancient castle's facade rose four stories above them. On the second and third floors, windows had been cut into the stone to give the skiers a view of the Alps. But here on the ground floor, security reigned supreme. One narrow window. A single heavy metal door.

He tried the lever handle, said, "Locked," and stepped back to allow her access.

She handed him the bag, pulled a long, stiff, platinum diamond pin out of her hair. Kneeling beside the door, she inserted it in the lock.

Her unflagging calm made her the best lock pick among the Chosen. Yet never had she worked under such conditions, with the lock, the pin, and the whole world trembling as death roared toward them.

Samuel flipped on the flashlight and aimed it at the window. "Glass is reinforced with mesh," he said.

She continued to work the lock.

"Need the light?" he asked.

"Please. No." The moonlight provided a clear, even illumination. Breaking a lock required a light touch and a narrow concentration, and the flashlight's beam would simply distract her.

The roll of the avalanche grew to a bellow. Above them, windows broke, raining shards of glass onto their heads. The castle stones were vibrating, shifting.

Samuel stood immobile beside her, ostensibly calm. Yet she could feel him straining, desperate to grab her and run.

Was it going to matter if they got inside? The building wasn't going to survive the impact of so much snow.

She found the mechanism with the tip of her pin. Lifted. Manipulated. Heard the lock click.

She opened the door.

Samuel grabbed her around the waist, lifted her

like a child, and dashed into the dim interior, lit by a pale night-light and the moonlight shining through the window. They stood on a metal landing with stairs going up to the main floor of the lodge and down to the basement.

Samuel vaulted down the first five steps.

She caught a glimpse of the lodge's locker room.

Then the avalanche hit like a nuclear explosion. Windows shattered. Moonlight disappeared. Electricity went out. Snow blew in with the force of a tornado, ripping at Isabelle's skin.

The stairs shook like a bucking horse. Samuel struggled to keep them on their feet.

Then the metal cracked. The steps disappeared out from underneath them.

They fell into nothingness.

Chapter 10

Samuel jumped, and twisted in midair, landing spine-down on the steps. He grunted on impact, then grunted again as Isabelle slammed on top of him. His teeth rattled as they skied toward the bottom.

The stairs ripped off the landing and fell to the floor.

She landed hard.

He landed harder. Something shattered in his spine. He thought he screamed.

Debris—plaster, metal, glass—rained around them, on top of them. Dust choked the air. The building shrieked as it buckled under the blast.

Then . . . then the massive avalanche moved farther down the mountain.

The shaking diminished.

Silence fell.

Isabelle coughed, wheezed, trying to clear her lungs.

Samuel lay absolutely still and quiet. His hands were numb. His legs felt as if they were attached at the wrong angle. He wanted to lift his head, but he was afraid to move. And the pain . . . he had never experienced such pain, coming in waves, hot, piercing stabs of fiery agony. Not when he dislocated his shoulder in the gym. Not when he had wrecked his Beemer and sliced his head open on the windshield. Nothing could compare to this. He wanted to die.

And very probably he would. *They* would.

Because it was utterly, absolutely dark in here. Because things kept falling out of the ceiling: big things, like steel beams and wooden trusses. Because they were buried alive and no one knew they were here.

"Samuel? Samuel?" Isabelle rolled off him.

He hadn't thought he could hurt any more.

He was wrong.

Her motions brought a fresh outbreak of suffering.

She groped for him. As soon as her hands touched him, he felt it—an easing of pain, like a salve on his damaged nerves.

"Uh." She grunted as the pain slashed at her. "Ruptured disks."

Thank you, God. Thank you.

Ruptured disks were bad enough—but he had thought he'd broken his spine.

The relief didn't stop him from snarling like a wounded lion. "I'm fine."

"You're not fine!"

"Don't touch me. Don't heal me!" He tried to push

her hands away. Waves of anguish ripped through him at the action.

And she flinched. When she touched him, she took his pain.

But she assumed she would do for him as she had done for Mathis. As she did for everyone. In incredulous tones, she asked, "Samuel, have you lost your mind? You need to be healed."

"I hate it when you—"

"Touch you? I don't believe that!"

"I hate it when you're suffering." He supported her when he had to, when others were hurt and she struggled to accept the pain that would cure them. But he *detested* having her suffer to help him.

"I know. But, Samuel. Think. I need you to be well. I don't know where we are, what condition we're in." Her voice wobbled as, not far away, something crashed to the floor.

"Where's the bag?" he asked hoarsely. "I lost the bag."

"Samuel, if you'll just let me—"

"Maybe we can get out."

"Let me see you lift your hands!"

He breathed hard, trying to control his helpless rage. "If you can find the flashlight, you can signal for help."

"Fine." She took her hands off him and groped along the floor.

He heard her moving away from him, slowly working through the debris.

"There's a lot of ice and snow splattered everywhere. Fallen boards. Crumpled metal." She hissed, a sound of pain.

"What?"

"There's broken glass. No big deal."

Which meant she had to pull some out of her hand.

"It's a mess in here," she said.

"No bag?"

"Not yet."

The floor beneath him was brushed concrete, hard and cold. The pain in his neck and his back burned like fire. He needed to move . . . so he did.

Pain blasted him, broke him, twisted him, fogged his mind.

But he thought he made no sound. He thought she wouldn't know.

Instead she snapped, "If you're not going to let me help you, then lie still."

His eyes strained, staring into the darkness. "No luck on the bag?" They needed the flashlight. They needed the survival gear.

"I'm widening the search area. These stairs just detached from the landing and fell to the floor."

"I noticed." He took long breaths, trying to get control of his agony. "Are you getting an idea of our situation?"

"What a delicate way of putting it, Samuel." Her tone mocked him. "We're in the locker room."

Impatience at her facetiousness gave a bite to his voice. "I *know* that."

"And we're in luck, because a row of lockers knocked over and exploded."

They *were* in luck. The chill from the floor was making him shiver in bursts, and each time he did, his torment ratcheted up. "Any blankets?"

"Skis. Ski boots. And a coat."

"Very good."

"If there's a way out."

"Right. If there's a way out." He kept his voice carefully neutral. Because he knew what she knew. In here, the air was frigid . . . and still. No drafts swept down a conveniently placed air vent. No sounds reached them from out-of-doors.

This was a tomb.

"Samuel?" She sounded brightly interested. "Where's your phone?"

As soon as she asked, he knew what she meant. He moved his hand toward the inner pocket of his jacket. Every inch was a lesson in agony, but he groped until he found the square outline of the phone. Slowly he pulled it out and hit the switch. The screen illuminated the darkness. He looked at her without turning his head. "Smart girl. Why didn't I think of that?"

"Because you're in shock. And I'm tired. And we're both . . . afraid."

She was right. He was afraid.

No one knew they were here. They had no air, no food, a billion tons of snow entombed them, and he hurt so much, he couldn't move.

Yet she smiled, a slow, satisfied curve of her lips,

and pointed. "There it is!" She grabbed the black bag, brought out the flashlight, and turned it on.

The glow was almost too much, and he flinched.

She saw his weakness.

Damn it. He hated that.

But she knew him too well. What was he supposed to do about that?

She knelt by his side. Dust streaked her sober face. Her hands hovered over him, waiting for permission to touch him, heal him.

He didn't want that favor from her. "Here's the phone. Call emergency. Get someone here to help us."

"Samuel, don't be an idiot." She took the phone, glanced at it. "There isn't a signal."

"There has to be."

"We're in the Alps in the basement of a stone castle that's been blasted by an avalanche. How many tons of ice do you think are on top of us? How many oak and steel beams are holding up the snow? A cell phone signal? Fat chance!"

He'd hoped to spare her this pain. Now his last shred of hope died. If they were going to survive, he would have to be healthy.

But more important, he couldn't endure the agony.

So he bared his teeth at her. "Go ahead and fix me. I need you."

She bared her teeth back at him, this clean, good, sweetness-and-light woman. "What did you say? I can't hear you."

Through his haze of pain and cold, he felt genuine

amusement—and pride. She could really be a bitch—
and he was the only person on earth who could drive
her to it. "I *said*"—he made sure he was good and
loud—"that I need you."

The building shuddered. Somewhere beyond their
circle of light, something fell, a beam, a wall, something that shook the floor.

She threw herself over his face, protecting him from
the showers of dust, debris, and ice that fell like har-
bingers of doom.

Slowly they ceased.

Slowly she sat up.

"I want you to heal me," he said. "Please. I need
to get us out of here before . . . *We* need to get out of
here."

She put her hands on his shoulders. "Relax."

Even before the sensation of healing swept him,
he experienced the pleasure of her touch. To have her
willingly stroke him . . . she made the world right.

Then he felt it: the gentle healing as she absorbed
his injury.

His eyes fluttered closed.

Heat billowed around him, around *them*, closing
them in a bubble where only the two of them existed.
As her hands cupped his neck, then slid over his chest
and down to his breastbone, the pain slipped from his
nerves to hers.

Distantly, he could hear her breathing grow harsh.

This was why he hated her to carry this burden. He
knew how she did it. She put her hands on the sufferer

and took the anguish as her own. Her body encapsulated his ruptured disks and healed them quickly,
generously.

Yet it was a cruel torture, for she suffered all the pain
that he suffered—and she knew she would. The first
time she touched him, she had tasted the anguish of
his injury, and yet she took the pain voluntarily.

He was a strong man, yet he knew he wouldn't have
had the courage to do what she did.

She was the bravest person he'd ever met.

He didn't know how long she kept her hands on
him, how long their hearts beat together, how long
they breathed with the same lungs, how long their
bones healed as one.

But when he opened his eyes, he was whole once
more—and she sat over him, swaying, face pale, eyes
weary.

"Come on." He pulled her down on top of him,
wrapped his arms around her. "Rest on me."

She was stiff, resistant.

"I won't grope you," he assured her. "At least until
you've recovered."

"Ass," she whispered. With a sigh, she relaxed and
turned her head into his neck.

Her voluminous coat enveloped them, cocooning
them in warmth. His body protected her from the chill of
the floor. . . . He liked knowing he could protect her from
something. He sure as hell hadn't kept her safe tonight.
Soon, he knew, they would be at odds again, but for this
moment, they had escaped death, and they were joined.

As her body grew warm and pliant, she asked, "How did you know?"

"How did I know what?"

"You knew about the tree across the road. You knew about the avalanche before they set the charges. You're not a mind reader. So how did you know?"

He grimaced. "I may not be a mind reader, but I was in that guy's mind tonight. It was not a pleasant place. I forced him to give me the information about Mathis, where they were keeping him, how many men were guarding him. He was fighting me, which made overcoming him kind of fun because . . ."

She tensed against him.

He continued. ". . . Because I knew he'd almost killed a child." He waited, curious to see whether she would chide him.

But she remained still, neither approving nor disapproving.

So he said, "At the same time . . . he was experiencing this sense of glee."

"So you made him tell you about it?" She had that tone in her voice, not quite accusatory, but not pleasant, either.

"I didn't bother. My mistake, but at the time, I was afraid the kid was going to die if we didn't get there in a hurry."

"If he didn't tell you, how did you know about the tree across the road? And the avalanche?"

"I didn't know. Not . . . really. But as I drove along, I started feeling that glee again. It was sick and it was mean, and I knew it was him. The farther I drove, the worse it got. It made me hurry—"

"That's why you were speeding."

"Yeah, I was on the run. Then . . . they must have been watching us with binoculars, because I got this huge burst of pure mean-ass pleasure, right before we went around that corner."

"You . . . read his mind?" She sounded politely incredulous.

For good reason. He wasn't a mind reader. Well, except for the weird connection with Dina, and he thought that was an anomaly, a meeting of their two talents. "This feeling was just an impression. I don't know why it had happened, or how. Maybe it was a hangover from me being in his mind."

"That makes a weird kind of sense," she conceded.

"In a gross way." Samuel didn't want any of that bastard clinging to his mind. Sitting up, he crossed his legs, settled her in his lap, and picked through his memory for the pieces of the puzzle. "I was going to turn around and run the other direction, because I knew they had set a trap of some kind; I just couldn't figure out what. If we'd hit that tree, the car would have been disabled and we would have been sitting ducks for whatever they had planned. Everybody up here knows that the wind blows the snow into the drifts that cause avalanches. I saw that tree cut across the road and the way the wind was blowing the snow, looked up at the mountain and that open stretch of pasture, and I knew. I knew. I figured if this castle was sturdy enough to stand all these years, it was our best chance to survive."

She looked up at the dark cavern of the ceiling. "I don't think the castle is still standing."

"Probably not. Not all of it. No matter how strong the structure—and it had to be formidable to withstand other avalanches that have surely swept down on it—it couldn't withstand such a large snowfield and such a maliciously placed charge." He looked up, too. "But it's holding its own."

"I guess that leaves two questions."

"How long will the building survive?"

"That's one."

"What's the other?"

"Why did the Others set a trap for us?"

Chapter 11

————— ◆ —————

Effortlessly, as if he'd never been hurt, Samuel rose, lifting Isabelle to her feet. "We were set up. Or rather—I was set up. The Others are trying to kill me."

Her hackles rose at his assumption he was the target. "Don't be so conceited. They hurt the boy to bring me to help."

"Maybe. I think it was simply to give urgency to the call."

"Oh, stop brooding." She put her hand to her forehead. Her brain felt heavy. Her eyes hurt from keeping them open.

"I'm not brooding. Just feeling stupid."

As the adrenaline rush faded, exhaustion dragged at her. She'd healed Mathis's not-inconsiderable injuries, then restored Samuel's ruptured disks. She didn't have the strength to be tactful. Besides, with Samuel, tact was a waste of time. "Tell me, what else would we have done? We rescue children. From bad situations. And from the Others. That's what we *do*."

"I should have been more cautious. I should have known they were watching me go to the bank to open the accounts." He saw the startled expression on her face, and said, "You didn't think of that, did you? That that's why we've been buried alive?"

"No. That didn't occur to me. I've had other things on my mind." She was so tired, she couldn't even snap at him with any fire.

Picking up the flashlight, he shined it around the locker room. It occupied the whole basement of the castle, with two dozen rows of lockers, half a dozen picnic tables and benches, and various changing rooms.

The open ceiling was fourteen feet over their heads: ancient, sturdy oak beams supported on oak columns with reinforcements of modern steel that spanned from wall to wall, and steel columns spaced to support the weight of the castle above. If she didn't know about the tons of snow that buried them, she would have thought they could walk out of here. But she had felt the blast of the avalanche, and as the flashlight played over the place the stairs had once been, a frozen waterfall of snow blocked the former entrance.

Lockers stood in double rows up and down the large room, except close against them where the lockers had fallen and smashed open. She saw an ax in the rubble, bricks and stones, broken glass, and, incongruously, one red ski still attached to its boot.

"Aren't you going to ask if the accounts transferred?" he asked.

"I never doubted you would succeed."

"I *did* succeed." Disheveled, his formal clothes
flecked with dust and snow, he looked like a corporate
pirate as he mocked her with his smile. "I met with the
bank president and presented our case. He refused."

She looked down at herself. The mink no longer
looked like a hundred thousand dollars. Tiny pieces of
castle clung to the fur; she shook it, brushed it, unrea-
sonably distressed by the chaos. "So you controlled his
mind and forced him to give you what you wanted."

"That's right. Why do you think I was chosen to
come on this mission? Who else could have done what
I did?"

"I didn't accuse you of anything," she said in a carefully neutral voice, but now she smoothed her gown,
admiring how the resilient silk had shaken off the
trauma to glisten once more.

"Didn't you?"

Her Jimmy Choo stilettos hadn't survived the night
as well as the gown; they were scuffed, the right heel
felt loose, and her toes hurt from exposure to snow
and ice and cold. Her whole body ached and throbbed.
And Samuel's hostility hit her like a blow, hurting her
when she could not bear to be hurt any more.

Of course, Samuel being Samuel, he didn't realize
he was being a jerk moron creep snake scumbucket. He
just kept on talking. "You were the acting leader of the
Chosen Ones for almost a year."

She stood by a table surrounded by benches, a place for the skiers to adjust their boots and eat their lunches. Wearily, she brushed the worst of the debris off the wooden surface. She tucked the length of the mink beneath her, crossed her legs, wrapped the wings of the coat around her. "Yes. So?"

"Did you ever hear anything about a safety-deposit box?"

She was hearing him, but at a distance. "No. Why?"

"There's a safety-deposit box at the bank in Zurich. The bank president took me down there. To open it takes some kind of combination or chanting or some silly-ass thing."

"What's in it?"

"That's the question that interests me. Not even Adelbrecht Wagner had a clue."

Her head drooped.

"He's the bank president," Samuel said helpfully.

She didn't care. She was waiting to die.

Samuel asked, "Do you mind if I wander away with the flashlight?"

"No." Belatedly she thought she should show some curiosity. "Why?"

"I'm going to see if I can find us somewhere to sleep."

"Right." Somewhere to sleep? Where? The Holiday Inn? She grinned to herself, and waved him away.

He took the light and disappeared down a row of lockers. For a few minutes she watched, then realized her eyes had drifted shut. No, slammed shut. Slowly she reclined on the table. This wasn't too bad a spot. She was so tired she didn't think she'd even roll off.

A second later, she opened her eyes to see Samuel standing over her.

"Come on, honey; you need to change and crawl into bed."

"Bed?"

He gestured. "I found the ski-patrol supplies. We've got a two-man tent with a raised floor, sleeping bags, and for you"—he held up oatmeal-colored long johns, top and bottom—"some socks and warm pajamas."

She smiled at him, so cold she was drifting away. "You didn't really find that stuff, did you? This is a hallucination."

"Come on, Isabelle." He helped her sit up. He groped her legs.

She knew she should protest, but she was too tired, and anyway, what difference did it make? He would have to get past her knees before she could feel anything.

Grabbing her ankles, he brought her feet out from under the coat, removed her shoes, and tossed them aside.

That roused a murmur of protest from her.

"I'll buy you some new ones when we get out of here," he said, and slid socks on her feet, first one, then the other. Then après-ski boots.

"They're too big," she told him.

"We'll find you the right size tomorrow."

She was sure that in a couple of years, her feet would get warm again. Polite as always, she said, "Thank you," leaned her head against his chest, and fell instantly asleep.

He pulled the pins out of her hair and worked his fingers through the stiff, hair-sprayed strands.

She half roused, and almost purred with pleasure. "Nice." Her voice was slurred.

"You can't sit here and freeze to death. I'm not done with you yet." He shook her, and when she lifted her head, he pressed something into her hand. "Drink this."

She lifted the bottle to look at it.

Perrier.

"How did you find that? That's *wonderful*."

He helped her tilt it to her lips. "I told you. I found the ski-patrol supplies."

Sure he did. She drank gratefully. Her fingers involuntarily loosened.

Catching the bottle, he set it down to the side. Made her slide, protesting, off the table.

"I want you to take the flashlight and go into the ladies' room." He pointed her toward a darkened entrance. "The water's not frozen yet. Better yet, the hot-water heater is down here, the water's still warm, and there are showers."

She squinted at him. His hair was damp and he looked considerably less grimy. "You took a shower!"

It sounded so good. To be clean . . .

She sighed and closed her eyes.

But it was too much effort.

He continued. "You can pee—"

Her proper upbringing rose in automatic protest. "Refresh myself," she corrected.

"Right. You can refresh yourself. Wash and change, then come back to me, and we'll go to bed and get some rest. Tomorrow we'll figure out a way out of here. Okay?"

She couldn't pull herself out of her malaise. She couldn't even try. Her knees sagged, and if he hadn't held her up, she would have fallen to the floor and stayed there until she died.

His hand tightened on her, holding her close against him. For a moment, she thought he actually empathized with her.

But no. In his amused, hateful, horny Samuel voice, he said, "I have been watching you all night long in this silk dress, and all I could think was—what have you got on underneath?" He pushed the mink coat off her shoulders and dropped it to the ground. "Before you go change, I'm going to find out."

A spark of surprise lit inside her.

He bent her over his knee. Swift as a striking snake, he ran his hand over her rear, down her leg, then under her skirt and up. His hand was on her bare butt before she had time to react. He stroked her, whispered, "Damn, that's a fine ass," then his fingers caught the elastic band of her thong and slid underneath, riding along the crack of her rear, pushing it down her legs, returning to stroke her clit.

She was awake now, aware, furious, fighting. She slammed herself out of his grip and almost toppled over. He caught her hands, pulled her back into him—and she kicked him right in the crotch.

He yelled, bent over, grabbed his balls.

And she kneed him in the face. She felt his nose crunch, saw the blood spurt, heard him yell in agony. All in all, it was a satisfying and exhilarating experience.

She didn't wait for him to recover. Snatching up the underwear, she stormed toward the ladies' room. "I hope you choke," she shouted.

"Wort ebry bita pain," he shouted back. "Come beck; I'll do et again."

"Jerk," she muttered, and went in to do what he said—pee, wash, and change.

When Isabelle climbed into the tent, she expected to have to fight Samuel off. After all, twenty minutes ago he'd been groping her intimately.

Instead, once he helped her remove her boots and zipped her into her own sleeping bag, he turned his back to her and went instantly to sleep. She knew he did, because right away he started twitching and moaning. And snoring and snorting. She waited for another few seconds, then snuggled against him, desperate for his heat, and fell into sleep on the lullaby of his nightmares.

Chapter 12

———— ❈ ————

Samuel's very first memory was of walking into the tavern, covered with the garbage he'd used to keep warm the night before, and hearing the regulars laugh at him. Laugh and point and laugh.

Humiliation. Incandescent fury. He bunched his fists and shouted at Fat Woman, "My mama's going to come and get me, and she'll kill you!"

But instead of giving him the clout to the head he expected, Fat Woman laughed louder and slapped her knee. "Your mama had you in the back of my garage like a stray cat; then she ran away, leaving me to clean up the mess. Stupid tall blond German woman gave birth to you. Look at you. You're a little troll. You haven't got a mama. You haven't got a family. You're nothing but a dark, dirty Gypsy bastard, and that's all you'll ever be."

He was only four, but he recognized contempt when he heard it. Contempt for him. Contempt for the pretty, kind, loving mother he'd imagined all his life. He flung himself at

Fat Woman, biting and scratching, and he was fast. He got her blood in his mouth and her skin under his fingernails.

But she was fast, too. Her fist swung at him like a wrecking ball, hitting him hard.

He flew across the room. Hit the wall.

But she stopped laughing.

In his sleep, Samuel ducked. But his face hurt anyway.

His dreams drifted to . . .

He slipped through the crowds. Tourists were everywhere. Bright-colored shorts, long legs, hemp sandals, all moving along the seawall overlooking the beach. He smelled sausage and ocean and flowers and sweat, and he concentrated on his mission.

Fat Woman wanted money. Lots of money. She'd trained him to pick out expensive handbags and wallets. That was the easy part. Pockets and purses were at eye level.

So he must have been about five, Samuel mused in his sleep.

Then he was back again, in the town, smelling the odors, seeing the leather bags, stalking the thin, tourist American lady because . . .

He'd taught himself to observe people first. Then what they carried. Whether they looked dangerous. Because if he stalked the wrong quarry, he would get caught. Put in prison. And tortured, raped, killed, and eaten.

That was what had happened to Fat Woman's last boy. That was what she told him.

He waited until the American lady was in the thickest

part of the crowd, then moved in. Lifting the flap of her purse, he removed her wallet.

Something snapped at his wrist like a mousetrap. A man's hand. The man lifted Sammy off his feet, and in a dispassionate English accent, he said, "Madam, this boy just picked your pocket."

"No. No. No!" Sammy dropped the wallet and kicked at the man, swinging wildly like a trapped monkey.

The man simply put his foot on the wallet and held Sammy out at arm's length.

"He did it," Sammy shouted. "He's trying to blame me. He did it!"

"He has a very good grasp of English." The American lady observed him through cool, intelligent blue eyes.

Sammy started shouting in Italian, then French, blaming the man over and over.

"Let him down, Darren," she said.

That was when Sammy realized he was truly caught, because American Lady knew the Englishman. "Gigolo!" Sammy shouted, then took another look at the man.

No, he wasn't handsome enough for a gigolo. He must be a bodyguard.

Sammy knew what that meant. Fat Woman had told him time and again. He was going to jail and there they would kill him. If he escaped, Fat Woman would kill him, because she expected him to do his job without getting caught. She couldn't stand bungling little snots.

"What's your name, boy?" American Lady asked, her blue eyes appraising him.

Sammy was going to die. But he didn't cry. He lifted up his chin and stared at her, lips clamped shut.

So Joey, the guy who sold flowers, answered for him. "That's Sammy the Gypsy. He's the best cutpurse in Capri. Thank God you caught him—he's bad for business. I called the police for you."

"He's filthy. He looks like he's starving. His parents should be ashamed," American Lady said.

Joey laughed like a braying donkey. "He's got no parents. He's just a little bas—"

Sammy rammed his head into Joey's 'nads.

Joey doubled over.

Sammy tried to scramble through the forest of legs that surrounded them.

But American Lady caught him by the hair and jerked him back.

He yelled in surprise. Then he tried to shame her. "That's not nice!"

Englishman grabbed his wrist again.

American Lady pulled a tissue out of her purse and wiped her fingers. "It certainly isn't. How long has it been since you've had a bath?"

Sammy looked at her blankly.

Joey recovered his breath and came roaring at Sammy. "Give me the little bastard. I'll take care of him for you."

"You mean you'll turn him over to the police?" American Lady asked.

"Yeah, that's what I mean."

Sammy backed toward her, away from the gleam in Joey's eyes.

"I think not," American Lady said decisively. "I'll handle this matter. Darren, take Samuel back to the hotel and see that he's bathed."

"Oh, madam. Not really! Look at him. He is a Gypsy."

"Romany is the correct term," American Lady said.

"Fine," the Englishman said in disdain. "But as the twig is bent, so grows the tree. This child will never be anything but a thief."

"I don't believe that." American Lady bent down to Sammy. "Samuel, I'm going to take care of you."

"Why?"

She laughed. "My husband would say I'm a pushover for small things in pain. He could be right about that." She straightened and said to the Englishman, "Take him to the hotel. I shall deal with the police and whoever has been caring for this child."

Samuel's skin hurt where the servants had scraped off a lifetime of dirt. . . .

No, wait. He was in a tent in the basement of a ski lodge. He'd faced off with an avalanche, and it was freezing in here. That was why his skin hurt. . . .

Samuel's third memory was American Lady telling him his name was now Samuel Faa, a typical Romany name, and that Darren and his wife were going to be his father and mother. Which he didn't understand at all, since Darren had supervised his bath and clearly wanted to murder Samuel by drowning.

But when Samuel asked Darren why, Darren sniffed and, in his formal stiff-ass English manner, he told Samuel that American Lady was Mrs. Mason and a powerful, rich boss with strong views about helping the helpless youth of the world, so Darren did as he was told. "As you will learn to do under my direction, Samuel."

Samuel didn't complain, because every day someone fed him food, real food, not leavings from someone else's plate. And not just once a day, either. They did it all the time.

He was a smart boy. He figured there were a lot of possible explanations.

Like the wicked witch in the story, American Lady was fattening him up to eat him.

She was going to sell him to a pimp.

Or his favorite—he'd died and gone to heaven.

But while he was scared, every time they put food in front of him, he ate it.

His memories of coming to the US were a blur—of driving in a car, of getting on a plane, his wrist held firmly in Darren's hand. Of seeing American Lady—Mrs. Mason, he now called her—go forward to the front behind a curtain while he and Darren moved to the back. Of arriving in the cold, dark city of Boston, driving to another huge hotel, going inside, and realizing this wasn't a hotel, but Mrs. Mason's house. He met his new mother, who seemed even less pleased than his new father to meet him.

He kept up a brave front until everyone's back was turned. Then he sneaked upstairs, looking for a place to hide. He found it in an empty room with a window seat overlooking the street. He closed the curtains, climbed in among the cushions, and cried. He cried in confusion, because he didn't understand where he was or what was happening to him. He cried in loneliness, because he couldn't know when Mrs. Mason and his new parents would realize he was truly a worthless bastard and throw him out in the street. And he cried in anger because he never cried. He never cared. It was easier that way.

When someone touched his shoulder, he jumped around in a fury and shouted a curse word he'd learned from Fat Woman.

A little girl stared at him, unblinking. It was Isabelle, four years old, wide-eyed, clean, and the prettiest thing he'd ever seen, and he no longer cared about Mrs. Mason or his new parents or this strange hotel. All he cared about was the humiliation of her watching him while he cried like a baby.

"Stupid bitch. What do you want?" he shouted, and wiped his nose on his sleeve.

He didn't seem to frighten her. "To make you feel better." Although he was twice her size, with calluses on his palms and the vocabulary of a trucker, she wasn't afraid of him. Instead she offered her hand, and when he didn't take it, she stroked her hand along his leg. "I'm Isabelle. I can make you feel better. I promise."

He'd heard the whores in the streets talking to clients. He'd seen people, all kinds of people, rich and poor, male and female, drunk and sober, humping and grunting in dark corners. Under the weight of his having seen beatings before and after, and women crying, his illusions about his mother had faded and died.

The little girl was saying stuff like the whores said to the johns.

But the little girl didn't seem to know anything about that. Instead she put her hand around his ankle and held it. And drew the hurt out of his bones, out of his heart. She absorbed his loneliness, his fears, leaving him erased clean as a chalkboard and ready to face this new world. As she did, her bright expression faded, leaving her gazing at him with tears in her eyes.

It was weird. It was frightening. "What are you doing?"

"I told you. I made you feel better. Didn't I?"

"Yeah." *So did she know about him now? He sort of felt like she'd soaked up some of him.* "Do you want me to pay you? I don't have any money, but I could get some."

"No. You don't have to steal anymore. But don't tell my mother that I helped you. She doesn't like it when I do what I do. She says it's different, and girls like me shouldn't be different."

She spoke so well. She was so smart. "What kind of girl are you?"

"I'm adopted, like you. So you shouldn't do anything different, either."

He thought he should warn her. "I'm just a dirty Gypsy bastard."

"No, you're not. I heard them talking downstairs. You're Sammy, and you're safe now." *She leaned over and kissed him on the mouth, a messy, little-girl kiss.* "I'll take care of you."

He liked the words. He liked the kiss. But she was nothing but a kid. "You're stupid. I don't need anyone to take care of me."

She didn't pay any attention to that. "I come here a lot. It's quiet and it's sunny, and no one makes me do anything. I can look out the window instead of studying books, or be warm in the sun instead of worrying about sunscreen, or sleep. . . . If you want, you can use my corner, too, when you want them to leave you alone so you can be yourself."

"I'm always myself."

"Then you're very lucky." Her smile blossomed. *"Will you read me a story?"*

Not to another soul would he have admitted it, but to this pixie, he was able to say, *"I don't know how to read."*

"I do. I'll read you a story." She picked up her book, the one with the colored pictures of knights and castles and dragons and princesses, and she read it to him. At the end of the book, the dragon was chased to his cave, the knight and the princess got married, and Samuel was in love.

Darren found them.

Isabelle was asleep on Samuel's chest.

Samuel was sitting absolutely still, terrified of waking her.

As her maid carried her away, Samuel would have followed her, but Darren put his hand on Samuel's shoulder and stopped him cold. *"Don't get any ideas,"* he said. *"She's not for you. You can't ever have her."*

Samuel didn't know where the words came from. From the heights of his soul, maybe, but more likely from the depths of his gut. But he distinctly remembered saying, *"I don't want to hear* can't *or* won't *or* don't *anymore. I'll be who I want. I'll have who I want. And I want her."*

He'd had her, too. She had been his, and he had been hers. They had lived together, and not just once. Both times, she had seen past the harsh exterior he presented to the world. They had had something real together. And the second time, when he could have kept her forever . . . he'd screwed it up.

Even in the depths of his sleep, Samuel knew this was his last chance to make things right.

The pain in his face eased. He sighed and opened his eyes.

In the darkness, Isabelle was leaning over him, her hands on his face.

"Whatryadoing?" he asked groggily.

"You're *snoring*. I can't stand it anymore. I'm exhausted. I need to sleep. So I'm *fixing* your *nose*."

Each breath he drew was clearer. "Thank you."

"Yeah, yeah." She lifted her hands away. Lay down, her back to him. "Don't even ask me to fix your balls. You deserve every bit of pain you're suffering."

He grinned into the dark, and pulled her close, her body relaxing against his, yet separated by the mummy sleeping bags that kept them alive, kept them warm.

She might not know it, but holding her made everything better.

Chapter 13

Isabelle reached out for Samuel in her sleep, and woke when her hands slid across the slick nylon of his sleeping bag.

She missed his heat. She missed the way he fought with his nightmares. She missed the fact that even when his nose was healed, he snored.

He'd been gone for a while, though, because his body warmth had faded from his side of the tiny two-man tent. She opened her eyes, frustrated that she cared. That she liked sleeping with him, holding him in her arms, being glad that of all the men in the world, she was trapped with him, that if they had to die . . .

Well. They'd lived through the night, and that was a miracle. They could get out of here, too. Somehow.

She looked around.

Light came through the thin nylon walls of the tent. Light that seemed focused off to the left side toward the table. Laid out beside her were clothes: a gold sweat-shirt, green ski pants, a purple thigh-length parka, all approximately her size, if not even close to her taste. She pulled them on over the long underwear, shivering as the chill of the clothes stole away the lingering warmth of the sleeping bag.

A camp lantern sat on the table, its LED light shedding enough illumination for her to see that the area around the tent had been swept clear of dust and debris. A breakfast had been placed on the table: a bottle of water, an energy bar, a battered apple.

Samuel knew how to forage.

She drained the water, then muttered, "No cappuccino?" She was grateful to be alive. She was glad to fill her stomach. But Dracula was wrong. Blood wasn't life. Caffeine was life, and she needed some.

She picked up the lantern and went in search of Samuel, wandering up and down the rows of lockers. She found him at the back, lit by another camp lantern, dressed in mismatched ski clothes, and using a pickax to pry open a series of lockers set behind a now-open wire mesh cage.

He looked her over, grinned, and nodded. "Nice."

"I feel like a Mardi Gras necklace."

"Beggars can't be choosers."

"No, and I'm grateful."

"Don't be grateful to me. Be grateful to the women whose lockers I've broken into." He showed her the point of the pickax. "It's not as elegant as your lock picking, but it's warmed me up." Walking over to her, he tucked his hand under her chin and turned her face from side to side. "You look like you're going to live. Last night, I wasn't so sure."

"I was fine." He looked good this morning, too, his nose completely healed and a twenty-four-hour growth of dark beard covering his chin.

"You had done too much. You were ready to lie down and die."

Vaguely, she remembered thinking just that. Vividly, she remembered him running his hand up her leg and rubbing her rear. And her flare of fury. For one wild moment, she almost asked him if he'd groped her merely to revive her.

But that would be stupid. Getting her on her feet might have been his primary objective. But he'd enjoyed himself, too, and she saw no reason to give him an opening to suggest a rerun.

He was still observing her, standing a little too close, breathing her air.

She pushed his hand away and stepped back. "Now—can I help?"

"That would be great. We're not going to starve to death—there are dry rations galore, not to mention energy bars and sack lunches. Water's a little more difficult. I think the blanket of snow is acting as insulation on top of us, so the temp has leveled off at about freezing. Fluids are slushy. Yet we can't light a stove to heat them up because—"

"Because it'll take oxygen." She sighed. He was right, but the choices down here were tough ones.

"I'll open lockers." He showed her the pickax. "You

sort stuff into piles. I've got it organized." He pointed. "Perishables go there. Obviously, we don't have to worry about refrigeration."

"That's enough fresh food to keep us for weeks." She looked around at the cavernous room, and added hastily, "Not that we'll be here for that long."

"No, of course not. Canned foods, energy bars, breakfast bars go there." He pointed again. "Bottled water, Cokes, juices."

She looked at the assembled bottles and licked her lower lip. "Any coffee drinks?"

"Maybe. What'll you give me for one?" He wore one of his patented clever-guy smirks.

"I won't kill you in a caffeine-deprived rage. How's that for a deal?" She smirked back, sweet as only she could be.

He reached into an empty locker, retrieved one of the bottles he'd stashed inside, popped the top, and handed it over.

Good to know she could make him fear her. Taking a long drink, she sighed with delight and contemplated the admirable qualities of coffee.

Abruptly he said, "I thought I had it figured out."

"What?"

"How to let someone know we're here. When I was at the bank, Dina was in my head giving instruction."

"She's a mind speaker. You're not."

"No, and I don't know why or how, but we were communicating. So I tried to put in a call this morning.

Sent it good and hard so it would get through." His mouth curled in disgust.

"No luck?"

"Think of the cartoon where the coyote thinks he's chasing the Road Runner into a tunnel, but it's an arch painted on the rock."

She flinched at the mental image.

"Exactly. I hit that wall so hard my brain bounced."

"What do you think happened to your lines of communication?"

"I don't know. I never have trusted Dina, but she had the perfect chance to betray us while I was at the bank and didn't. Now we're here, and I don't know if she was so freaked about *me* talking in *her* head for a change that she shut me down. I don't know if she set us up to be killed in this avalanche. For all I know, the cigarettes finally caught up with her and she dropped dead of a heart attack."

"Or the Others found out she was helping us and killed her." She was pleased to note that the caffeine was moving through her veins, because she was putting logical thoughts together.

"That's possible, too. Have you ever heard how she got her nose sliced in half?"

"No, have you?"

"No. Last I learned about Dina was when Genny realized she and Martha were sisters. I didn't even realize there was a similarity."

"I didn't know either, Sammy."

"Really?" He moved his head back and forth. "That makes me feel better. Not quite so insensitive."

She smirked at him. "I wouldn't go that far."

He smirked back at her. "As soon as I said it, I knew you were going to hit that one out of the ballpark. Now—ready?" he asked, and gestured toward his well-sorted piles.

"Sure," she said expansively.

"Here's where I put the alcoholic beverages."

"Wow." She surveyed the veritable mountain of whiskies, schnapps, wines, and beers.

"Skiers do like their libations." He grinned. "Clothes and blankets there. Any tools you run across—there." He grabbed an energy bar, opened it, and took a big bite. "Don't forget to eat. Maintaining body heat at this temp will really burn the calories."

"I'm not fragile, you know. I work out and my body mass index is right on target." And why did she feel like she needed to defend herself to him?

He swung the pickax and broke the lock. "You look great."

What was she supposed to say to that? "Thank you," she said.

He gestured to her. "See what you can find." He started on the next locker.

She went to work. She drank her iced coffee—might as well put a good face on it—looked through the clothes, found a wool scarf, and wrapped it around her neck and head. Found a good pair of gloves, warm but tactile, and went to work. He was right: The problem wasn't food or water. It was heat and light. If they didn't get out soon enough, they were going to freeze to death in the dark. She looked up at the ceiling again, at the heat ducts hung from metal straps and the steel and oak beams. "Samuel, why isn't anything creaking? This whole place seems solid as a—"

"Tomb?" He turned back to the locker he was excavating. "I'm not a structural engineer, but here's my theory. You've got a medieval castle, some major construction, reinforced for modern life. An avalanche comes down, because it had a little help from our boys with the Others. It wipes out the castle all the way to ground level. But it's like a tornado: It doesn't dip down; it blasts past. The beams and the floor hold, the heat down here rises, and the snow melts, then refreezes into ice. I think we're in an ice cave."

"So we can't even dig our way out."

"I've got the ski patrol's shovels and pickaxes. We'll give that a shot, but if it doesn't work"—he grinned like a boy—"I found the dynamite."

Chapter 14

"The dynamite?" Isabelle carefully placed the empty glass bottle, formerly full of cappuccino, on the ground.

"Yeah! The ski patrol are the people who set off charges to create *controlled* avalanches. They stored their dynamite down here in their lockers." His eyes sparkled with glee. "I've got it."

"Samuel. You are a lawyer." And lawyers were supposed to be logical, although she was starting to think there was as much chance of that as of *men* being logical. "When did you learn to use dynamite?"

"How hard can it be?"

She needed to remember that he was also a boy at heart. "To blow things up? It's easy. Not to blow yourself up at the same time? It's a bitch."

"Isabelle." He imitated her patient voice. "How would you know?"

"I *did* learn how to use dynamite."

"Where did you learn that? In finishing school?"

"I learned in basic training." She really enjoyed telling him that. Enjoyed watching expressions of amusement, skepticism, and dawning belief chase across his face.

He put down the pickax. "Basic training? Like . . . in the military?"

"Like in the military," she confirmed.

"Pull the other one."

She stepped up to him, challenging him toe-to-toe. "Let's face it, Samuel. We occasionally collide like dual suns in a single orbit. But we've spent years apart, and you don't know everything about me."

He leaned down so his nose was close to hers and challenged her right back. "I know Mrs. Mason's little girl wouldn't join the military."

The smug, nasty rat. "I didn't join the military. After I realized you'd betrayed me, I needed some way to take my mind off the humiliation. So I joined a basic-training course run by an old marine drill sergeant up in the Rocky Mountains in Wyoming. Three months of physical training, survival preparation, and hell. When I was done . . . you weren't so important anymore." She relished the way he looked, brown eyes wide, mouth half cocked open. She'd astonished him at last.

Take that, Samuel Faa.

Being Samuel, he recovered at once. "So you can set the charge. Even if the blast doesn't break through the ice, the sound should get the rescuers' attention."

"First of all, Samuel, there are no rescuers." In the

depths of the night, while she was listening to Samuel snore, she'd thought out the situation. "No one knows for sure where we were when the avalanche swept through, but since we've disappeared, they're pretty sure we were buried in snow. And not in a good way. In a *'they're frozen or asphyxiated'* way."

"Or in a *'they were swept off the road and down the chasm'* way."

Good. He wasn't under any illusions. "More important, we're trapped in what apparently is an airtight room. We've only got so much oxygen in here, and an explosion will use it up. We'd be lucky if the rescuers, supposing they heard or saw the explosion, could dig down to us quickly enough to get us out before our oxygen was depleted."

"Don't sugarcoat it. Give it to me straight." He was joking around. Of course.

She wasn't. "We've got to save the dynamite until there's no hope left."

He stared wistfully at the box of dynamite. "All right. Fine. But in the meantime"—he slung the pick over his shoulder—"hey-ho, it's off to work I go."

She followed him as he headed toward the far corner. "What are you going to do?"

"I don't know where these double doors go, but the snow didn't bust them in, so I'm prying them open."

"Have you thought about just unlatching them?"

"They swing out."

"Of course they do." Because exits always swung out. "Something's blocking the way?"

"It might be snow and debris from the castle. But it might lead to a tunnel or something. Aren't castles supposed to have secret tunnels?"

"I wouldn't hold my breath." Because that would be too convenient. "What happens if you get it open and snow fills the room?"

"Then I guess we don't have to worry about whether to use the dynamite." He sounded cheerful.

"You don't think this is going to work."

"No." He stopped by the doors. "But we have to try the obvious stuff before we go on to do the difficult stuff."

She nodded, seated herself on an overturned bank of lockers, and watched as Samuel hooked the point of the pickax into one door near the bottom and started prying the metal back layer by layer. As the gap widened, he shed his cap, his coat, his ski pants, and he was down to a long-sleeved T-shirt and a pair of too-loose jeans that sagged on his hips and gave her glimpses of black, tight underwear. Sweat stained his chest and back.

And she wanted to lick it off his skin.

Damn him. He had no business looking so good.

"You're still boxing?" she asked.

"It keeps me off the streets." He flashed her a smile.

"Really? I thought that's what sent you into the streets."

His smile disappeared. "Honey, I was picking pockets as soon as I could toddle. The *bitch* who kept me until I was five used to send me around the clients in her shithole of a bar to pull their wallets."

She swallowed. Sometimes she forgot about his background before her mother plucked him out of the gutter. "I didn't mean then. I meant in Boston. When you were in high school."

"No. Boston was a whole different ball game. I was going to a rough public school. I was Romany. I was short for my age. And I went through puberty late." He smashed the flat end of the pickax into the door, pulled it out, smashed it again. "I was getting killed every day, and I did something about it. I learned to defend myself. I would think you'd approve of my taking such rational action—as opposed to buying a gun and blasting those bullies to hell. Which, if you watch the news, more than a few kids do. I was an adolescent like them, with more than a few reasons for rage."

Which, if the way he was hitting that door was any indication, he still fought. "Why *did* you go to a public school?"

"My father wouldn't pay for a private school, and he wouldn't let your mother pay for one, either. He said it would give me illusions above my station."

"Your father is medieval."

"He's an English butler. He comes from a long line of English butlers. And what's good enough for him should certainly be good enough for an illegitimate Rom pickpocket."

She half expected him to shoot her a rueful grin.

He didn't. Instead he swung the pickax as hard as he could and smashed the door again.

So he was still hacked off about that. Not that she blamed him.

"I wonder what your father thinks of me?"

Samuel placed the pickax head on the floor, leaned on it, and considered her unsmilingly. "It's not a discussion we ever conducted. He would consider it impertinent to"—Samuel's voice changed, became upper-class English—"converse about his employers and their progeny."

She didn't really want to ask. She knew she wasn't going to like the answer. "But?"

His voiced changed back to his own. "But if I were guessing, he would say you're an orphan who has the wisdom to appreciate your good fortune and those who gave it to you, and he would commend your sincere desire to repay them with obedience to their wishes."

"Samuel, that's awful!"

"You asked."

Her feelings were hurt, yet she asked, "Is that what *you* think of me?"

"I think you're overly worried about your mother's good opinion." He didn't choose his words carefully. But that was Samuel. Truth above all—or at least what he perceived as the truth.

"My mother has always done what she thought was right for me!"

"Who would you be if your mother had encouraged you to do whatever you wanted?"

Isabelle got to her feet, her fists clenched at her sides. "I would be who I am, Samuel. I would raise funds for the World Children's Literacy Foundation. I would work for the Gypsy Travel Agency as a healer. One has my mother's blessing. The other does not. But they're both who I am."

"Why *did* you join the Gypsy Travel Agency?"

"I always knew I was given my gift for a reason, and the Gypsy Travel Agency provided a chance to use it for the good of mankind." She lifted her chin. "And I don't care if you think it's corny. It's the truth."

"I know you, Isabelle." He took a step toward her.

She held up her hand against his words.

He halted. "I know you better than anyone else knows you. I know it's the truth."

"And you know it's corny?"

"That, too."

"At least I didn't have to practically get thrown in prison before I would join."

"The Gypsy Travel Agency directors set me up."

"They had to, didn't they?"

"No. Really. Why would I be reluctant to give up my quite profitable law practice for all this?" He swept his hand around the room. "Didn't it occur to you that I might be picked for the team?"

"Yes, but I thought the Gypsy Travel Agency was going to be a big, bustling concern and I would hardly ever see you." She remembered this all too well. "Then the building blew up, everybody was killed, and you and I were together all the time."

"Without your mother's encouragement, you wouldn't have gotten engaged to that pissant senator."

He hooked the point of the pickax in the widening edge of the door and yanked, peeling back metal in a teeth-grinding racket.

"True," she said pleasantly. "But I also wouldn't have gotten engaged to that pissant senator if I hadn't been royally screwed over by the man I loved."

He yanked again, curling away a good-sized piece of door to reveal a patch of frozen-solid, immobile avalanche. "Son of a bitch!"

Although she knew he wasn't really cursing the snow, she said, "We knew this probably wasn't going to work."

He slammed the pickax at the ice. And swore louder when it bounced back and punched a hole through his jeans and into his thigh.

He jerked it out.

Blood spurted.

"Sammy!" She ran toward him.

He looked up at her, wildly surprised that his temper had produced such results. "I'm sorry!"

"Don't apologize." She reached for him. "It's okay."

"No, it's not." He held a hand out to stop her. "Don't touch me!"

"Honestly, Samuel! Lighten up. I fixed your last injury and survived."

"Yeah, but this one hit the femoral artery. It's a fatal wound." He went down hard on the floor. "If you try to help me, you'll die, too."

Chapter 15

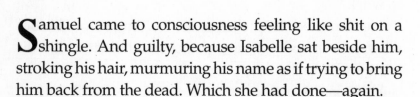

Samuel came to consciousness feeling like shit on a shingle. And guilty, because Isabelle sat beside him, stroking his hair, murmuring his name as if trying to bring him back from the dead. Which she had done—again.

The effort left her looking as white, drawn, and as close to death as she had appeared last night. Only this time she was covered in blood. His blood. Both of them were going to have to strip down in this frozen prison and wash themselves in slushy water—and it was his fault.

He hated when it was his fault, and with Isabelle, it seemed like it usually was.

Taking a deep breath, he looked into her eyes.

"You're going to be okay," she whispered.

"But are you?" he asked.

"Soon," she said.

Fact was, her healing always lagged behind her patients', so he was probably feeling better than she did.

He dragged himself into a sitting position, and the effort was even more than he'd imagined. "We almost died that time, didn't we?"

"It was deep and gross, but it wasn't as bad as you thought."

"What would have happened if I had been right?"

"I don't know. I've never had to heal a femoral artery before."

His temper rose. "You should have kept your hands to yourself. You could have died trying to help me."

"Don't yell at me." Color blossomed in her cheeks as she got mad, too. "You know I have had to make the decision to let people go. If they're hurt too badly, I just . . . I'm not going to do any good in this world if I'm dead."

"So you would have let me go?"

"It was a dilemma, since I so frequently want to kill you," she snapped.

Like any good lawyer, he interrogated her with his silence.

She caved, of course. "Okay. There wasn't a good choice. I figured I had to heal you for selfish reasons."

"What kind of selfish reasons?"

Reaching out, she once more stroked his hair back. "You're my best chance to get out of here—if you will stop throwing the pickax."

He laughed. "Oh, honey, I do love you."

She stiffened, pulled her hand back, offense in every line of her body.

And he didn't know how to recover. It was nothing

more or less than the truth, but she didn't want to hear it. She didn't believe it.

Somehow, he would make her believe it. He was smart. Brilliant, in fact. Being trapped down here sucked, no doubt about it. But he also recognized the opportunity he'd been given.

Before they got out, he would convince her to give him another chance.

Hefting himself to his feet, he picked her up and headed toward the tent.

She lifted her head as if to protest, then dropped it back on his chest.

"Smart girl," he said.

"There's no use talking sense to you. You can't even hear me."

"I listen to every word you speak. I just don't always do what you tell me."

"Don't I know it." Her mouth curled in a smile. "Unless I'm talking about my underwear."

Sixteen-year-old Isabelle walked into the house, dropped her backpack on the chair, shed her coat, ignored her mother's call, and ran up the stairs to the third floor. Striding into the bedroom, she pulled open the curtains on the window seat. Hands on hips, she glared at Samuel's long length stretched out in the sun. "Have you lost your mind?" She got a good look at him. "And what did you do to your hair?"

"I shaved it off."

"I can see that. But why? I loved—" She stopped. He did not need to know she loved his hair, so black and thick.

"Because it's a liability when I fight."

"You shouldn't be fighting!"

"Yeah, princess. You would think that." Putting his finger in his book to hold his place, he looked her over, a slow, appreciative sweep that lingered on her prep-school white shirt, blue sweater, pleated plaid skirt, and knee socks.

"Knock it off." He'd started doing this, trying to distract her when she gave him trouble about stuff. His grades. His clothes. His attitude.

He patted the cushion. "Come in and shut the curtains behind you."

She hesitated. They hadn't met here in years, ever since he got too big to bother with her, while she turned eleven and went to St. Theresa's Girls' School.

"Come on." He lifted the book and showed her the title—Machiavelli's The Prince. *"I'm just reading."*

He was going to bother with her now. She was going to make him *bother with her.*

She climbed in and shut the curtains. "I talked to Mother today. She said you had quit school!"

"News travels fast."

"The saying is 'Bad news travels fast.' I guess that's right."

"Are you really surprised?"

"Yes, of course I am! How else will you be able to get into college and make something of yourself?"

"Why would I need to go to college to wait on the table while you have a party?"

She caught her breath.

"Had you forgotten? Or did you merely think it was nothing more than my proper place in life?"

Yes, she remembered. Every year at her birthday party, Samuel would be forced into a miniature suit and sent in to serve the other little girls at the table. None of the children or the attending parents thought anything was amiss; indeed, most of the mothers cooed over him. But Isabelle always saw his resentment in the flash of his dark eyes.

"I am not a servant," he said. "Specifically, I'm not your servant."

"I never thought you were. You know I didn't. I told Mother to stop having you work at my parties, but she said—"

"She said it was Darren who insisted. Yes, it's true. He believed I would realize how truly honorable a job it is to serve and serve well." Samuel showed his teeth in what looked like a snarl. "I did not."

"I know." Isabelle looked down at her hands.

Eventually Mother had put a stop to using him to wait on Isabelle's guests. It happened at Isabelle's eleventh birthday party. One of the little girls wasn't little anymore and she reacted to his dark beauty by flirting with him and he flirted back with a natural aptitude that upset the parents, upstaged all her mother's carefully planned entertainment . . . and made Isabelle rigid with a tension she didn't comprehend. "My mother's a snob. I know that. But not as bad as your father."

"No one's as bad as my father." Samuel was still reclining, but he was no longer relaxed. His whole body vibrated with suppressed fury. "My father honestly thinks that being a butler is the best I can aspire to. Doesn't understand why I don't. He won't even listen to me."

"But still I don't understand what this has to do with your quitting school. Surely if you want to improve your lot in life . . ." She realized how patronizing that sounded, and stumbled to a halt.

"No. I'm determined to go to hell in a handcart," he said bitterly.

Her temper flared. "You're going about it the right way. Mother said you got a tattoo!"

Turning his head, he showed her. Five black marks on his skull, spaced like fingerprints from the back of one ear to the other. "It's not a tat."

"It is, too!" How stupid did he think she was?

"I got it last year. It came naturally. When I got my power."

That froze her in place. "What power?"

He stared at her as if not sure how to explain. Finally, he said, "Do you remember the first time we met? Here in the window seat?"

She shook her head no, although the faintest memory niggled at her mind.

"You made me feel better. You healed me."

"I shouldn't have, I suppose, but I was little and didn't know better."

"I know. Your mother doesn't like you to be different."

"For my sake! So I can fit in!"

"Believe me, I know about not fitting in, and you fit in fine."

For the first time she looked at him, really looked at him, stretched out there on the cushions.

He was tall, well over six feet, and fit, with muscled

shoulders that strained at his short-sleeved T-shirt, thick wrists, and powerful, long-fingered hands. His nose was squashed from the soccer ball hit he'd taken full on the face in fourth grade, and his lips pouted like a young Jagger's. Long, dark lashes fringed his brown eyes. His lids drooped with a knowing, cynical cast—and he was only seventeen. When had he turned into a man who viewed the world so scornfully?

"I do fit in," she acknowledged. "I work at it. What about you?"

"Not so much. Remember last year, when my voice changed overnight? That wasn't the only thing that happened. Not by a long shot."

She arranged the pleats on her plaid skirt. "You don't need to spell it out. I know about the other stuff."

"I wasn't going to tell you all that stuff. Prude." He laughed at her, but kindly. "The thing is, every other guy at the gym had already hit puberty, so I was glad to finally stop squeaking when I talked. For lots of reasons, but mostly because there was this kid. Little, skinny shit with a smart mouth that never stopped, and he picked on me all the time, razzing me about being a Gypsy orphan."

"What was he?"

"Greek, I think, but his parents were married, so in his opinion, that made him hot shit." Those beautiful lips, the ones she had just noticed, folded into a grim line. "I couldn't do anything about it; he was too short for me to beat up and he knew it. So after this overnight transformation, he saw what was going on and he was just relentless." He imitated a falsetto voice. "'Hey, Faa, did the hairy fairy visit you?'— and that was the cleanest of it. So I very politely suggested

he beat himself up. And I really, really, really"—he put his fingers on his forehead—"wished he would."

She leaned forward, intent on his face. "And he did?"

Samuel sat up, crossed his legs, and stared back into her eyes. "Yeah, he did. At first we all thought he was trying to be funny again, but then he started crying and he had bruises, and I wished he would stop, only this time I didn't wish it so much as command him with my mind. And it worked."

When Isabelle heard Samuel's confession, she knew she should say something comforting. Something about him. Instead she blurted, "Thank God I'm not the only freak in this world."

"I wouldn't say that." He grinned at her.

She punched him in the arm.

"Good shot." He rubbed the spot. "I did the research. Do you know who we are?"

"Who are we?"

"We're the Abandoned Ones. We were given gifts because our parents, our real parents, threw us away."

Each word was like a stab to her tender heart. "Why do you think that?"

"Ever heard of Joseph Campbell?"

"Of course. He did research on pervasive myths that cross cultural boundaries and appear to be part of the human psyche regardless of background or geological location."

"So they taught you a few things in that fancy school of yours, huh?"

He didn't seem to expect an answer, which was good, because she didn't have one. She was the Masons' only child.

He was the butler's only son. She went to a posh private school. He went to one of Boston public's finest. The disparity made her uncomfortable, but what could she do? Her mother told her she'd offered to pay for private school. Darren had refused. And Patricia Mason had said she'd interfered enough when she urged the reluctant Darren to adopt Samuel.

Isabelle had hotly replied that Darren should give Samuel the best start possible, but Patricia said that was a line she could not cross.

"*The thing about the Abandoned Ones,*" *Samuel continued,* "*is that it's an ancient legend that crosses cultures. Trust me. I've read a lot about that legend now. Supposedly, our gifts make us possible recruits for the Chosen Ones, which is this ancient society of do-gooders.*" *Samuel's cynical face was abruptly more cynical.* "*We can also be recruited by the Others, which is this ancient society of assholes.*"

He was distracting her. Or she was pretty sure he was. "*What does this have to do with your hair?*"

"*After I made Jermaine beat himself up, I got this itching on my head. I reached up and my hair was falling out in clumps. So I got Steve to look, and he said it looked like fingerprints on my skin.*"

"*Let me look at them.*"

He turned around. "*I was . . . well, I was scared. I covered up the bald spots no problem, my hair was long enough but Steve told one of the guys, and pretty soon it was all over the school that I was a . . . freak.*"

His head looked like the sheets she used when she volunteered at the school carnival to fingerprint little kids for their parents' records, except these marks weren't made by small fingers. It looked as if a man's hand had pressed hard to make these prints, even leaving little indents in the skin.

"This is so weird. Did you tell your father?"

Samuel laughed, a short burst of nasty amusement. "Oh. Cara. Like he would understand or believe me."

She bit her lip. Samuel and Darren had always been at loggerheads, more so now that Darren's wife had left him and blamed the divorce on Samuel.

"Have you compared these prints to yours?"

He sighed in exaggerated exasperation. "It's a little tough for me to get a good look at them." He held his right hand up. "You do it."

She did, examining each finger and comparing it to his head. "They're your prints."

"So I am a freak."

"I guess we both are." She returned to the subject at hand. "But that's no reason to quit school."

He turned. Leaned in until they were nose-to-nose. "I'm not stayin'. They haven't taught me a damned thing for years, and the whole world is out there calling me."

She leaned right back. "No. No! You can't do anything without a high school diploma."

"I can't do anything with that high school diploma. People don't get into college from that school."

"Listen to me!"

"I will." Putting his hands on her arms, he smiled at her. No . . . he smirked. "If you tell me one thing."

"What?"

"What are you wearing under that extremely hot skirt?"

Chapter 16

Isabelle stared at Samuel. Was he kidding?

Of course he was.

Huffily, she said, "You're making fun of me." She started to flounce off the window seat.

He lunged, wrapped his arm around her waist, rolled, and put her under him. He stared into her indignant eyes and with slow emphasis said, "I am so not laughing at you."

I don't know what you mean. *But abruptly, she did. She was young, she was a virgin, but she wasn't stupid. She'd read the books. She'd checked out the Internet. She'd talked to her friends. And even if she hadn't done all that stuff, her instincts jingled insistently. Her voice quavered as she said, "Well . . . good. Because I don't like to be laughed at."*

She and Samuel, they hadn't ever made out. In fact, after they got to be teenagers, their early, easy affection had changed, become a distance that didn't encourage contact. When their eyes met, her gaze slid away. When they bumped into each other, she leaped back. She thought people—people like her mother and father—saw how uncomfortable she was, because they never allowed them time to be alone anymore. Having anyone see her discomfort . . . well, that just embarrassed her. So did the dreams she had sometimes.

Now Samuel's body was hard against hers, his skin warmed by the sun. He pushed her hair off her forehead, tucked it behind her ear, yet his brown eyes were hot, intense, focused on her as if he wanted to dive into her soul.

He made her nervous. He made her aware of every breath she took, of every breath he took, of the way their chests moved against each other.

She wanted to look away. She wanted to push him away. She wanted to pull him close. She didn't dare move, except to chew at her lower lip.

His gaze dropped to that betraying little movement. His head dipped. Paused.

He was thinking about kissing her.

Her heart thundered in her ears.

She wanted him to kiss her.

She lifted her head a little.

Their lips met in the middle.

Samuel. Her first kiss. Samuel. First kiss. With Samuel.

She didn't remember a time when she hadn't known him. Loved him. Now this . . . her first kiss. Their two mouths, pressed together . . .

Lifting his head, he smiled at her, darkly satisfied. "There. That's done."

Wait. *"We're* done*?"*

"Do you want to be done?"

"No! Yes! No!" She frowned at him. "Did you do it wrong?"

"Kiss you? I don't think so."

"You've kissed other girls?"

"A few."

She didn't like knowing that. But he had experience, so she guessed he knew what he was doing. So it was her. "Is there something wrong with me? I . . . wasn't I supposed to . . . ?"

"Supposed to do what?"

"You know . . . experience overwhelming passion?"

All of a sudden, he was fighting a grin.

Which made her mad. He didn't need to act like she was dumb. "I'm just saying, in the books, when a guy grabs a girl and kisses her, the girl always experiences overwhelming passion."

He lowered his head again, until his mouth was barely above hers, so she felt his breath and the brush of his lips as he spoke. "Let's see if we can find out about that."

This time when he kissed her, he pressed his lips to hers more firmly, then used his tongue to tease her with little wet touches that made her stiffen in alarm because that felt really, really . . . real. She wasn't hearing the music swell. She wasn't behind a camera watching, or holding a book reading; she was here, on the familiar window seat, with Samuel, whom she had known forever, and his mouth was opening over hers, and she was opening her mouth back, and there was no overwhelming passion, just this shaky kind of panic. . . .

Then.

Wow.

It was weird, but she remembered kissing him when she was little. She remembered the taste of him. This was Samuel. She hadn't simply known him forever. Long ago, she had healed his fears and absorbed a part of him.

And she relaxed.

He smelled good: clean brown skin and muscles over strong man bones.

As she let his tongue move freely in her mouth, a faint scent of sweat or something so intimately Samuel made her press her knees together. Not because he was making any moves on her—his fingers were tangled in her hair—but because sensations rushed at her: hurried breathing, heart pounding, blood thundering in her veins, and need, burning need.

This was just like the books. Overwhelming passion . . .

Which was . . . overwhelming. It wasn't what she expected. Being swept away sounded romantic. It felt . . . frightening. She hadn't realized that she would want to . . . to forget the morals her mother had so carefully instilled in her and do things with him. Almost of their own volition, her hands stroked his neck, his shoulders, his arms. She explored his muscles rippling under his shirt. Rubbed her legs against his.

His whole body became so rigid she might have thought it was rejection.

But she could feel his heart slamming against his chest, taste his hurried breath, and he kissed her as if he wished to feed her his whole self.

Never in her life had she felt so much a part of another person.

Then he broke it off. Simply lifted his head and stared down at her, his eyes wide.

"Don't stop." Then she was embarrassed. She had whimpered.

"Your mother's calling you."

"What?" Isabelle wasn't quite processing his words.

"Your mother's calling you."

"I didn't hear her."

"Trust me. I have good ears."

She did trust him. But she didn't want it to be the truth.

"Come on." He got onto his knees, pulled her into a sitting position. "You don't want her to catch us."

"Right!" He was so right. She didn't even know what her mother would do if she realized Isabelle had been kissing Samuel.

Make Isabelle feel guilty.

Make Samuel leave the house.

No!

"Right." She catapulted off the window seat, then discovered she had to steady her legs. They were shaking. She was shaking. With anxiety, with sexual need.

How had she come so far so quickly?

Had she been ready? And waiting for Samuel? Was he all she needed?

She whirled and looked at him.

He stared at her, so much passion in his gaze her knees buckled again.

She backed away from the window seat, then turned and stalked to the door. Yanking it open, she yelled, "Coming, Mother!" Then she turned back to him. Her chin trembled with nerves, but she spoke clearly. "White cotton panties."

He froze in place, staring at her as if the three words had scrambled his brain.

Then she saw him remember his earlier question.

What are you wearing under that extremely hot skirt?

"White cotton panties," *she repeated.*

Color surged in his face. His long, dark lashes fluttered closed. He groaned as if he were in pain.

She walked out the door, slammed it behind her, and smiled.

Quit school, would he? Leave Boston, would he?

She had given him something else to think about.

Chapter 17

"**D**o you mind not hogging the whole tent?" Isabelle rolled over in frustration, digging her elbow at Samuel, then realized that his down sleeping bag protected him.

"How can I hog the whole tent? This bag is keeping me confined."

"Then scooch your bag over."

"There is no *over*. It's a two-man tent."

"What two men could fit in here?"

Neither Samuel nor Isabelle slept very well. They weren't as tired as the night before. It wasn't her dreams of Samuel that kept waking her. No, not at all. The lingering pain from Samuel's injury made them restless. That was it.

And five and a half years ago, when they had slept together . . . they *slept together*. So for Isabelle, the forced proximity proved irritating and . . . tempting. If there was one thing she knew from past experience, being tempted by Samuel led to two things. Great sex. And heartbreak.

So no. *No.* And no.

"What are you muttering about?" he asked.

"Is it time to get up yet?"

"What difference does it make? If you want to get up, we'll get up."

"True. It's not like we have a full schedule."

"Actually, I have an idea. . . ."

Which was why Isabelle found herself side by side with Samuel at the double doors, digging a tunnel through the snow toward the surface.

Samuel and Isabelle slept *that* night.

And she didn't dream of him at all. Not at all.

Chapter 18

Samuel and Isabelle woke groaning as they dragged their aching bodies out of the tent and back to their tunnel. They had agreed they had to make the tunnel big enough to use a shovel effectively. At first, in a hurry to succeed, they both dug using the ski patrol's folding shovels. A minor cave-in set them back—and scared them—and they agreed that one would dig while the other placed the snow onto a tarp (the ski patrol rudely did not include buckets in its supplies) and dragged it into a pile between rows of lockers. That way, if a cave-in occurred, the dragger could come to the rescue of the digger.

But as they worked in the hard-packed snow, their confidence grew.

When day three was over, they had created a tunnel that burrowed into the avalanche until it reached the stone steps built into the earth, then followed them to ground level and from there took a gradual slope toward the surface. Toward freedom.

They went to bed exhausted—and hopeful.

Chapter 19

———◆———

"We've been in here four days, right?" Isabelle shoveled snow onto the tarp.

"Right." Samuel flexed his shoulders, ate an energy bar, and tried to recover enough to take over.

"I'm thinking my role in *Indiana Jones and the Ice Temple of Blisters* is about over."

"Nice." He nodded his appreciation. "You might say it's time to *Dial M for Meltdown*."

They were inching their way toward the surface, making the angle a little sharper, joking around because it helped get their minds off their aching muscles.

"Heh. Good one. I'm tired of starring in *A Ski Lift Named Desire*."

She was slowing down.

He was slowing down.

But it was hard to quit when they both thought they might break free today . . . or tomorrow . . . or the next day. . . . "I'm tired of *Saving Private Frostbite*."

Isabelle rested her shovel on the ground, leaned on the handle, and laughed, long and hard.

He grinned as he watched her.

"You look great." Thinner and paler than she had been when they'd fallen into the set of *It's a Wonderful Popsicle*, but her indomitable spirit continued to shine like a beacon in this darkness.

"So do you. I had no idea you could grow a full beard in four days."

He rubbed his hand across his chin. "If I'm making court appearances, I shave twice a day."

"Or impressing women?" she asked.

"No, honey, you know it's not my *beard* that impresses women." He grinned as she sighed with exaggerated disgust.

"Let me take a turn," he said.

"Rest a little longer. I'm okay." With her shovel, she reached up toward the front of the tunnel and dug into the snow.

The metal hit something hard.

Snow fell off in chunks, revealing a tree branch as thick as his thigh.

He straightened. It wasn't the first time this had happened—a lot of debris had been swept down with the avalanche.

But under the force of her blow, the branch shifted.

The snowbank in front of them shimmered.

She saw it, too. She said, "Oh, no, you don't." She lunged for the branch, tried to steady it.

Samuel grabbed for her.

But he was too late.

With a roar, the tunnel collapsed.

She went down, buried under chunks of snow and ice.

He grabbed her feet and started pulling, blindly dragging her backward.

The collapse continued, moving from the far end of their digging toward the door, filling in every space.

Five feet from the door, he lost his grip on one of her feet. He stumbled backward. Lost the other foot.

She vanished in the whiteout.

The snow continued to tumble, trying to bury him.

He sputtered and fought, desperate to get back inside the locker room. Grabbing the waiting shovel, he ran back into the chunks of still-settling snow.

The cave-in had stopped—but there was no sign of Isabelle.

Fueled by mania, he dug. The distance it had taken them two days to cover he cleared in twenty minutes.

He told himself that she had freed a space for her face so she could breathe, she had special healing powers because she was Chosen, cold slowed a human's metabolism so they required less oxygen, he would find her in time.

I have to find her in time.

God could not be so cruel as to take her from him. Not now.

He found her thigh with his shovel, striking with the metal.

She flinched.

She is alive. Thank you! She is alive.

He pulled, but the snow weighed on her too heavily and he couldn't budge her. So he dug toward her head, stopping to tug occasionally, moving quickly yet cautiously.

Be careful.

When he'd unloaded enough of the snow, he pulled her free and turned her over.

She was white. Cold. Still.

"No. Listen. Baby." He put his head to her chest and heard the slow, slow beat of her heart. He tilted her head back, cleared her airway, and breathed into her mouth, into her lungs, heating her, bringing her back to the land of the living. Three breaths and she coughed, struggled, coughed some more. Flipped over onto her knees and gasped, over and over, while he held her shoulders and said, "Isabelle. Come on. You're okay. Talk to me. Tell me you're okay. Baby . . ."

She turned on him ferociously. "I'm okay!" she shouted, and coughed again, her chest heaving as if she could never again get enough air.

He pulled her close, yanked her out of the tunnel. He brushed snow off her frozen skin, finger-combed chunks of ice out of her hair. And held her, breathing hard, trying to calm his racing heart, knowing he would never be calm again. Then he shook her. Shook her hard. "What were you *thinking*? When that snow moved, what were you thinking, trying to stop it? Are you *crazy*? Why didn't you just *run*?"

She turned on him, teeth bared. "I was *thinking* how

close we were to getting out of here. I was *thinking* I was sick of energy bars. I was *thinking* we were running out of air. I was *thinking* we're going to die down here! That's what I was thinking!"

"Let me do the thinking from now on!"

"Because you've done such a great job of getting us out?"

"I'm working on it!"

"So am I! Now—I'm going to bed." She stalked away, stiff-legged with rage and limping from the blow from the shovel. "And I hope I don't wake up dead!"

He followed her, still sweaty from the exertion of digging her out, still angry at her for taking a chance, and furious at himself for endangering Isabelle.

Isabelle.

He'd known her his whole life. He remembered the charming little girl. The gawky adolescent. The prep-school uniform . . . *My God.* That summer, they'd spent every day huddled in the third-floor window seat. Even today, those memories shone like old gold, untarnished by the events that followed.

Today Isabelle had almost died because of his plan, his carelessness.

He had to find a way out.

He had to save them.

Chapter 20

───────◆❈◆───────

*T*he door to the third-floor bedroom opened.

Inside the window seat, Samuel tensed. Waited in silence.

The curtain opened, and Isabelle smiled down at Samuel's outstretched form. "Hi, there," she said.

He stared at her in her summer shorts, her long, slender legs tanned and smooth, and tried not to think about how they would feel wrapped around his hips. Romancing her was the hardest thing he'd ever had to do . . . literally. He wanted to grab her. He wanted to take off her clothes. He wanted to have sex with her, then have sex again, then . . . He didn't know how often he could have sex in a row, but with Isabelle, he was pretty sure it was a lot.

Instead, he read poetry because she liked it, and to return the favor.

The first time they met, she had, after all, read him a fairy tale.

They'd spent hours stretched out in the window seat, her

head on his chest, his arm around her, while he read Yeats aloud. Now, in a normal voice that showed no sign of his agitation, he asked, "How did you get away from your mother?"

"I told her I had cramps." She must have seen his alarm, for she gurgled with laughter. "I don't really. I'm okay." She climbed onto the window seat beside him, reached up to pull the curtains closed.

Her really fine ass was almost in his face, and he bit his lip on a groan. He used to think she was clueless. Now he wasn't so sure. He was kind of getting the feeling she was using her first-class young body and his obsession to lead him around on a leash.

Funny thing was, he was good with that. When he was with her, his rage at his parents, biological and adoptive, calmed, and he faced the fact that he could easily enjoy being domesticated . . . by Isabelle.

He really needed to distract himself or an already painful hard-on would turn into a major case of blue balls—and he preferred to wait a little longer before he was in major agony. "Do you want to read poetry?" he asked.

"Not today." She knelt beside his outstretched form.

He picked up Romeo and Juliet. *"Shakespeare, then." They recited the plays, each taking different parts. Not that he would ever tell the guys.*

"No, although I love to hear you do the 'Wherefore art thou?' speech. You're developing a real dramatic flair."

He shrugged as if indifferent to her praise. But weirdly enough, in Shakespeare's works he discovered the voices of other men like him—impatient, angry, ready to burst out of their lives and do what they wanted.

He did this stuff to make her happy, and tried not to freak out when he realized he liked it. The poetry, the plays—they were souls encapsulated in words, and through them he saw a different future for himself.

"What do you want to do?" he asked, and tensed as she leaned over his long form and kissed him with her warm, soft mouth. Once. Twice. She kissed his eyelids, his chin, his throat. Gradually, as she kissed him, she reclined beside him, stretching her legs beside his, leaning her hip against his, pressing her breasts against the side of his chest.

His heart pounded as her warmth enfolded him. This felt like more than lust to him; this felt like real affection. This felt like . . . love, and he wanted to hold her in his arms forever.

Taking a fortifying breath, she really kissed him with her tongue and her teeth, nibbling on his lower lip. She let him taste her, sucking his tongue into her mouth until they performed intercourse with their mouths.

He'd taught her everything he knew about pleasure with your fly zipped, and now she proved that when she let her instincts lead, she could reach far beyond his teachings.

God.

He could kiss her forever, but he didn't dare. Or he would forget who she was, forget who he was, forget his goals and his needs, and become nothing more than Isabelle's boy toy. So he took her shoulders in his hands and pressed her away from him. "We can't keep doing this."

"Why not?"

"Because you're a virgin. And I'm not. And I want to have sex with you." A silence fell between them: deep, dark, frightening . . . exhilarating.

She chewed her lower lip, her expression considering. "What about . . . if I . . . if I have sex with you, will you stay? Here in Boston? And graduate and go to college?"

He sat up, angry and . . . hurt. "Because I'm not good enough for you unless I graduate and go to college?"

"No!" She grabbed his thigh, squeezed hard. "I don't mean that at all. I just would like to help you make the right decision."

In the two months since she first found him here, his hair had grown back to a short shag, and he pushed it back with an outraged motion. "I'm not making deals with you. You're not going to tell yourself that you're sacrificing your purity for my sake. You either want me or you don't. You either trust me to do the right thing or you don't."

"I do want you. I do trust you." Reaching up, she took his shirt and tugged him down to face her. "I don't think that I'm more important to you than your destiny."

Of course. There was a reason they resonated on basic levels. They shared a common uncertainty, for if their biological parents had despised them so much as to toss them away . . . was that their fate from their adoptive parents? From their friends? Would they ever truly know security?

He leaned his forehead on hers. "You're the most important thing in my life, and I've wanted you since the first time I saw you. I love you, Isabelle, and I want you to love me, too."

"You love me?"

"For so long." Since the first time he saw her.

"I love you, too." Her smile blossomed. Her blue eyes sparkled.

She made him feel powerful, beneficent. Because he had

never made anyone so happy. "So I need to read to you, or . . . Well, I need to read to you."

He tried to sit up.

Her fingers tightened on his collar. "Sammy. Please. Would you . . . ?"

He stared at her so long, so hard, he felt faint. Finally he realized he needed to breathe—and gasped like a fish.

"Are you okay?" *She looked concerned.*

He felt himself turn red. Him, the guy voted most likely to score.

"What do you want?" *he asked hoarsely. He was pretty sure he knew, but this was too important to screw up.*

Her lids fluttered down, her dark, long lashes resting against her skin, then fluttered up, and she gazed at him with those amazing blue eyes. "Would you teach me to make love?"

He needed to say something warm and romantic and re-assuring. Not, Yeah! *Or,* Take off your clothes! *Or,* I just came in my shorts. *But it was tough, because this wasn't like the other times. This wasn't a score. This wasn't screw-ing. This really was . . . making love. And he needed to do it right.*

Apparently he'd paused too long, because her chin trem-bled and her eyes filled with tears.

So he blurted, "I really want to, but I'm nervous because it's you."

She blinked her tears away.

Her eyes looked the color of the cobalt pastels the girls used in art class.

She got up on one elbow and stared at him. "You're ner-vous? I didn't know you ever got nervous!"

"Don't tell anybody." He eyed her, serious as death. "Or I'll have to kill you."

She smiled, obviously not alarmed. "I won't, because . . . I'm nervous, too."

A reluctant grin tugged at his mouth. "We're perfect for each other, aren't we?"

"Yes." She put her hand on his shoulder. "We are."

Her T-shirt pulled tight across her breasts.

He hoped she wasn't turned off by sweat, because he was sweating with arousal and nerves.

He'd gotten laid before. Enjoyed it thoroughly. How could he be so freaked this time?

But he knew the answer. This was the first time it was important.

Everything he'd read about girls said he had to go slowly, which meant he'd probably come three times before he got her bra off. But he didn't, and managed the T-shirt and the bra— it was plain white, which made him think she was telling the truth about her panties—and her breasts looked like perfect caramel ice-cream scoops topped with pink sugar roses.

He had to freeze for a while, keep himself carefully arched over her body, before he could kiss them, lick them, say, "They're beautiful," in a voice so sincere he felt like a preacher . . . but he'd never meant anything so much in his life.

He had to pause again while she pushed his T-shirt up his chest—her palms brushed his nipples on the way past and he almost finished right there—but luckily for him, she was quick and efficient and his suffering was brief. Except then she ran her hands over his arms, over his chest, and *winced at the bruise on his breastbone. "I didn't think you were fighting anymore," she said.*

"I practice every day, and fight every Thursday night." She didn't realize it, but he had compromised for her. He wanted to fight three nights a week.

Instead he read poetry.

Nevertheless, her lip trembled with disappointment, and he had to steel himself not to promise to quit altogether. But his trainer thought he had real promise, and it was the only way Samuel could see to get out of this stultifying town without being indebted to anything or anybody.

So he changed the subject by making fast work of the zipper on her shorts. Pressing his palm flat on her belly, he looked into her eyes and slid his fingers down until he touched her clit.

She was damp and warm, and she clamped her legs together. Then she half closed her eyes as if it felt good.

So he moved really slowly, touched gently, and after a while—okay, after forever—he got her pants off—and proved to himself once and for all that she really did wear white cotton panties, boy cut.

Then she wanted to take off his jeans.

He wanted to rip off his jeans.

But that would frighten her.

So he got onto his knees and let her unzip him, touch him through his underwear, then push the denim off his hips. And his underwear. Then she stared at him and said—honest to God, she said—"It's too big!"

He didn't know whether she was being funny or if she thought that was something he needed to hear—he most

definitely didn't; he didn't need one more bit of encouragement—so he said, "It's standard-issue. Haven't you looked
at any porn ever?"

She ducked her head and blushed. "Yes, but it's gross, and
everyone knows they do stuff with Photoshop, so I didn't
think . . ."

He was not in the mood to discuss whether the stuff on
porn sites was faked, so he climbed out of his jeans, shoved
them over the edge, and smiled at her. Then he realized—
smooth move—the condom was in his pocket on the floor.

She giggled when he dove for it.

She still giggled when he came back with the foil packet
in his teeth. She took it away from him, placed it on the win-
dowsill, wrapped her arms around his neck, and kissed him.
"I'm so glad it's you," she said.

Me, too. But he couldn't talk. He was too busy trying not
to feel her hard little nipples poking into his chest, and the
way she squirmed as she kissed him, and . . . Oh, God. She
opened her legs and let him settle against her.

"I like the way your skin feels against mine." Her eyes
looked rapt, her mouth puffy from kissing.

For the first time, he relaxed a little. Because she was lik-
ing this, she was feeling the passion, and more than that, she
was feeling the closeness between them—and so was he. So
he caressed her breasts some more, touching as much as he
liked—which was a lot—and when he slid his fingers down
to her hips, she was breathing hard and whimpering softly.
Which was good . . . and bad, because it made him have hal-
lucinations about doing this now.

He didn't, though. He sat up between her knees and got

his first glimpse of her soft, pink woman parts. "Perfect," he whispered, and touched her clit some more.

She tried to clamp her legs together again, and when he slipped his finger inside her, she gave a hip roll that made him break a sweat. When she moaned, his control cracked. He tore open the condom and rolled it on fast, then positioned himself and pressed hard.

Her eyes flew open.

"Hurts?" He was surprised he could still speak.

"Yes."

"Stop?" Shit. Why had he asked that?

She shook her head, braced her feet against the cushion, and lifted her hips to his.

She was helping him. Which made him want to go as fast as he could. Which was really fast.

Instead, he held himself still, let her do the work, and hoped she didn't notice the tremor as he leaned on his arms. Finally she whispered, "You can move now."

So he did, nice and slow, and that was the most difficult thing he'd ever done in his life . . . and ultimately the most rewarding, because when they were finished, he knew Isabelle was his love . . . forever.

Chapter 21

<hr>

The raucous sound of a power tool woke Isabelle. Her eyes sprang open.

Power. Electricity.

Rescuers had found them?

She blasted out of the tent in her long johns and socks. She looked around.

The lantern sat on the table. Food sat beside it: one of the endless energy bars, a juice box, and something that looked like a former banana.

No light. No heat. No voices. Just the sound of that damned saw or drill or whatever from the back of the locker room. As she stood there in her long underwear and her socks, her excitement wilted around her.

The sound was nothing but Samuel doing . . . something.

Hugging herself, she ignored the food. Climbed back in the tent. Huddling back into the sleeping bag, she tried to get warm again. To go back to sleep. Because what was the point of getting up?

They had tried to dig out. After days of blistering exertion and foolish hopes, they had failed. They were trapped here on the set of *Silence of the Lamb-lined Boots*—she made an internal note to tell Samuel that one—and she wanted to die in peace.

But that power tool went on and on, the screeching high and constant until she was grinding her teeth. When some piece of metal slammed to the floor, she jumped so hard she gave herself a kink in the neck.

"Honestly!" She slapped on her clothes, crawled out of the tent, and went in search of Samuel.

A tall ladder leaned against the wall at the back. He was perched on top of it, cordless saw in hand, chopping open the huge tin heating duct strung across the ceiling.

"What are you doing?" she shouted.

He continued working.

"What are you . . . ?" *Oh.* He was wearing orange earmuffs.

She put her hand on the ladder and shook it slightly.

He cut the power to the saw. Grabbed at the ladder. Pulled off his earmuffs with controlled exasperation. "Do you mind not scaring me into next week? For a second there, I had visions of falling and rupturing another disk."

"I've been calling you for five minutes and you couldn't hear me." It had been more like thirty seconds, but she was too aggravated to be honest. "What are you doing?"

"I'm going to see where this ductwork goes."

Her heart leaped with improbable hope. "You think it goes out?"

"I don't know. Probably not. But it's worth a try."

She sank down on a stuff sack with a stowed tent inside. "Where did you get the saw?"

"Ski patrol. Batteries were charged, so I thought I might as well put it to use." He actually looked pretty good—bright eyed and confident, with his jacket flung at the base of the ladder and someone's red plaid flannel shirt stretched across his broad shoulders. In fact, with that black beard covering his chin, he looked like . . . like . . . He looked like the lumberjack in that paper towel advertisement.

Probably he looked so animated because he was making a horrible amount of noise and using power tools.

She'd look that way if she were putting on makeup and getting ready to go dancing instead of sitting here miserably wondering whether it was worse to be dirty or wash in the freezing water. Thank God she'd taken that shower the night the avalanche hit. Because if her hair were still that sticky and disgusting, she would be going insane.

What was she talking about? She *was* going insane.

"If you're going to sit close," he said, "grab the ear protection over there." He pointed toward the neat piles of tools and batteries.

She stood and rambled over. "Did you know I'm claustrophobic?" she asked in a conversational tone.

"No." He sounded dubious.

"I didn't, either. But I do now." She picked up the ear protection and held it against her chest.

"Did you eat the breakfast I left you?"

He might as well have asked if it was *that* time of the month. Which it wasn't, not for another week, and if they weren't out by then, wouldn't *that* be lovely, scrounging through the lockers for tampons? "This isn't about food. I just . . . I want to know what day it is."

He pushed back the cuff of his work glove and glanced at his watch. "It's Thursday, about eight."

"Morning or evening?"

"Evening."

"Are you sure? Because I can't tell. I can't tell! I want . . . to see . . . some light." When he started to point to the lantern, she charged on: "Not those stupid LEDs that are burning through our batteries faster than we're getting out of here. I want to see the *sun*."

He descended the ladder and put the saw down. Walked toward her. "You know, I've been thinking. I bet they've found my rental car and deduced we're here."

"*No*, they *haven't*. They haven't, or you wouldn't be doing ridiculous stuff like thinking of climbing into a heating vent in the hopes of finding a way out."

"Actually, I was trying to hide from you."

She sighed. "You're not funny."

"I'm not trying to be. You complained I hadn't done a good enough job of getting us out of here. I'm trying every avenue." He didn't raise his voice, but his eyes got intense and heated, as if the solitude and darkness and cold were getting to him, too. Oh, and the threat of death hanging over their heads might be commanding his attention, too.

She intended to apologize for being a bitch.

Then he added, "I hope that suits you, *princess*."

Her teeth snapped together. "I *hate* it when you call me that. Like I'm some kind of spoiled brat."

"You? No. Not you." His tone mocked her.

The way he put his hand on his hip, imitating her own pose, made her temper rise. "I put in the work. I've got the blisters to prove it." She thrust her hands under his nose.

"I remember the first time I saw you. I was five. You were four, and so pretty, so sweet, so loving. Darren told me you weren't for me."

"I guess he was right." She smiled sweetly.

"I guess he was." He smiled back, all shark teeth. "But I guess the question is—what color are your panties *today*?"

That was Samuel. He *had* to remind her there had been a time when her underwear had been of intimate concern to him.

Well, not anymore, buster. "My panties are not now nor will they ever again be your business." Turning, she stormed away.

Until he grabbed her arm and swung her around, dragged her until she was face-to-face with him, and asked, "Why did you leave me?"

Chapter 22

———✦———

Isabelle's eyes lit up as if she were a spitting cat. "You know why I left you. Because you used me."

"Wait. You only want to remember that *second* time." Samuel was just as angry as she was, and for just as good a reason. "For a refreshing change, let's talk about the *first* time we broke up, after that summer we spent on the window seat."

"Oh. That." She wrapped her arms around her waist and turned away.

Yeah, she was guilty as hell, and she knew it, too. "So, princess. Tell me all about it."

"It was a long time ago."

"You don't remember?" He paced around her so he was looking at her downturned face. "Because the memory burns like fire in my gut."

"I remember. Everything was new and bright, and we were so young and . . . ."

"In love?" he asked harshly.

In a low voice, she said, "Yes. I was so desperately in love with you, I was afraid to look my mother in the eyes. I never understood why she didn't see the truth."

The whole crap-ass situation always led straight back to her mother. "She didn't see it because it was beyond her comprehension that her daughter could find anything in common with the butler's son."

"She's not so . . ." Isabelle faltered.

"Yes, she is," he said unequivocally. "I appreciate that your mother lifted me from the gutter, but whosoever she chooses to elevate to the status of daughter is above all others in this world, and all the more reason for her to remember the contrast between you and me."

"She does have her reasons for being a snob," Isabelle reminded him.

"Don't I know it? I've heard it a hundred times." He circled her again, a slow tour that kept him from exploding in frustration. "Her ancestors landed on Plymouth Rock in the *Mayflower*."

"She doesn't talk about her background all the time!"

"She doesn't have to. My father told me time and again who Patricia Mason was and how that placed her—and you—far above any aspirations I might harbor. Because, you know, I'm a half-Gypsy bastard with a talent for picking pockets." Even now, so many years later, Samuel could taste the bitterness on his tongue.

"Darren's so much worse than my mother!"

He stopped pacing. "Amen to that."

The moment of silence that followed was almost like the end of a prayer where they remained in thoughtful accord.

Then Isabelle had to screw it up. "Mother's a good person. She's a primo organizer. She's raised hundreds of thousands of dollars for international children's literacy. She's assisted in dozens of adoptions. If she had the right staff, she could run the world."

"She runs your life."

"I owe her everything!"

"She makes you pay with obedience."

That brought her face up to stare at him hotly. "I am not obedient."

"Remember when you were little, and she told you healing was vulgar because it involved touching people and enveloping their disease or their wound to cure them?"

Isabelle sighed. "She's not big on physical contact."

"I gathered that. That must be why your dad looks so gaunt. He hasn't been laid for years. And you—does she ever really hug you, or is it that cheek-touch thing I always see?" Before Isabelle could get indignant, he said, "I can't even imagine what Patricia thought when she realized you had a gift. It's different, and different is not something of which she approves."

"No. She is quite—"

"Stuffy? Medieval? *Congested?*" He started pacing.

"If you want to be that way, fine." Isabelle's voice rose. "But her goals and mine frequently coincide."

So now they were back to the subject at hand. "Is that why, when things got too real, you ran away? Did she give you the excuse you were looking for to get away from me?"

"Are we talking about when I was sixteen? Again?" Isabelle pushed her hair out of her face. "Samuel . . . I was only sixteen!"

"Yeah, and I was seventeen—and you left me to face your mother and my father." He turned and paced around the other way.

Isabelle spun on her heel, observing him warily. "My mother found us. In the act!" It was clear her humiliation still burned.

"She didn't find us. My father told her about us." He walked away from Isabelle. "What does it matter how we were discovered? Who told on whom? What's that got to do with it? You didn't have to run away."

"I didn't run away. She took me away." Isabelle looked sullen.

She never looked sullen. Good. He was getting to her.

"You let her. You could have let me know." He leaned his knuckles against a table and stared at her, chin down, eyes narrowed. "Do you know what it was like, sitting at that table when Darren and your mother told me you'd *gone away*? That you were beyond the reach of my grubby paws, and to make sure I stayed away, your mother was willing to pay for me to go to prep school and college? They paid me off like you were the lady and I was the stable boy."

"You took the money, didn't you?" She had the guts to sound resentful.

"Hell, yes!" He stepped around the table toward her. "In cash! Then I gave them both the finger and got out of there. What did you think I was going to do? Be noble and refuse? Obviously you knew what kind of guy I was or you wouldn't have abandoned me."

"I guess I did know." She stepped away, ready to run away again.

The little coward.

"And all those afternoons sitting around reading each other fucking poetry were nothing but bullshit," he spat.

She spun around. "I thought you liked poetry."

"I do like poetry." He stalked toward her. "I'm a fucking sensitive guy."

"Stop saying that word!" She backed up.

"Really? That's the problem here? My *language*?" That shut her up, he was pleased to see. "You ran. You ran like a scared rabbit."

"I wasn't scared."

He flexed his gloved hands as he herded her toward the corner.

She went one slow step at a time. "I was smart enough even then to know we weren't a good match."

It was like a dance without music. They never took their eyes off each other, but it didn't matter. They both knew the motions.

"We were a great match. That's what scared you."

"We were too young!"

"We were young, but we had everything in common. Our souls were one. We could have made it."

"You don't know that."

"No, I don't. But I know this." In one swift motion, he closed the gap between them. Grabbing her coat, he pulled her close and up onto her toes. He gazed into her eyes. "The sex was great."

"It was great because we were teenagers. It would have been great no matter . . ." She faltered, unable to finish the lie she had told herself.

"You can't even convince yourself."

Her pupils were dilated, swallowing the blue of her eyes.

Because she was frightened? She should be. The old rage welled in him, sharp and acrid on his tongue.

But it wasn't merely fright that had her trembling against him.

It wasn't cold, either.

The heat, the desire, the pure, raw sexuality they so carefully controlled fought to be free, and he could almost taste her need.

"I had you," he said. "Lots of times. And oh, princess, how much you loved it."

Chapter 23

―――――❦―――――

The moment stretched between them.

Isabelle's breath quickened. Her heart hammered. Her cheeks got hot, and her fingers clutched handfuls of the soft flannel on his shoulders.

Then, in unison, she and Samuel closed the distance between them.

And they kissed.

Heat. Blazing heat.

Mouths open, tasting. Tongues probing. A rhythm so familiar, yet new.

He stripped off his gloves. Pushed the zipper down on her coat so hard he created sparks. He didn't bother to drop it off her shoulders. Just found her breasts through her sweater and held them, stroked them, explored their contours.

Glorious. Old times remembered with a new lust.

She pressed herself into his hands, needing his touch with a desperation that had built during the days and nights of being too close, fed by too many years of missing him.

His touch felt good. So good.

She reached for his ski pants, unzipped him.

He grabbed her hands. "Wait."

"No."

"We've got to think this through."

She was finished with waiting.

"It is far too late for that." Sliding to her knees, she pressed her mouth to the underwear stretched taut across his erection.

The heat of her breath made him suck in air. "You're killing me."

"You'll survive. At least long enough for me to get what I need." Pulling her hands out of his, she pushed his pants and underwear down onto his thighs; then, starting at the base of his penis, she licked it like an ice-cream cone, stopping only to swirl her tongue around the head.

That was what it took to kill his initial resistance.

Wrapping his hands in her hair, he pulled her head back and looked down at her.

His eyes glittered like dark stars. Color surged in his cheeks. "In the tent. Now."

"No. Here."

"It's too cold. We'll freeze."

"Here," she said stubbornly. Because she didn't dare make the walk to the tent. A delay and the cool air might return her good sense.

No. She wanted this. *Now.*

She could see him wavering again. Because he knew her. He knew why she didn't want to think about it.

So she cupped his testicles and sucked his penis into her mouth. She pulled him deep, savoring the flavor of his skin, the drop of come that eased from the tip, the well-remembered ridge of the head, the veins that ran the long length of him. The taste of him set off memories of hours spent in the window seat, on the bed, anywhere, exploring each other's bodies, discovering the depth of their emotions, their passions. That memory made her body tighten, made her grow damp in anticipation.

The sound of his heartfelt groan was sweet surrender. "All right. You win."

Reluctantly, she released him.

As soon as she did, he yanked her to her feet and marched her to the packed tent sack she'd used as a seat. Turning her to face away from him, he urged her to her knees on the concrete. He knelt behind her, his knees outside her knees. He held her in place. Pulled down her zipper. Bent against her, his front against her back, enveloping her in his warmth.

She leaned against him, reveling in the sizzle between them, in his arms embracing her.

His callused hands skated across her belly to her hips. He pushed her pants down, but only to the tops of her thighs.

Not far enough.

She almost objected.

Then his hands glided between her legs and he used

his fingers to open her lips and subtly, gently stroke her.

She pressed herself into his touch, already so close to orgasm she was shuddering with need.

"No, you don't." His voice came from behind and above her. "Not without me." She heard the crinkle of foil and turned in astonishment.

He was opening a condom, putting it on.

"Where did you get *that*?"

"Almost every locker had at least one."

"Right." Of course they did. Because they were ski lockers.

But why was he carrying it in his pocket?

He shoved her pants down to her knees.

The cold struck her, giving her goose bumps.

He bent her again, opened her from behind.

She suffered a moment of acute awareness. She was too exposed, too vulnerable.

Then he found her with his fingers, then with his erection. . . .

Discuss the condom later. . . .

His penis opened the first resistant inches with a firm, inexorable momentum. Once he had breached her defenses, he advanced into her, a slow, steady progress as her body unlocked itself for him, for his heat, for the unrelenting tightness caused by his knees clamped around her knees.

By the time he reached the limit, she was gasping aloud. She tried to move. He wrapped his arm around her waist and held her still.

"Please. Samuel. Please." She was praying to him as if he were a deity. "I can't stand it. You've got to hurry. *Now*."

His voice was smooth, unimpressed. "Tell me you're sorry."

She lifted her head. "What?"

"Tell me you're sorry you ran out on me and left me to face the consequences."

She tried to straighten up.

He held her absolutely still, and slowly, so slowly, pulled out almost . . . all . . . the way. "Tell me."

His chest rumbled against her back, and she could imagine how his eyes gleamed with the satisfaction of holding her helpless.

"You're a sleaze." She tried to shove herself out of his grasp.

No way.

"Not a doubt about that." Slowly, just as slowly, he pressed back inside.

She squeezed herself tightly, trying to hold him back, but that increased the friction, and inside she quivered with an eagerness so compelling the world constricted to this place, this moment, their union.

"I feel how close you are," he whispered as if every word were dirty. "I can send you over the edge. One firm thrust is all it would take. Once you started coming . . . Isabelle, are you listening?"

She leaned her forehead on her clasped hands, stared at the blue nylon sack beneath them. "No."

He stopped talking. Stopped *moving*.

Her fingers tightened on one another as she fought the compulsion to yield.

He must have had respect for her self-control, because he leaned in so close his voice murmured in her ear, and he incited her. "Once you started coming, you wouldn't stop. Every time I went deep inside, my balls would be crushed against your clit, and—"

"All right!" She grabbed the nylon with both hands so tightly her knuckles turned white. *To hell with pride.* "I'm sorry I left you alone when we were teenagers to face the inquisition."

"Nice." He shifted smoothly, his hips clenching, his erection lifting, until he was, as he promised, crushed against her exposed clit.

So close . . .

On a gasp, she said, "I've been ashamed ever since I abandoned you. I was afraid. . . . What we had between us was so intense and I wasn't ready. . . . I was a coward. I *am* sorry. Oh, please, Samuel, I really do mean it." She did. It had been her ugly secret for so many years, and it felt strangely liberating to admit it aloud to him.

"I believe you." He was moving now, still unhurried, still a torment. "You said everything I've waited years to hear." With his arm around her, he forced her to remain still, but his motion was constant . . . and gradually increasing.

With his free hand, he caressed her rear, smoothed the skin, found the crack at the base of her spine, and ran his thumb up and down.

She fought him, whimpering, frantic to be more than a recipient, to move with him and seize the climax that eluded her.

Reaching beneath her, he pushed up her sweater and found her breast. Firmly he squeezed.

Jolted by the contact, she bucked beneath him.

At last he released her, straightened up, and thrust. *Hard.*

She pushed back. *Hard.*

He groaned.

Good.

They thrust again.

For one eternal second, they hovered on the edge of anticipation. Then, in unison, they moved together, clashing in a battle both would win.

The first orgasm swept her. She tightened her body, arched like a cat, moaned and wept.

There was nothing romantic about this. It was swift, dirty, sweaty . . . exhilarating. It was sex without frills, rampaging toward the ultimate satisfaction, and each climax racked her like a fever, erasing thought, building heat. She was going to implode with lust, with constantly building need.

Then his orgasm began. He rocked her against him, bringing them together hard and fast, and each time he did, she came again. It never stopped, this battering of the senses, this bliss that was too much—and yet never enough.

He lifted her, remorselessly forced her against him.

Inside her, she felt the jump of his penis as he came—
and she came, too, clamping down on him, milking
him, until the ride was over.

Then, by mutual consent, they wilted down onto the
tent bag.

His large, splayed hand protected her naked belly
from the cool nylon. His other arm he slid under her
head. He rested on top of her, his legs still tight against
hers, his penis deep inside; everything about his posture spelled *mine*. Samuel had always been possessive.

Today, his attitude felt like protection.

Chapter 24

Before Isabelle was ready, Samuel lifted himself off of her.

She moaned as his body left hers, then moaned again as the cold air she now knew so well struck her once more, surprising her with its chill.

A thought, coherent and full-formed, jolted her—*I am not going to be sorry. I am not going to be guilty. I am glad we did that, and no matter what happens now, no one can take that away from me.*

Her earliest memory was being told by someone—a nanny, a teacher—that she was the luckiest little girl in the world because Patricia Mason had adopted her, and that that adoption saved her from a dire childhood or possibly death. She remembered crying because she wasn't really her mother's baby, and remembered, too, how angry Patricia had been when she found out.

But the damage was done. Isabelle had grown up steeped in responsibility and guilt . . . but for the first time in her life, she refused to feel guilty about Samuel.

She lusted after him, and that lust had just given her the one thing she craved—forgetfulness.

For a few passionate moments, she had been unaware of the cold, the dark, the fear, the desperation. Only he had existed, he and the pleasure he gave her.

As he helped her up, he looked into her face. His eyes widened. "Did I hurt you?"

"What?" She wiped the tears off her cheeks. "Oh. This. No. It just felt . . . It's been a long time. It was good."

He nodded. "Okay."

Okay? Really? No, Yes, it was fabulous, the moment I've been waiting for all my life? Or even a swagger and, Hey, I'm good? Just . . . Okay?

That didn't sound like the confident, aggressive man she had always known. Wasn't he going to follow this lovemaking with a pitch for another romp in his bed?

But no. He didn't say anything. Instead he tucked her into her pants, into her coat. Zipped her up. Behaved like a man who wanted to get her covered as soon as possible.

She didn't know what to think.

But she wanted him to realize she wasn't blaming him or wallowing in guilt or anything, so she said, "That whole thing felt really good."

"It did. Felt great!" he agreed too enthusiastically. Almost . . . awkwardly.

Well. That was probably better. Because no matter how glad she was that they had had sex, they couldn't do it again. It wasn't right for them to attack each other like ravenous beasts. . . .

Or rather, it wasn't right for her to attack him. Because she had to be honest with herself. That was what had happened.

She tried to think what to say, how to phrase her thoughts. "We have to talk."

At the same time, he said, "Look, I'm sorry, but having sex with you was stupid."

She felt as if she'd been slapped.

That was exactly what she was going to say, although she wouldn't have put it so bluntly—and she never expected to hear it from him.

"I know what we're both thinking, so let me say this." He lifted his eyebrows, asking for permission.

Still stunned, she nodded.

"We both . . . well, I can't speak for you, but I know I'm anxious about being trapped for so long with no help in sight and no viable plan to escape."

She gestured for him to continue. Really. She was going to say this. Exactly this.

"The tension is weighing on us. On me." He was serious, intent. "After the disappointment yesterday when the tunnel caved in—"

"Gone with the Windchill," she joked, trying to cover up her hurt and surprise.

"Right." He didn't even admire her movie title; he merely smiled perfunctorily. "I think we can probably agree that the sex was an aberration caused by anxiety."

An aberration? You had a condom in your pocket.

But what good would it do for her to be sarcastic? At least he'd been prepared. If he hadn't been . . . She shivered. If he hadn't been, she might be pregnant right now.

There was a thought to keep her awake at night.

Choosing her words carefully, she suggested, "So we used each other as an antidote to depression?"

"It was a much-needed release of tension for us both."

"Right. And we don't want to do it again because we might frostbite our parts."

"That's the least of our worries, I would say."

"Right," she said again, and smiled brightly. "Why don't we just agree the sex didn't happen? Probably if we were trapped with someone else, we'd have had stupid sex with them, too."

"Stupid sex. Exactly." Picking up the saw, he started toward the ladder.

Startled, she stared at his back, then called, "What are you doing?"

"I'm going back to work. We need to get out of here before we get stupid again."

She didn't know where the words came from, but once they were out, she was glad she'd said them. "I think it's time to use the dynamite."

Chapter 25

Once Isabelle had started, the words spilled from her. "I know there's a chance, a good one, that when we use the dynamite, the building will collapse on us. And if that doesn't happen, the explosion will use up our remaining oxygen and we'll suffocate."

He started to speak.

She held up her hand. This time, it was her turn to be honest. "But I'm sick of eating half-frozen dehydrated rations. I'm tired of being cold except when I'm in my sleeping bag. I don't want to spend all my time thinking up corny movie titles to make you smile—and anyway, it's not working anymore. I'm scared we're going to slowly fade away, be discovered in the spring, and be a footnote in some Swiss newspaper article. My lips are chapped because all the lip balms we've found were someone else's and open, and I don't want to get a disease, but what difference does it make if we're going to die anyway?"

"Okay, we'll use the dynamite."

"We can either die slowly, one by one, or we can take this one chance and maybe the rescuers will find us, or even better, maybe we'll blast our way out—" Her head snapped around. "What did you say?"

"I still plan to look in the venting." He stood, looking up the ladder, his jaw squared as he contemplated his mission. "If we could find an outlet up by the ceiling, one that goes outside the building, that would be our best chance *not* to destroy the roof over our heads. There's no point in alerting the rescuers while killing ourselves in the process."

She stared at him, wide-eyed.

For so long, she'd thought of Samuel as a slick lawyer who wore expensive suits, swam with the sharks, and had the moral integrity of a tomcat. But right now, dressed in black ski pants and a red plaid flannel shirt, he looked tough and capable, the kind of man she could depend on to rescue her in any crisis.

Come to think of it, in the past he'd always been there, even when she didn't want him. Always she had known that if she called him, he would come.

In so many ways, he was the best man she'd ever known.

If only she could trust him.

She must have contemplated him a little too long, because he asked, "What? You think I haven't thought of everything you said?"

"I . . . I think you're a good guy."

"I think if you're saying that, it's definitely time to

get you out of here." He sounded humorous, but he looked at her as if her sanity were in doubt.

"No, really. This has been like a retreat in a convent . . . er . . . other than the sex that we didn't just have. I've had a lot of time for contemplation. What happened between us—you nailed it. The first time we separated, it was my fault. The second time, it was yours."

He muttered something dark and crude.

"But you've been my friend, always." Quickly she added, "Which is why I'll set the charge."

"The charge on the dynamite?" His voice rose. "Why don't you just cut off my balls?"

Just when she was starting to feel charitable . . . "Are you insinuating that I'm trying to emasculate you?"

"After what the two of us just did there?" He gestured toward the tent sack. "No. But you know how you have to coddle my ego."

She snorted in unladylike amusement. "You've got an ironclad ego. Do you really think anyone out there"—she waved vaguely toward the ceiling—"is ever going to know who made it go boom?"

"*I'll* know."

She gathered the shreds of her patience around her. "You aren't familiar with dynamite."

"I agree. So you tell me what you learned about it in boot camp. You know me well enough to realize I'm not going to hide while you put yourself in danger, so you might as well give me a crash course on how to blow stuff up, or we'll be stuck down here forever."

*   *   *

Isabelle prided herself on being calm. Collected. Reasonable.

In the past (aboveground), she had admired herself, *actually admired* herself for moving beyond the anger and the pain her time with Samuel had caused.

Now, five days alone with him and she had transformed into a screeching, ranting, grudge-carrying bitch who hated the man so much she dropped her pants at the first opportunity.

She sat on the stuffed tent sack, her elbows on her knees, her chin in her fists, staring at some unspecified point. . . .

She hadn't really dropped her pants at the *first* opportunity. She'd managed to hold off for five days.

But it hadn't been easy and it hadn't been fun, and if she had any integrity she would admit that living in a giant deep freeze had been the only reason she'd held off so long.

Above her, the tin heating vent snapped and crackled like breakfast cereal.

She shot to her feet. "How's it going?" she shouted.

"Fine." His voice sounded distant and abstracted. "Now if only I could remember whether the red wire connects to the green cable or—"

She stood frozen in horror.

As if he read her reaction from there, he said, "Chill, Isabelle! I know how to use a timer."

Which meant he had been joking, which wasn't funny. Unless she'd completely lost her sense of humor . . . and that was certainly possible. She wrung her hands and stared at the ceiling. Definitely, certainly possible.

Samuel had explored the vent that exited through the ceiling and ended in the snow, then called it their first piece of real luck.

The plan was for him to place the dynamite into the snow above the roof, set the charge on a timer, and get out of the heating run. He had insisted that ninety seconds was long enough for him to reach the ground and for the two of them to go to cover; any longer and he said they'd be hyperventilating by the time the blast occurred.

He had a point, but she was hyperventilating now. If he died . . . She didn't think she could survive if he died. Because he was a part of her. An integral part of her. A really, really important part of her.

"Okay!" he shouted. "Ninety seconds! Go to cover!"

Above her, she heard the tin crackling as he slithered along. He cursed once, shouted, "I mean it, Isabelle, go on!"

She wrung her gloved hands, desperate to see him appear.

His feet popped into view. His legs.

She put her hands on the ladder to steady it.

He slid out of the vent, glanced down, and his dark eyes kindled with anger. "Isabelle . . ." But he didn't take the time to shout at her. Instead he wrapped his legs around the sides of the ladder and slid down in one motion.

She sprang out of the way, turned, and ran for the far side of the basement.

He was hot on her heels.

They got under the table they had wedged in the corner, covered with blankets, cushioned in every way possible. They donned their ear protection. He flipped off the LED lantern and, ignoring her protests, flung himself on top of her. Unerringly, he found her mouth and kissed her.

It tasted like a just-in-case farewell.

And the explosion rocked the floor.

Chapter 26

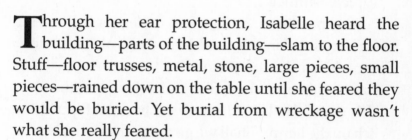

Through her ear protection, Isabelle heard the building—parts of the building—slam to the floor. Stuff—floor trusses, metal, stone, large pieces, small pieces—rained down on the table until she feared they would be buried. Yet burial from wreckage wasn't what she really feared.

What held her stiff and still was the imminent collapse of the ceiling and all the snow piled atop it.

She didn't want be buried alive.

She didn't want to die at all.

Her heart thundered. Her hands trembled. She held on to Samuel as if he were her only hope of heaven.

Gradually the hailstorm of debris ended.

They were still alive, uncrushed . . . and the explosion was done and they needed to get out and survey the results.

Except she *was* crushed. By him. He stretched out on her, covering every inch of her so that her nose was pressed into his chest and his arms protected her head.

Chivalrous?

Yes.

Stifling?

Also yes.

Nerves jangling, she removed her ear protection. "What good is you lying on top of me going to do if the ceiling collapses?" She shoved at him.

"Hey, at least I'll get a farewell feel." He ran his hands up and down her sides, bold and insulting.

Typical Samuel.

Funny, but he made her feel better, as if knowing Samuel was still in this world, his same old obnoxious self, made her life complete.

Her heartbeat calmed. She took a long breath.

"It's over." He lifted himself off her and flipped the switch on the lamp. "Shall we go out and see what we've done?" He looked different to her. Austere, intense, not at all the sarcastic, flippant Samuel she knew so well.

"Let's go," she said.

They dug their way out of the padding over the table and out into the open air.

The basement had been changed by the shock wave—yet it was the same. Dust swirled in the air. All the lockers had been flattened, tilted away from the explosion like a forest of trees blasted by a volcano. In the far corner, the heating runs were crumpled piles of metal crushed beneath massive chunks of the ceiling.

Yet . . . yet . . . no sunlight shone into the basement

locker room. No fresh wind blew in their faces. Even from a distance, even in this dim light, it appeared the snow, although blackened and jagged, remained essentially intact.

No. Oh, no.

They picked their way through the wreckage, staring incredulously as they approached the site of the explosion. Heads craned up, they circled beneath the shattered ceiling and the igloolike dome of ice.

"How is this possible?" she whispered.

"I had to work hard to get the dynamite into the snow. As I said, I think on the first night, a shell of ice formed over what remains of the ski lodge." The explosion had tossed the ladder into the wall and slightly crumpled the aluminum, but Samuel set it up under the hole in the ceiling. "Would you steady this?"

She leaned on it as he climbed, and she speculated, "Since then the weight of the snow above has crushed the snow below, packing it into an even more impermeable layer. So the ice didn't yield, which forced the blast of the dynamite downward. We're at the bottom of a glacier."

He stood at the top and slammed his fist into the ice. "With no way out."

As he descended, his simmering frustration scalded her.

She looked around at the debris. "I guess we'd better set up the tent again."

"Why? If we're right, and the explosion used all our oxygen, we're going to suffocate."

"Not yet." Although she already felt light-headed. But maybe that was disappointment.

"But soon." He headed toward the far corner where they'd stashed all their "just in case this doesn't work" stuff.

Most of the time, Samuel was such a cocky jerk, she couldn't stand him. Or she told herself she couldn't stand him. But right now, he looked so *guilty*.

She picked her way through the mess, thought briefly about making an attempt to clean it up.

Then she re-sorted her priorities and crawled under the table that had protected them from the explosion. She found the stash she'd so carefully collected. She gathered a half dozen bottles, and came out with them held between her fingers.

She found Samuel on his knees stoically, deliberately rebuilding their tent. "What do you want?" she asked. "Scotch? Aquavit? Ouzo? Schnapps?"

He surveyed her, standing there smiling like a waitress in a German beer hall. "You came prepared."

"For celebration—or forgetfulness."

"Of course. You are always prepared."

"You were the one who had the condom."

"Old habits die hard." He reached up and with one finger tapped the thin, tall, clear bottle. "Since this is a ski lodge, schnapps is called for."

"The perfect choice." The schnapps was from one of the hundreds of small German families who distilled their own brand, and as she pulled the cork, the scent of peppermint did not so much rise to fill her nostrils as assault her. She sipped. Peppermint exploded on her taste buds. "Ah. A good vintage."

He snapped the tent poles together, then took the bottle from her, staring at her as if he didn't know who she was.

"What?" She knew what, but she wanted to distract him. Make him notice her and not the mess they were in.

He sipped cautiously, then handed the schnapps back. "I've never seen you drink from the bottle before."

"Probably because I've never drunk from the bottle before. But I want to try everything once before I die, so I guess I'd better hurry." She took a swig and coughed. "You know, I have to say something here, and I want you to listen very carefully."

"Go ahead." He slipped the sleeping bags into the tent, laid them out, side by side.

She enunciated clearly. "This is. Not. Your. Fault."

He spread a blanket over the top of the bags and made everything look as it had before.

He wasn't listening.

She would make him. Kneeling beside him, she handed him the bottle. "Look. I'll blame you for everything you deserve. You know that. But you're not responsible for the avalanche. You had no way of knowing what the Others intended. You gave us a few more days with your quick thinking getting us here. I know what I said, but I was mad and I also know that once we were trapped, you did everything you could to get us out. We waited until there was no other choice before we set off that dynamite, and I'm the one who said it was time, and I told you how to set the blast. It didn't work. We're stuck and our oxygen is seriously depleted." She leaned in until he had to look her in the eyes. "There's no one I'd rather face death with."

He clutched the bottle as if his icy fingers didn't comprehend what they held. "Do you mean that?"

"Why would I say it if I didn't mean it?"

"You're incredibly polite."

"Not to *you*."

He laughed. A brief, harsh chortle, but it was a laugh. "That's true."

"Too right."

"Here's to honesty." Lifting the bottle, he drank. "I love you."

"What?" She sat back on her heels.

"I love you. You know that. I've always loved you. I'd rather live with you. But if we have to die together . . . yeah, that's good, too."

Her eyes filled with tears.

This knowing they were going to die—it brought so many emotions to the surface. Raw emotions. True emotions. The old hurts seemed less important. She remembered the golden moments.

He contemplated her, his eyes serious. "About that last time we were together and what I did—"

"No!" She held up her hand. She was feeling good. She was feeling mellow. She couldn't remember *that*. His betrayal had been so unexpected, so cruel. . . . "Let's just remember the good times."

Chapter 27

———◆———

"We have no future. I don't want to talk about the past. So what should we do on our last night on earth?" Isabelle leaned against Samuel, grinning foolishly.

He regarded her affectionately. She wasn't drunk. But she was uninhibited. The woman had no head for liquor. "I don't know. What do you want to do?"

"I was thinking we should do something stupid!" She leered, actually leered at him. "But for longer this time!"

"That sounds like a good idea." He wrapped his arms around her, kissed her on her chilly nose, her cheeks, her eyelashes. When she was straining toward him in frustration, eyes closed, lips slightly open, her expression an open invitation, he asked, "Could I get you to do something for me?"

"Sure!"

Her enthusiasm made him grin. "Listen before you say yes. In this cold, it's a big favor."

She opened her eyes. "What is it?"

"When I saw you at the party the other night . . . you looked wonderful, like the princess you are."

"Am not," she said truculently.

"I wanted to kneel before you, kiss you through that gown. I wanted to have you push me over and straddle my face. I wanted to pleasure you so thoroughly you would always feel my lips on yours, my tongue in your mouth, my dick in your pussy. . . ."

"Samuel, you shouldn't say things like that. . . ." But she stared up at him, rapt.

He finished, "I want you to put on the dress."

"Okay."

"I want to feel you through it, know there's only thin silk between us."

"Okay."

"Push it up over your hips and—"

"I said okay. Okay." She backed away, smiling. "Oh. Kay."

He watched her vanish into the depths of the ladies' room.

They were going to die, and no matter what she said, he was responsible. He had failed to realize the Others would figure out his mission to release the Gypsy Travel Agency's fortune. He had failed to realize that they would stalk him, entrap him, murder him to stop him from succeeding.

At least they had failed in that. He could go to his death satisfied that he had done his best for his friends, the Chosen.

But he hated that he had brought her into this. Because whether Isabelle liked it or not, he was her man. He was responsible for her safety. He had dragged her with him on the mission to rescue little Mathis Moreau from his kidnappers. He hadn't recognized the danger, and when he did, he hadn't reacted fast enough to save them. Worse, every attempt they made to escape had been thwarted.

So he could make her last night on earth a night she would carry as a treasure into the next world.

Like a courting bird, he hustled around, making their nest inviting. He lit the heater and placed it just outside the tent—it might burn oxygen and batteries, but what did it matter now?

What mattered was having the first warmth they would enjoy in days.

He spread out the sleeping bags so they could sleep together, fixed the pillows . . . shook out the fur coat and placed it over the top.

The fur . . . Remembering how he had stolen it from the closet, then found out he'd inconvenienced some pompous rich bitch who paid a hundred thousand for it . . . that made him smile.

Then his smile faded. He and Isabelle would go to sleep in each other's arms, and they wouldn't wake up. . . .

Damn! He didn't want this to be the end. He didn't want the Others to win this battle. He wanted to live with Isabelle at his side. He wanted them both to get their full marks, their powers. He wanted them to be forever mated, forever as one.

And now that would never happen.

"Samuel." Isabelle's warm, intimate voice brought him back from the edge of despair.

He turned. He gawked.

After so many days of seeing Isabelle in bulky coats, sweaters, and ski pants, this was his first glimpse of heaven.

Yes, the dress was smudged. Yes, it had a tear. But the designer gown flowed over her body like a wash of gold, shimmering as it lovingly outlined her breasts, her waist, her thighs. She wore the foolish heels, making the line from her hips to her toes even longer, and like a model she turned, encouraging him in his gawkery. The silk trembled with every movement, and every moving shadow hinted blatantly of that which was just beneath.

He trembled. "My God," he said hoarsely. "It doesn't look like you're wearing anything under that gown."

She stopped, and like a thirties pinup girl she looked over her shoulder at him, one finger to her pursed lips, eyes widened in falsely innocent dismay. "Oh. I didn't know you wanted me to wear underwear. I'll have to go find my panties." She took a step.

"Wait!"

She turned to him, a spin that made her gown swirl around her calves.

"If you do that," he said, "I'll be done by the time you get back."

She laughed warmly, low and soft; then, as he held the tent flap open, she slid in in one graceful motion.

He followed, ridiculously pleased at her willingness to enter his domain.

"At last, a use for this coat." She sat on the fur and petted it with her hand, then rolled back and stretched like a cat, one arm, then the other, her right leg, then . . .

As she stuck out her left, clad in the foolish Jimmy Choo gold spike heel, he caught her ankle and ran his hand up her calf, pushing the silk aside as he went.

Her hand went to her heart as if to contain the tumult.

Good. He wasn't the only one blasted by need, by sentiment, by the rush to seize satisfaction before they died . . . and yet, he intended to make this last as long as possible.

He bent her knee so that the silk fell in a sleek rush onto her hip, half baring her to his gaze. He halted to admire the soft lips lightly covered with fine curling hair, her blushing clit, the shadowy, mysterious entrance to her body.

"Samuel, I can feel you looking." Her voice was slightly slurred, and as he watched he saw the pale pink of her inner flesh heat to a rose.

With one hand, he traced the inner length of her other leg from her ankle to her thigh, a long run of skin colored by loving nature with burnished warmth.

The fullness of her skirt now rested on her belly, and he lifted her ankle to rest on his shoulder. He slid his finger along her slit . . . and in an arrested voice, he said, "You're icy."

"Oh." She stirred in embarrassment. "I wanted to freshen up, so I washed. . . ."

"With snow?" He was horrified at her feminine insistence on cleanliness—and intrigued.

"Don't be silly. With water."

"You used slushy water to freshen up?" More horrified. More intrigued.

She paused, then purred, "Am I fresh?"

Never in his life had he heard an invitation more artfully delivered. He slid down to rest between her thighs, stretched out with his mouth inches above her, and slowly dipped his head to inhale her scent. "Yes."

"Then I guess it was worth it."

He laughed helplessly. "There is not another woman like you in the world."

She watched him, eyes half closed and smiling. "That is quite true."

Now was the time to say all the things he'd always meant to tell her. Now . . . because there was no tomorrow. "All these years, I have dreamed of your taste, of the way you move when I take your clit into my mouth and suck it, the way you grow damp and needy, and best of all—the way you clamp down on my tongue when you come."

"You make me hot from the inside out."

"I always enjoy the taste of you, and it is a flavor I have long craved."

She moaned softly.

His breath brushed her skin, and he said, "As long as I've got a face, you've got a place to sit."

Tilting her head back, she laughed helplessly. "How can you be so romantic one minute and so crude the next?"

He kissed her between the legs. "Because with you, I want to be everything I am—romantic and crude, serious and funny, loving and in love. I want to buy you gifts when I've had a good day, gripe at you when I've had a bad day, be a jerk and know you'll slap me, know that no matter what I do, you'll love me anyway."

"You want everything," she whispered.

"Yes. I want everything." He kissed her belly. "But I want everything for you, too. I want you to come to me when your friends are a pain. I want to hear you laugh too loud at silly jokes and hold you while you cry over a chick flick. I want you to feel free to be bitchy when you've got PMS. I want to hear you scream when you're angry at me and know you're not going to walk out because we're meant to be together forever. I want everything for us . . . and all we've got is tonight, so let's make this"—he kissed her again—"a good night."

Chapter 28

A t Samuel's declaration, at his vision of a whole life of love, sentimental tears welled in Isabelle's eyes.

Then he opened her with his fingers and used his mouth and lips and teeth to make her crazy. She twisted on the fur, insane with need, as he probed and sucked. Passion built in her veins, making her heart race, her hands clench. Bringing orgasm too fast, yet not fast enough. She hovered on the edge as he built her frenzy bit by bit, teasing her with a retreat, blasting her more intensely, using his tongue in ways she had never imagined.

He had always been like this, wanting to know she'd found her bliss, over and over, before he found his. But today he used skills she didn't know he possessed until she begged, "Samuel, please. Please."

"Please what? Please . . . this?" Lifting his head, he thrust one finger in her.

That was all it took. His finger inside, moving, stroking . . . and she came. It was bliss. It was magic. It was release and pleasure. And when she thought she was done, he used his thumb to circle her clit and drive her higher, longer, until she dug her heels into the fur and lifted herself to him, an offering, a seduction.

When she subsided, she rested, panting, on the fur.

"What shall we do now?" He sounded amused.

She opened her eyes a little.

He *looked* amused.

The bastard. She'd show him.

She used her toes to push first one shoe, then the other off her feet. Wrapping her legs around his neck, she trapped him in place. "Again," she said.

And he obeyed.

She let him go when her legs were too weak to hold him. As he rose above her, she heard him chuckle.

Had he so firmly kept control over his lust?

She would fix that.

Smiling, she let her hands wander over the edge of her bodice, knowing his gaze would track her movements.

It did. His eyes glazed with desire as her fingers glided over the silk, around her breasts, over her nipples, pinching them gently until they were erect and thrusting at the thin material. She skimmed her palms down her rib cage in a slow, sensuous motion, stopping short of her slit. She lifted one leg so he could see . . . everything, then slid the silk up and down, back and forth, almost touching herself.

But.

Not.

Quite.

His breath was harsh in the chill air. He sat up abruptly and stripped off his shirt, pants, long underwear, leaving him clad in only a pair of navy blue boxer shorts that tented over his erection.

Now her breath was harsh; she hadn't seen him naked since she'd run away from the home they shared, her heart shattered by his betrayal.

He looked the same: big-boned, heavily muscled, with long arms and large, capable hands. Yet she saw the subtle changes. His shoulders and chest were bulkier, as if to prepare for this job he had worked to build himself into a formidable fighter.

Politically correct or not, knowing that he could protect her gave her a thrill.

Sitting up on one elbow, she reached out and lightly ran her palm over his shoulder and down his arm.

At her touch, his eyes half closed.

"What is your pleasure?" she whispered.

"To make you happy."

"As you wish." Taking his hand, she placed it on her breast.

He groaned, a deep, beastly groan, then used the silk to rasp softly over her skin and rouse her nerves from their long slumber.

"Good man," she said. Wrapping her hand around the back of his neck, she drew him close, directing him, and he followed instructions willingly, kissing her nipple, wetting the silk, then slipping his hand beneath the strap and sliding it off her shoulder.

"Lovely. So lovely." His voice caressed the words.

This time when he kissed her breast, it was nude, the nerves were wide-awake, and he suckled so skillfully, she thrust herself into his mouth in ravenous demand.

When he lifted his head, his brown eyes gleamed with satisfaction. "Greedy."

She surged forward, rolling him onto his back.

He let her climb on top, her knees straddling his hips.

Leaning down, she kissed him.

His lips opened.

She became the aggressor, baiting him with feints and retreats. She twisted her fingers into the smooth, straight strands of his hair, the pure tactile pleasure intensifying her passion. When the kiss became . . . not enough, she lifted her head and wondered if she should say the things she would never admit . . . if they were going to live until tomorrow.

But they weren't going to live.

So she said, "The first time I saw you, back before I even really remember, I wanted to hold you. Then . . . the first time we made love, you imprinted yourself on me."

"Yes," he whispered.

"There's never been another man for me. That's why, all these years without you, I've been so angry. Every minute we've been apart, I longed for you." She kissed him again. "I knew you were the only man I could ever love."

Wrapping his arms around her, he rolled over, putting her beneath him. He looked into her eyes. "You love me even knowing I'm the one who trapped us here on the set of *Harry Potter and the Chamber of Dehydrated Rations*?"

"You didn't trap us here; the Others did." But she gurgled with laughter at his silly joke. "Here, where I've become one of the *Raiders of the Lost Lockers*."

Beneath her, the fur tickled her neck, her back, her arms. The cool silk brushed her sensitive nerve endings.

Between her legs, his erection nudged at her.

Abruptly, she lost her sense of humor. "I love you, Samuel Faa, and I always will—in this world, and in the next."

Chapter 29

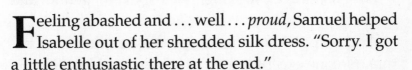

Feeling abashed and ... well ... *proud*, Samuel helped Isabelle out of her shredded silk dress. "Sorry. I got a little enthusiastic there at the end."

"It's okay. I don't plan on wearing it again." She flopped back onto the fur, smiling a deeply satisfied smile.

He had done that. He had made her happy.

He smoothed a hand across her shoulder, over her breast, and followed its progress with his gaze as he stroked one of her strong, shapely thighs.

Now that she was naked, he wanted her again.

He wanted her ... always. "We should have done that sooner, because I'm sure we saved ourselves."

"How so?" she asked.

"We must have melted all the snow over the locker room."

She chuckled deep in her throat. "The satellites can see the hot spot from space."

"We've been transported into a James Bond movie."

"I am quite sure that this"—her hand slid down his hip and grasped his stirring erection—"is not your *Goldfinger*."

She looked so deliciously naughty he laughed out loud. Leaning close to her ear, he whispered, "Yet I've been trapped with Pussy Galore." And he nipped at her lobe.

"Ouch!" She shoved at his shoulder. At the same time, she stroked his cock, long and slow, and when she found a drop of semen at the tip, she picked it up with her finger. Her gaze challenging his, she lifted that finger to her lips, and sucked it into her mouth.

Isabelle, fragile-looking, well-spoken, gentle and courteous . . .

And no one knew the deeply erotic side of her nature. No one except him . . . and Senator Noah Noble, and whomever else she'd slept with after Samuel had driven her away.

His fault.

Possessive of her, angry at himself, he pulled her on top of him, thrust inside her, gloried in her tight heat, and knew that for this moment, she was his.

Caught by surprise, she arched on top of him. Then she saw the emotions that goaded him, tightened her legs around his hips, and vowed, "I will drive every last thought from your mind."

When she was done with him and he gasped by her side, he said, "The oxygen must be fading, because if we do that again, I'm going to die."

Curling up next to him, she put her head on his shoulder. "It's a good way to go."

Chapter 30

———————⟨≈⟩———————

"**S**amuel?"

Isabelle's voice pulled him out of a deep slumber. "Hm?"

"I don't want to alarm you. But we're still alive."

He opened his eyes.

Isabelle was sitting up in her sleeping bag, a flashlight in one hand and his watch in the other.

She was also naked, and his ability to process information was temporarily impeded by the gleam of her skin, the shadows and peaks of her breasts.

She recognized his problem, because she covered herself with the blanket and repeated, "Samuel, it's twelve hours since we set off the dynamite, and we're still here."

Distraction removed, he was able to think. "There's air coming from somewhere."

They looked at each other.

In unison, they pulled on their clothes and scrambled out of the tent.

Samuel halted, hands on his hips, and told her, "Douse the light."

She turned it off. "Why?"

"I want to think without the distraction of my eyesight." He took long breaths, trying to feel the draft of oxygen that was keeping them alive. "Where would there be a vent or a passage? Not near the top. I've looked. No doors. No windows . . ."

"It's a castle. It *has* to be a secret passage."

"The only place we haven't looked is below us."

She flipped on the light, blinding him. "There's a dungeon." She said it so simply.

Right. It was so obvious.

He picked up the LED lantern. "There's an overflow drain in the men's room."

"And the women's room."

They split, heading for different restrooms.

She looked back at him. "The women's room is going to be cleaner."

He'd give her that one. He'd already noted that male skiers saved their precision for the slopes.

He followed her.

The drain was set on the floor between the sinks and the toilets, a five-inch round black grate in a seat of gray ceramic tile.

They knelt beside it, leaned over it—and felt the faintest brush of damp, cool air.

Samuel wanted to groan with relief. Instead, he said, "We're going to have to look down there."

"I'll get a screwdriver."

"What for?"

"To loosen the grate."

"Never mind that. Bring me the pickax."

She blinked at him. "On one condition."

"Sure. What?"

"You let me pound on it for a while."

The white glare of the LEDs bled the natural gold out of her skin, leaving it flat and lifeless. She had scraped her hair back into a ponytail, she wore no mascara, her lashes were almost nonexistent, and the ski clothes hid every curve and muscle of her glorious body.

Yet never had she looked better to him. "I'll let you take as many whacks as you want."

She started to walk away, then returned. "You know what gets me? We could have been running a heater. And a stove. We could have been warm. We could have been cooking."

"We could have been *out*."

"That, too." She disappeared, a single light flashing back and forth in the eternal dark.

He dug his work gloves out of his pockets. He discarded the coat. His hat. Looked up when she came in, pickax over her shoulder.

"Which of the Seven Dwarves am I?" she asked.

"Grumpy," he said. "And I'm Dopey."

"Get us out of here, and you can be Happy."

"Smart-ass." He grinned. Taking the pickax from her, he set it down, caught her head in his hands, and kissed her. Hard. Passionately. Reminding her of all the things they'd said the night before.

Drawing away, he grabbed the pickax, lifted it high over his head, and smashed the blunt end right on the grille.

It broke through the floor, which crumbled down in a shower of tile and landed . . . down there. Far, far below.

Samuel and Isabelle looked at each other.

He offered her the pickax. "Your turn."

She took it, gave a few good blows around the hole. She didn't have his body strength, but she sent chunks of the floor crashing down.

He held out a restraining hand. "Stop. Let's look."

She pulled the flashlight off her belt, knelt beside him, and shined it below.

Black rock floor. One black rock wall. A few rusty iron bars.

"I was right," she said. "It's the dungeon!"

She looked so pleased, he hated to dampen her enthusiasm, but he was nothing if not ruthlessly practical. "Yes, but the passage—is it an air passage only? Here, we're below ground level. One floor below . . . that's a long way down. I don't think we can excavate our way out of here."

"Even if that's true, maybe the tunnel slants up. Or it goes straight, and comes out on a slope near someone's house or something and we'll be able to yell at them." She pushed his shoulder. "Come on, Samuel, this has to work out."

"It already has. My turn." He worked the pickax again; then, when he'd opened a hole big enough to work with, he fetched the battery-operated saw and a coil of rope. Using the saw, he cut through the floor deck until he had a hole large enough for his shoulders. Taking the flashlight, he stuck his head in and shined it around. "It's probably a cave and they used it for their wine cellar and dungeon."

"There's wine?"

He lifted his head and looked at her. "No."

"Oh."

"No skeletons, either, that I can see."

"Good," she said fervently.

"Nor any way out. I'm going to have to go down and scope it out."

With air, they had hope. Surely they could live long enough to somehow get out of here.

As he looped the rope around the metal toilet stalls, she asked, "Do you want me to go down?"

He dropped the length into the hole. "You'd be easy for me to pull up, but we don't know what's down there. Spiders for sure. Snakes, maybe. Roaches? I dunno. Do you want to go?"

She shook her head.

He tested the strength of his knots. "I can climb back up, so you stay close and don't drop anything on my head." He grinned at her. "No matter how tempted you are."

She didn't smile back. "I won't."

He dropped into the darkness, going hand over hand until his feet touched down. "I'm here," he called, and turned on the flashlight.

Her head popped into the opening, blocking the ambient light from above.

But he didn't complain. He understood her anxiety; his heart was thumping, too, with hope and anticipation.

The ceiling was about twelve feet above him. The floor beneath his boots was slick and uneven, rough-hewn granite with pockets of soil and dampness. The earthy smell surrounded him, and here and there iron rusted in piles.

"Do you see anything?" she asked. "And by *anything*, I mean a door marked by a blinking green exit sign."

"I see where stairs used to go up to your level." He shined the light at the ceiling. "But nobody's been in or out of here in years."

"Can you feel a draft?"

"No, but the air is fine, no gases, so there is an outlet." Slowly he started a circuit of the walls, wandering down one side, taking the corner, exploring the second side, turning the corner—

He stopped. Just stood there.

"Samuel? What's wrong?" Her voice sounded urgent. "Samuel? Is it a skeleton? A giant spider? Samuel, are you hurt?"

"Not at all." Even to himself, his voice sounded disembodied. "Far in the distance, at the end of a tunnel . . . I can see sunlight."

Chapter 31

———⟞⟝———

Samuel didn't fit through the narrow tunnel. For once in his life, his size, his big bones, his superior strength weren't an advantage. He just by God did not fit.

Isabelle did. At least, she fit through the first few feet, head down, crawling on her belly through the channel cut into the rock.

Then he pulled her out. Outfitted her with the proper passage-squirming clothes: a ski jacket with a tight-fitting hood to keep spiders from dropping into her hair or down her neck, a full-body waterproof ski outfit to keep her from getting damp, hiking boots, and insulated gloves. They worked fast, wanting to give her as much daylight as possible, not knowing where she would come out, not knowing how long she would have to hike before she found help, uncertain of any oncoming winter storms. . . .

When Samuel thought of all the things that could go wrong out there, he felt the savage in him rising.

But what good did it do to complain? This was how it had to be, and who knew if the tunnel was even passable all the way?

"If it gets tight," he said, "come back. If you get scared, I'm right here. I'll come for you somehow."

"What are you going to do? Chop off your shoulders?" She patted him comfortingly. "I'll be fine."

He kissed her again.

She looped her arms around his shoulders, kissed him back.

He didn't like the way she threw herself into that kiss, as if she believed they would never have a chance to kiss again.

When she pulled away, he said, "You don't have to go."

"Yes, I do."

"Yes, you do." He put his forehead to hers and started in again. "If it gets tight, come back. If—"

"Samuel." She shook him. "I'll be fine. We're going to get out. Pretty soon, this whole week is going to be nothing but a nightmare."

He didn't quite like the sound of that. Not all of it had been a nightmare. Not for him, anyway. So he kissed her again, using his passion, one last time, to carry her away from the darkness, the bugs, the peril she faced.

Then he did the hardest thing he'd ever done in his life.

He let her go.

He watched as her silhouette, highlighted against

the sunlight, squirmed along through the tunnel. Occasionally he called, "How's it going?"

"Okay." But her voice sounded as if she had turned her back on him.

Which was dumb, because she was moving away, so of course she would sound distant.

Once she stopped for so long, he leaned in and shouted, "What's wrong?"

"Spiderweb." A long pause. "I think I ate the spider."

Now that she said that, he could see her shuddering. "A little extra protein," he called cheerfully, and wished it were him facing this ordeal instead of her.

"You're a jerk."

"Everyone knows that!" he replied.

Bracing herself, she went forward, farther and farther away from him.

How long was this passage? A quarter mile? Half mile? Her ordeal seemed to go on forever.

Suddenly—she was gone. No wriggling silhouette. No distant voice.

"Isabelle!" he bellowed.

Her head popped up, and clearly, she was standing on the other side facing him. "I made it!" She wildly waved her arms.

"Where are you?" he called.

"I can see a house down below. And people. I think I came out on the other side of the highway."

"Makes sense!"

"I'll send someone to dig you out right away!"

"I'll see you on the outside."

She stood there as if undecided about . . . something.

"Go on now," he called. "Be careful!"

"I am. I will. Bye, Samuel. Bye!" One moment she was there.

Then she was gone . . . leaving him with the irritated sense that something had just gone very wrong.

Chapter 32

The sign read:

**WELCOME TO HOLYROOD, WEST VIRGINIA
POPULATION 14**

Aaron Eagle pulled the van to a stop, and the Chosen Ones peered out the front window and down the main street—the *only* street—of the town.

"This is the place." Charisma could feel a tingle in the stones that ringed her wrists.

Holyrood hid secrets, special secrets. She didn't know what they were, but the earth knew. She could hear its singing.

"Where are the fourteen people who live here?" John Powell was their leader, the man who had received the e-mail asking for help and made the executive decision to make the drive from New York City to this tiny hamlet deep in the Appalachians.

He didn't have to do it. Maybe it was bad idea. But he had said, *There's no use us sitting around worrying and grieving about Samuel and Isabelle. We've got to go out and do something, and this message*—he tapped the paper he'd printed out—*if it's really from one of the Chosen who has retired . . . well, we need to respond. He asked for our help. We need to make contact.*

"More to the point, where's this Billy Pemrick character?" Caleb D'Angelo looked like what he was—a bodyguard, tough, strong, fierce, and right now tense with suspicion. "He said he'd meet us at the mayor's office, but surely he heard us coming up that last grade."

Everyone nodded.

There were six of them in the van: their driver, Aaron, an art thief with an impressive extra talent; John Powell, the guy with the power; Jacqueline D'Angelo, their psychic; Aleksandr Wilder, Chosen but not gifted; and Caleb, who wasn't one of the Chosen at all, but was Jacqueline's husband and the man they depended on to have their backs.

And Charisma Fangorn, well aware that she was out of place in this rural environment. She was out of place almost everywhere she went, no big deal, but some people really did have problems with her tats, her piercings, her pop clothing, and her black-and-yellow hair. She figured once they got to know her, they would love her.

And usually, they did.

The ones who didn't were stupid.

"So is this a trap?" Aaron asked.

"If the Others are going to set a trap for us, it would have been easier in New York," John said flatly.

John was nothing if not logical.

"It's not a trap for us. But everything is not as it seems." Jacqueline stared out the dark-tinted side windows at the forest that pressed close to the road.

"Are you having a vision?" Caleb hovered close to his wife, always ready to protect her when a prophecy seized her.

"Not exactly." She put her hand on his arm. "But I've got some really strong intuition working here."

Charisma cranked around in the seat. "It's wonderful the way your gift keeps developing!"

"Either it's developing or I'm wrong and we're driving into a minefield," Jacqueline said.

"Don't sugarcoat it, honey; give it to us straight." Caleb opened the panel in the floor and pulled out the firearms—cleaned, loaded, and ready. Since the Chosen Ones had first come together, Caleb had been training them in the use of firearms. Some of them were better than others, and Caleb decided who got what. He handed out pistols to everyone, rifles for him, for Aaron, for Jacqueline, for Aleksandr. Charisma had an astigmatism that made her pull to the right, and John, with his ability to project power, was more useful with his hands free.

They all wore bulletproof vests, now standard equipment for the Chosen Ones.

The trip into the Appalachians had been everything

they'd expected. The freeway had become a highway, the highway had become a road, the road had gone from two-lane paved to gravel washboard, and the higher they climbed, the denser the forest, the more primitive the atmosphere, and the narrower and more winding the road. During the trip, Charisma had felt as if she'd gone from twenty-first-century New York City to colonial America—or even earlier.

"Is the town empty?" Aleksandr moved his shoulders uneasily.

"No, there are people here." Aaron eased his foot off the brake and let the van glide forward at an idle.

"Are *you* developing a psychic gift?" Jacqueline asked.

"Better than that, I'm a thief." Aaron's eyes shifted from side to side, scrutinizing every bush, every window. "And if a thief doesn't have a pretty solid sense about people watching him, he's soon going to be dancing with Bubba at the prison prom. Or be pushing up daisies at the local cemetery."

Holyrood was a pretty standard old mountain town. The newest building was the store, built in the forties after the war. A dozen small, square homes in various states of old age and disrepair sat back from the street. Picket fences surrounded each patch of grassy yard. The garages were set toward the backs of the long, narrow lots.

"Someone is watching us," Aaron concluded, "and watching us really hard."

"Yes, and there's been gunfire," Charisma said.

"Your stones are telling you that?" Aleksandr asked incredulously.

"Bullets are made of lead, lead comes from the earth, and . . . Yes, the stones are telling me a lot of stuff. Mostly to be careful." Charisma glanced in the back. "So be careful."

"Instead of the usual reckless idiots we usually are?" Aleksandr suggested.

She turned and grinned at him.

He didn't grin back, and that startled her.

Aleksandr was the youngest member of their team, now in graduate school at NYU. When he'd first joined the Chosen Ones, he had been raw, gangly, an over-grown boy with overgrown brains. He'd been brought in because he was one of the famous Wilders, but Aleksandr had no gift. He'd been born into a loving family; magic gifts weren't given to infants who were welcomed and loved.

Yet because of his background, everyone liked him. He was polite, he was generous, he was inventive, he didn't have issues. He was great with the computer, which as far as Charisma was concerned was better than woo-woo. . . .

But today, he appeared to be different.

Maybe she just hadn't really examined him for a while, but he didn't look like a kid anymore.

He was a man, tall, broad-shouldered, serious.

It made her feel funny to stare him in the eyes. She'd

always felt older because her early life had been so rocky, but they were actually close to the same age. She was almost twenty-three, so he must be twenty-four.

She faced front.

Probably he had grown up so abruptly because they had lost their friends and allies. Because with every day that passed, it looked more and more as if Samuel and Isabelle were . . . gone . . .

Charisma couldn't believe it. She couldn't. She would *know* if they were dead.

"Any bets that that's the mayor's office?" Caleb pointed at the sign on the small, square building next to the store. "Park off to the side of the garage. Um, to the right—there's an old truck parked to the left."

Aaron turned abruptly, changing from a leisurely drive down the street to a fast skid into the driveway and into the unoccupied spot beside the garage.

He turned off the motor and waited.

Nothing. No sound, no motion.

Twisting to face the back, he asked, "What do you think?"

"I think no one can see in the van, the Others can't see who we are and there's a pretty good chance they don't want to fire on innocent people," John said.

"Because they're such nice folks?" Aleksandr asked sarcastically.

"Because we might be tourists, and they have instructions to keep this operation as clean as possible," Caleb said.

"Right." Aaron nodded. "So Charisma and I are going in. Cover us."

Picking up his rifle and the rounds of ammo Caleb had placed beside him, he concealed them beneath his coat, then swung the door open.

Charisma did the same.

Still nothing.

They got out and walked toward the mayor's side porch.

The back of Charisma's neck itched with the knowledge that too many eyes were upon them.

They climbed the steps, tapped on the door.

No one answered.

"Mr. Pemrick?" Charisma called. "You sent an e-mail to John Powell asking for—"

The door flew open.

A broad-shouldered old Clint Eastwood sort of a guy grabbed her by the wrist and pulled her inside.

Aaron followed.

And a blast of buckshot followed them both.

Chapter 33

The old guy got the door shut and glared at Aaron. "You John Powell?"

"I'm Aaron. This is Charisma." Aaron gestured. "John's in the van."

Aaron and Charisma stood in the mayor's office, all right: a single large room, three desks, six chairs, one large metal file cabinet, and, through a narrow, open door, a tiny restroom.

Glass and shards of wood crunched under Charisma's feet. Every window had been shot out. Chunks of the windowsills had been blasted away. The shades were peppered with holes, hanging crooked or fallen to the floor. Rifles and ammunition had been strategically placed throughout the room.

"It looks as if you've already been through a war," Aaron said.

"Sorry I didn't tidy up. I wasn't sure I was having visitors," Billy said in his slow West Virginia drawl.

"Or at least—I wasn't sure I was having *welcome* visitors. If we stay back here a ways, they can't see us. But it's a good idea to stay down, because they send in a shot every once in a while."

"You're hurt." Charisma didn't need to see the blood matted on the back of Billy's shirt to know that. Her stones were vibrating.

"They got a few shots in," Billy allowed. "Mind if I sit down?" But he didn't wait for an answer. He slithered down on a desk chair.

His thinning hair was still red, his faded eyes were blue, but what should have been a ruddy complexion was gray with exhaustion and drawn with pain.

Aaron pulled out his cell. "So I can bring in my people—where are the shooters?"

"I've got three in the house across the way. Two in the houses on either side." Billy used four fingers to point. "One somewhere in the general store, although I think he isn't doing as well as he thought he would when he went in. Might have got a good shot in myself."

"None in the woods around us?" Aaron asked.

"No, they're city folk. They don't like all them trees and such." Billy's face crinkled in disdain.

"Anyone out there with powers?" Aaron was assuming the worst.

"The sweetest-faced little gal you've ever seen—she's about eighteen, but I can't quite figure out what her job is. She's sitting in the house across the way, watching the whole operation and waiting for . . ." Billy sighed. "I don't know what she's waiting for, but she scares me. I think she's here to make me talk, and I think she's got some kind of pretty nasty gift that could do it. I've been thinking that today was a good time to die. My Ruby Lee is going to be glad you got here before I did."

While Aaron dispensed the information to the group in the van, Charisma commanded, "Billy, take off your shirt."

"If I had a dime for every time a pretty girl like you said that to me." Billy pulled his shirt out from beneath his belt, unsnapped it, pulled it off.

"Wow!" She ogled the carefully etched marks across his belly. "Awesome tat!"

"Thank you, little lady, but as I'm sure you must know, it's not exactly a tattoo." He said the word as if he were correcting her grammar. "Had a dag-blasted Varinski shape-shifter attack me while my attention was elsewhere. Gave me my mark and taught me a lesson I never forgot."

"What was that?"

"Don't assume an enemy's going to attack from the rear." He turned the chair and straddled it so she could view the damage.

He'd been peppered with buckshot more than once, and from close range. Blood rose from wounds that looked like hamburger, and buckshot clustered so closely together he would need surgery to get it all out.

"Those bastards," Charisma said softly. She didn't really know what to do, how to fix him.

If only Isabelle were here.

But Isabelle was . . . missing. Not dead. *She was missing.*

"One of the silly fools with a shotgun *did* attack from the rear. He sneaked up to the window while I was firing out the front. Brought me to my knees, he did." Billy turned his head and smiled coldly. "But if you go look out in my garden, you'll see he is now fertilizing my roses. The first-aid kit is right there on the desk. I was trying to fix myself up for another go-round."

Aaron stepped to the door. "The rest of our group is coming in."

"I wish I could help protect 'em"—Billy's head sank onto his arms crossed on the back of the chair—"but I'm starting to feel sorta poorly."

"I imagine you are." Charisma ran her hand over his back, feeling the lead pieces, flicking the easiest ones out with her fingernail.

The shooting started, loud, abrasive, so many blasts it sounded like a machine gun.

"Unless you brought something to stop those bullets, your people are dead," Billy said.

"John Powell will stop the bullets. He's like Darth Vader without the breathing problems," Charisma told him.

Aaron yanked the door open, and called out names as the Chosen entered, introducing them as they piled in. He slammed the door on another barrage of shots.

Caleb pointed Jacqueline, Aleksandr, and Aaron toward windows. They took their places in the shadows.

Caleb strode to the front door, cracked it, knelt, and shot.

Across the street, someone screamed.

Billy looked them over. "There aren't enough of you. There aren't seven."

"Two of our team are gone," Charisma told him. "In Switzerland."

"Gone? Is that a euphemism for . . . ?"

"No! The rescuers are still looking for them." Charisma didn't say the search had officially changed from rescue to retrieval.

"John?" Jacqueline beckoned. "Can you come over here and push over that gardening shed next to the house on the left? If you can do that, I've got a clear shot."

John went over, looked out. Gently he moved Jacqueline aside, lifted his hands, and from across the street, Charisma heard wood creak, then blow apart.

Someone yelled.

Jacqueline moved into place and shot.

The yelling stopped.

"I take back all the bad things I've said about the younger generation." For the first time, the muscles in Billy's broad back relaxed.

John strode forward and shook Billy's hand. "Mr. Pemrick? John Powell. It was good to hear from you. Really good. We thought we were pretty much the only Chosen left alive."

"There are a few of us hanging around, out in the sticks mostly, the ones who didn't much approve of the

Gypsy Travel Agency and how they handled matters," Billy said.

Charisma picked up the tweezers. "How did you find us?"

"It took me a while," Billy said. "I tried to contact the Gypsy Travel Agency. But they're gone."

"For almost three years," John told him.

"For a while I thought the Gypsy Travel Agency had managed to destroy themselves and the Chosen Ones completely. But then I figured, no, we're isolated up here, and we're hillbillies"—Billy's West Virginia drawl grew more exaggerated—"but I would have heard if the country had collapsed completely. Would have seen it on my computer machine."

Charisma laughed softly.

"What?" Billy turned around to look at her, and his faded blue eyes twinkled. "You don't believe I'm a hillbilly? Born and raised right here in the heart of the Appalachians."

"No, sir, I believe you are a hillbilly if you say you are. But I think you might have seen a little of the world in your day." Charisma picked more buckshot out of the old man's powerful back.

Aleksandr smoothly raised his rifle and shot.

Billy said, "I'm glad to know someone taught the Chosen Ones how to use firearms. It's a useful skill."

"Yes, sir," Aleksandr said. "My grandfather was a stickler about useful skills."

"Who's your grandfather?" Billy asked.

"Konstantine Wilder," Aleksandr said.

Billy twisted away from Charisma's touch. "Really? You're a Wilder?"

"Yes, sir."

"Last I heard about the Wilders, they'd broken their deal with the devil and caused old Lucifer a whole lot of heartburn."

"We do what we can," Aleksandr said.

"So you can't shape-shift?" With each piece of shot Charisma extracted, blood trickled down Billy's back.

"Don't know. Never have. Never tried." The tone of Aleksandr's voice was off.

But Charisma was too busy slapping first-aid tape on each bleeder—lousy nursing, but she had little practice—and she didn't have time to delve into whatever was bothering him.

"You keep it that way," Billy said. "A deal with the devil is a slippery road right to hell."

"You and my grandfather would get along really well," Aleksandr said.

"Since when do you *want* to change, young Aleksandr?" Caleb must have heard that tone in Aleksandr's voice, too.

"I don't," Aleksandr said coolly. "I just want to get out of here alive."

"That makes two of us," Billy said. "I got my civilians out of town, but I couldn't leave and at the same time keep the Others busy, so here I am with buckshot in my ass, a pretty girl working on me, and no way out."

"Oh, I wouldn't say that." Charisma finished off the roll of adhesive and handed Billy his shirt.

"What did you have in mind?" Jacqueline asked.

"I'm not a psychic, but I see a truck in our future." In her mind, Charisma pictured the truck parked on the other side of the garage from their van. "A 1968 three-quarter-ton crew cab Ford pickup, formerly white, now sort of rust-colored. Because of the rust."

"You're talking about the vehicle I love," Billy warned. "Ain't she a beauty?"

"She is. Is she still in good shape? No shots to the carburetor?" Charisma asked.

"I believe she's been spared," Billy said.

"Sweet-talker." Man, Charisma loved a good old pickup with a lot of power. "Where are the keys?"

"Under the driver's-side floor mat." Billy hoisted himself to his feet and stood, wavering. "Don't have much crime here in Holyrood. Well, except for this bunch of evil hooligans trying to take over the town."

John hurried over, took the shirt, helped Billy into it. "What are they here for?"

"They're searching for something, and seem to think it's in one of the caves in the area." Billy added, "There are a lot of caves in the area."

"Why would they think that?" John sounded casual. He was not.

"We're close to an entrance for the sacred cave." Aaron watched out the window, but his voice was grim and sure.

"Now, how did you know that?" Billy was clearly taken aback.

"Wherever I am, the sacred cave calls me." Aaron

watched Charisma tighten her bulletproof vest. "What's your plan, Charisma?"

"I'm going to get the truck, bring it around to the entrance, get Billy and the rest of you inside, and drive us out of this valley."

"It's not a valley. It's a holler," Billy corrected. "Get this hillbilly terminology correct. Anyway, your plan won't work. They'll pick us off as we go out the door."

"I'll go with you, Charisma," John said. "Protect you from the bullets."

"Someone has to get Billy into the truck. He needs to get to a hospital, John. He needs to go soon." The Chosen healed faster than most people, but Billy was older, he was exhausted, and he'd been badly hurt.

And Isabelle wasn't here to heal him.

Charisma wasn't going to think about that now.

"A couple of us will stay here and provide cover while you get in the truck and get out of town," Caleb said.

"Suicide mission," Billy said.

"Not at all." Aaron smiled briefly. "Caleb and I are good shots, and when the time comes, I can provide camouflage for him."

"You can make the two of you disappear?" Billy asked. At Aaron's nod, he said, "I had forgotten how much fun it was to work with a whole danged group of Chosen."

"I can stay, too," Aleksandr said.

"I can't cover you both," Aaron said. "I can't spread

myself thin enough. Besides, you're young; you need to get out."

"I should drive then," Aleksandr said. "I was raised in Washington in the Cascade Mountains; I know how to drive narrow, steep, winding roads—"

While he was talking, Charisma slipped out the back window.

Chapter 34

———⟨⟨⟩⟩———

Charisma dodged from bush to bush toward the ragged old pickup. The Chosen fired a barrage of shots to distract the Others, but she focused on the music the bullets made as they whistled toward her, bullets that lifted bits of grass and dirt close to her feet. She'd never heard the bullets before, but then . . . well, in her life, she hadn't really been shot at a lot.

Flinging open the truck's door, she jumped in and shut it behind her. The key was exactly where Billy promised, under the floor mat, and the motor started right up.

The truck might look like crap, but it was an extended-cab, which they desperately needed, and Billy kept the works under the hood in primo shape.

Charisma slammed the gearshift into reverse and peeled out, eyes glued to the rearview mirror. Bullets from the store were rocking the truck, so she kept it in reverse, cranked the wheel, and smashed into the building right below the window.

The firing stopped.

She figured either she'd gotten the guy, or he was still running backward through the store. She hoped he'd stained his underwear.

Putting the truck in first, she pushed the accelerator to the floor and plowed right through the picket fence to the front porch.

The door opened.

John stepped out first.

The bullets flew at him. He flung up his hands and they flew back with equal force.

Before the yells from across the street had died, Aleksandr had opened the truck's back door, and everyone was inside.

Aleksandr climbed across the back of the seat to sit by the other front door, his rifle pointed out the open window. He was, literally, riding shotgun.

Jacqueline kicked the seat behind Charisma. "We're in; let's go!"

Charisma let off the clutch, hit the accelerator, and took out the front lawn and the rest of the fence before the wheels hit the road.

From the backseat, Billy groused, "If I don't die, the little woman is going to kill me."

"Let's make sure the first doesn't happen before we worry about the second," John said.

As they flew past the Holyrood city sign, Charisma asked, "Everyone got their seat belts on?"

The satisfying sound of clicks answered her.

Charisma blasted down the grade and around the

first few curves, driving the way she'd learned in Oregon and Alaska and a few of the other places her mother had dragged her through. It took a few minutes before the Chosen realized she knew what she was doing, and she could almost hear their collective sigh of relief.

Then, in a conversational tone, John said, "So finish your story, Billy."

"About how I found you?" Billy seemed cheerfully unconcerned when all four tires left the ground. "It was this way. After the Gypsy Travel Agency was gone, there was no sign of the Chosen Ones, so I started thinking about where they could be. Finally decided to ask Irving Shea, sent an e-mail, and got young Aleksandr Wilder's response." He sounded more serious when he said, "Glad I was to hear you still existed, what with the Others getting so bold. Even down here, I've seen that they have hired help and are getting reckless, looking for . . . Say, what do they want?"

"We don't know," Jacqueline said. "I had a prophecy a few months ago, but we don't quite understand it."

Billy chuckled. "Good to know prophecies are the same as they used to be. I remember one time when our seer—her name was Zusane—"

Jacqueline sucked in her breath.

Billy stopped. "You knew Zusane?"

"She was my mother."

Billy sounded charmed. "You're little Jacqueline Vargha? I remember you. Saw you when you were about three, your hair as yellow and fluffy as a dandelion. My, oh, my, you grew up as pretty as your mama."

"No, sir, I didn't. No one will ever be as pretty as Zusane." Jacqueline's voice choked a little. "But thank you for the compliment."

Before Jacqueline, Zusane had been the psychic for the Chosen Ones, a woman of beauty, style, grace, and outgoing sexuality that had netted her five husbands. Or was it six? Charisma couldn't remember.

"I'm sorry to hear of your loss." Billy's Southern courtesy was sincere and warm. "She was a lovely woman in every way."

"It's not really a loss," Jacqueline said. "She visits every once in a while."

A pause. "She always broke the rules," Billy said admiringly.

"That's for sure." Jacqueline's voice was full of wry acceptance.

Death had improved the contentious relationship between mother and daughter, but as in life, Zusane was never around when needed.

"Why don't you tell Billy about your prophecy, Jacqueline? We so seldom have access to someone from before the Gypsy Travel Agency went up in the explosion. . . . I am wondering why you weren't in the building, though." John allowed his inquiry to hang in the air.

"You mean you're wondering if I was tossed out on my a— Pardon me, ladies." Billy excused himself with old-fashioned courtesy. "If I was tossed out on my heinie. No, I left on my own. Most of us who are still alive left on our own. We didn't approve of the cra— Pardon me, ladies. We didn't approve of the stunts the agency was pulling. Finding archeological sites, stealing the artifacts and selling them. Using mind tricks to pressure old people into leaving their fortunes to the company. Making money when they should have been doing no more than supporting the Chosen Ones in their endeavors."

"Okay," Aleksandr said.

"Okay," John said.

"Okay," Jacqueline said.

Billy must have been taken aback, because it was a few minutes before he asked, "Is that okay with you, Charisma?"

"I have no problem with it at all. We already figured out the Gypsy Travel Agency had a few moral issues that needed fixing." She whipped around a hairpin turn, back wheels skidding perilously close to the edge of a twenty-foot drop.

Aleksandr hissed.

"Shut up, Aleksandr," she said. "Billy, from what we can tell, the Gypsy Travel Agency was quite the profitable operation, and while we never got the whole story, what with us not being involved and everything, we're doing what we can to put things right."

"You're living with Irving Shea," Billy said neutrally.

"He's doing what he can to make reparations," John said.

"Right." Now Billy's scorn clearly sounded in his voice. "Irving Shea was the mover and the shaker of the Gypsy Travel Agency."

"He blames himself for what happened," John answered. "He sacrificed his health in the hopes of helping us find out what we need to know. I assume you know the power of deliberate self-sacrifice?"

"Yes. I do. Did it work?"

Jacqueline twisted around. "My prophecy occurred in his hospital room."

"Tell me," Billy said.

"*The world is changing. The rules are changing. The gifted are changing.*" Jacqueline's voice became deeper, dreamy, as if she were no longer in the car. "*Some will develop gifts who are not gifted now. The Gypsy Travel Agency is sacrificed to one man's ambition and his unwillingness to trust in the ultimate triumph of good. Now the Chosen Ones pay the price. Yet the sacrifice he offers might save them. . . . In that, the fledgling Chosen can find hope. Before their seven years are over, each of the seven must find a true love. They will know they have succeeded with the blossoming of their badges and their talents. And some must find that which is lost forever. For rising on the ashes of the Gypsy Travel Agency is a new power in a new building. Unless this hope takes wing, this power and this building will grow to reach the stars, and cast its shadow over the whole earth, and evil will rule.*"

The silence in the interior was profound.

Then Jacqueline shrieked, "Are you crazy, Charisma? You're headed right toward that truck!"

"Yep." They were headed down a steep grade that took a hundred-and-eighty-degree turn and went back up the next steep grade. Facing them on a bypass was a half-ton Chevy truck with two ugly-ass guys pointing weapons out the windows.

The Others *really* wanted Billy for something, and if they took out the Chosen, that was fine, too.

"You've got a brush guard on the front of this vehicle, Billy?" Charisma asked.

"Yep."

"Reinforced?"

"Chrome reinforced. Hate to lose that chrome."

"Sucks to be you." She accelerated right at the enemy. "Better duck, everyone; they're loaded for bear."

Aleksandr got off a shot, then pulled himself into the fetal position.

The shotgun blasts hit the windshield, spraying glass and shot all over the truck.

Charisma was pretty sure she was hit, but not badly, and as she slammed into their truck, her blood was pounding with pure pleasure.

Thank heavens this vehicle was built pre–air bags or she would have been blinded. As it was, the seat belt caught her and slammed her ass against the seat so hard she saw stars.

But as her ears cleared, she heard Aleksandr yelling, "Back up! Back up! Back up! Back up!"

She could do that without seeing well. And she did, reversing back onto the road, taking the corner, and heading up the grade.

The truck was rattling a little louder now—apparently parts had been loosened by the collision—but from the backseat, she heard Billy say, "No wonder you let this little gal drive! She could be runnin' moonshine. She's a pistol!"

"Why, yes, I am," she said. "You okay, Billy?"

"Doing good, sister."

Charisma glanced in the rearview mirror at Jacqueline.

Jacqueline shook her head slightly.

He wasn't doing as well as he claimed.

"Now—that's quite the prophecy." Billy picked up the conversation as if nothing had ever happened. "The gifted are changing, huh? New people will become gifted? I get all that, and I'm glad to hear it. It sounds as if Irving's sacrifice is working for you. But the rest of it . . . I haven't got a clue. Do you?"

John said, "We know that when we find our true loves and face what we most fear, we get enhanced powers and enhanced marks."

Jacqueline must have shown him the marks on her palms, the marks that looked like eyes, for Billy said, "Those look exactly like I imagined the first female seer would have in her hands."

"Yes, I got my powers because of Caleb, and I hope . . ." Her voice quavered.

"Those men will hold off the attackers, and if the attackers do overwhelm them, Aaron will hide Caleb in plain sight," John said firmly.

"I know. I just . . . I worry," Jacqueline said.

They all worried about one another all the time. In some ways it was the worst part of the job.

Or . . . no. The worst part of the job was losing their friends. Losing Samuel and Isabelle.

But they could still be found. Charisma was determined about that.

Glancing in the rearview mirror, she announced, "Bad news. That crash didn't disable them. They're after us again."

"That can't be good." But Billy didn't sound too concerned.

"They do look a little worse for wear." Charisma smiled savagely. "Those half-ton pickups simply don't hold up to a little crunch from a three-quarter-ton like this baby."

"Keep up the good work, little girl," Billy said. "You all seem to have a pretty good grip on this prophecy. Tell me what the other part of it means."

"We don't know." John opened the sliding back window and put the eye of the rifle out. "That's the enigmatic part."

"Wouldn't be a prophecy if there wasn't a mystery." Billy sounded almost pleased.

"So you've got no guidance to give us?" Jacqueline sounded as if she'd scootched down.

"You seem to be doing all right on your own. Plus you've got good folks like me playing hardball in the backfield for you. You'll probably make it through. If you don't—well, face it, it'll be the apocalypse and the world will be overrun by the wicked. So you'd better get it right!"

Charisma looked into the rearview mirror into Billy's twinkling eyes. "You got a trailer hitch on the back of this thing?"

"Sure do."

"Good-size one?"

"Sticks out eight inches."

"Right around this next corner, brace for impact." Charisma took a ninety-degree turn, slammed on the brakes, and waited.

The pursuers raced around the corner and rammed them hard enough to crumple Billy's truck bed—and drive the trailer hitch deep into their radiator.

John shot his rifle through their windshield, then shouted, "Go!"

Charisma put her foot to the floor.

The engine raced, but for a moment, they didn't move.

Then, with a lurch, they pulled free.

Shotguns blasted as they pulled away, but in the rearview mirror, Charisma saw steam and smoke rising from under the Others' hood.

They were dead in the water.

Aleksandr crowed with laughter and shoved Charisma's shoulder. "Good driving!" For a moment, he looked as young as he had the first day she'd met him.

She was glad. So glad. After the loss of Samuel and

Isabelle, she couldn't stand to lose more people she loved.

They made it to the hospital in record time.

As Billy went into surgery, he took Charisma's hand and said, "Looks like you kids have got a lot of work in front of you. If I make it through—"

"You'll make it through," she said.

"If I make it through, I will enjoy watching to see how it turns out."

He was out in record time while the doctor muttered about miraculous recoveries and how he'd never seen a man of Billy's age with such recuperative powers.

Caleb and Aaron walked in, smirking about disabling the goons hired by the Others, although they didn't want to talk about the spooky girl Billy feared or how she'd escaped them.

Most wonderful of all, John got a text that brought him to his feet right in the waiting room. "Isabelle just walked into a rescue station. She's alive! She's fine. She's relieved. And they're going back to dig Samuel out of a snowy grave right now."

Chapter 35

————◆❦◆————

Samuel crawled out of the basement to cheers, grins, shoulder slapping, and camera lights.

But no sign of Isabelle. She didn't rush forward to fling her arms around his neck, kiss him, tell him she had worried about him, declare her love.

She was fine. She had to be, or the crowd wouldn't be so happy.

So where was she?

He played to the cameras, smiling and waving, saying all the right things while walking through the crowd: "So glad to be out. . . . Thank you to all the noble rescuers. . . . Never gave up hope. . . . Just want a hot meal and a shower . . . and a milk shake." Catching sight of Mrs. Mason, he cut off the reporters. "Now, if you'll excuse me, I see someone who's here for me."

Not a lie. Mrs. Mason was there for him. She stood beside her long limo, door open, chin tucked into her ankle-length down coat, her large dark glasses covering her eyes.

Darren Owen stood beside her, dressed in a chauffeur's outfit, even now clearly disapproving of Samuel.

What did Samuel have to do to gain his praise? Rescue a dozen infants and die in the attempt?

Yeah. That might do it. Especially the dying part.

A member of the ski patrol grabbed at Samuel and said, "We need to perform a physical."

"But first, this is very important." Samuel indicated Mrs. Mason, pulled away, strode toward the car.

Mrs. Mason slid inside.

He followed.

Darren shut the door on them, ran around, got in, and while reporters and ski patrol shouted, Darren drove them away.

Samuel didn't even have to glance around the interior of the limo. He knew Isabelle wasn't waiting inside. Turning to Mrs. Mason, he bared his teeth. "She's not there when I get dug out. She's not here with you. Where is she?"

Patricia Mason should have been afraid of his anger.

She wasn't. As far as he could tell, Patricia Mason wasn't afraid of anything. "She's on her way back to New York."

"What did you do? Hug her, say, 'Honey, I'm glad you're alive,' fling her into a car, and send her away? As soon as you confirmed she'd spent five days trapped with me?" He leaned toward Mrs. Mason, ignoring the oversize sunglasses to keep aggressive eye contact. "Anything to get her away?"

"That's not the way it worked."

"Tell me how it worked."

"She wanted time to think."

"Time to think?" He was so angry—at Mrs. Mason, but mostly at Isabelle for allowing her mother to control her again. "Is that your euphemism for, 'I don't want my daughter sleeping with you no matter how right it is'?"

"It wasn't me!" Mrs. Mason whipped off her glasses. Her pale blue eyes were indignant. Insulted. "I didn't tell her to run away."

"Oh, really. This from the woman who made sure her daughter got away from our teen romance without being besmirched by any rumors about the butler's son."

The glass partition between the seats was down.

Darren cleared his throat, and, when Samuel glanced up into the rearview mirror, he glared meaningfully.

"Forget it, Dad. It's way too late for *decorum*." Samuel placed a heavy, scornful emphasis on his father's favorite word.

"I won't lie to you," Mrs. Mason said. "I don't want you two together. But she told me what you did to save her. I thought she should stay and thank you. And talk about . . ." She waved vaguely.

"About our *relationship*?" He shot the word at her.

"Well . . . yes. Isabelle doesn't seem to be able to settle, and it's because of you." When he would have spoken, Mrs. Mason lifted her hand. "I don't want her to be with you. But I do want her to be happy. So I did not send her away."

He leaned back, shoulders tight, and mulled over Mrs. Mason's words.

The woman didn't lie. She didn't have to. Such a powerful personality never needed to stoop to deception.

Isabelle always did the right thing. And the right thing was to stay here, make sure that he was rescued unhurt, thank him, and speak to him seriously about their time together. The truth was, he had half expected her to tell him the conversation and the sex and the vows were all a fluke built on the belief that they were dying and might as well seize every moment. . . .

The fact that Isabelle Mason had disregarded her mother's advice and *run* rather than face him meant . . . it meant she was scared.

Not of him, but of herself. Of her feelings for him. She still didn't trust him. Obviously. But she'd confessed she loved him, had always loved him, and he believed her.

So Isabelle was running in panic.

And he would give chase.

He smiled.

Mrs. Mason saw his expression. She apparently interpreted it in a correct manner, because she gave a huff of distress and turned her head to look out the window.

He relaxed against the leather seat. "Guess I need to go back to New York and check in at Irving's and see what's up."

Chapter 36

Isabelle watched the rescue from the news feed on the airport monitor.

Samuel looked good. A little thinner, a little paler, with a full pirate's beard. And when he realized she wasn't there . . . his expression was quite savage.

She knew she shouldn't be running away. It was cowardly and unlike her. She and Samuel had said so many things to each other: admitted their mistakes and their regrets, declared their love, and done everything to make each other happy.

It wasn't that she didn't mean everything she'd said about loving him forever. She did.

But she'd thought they were going to die!

She didn't have the intestinal fortitude to try another relationship with him. No other man could break her heart like Samuel, and she didn't trust him not to do it again.

The television camera zoomed in on his face.

As if he knew she was watching, he looked into the lens and smiled with all his teeth.

She stepped back, away from the impact of that ferocious message he was sending, stumbled over a flowered duffel bag, and slammed into a guy walking past. "I'm sorry," she said. "I wasn't watching."

He was a big man, taller than Samuel. Beefier, too, and he looked Polynesian or Japanese, she didn't know which, but for sure he could be a sumo wrestler. He steadied her with his hands on her arms. "No problem." His accent was American, and he hurried toward the gate, where they were giving last call for the flight to Amsterdam.

She rubbed her arms where he'd touched her. The contact had been brief, but unsettling. He was . . . odd. Not quite right.

But not her business, and anyway, they were calling her flight to New York City.

She glanced toward the television once more, where reporters chased Samuel for the chance to interview him. Then she hastened toward the gate and away from the image of Samuel and his fury.

"Excusez-moi, mademoiselle!" a young man's voice called.

She paid no attention.

"Excuse me, miss!" This time the call was in accented English. Footsteps pattered behind her, and someone caught her sleeve.

She turned to see a teenager holding a flowered duffel bag.

He held it toward her. "You left this."

"It's not mine," she said.

"You have no carry-on?"

"This purse." She lifted the cross-body bag she'd picked up in the gift shop.

She had refused to go back to her parents' home to pack. She knew if she paused so long . . . Samuel would catch up with her.

The young Frenchman held the flowered bag and looked around in dismay. "But whose?"

An older woman rushed down the concourse toward them. With a scowl, she snatched the bag from the boy and headed toward the Amsterdam flight.

Isabelle and the boy looked at each other and shrugged.

Isabelle continued on to her airplane, settled into first class, and tried to sleep. Instead she found herself watching the blue waters of the Atlantic and wondering what would happen when she once more saw Samuel . . . and he saw her.

When she landed in New York City, security was swarming the airport.

The flight to Amsterdam had exploded in midair.

Chapter 37

McKenna opened the door to Irving's nineteenth-century Upper East Side mansion and came as close to smiling as the dour Scotsman ever came. "Well met, Mr. Samuel! And such good timing. Mr. Irving is on his way home from rehabilitation and the Chosen are gathered to greet him."

"Hey, great, thanks, McKenna." Samuel shed his coat into McKenna's waiting hands. "Did Isabelle make it here okay?"

"Miss Isabelle arrived with no problems and has done nothing but sing your praises for your gallantry and courage. Congratulations, sir, for stepping so nobly up to the plate!"

That explained McKenna's enthusiastic welcome. Isabelle had been assuaging her guilty conscience by touting his heroism.

Good move, Isabelle. But it isn't going to save your ass.

"Where are the Chosen Ones?" Samuel asked.

"In the library. When Mr. Irving arrives, I am allowing a brief welcome only; then Mr. Irving is to rest from the ordeal of his return." McKenna sounded firm, and he'd get his way . . . if Irving allowed it.

Samuel headed across the foyer.

McKenna followed. "At Mr. Shea's age and in his condition, merely the act of leaving one bed and going to another will be fatiguing beyond his capacities."

"Agreed. Let's hope he thinks the same way." Samuel walked into Irving's spacious, well-appointed library, flung out his arms, and smiled narrowly.

Isabelle saw him first. Of course she did. Her face lit up with joy. Next the joy faded and shame took its place.

If nothing else happened in his life that was good and just, he would always remember that first instinctive response.

Caleb D'Angelo nodded, a brief jerk of the head that acknowledged his relief at Samuel's return.

Charisma Fangorn threw herself at him, bracelets jingling, and wrapped her arms around his neck. "I knew you were okay. I knew you were. The earth stones told me you had survived."

"It's a long way from Switzerland's earth stones to New York City's earth stones," Samuel said.

"Not when you measure the distance in light-years," Charisma assured him.

"Good point." Samuel shook Aleksandr Wilder's hand.

"Good to have you back," Aleksandr said.

"Good to be back," Samuel replied, and noted that Aleksandr had lost weight. In fact, he was looking gaunt, not a likely situation for a grad student who ate at Irving's table.

Had he looked like this before Samuel left for Switzerland? Should Samuel be asking the kid what was wrong? Not that Samuel was good at that empathetic thing, but if everyone else was oblivious, perhaps he was elected.

Their seer, Jacqueline D'Angelo, hugged him next. "I knew you'd be back."

"Yes, but you and your crystal ball—you cheat." He grinned at her.

"For you, it was sort of a science project. I had to look in the entrails of worms." She grinned back.

Rosamund Eagle put down her book, stared at Samuel, and said in her vague way, "I thought you were gone."

Aaron pressed her shoulder. "He was, honey. He returned." Stepping forward, he shook Samuel's hand. "Welcome, man. There was no one here for me to be an ass with."

"Everyone has their place in the food chain." Samuel pressed Aaron's hand solemnly.

Their leader, John Powell, stood apart, waiting for Samuel to finish his greetings. Stepping forward, he enveloped Samuel in a bear hug. "Good work all around," he said.

"No problems with the cash flow?" Samuel asked.

"It's clean. It's good. Not a glitch." John lowered

his voice. "I got your message about the safety-deposit box, and right away set Rosamund to doing the research. She'll get it figured out soon . . . I hope."

"Hm. Yeah." John seemed shaken, a most unusual occurrence for their stoic leader. What was in that safety-deposit box?

John indicated Isabelle. "We're grateful you brought our healer back alive."

"I know you are." Samuel reached Isabelle.

Isabelle of the dark blue downcast eyes and trembling smile. "Samuel. So glad you made it back."

"Made it out, you mean? From under the avalanche? The rescuers collapsed more than half the ski lodge before they got to me." He allowed his irritation to color his words. "I thought for sure I was a goner."

She stared at him, stricken.

He smiled pleasantly, wrapped his arms around her, pressed his cheek to hers. He spoke in her ear. "We'll talk . . . later."

She nodded as if numb. Or maybe she was resigned.

John's wife, Genny, scrutinized Samuel as if seeing something she didn't understand. Then her face cleared. She smiled and said, "You've got Isabelle in you!"

Everyone turned to look at her.

Isabelle flushed.

Genny laughed a little. "That didn't come out like I meant. I *mean*, Isabelle healed him and now he has her inside him."

Genny was not Chosen, yet after meeting John and going through hell to return to his side, she had developed a most interesting talent. When she looked at one of the Abandoned Ones, Chosen or Other, the gift given at birth manifested itself before her . . . somehow.

Spooky.

Samuel patted his stomach and raised his eyebrows inquiringly. "In me?"

"I know what I see," she told him. "I'm not wrong, am I? She did heal you recently, and from a grievous wound."

"That's right, but she's healed me before."

"A long time ago," Genny said. "That's why she's at the base of your being."

"Yes." Samuel stared at Isabelle. "She is."

There was a silent, awkward moment as everyone looked from Samuel to Isabelle and back again.

From the foyer, they heard the door open and McKenna say, "Mr. Shea, welcome home!"

As if galvanized, the group rushed out and lined up like school kids for inspection.

At the first glimpse of Irving, Samuel's exultation faded.

Two burly men carried the old man up from the street. Irving looked old, frail, slumped in his wheelchair, a survivor of an accident that everyone now knew was not an accident, and only his incredible will to live had kept him clinging to life.

Dina walked at his side.

She looked rougher than she had the last time Samuel had seen her. She was Romany, short and stout, with dark hair now streaked with gray and the damaged skin of a lifelong smoker. Her dark eyes were beautiful, but long ago, someone had split her nose from top to bottom. It had healed, but no one could look at her without knowing this handsome woman had suffered pain, humiliation, and indignity. She looked at Samuel as she passed, and he thought she had the most cynical gaze he'd ever seen.

And he was a lawyer. He knew cynical.

Another woman came in last. She was young. She was tall. She was pretty. Her blond hair looked natural, and she wore it in a neat coil at the back of her neck.

"Have you been picking up girls again, Irving?" Samuel asked.

Irving lifted his head, and in slow, slurred speech, he introduced her. "Amanda Reed. Private nurse."

The Chosen Ones and their mates nodded, murmured hellos and their names.

She looked at them coolly, her gray eyes commanding. "Mr. Shea needs to rest after his trip. Perhaps it would be better if you visited tomorrow, one at a time."

"No!" Irving struggled to speak. "Want them. Talk. Now."

"Mr. Shea—" Amanda began.

"No!" His dark skin was almost gray with exhaustion, but his brown eyes blazed. "Want a report!"

"We'll be fast," John assured Amanda.

"And we live here, so we can easily visit when he's not so tired," Charisma said.

"You *all* live here?" Amanda looked them over as if they were a bunch of freeloading relatives.

"Not all. I mean, John and Genny have their own place, and the rest of us are in and out all the time. Aleksandr's hardly ever here anymore—he sort of lives at his girlfriend's—and Aaron and Rosamund have talked about getting a place, but Aaron's afraid Rosamund would forget to eat if we're not around to remind her . . ." Charisma trailed off.

"It would be best if you all came by later, and one at a time," Amanda said again.

"Report now!" Irving insisted.

"You might as well forget it, sister," Dina advised. "If you try to stop him from getting his report now, he's going to get more agitated. These people care for him; you can trust in that. They'll protect him from harm in every way possible."

"Of course. I never thought any differently." All too clearly, Amanda was only mouthing platitudes.

With impeccable timing, McKenna stepped into the developing situation. "If you would allow me, Miss Reed, I'll take you to Mr. Shea's room. I'm sure you'd like to verify that the medical equipment you requested has been delivered and set up correctly."

She gave up with very little grace. "Of course."

"This way." McKenna led her toward the stairs.

Charisma moved over by Samuel and, in exaggerated terror, said, "She's scary."

"I'll bet she's going to get scarier, too," Samuel answered.

Irving waited until Amanda was out of earshot, then waved an imperious hand. "Library!"

Jacqueline pushed the wheelchair.

The Chosen Ones followed.

John shut the door, closing them in with the shelves of books, the comfortable seating, the cozy, familiar room.

Irving pointed a shaking finger at Samuel. "Now. Report."

Chapter 38

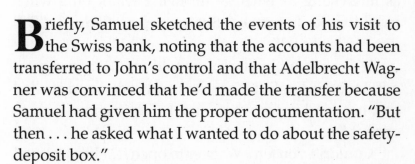

Briefly, Samuel sketched the events of his visit to the Swiss bank, noting that the accounts had been transferred to John's control and that Adelbrecht Wagner was convinced that he'd made the transfer because Samuel had given him the proper documentation. "But then . . . he asked what I wanted to do about the safety-deposit box."

"The safety-deposit box?" Charisma looked around the room. "Is that something we're supposed to know? Because we've read every word of *When the World Was Young, A History of the Chosen Ones*—"

"*You've* read," Samuel corrected her.

"—*I've* read every word of *When the World Was Young, A History of the Chosen Ones*." Charisma was enthusiastic, intelligent, and interested in everything. "I don't remember anything about a safety-deposit box."

Irving closed his eyes wearily. "John. Talk."

"The safety-deposit box. When I was with the Chosen

Ones before the tragedy"—no one knew whether John was speaking of the explosion of the Gypsy Travel Agency or his own personal tragedy—"the safety-deposit box was nothing but a myth, one of those things that came up when we were sitting around Davidov's having a beer and discussing how to catch a unicorn." He turned to Jacqueline. Both had long histories with the Gypsy Travel Agency. "Do you know anything? Did your mother ever mention the safety-deposit box?"

Jacqueline shook her head. "Like you, I had heard rumors, but for a kid, a safety-deposit box isn't nearly as interesting as whether throwing water on a witch would make her melt." She turned to Samuel. "Did you really see it?"

"It's in a vault by itself," he told her. "Wagner got it out. I touched it. But it's locked and coded and spelled and heaven knows what, and I didn't know how to open it."

"Couldn't you *force* Wagner to open it?" John tapped his forehead.

"With the mind control? I tried. He doesn't know." Samuel looked between John and Jacqueline. "What's *in* the mythical safety-deposit box?"

John sighed and shrugged. "Don't know."

Jacqueline shook her head. "Something important. Something the Gypsy Travel Agency was guarding in the most secret of ways."

Samuel glanced at Irving. He appeared to be dozing. Or maybe he was just listening. But clearly, he wasn't going to talk, at least not yet.

"You're the seer," Samuel said to Jacqueline. "Can you *see* what it is?"

Jacqueline glowered at Samuel. "You know it doesn't work that way. I see what is given me to see—and that's not something that has been given."

"Have you thought about trying to use the hand?" Samuel asked.

"Now why didn't I think of that?" Jacqueline's voice rose. "It's so simple! Just pick up the hand bones of the first prophetess, jiggle them like dice, and that exact moment in the past will fall out."

"It might work!"

"Why don't I just use a Ouija board?" Jacqueline had never had a vision before she became the seer; she got a little defensive sometimes.

"I've wondered that." Samuel was starting to enjoy himself, to feel normal for the first time in two weeks.

"A few months ago I saw the whole prophecy that we needed, and I'm pretty proud of what I've accomplished since I took over the position of seer." Jacqueline flushed with anger. "So put a sock in it, Samuel Faa!"

Isabelle slid her arm through Samuel's and grasped his hand. "Samuel? She's right. Shut up. This is Irving's first hour home, and he's not well."

Samuel looked at Irving.

The old guy sat with his eyes closed, wearing a slight smile.

"I'll bet he hasn't enjoyed himself this much since he took a header down those stairs," Samuel said.

Irving nodded in agreement.

A faint knock sounded.

John opened the door.

Martha pushed in the tea cart. As always, she'd prepared a delectable selection of foods. Hot water and coffee were in the correct carafes. Cokes were on ice. But rather than silently serving, as she always did, she stood staring at Irving, tears in her eyes.

"Good to be home, Martha." He took more care in enunciating for her than for the rest of them, and he smiled a lopsided smile.

"Good to have you home, Irving. It hasn't been the same without you."

"Going to be without me someday," he told her.

"Not yet." Martha looked around at their little group and spotted Dina, sitting with her back to them, reading a book. "What is *she* doing in this house?"

"With me," Irving said.

Martha's expression passed from affectionate respect to stiffest formality. "Of course, sir. Forgive my impertinence."

Irving sighed. "Nothing to forgive. You're not servant. Friend."

Martha rejected his kindness as much as she begrudged Dina her place here. Dina, her own sister. "May I pour your tea, sir?"

"Martha . . ." Irving made puppy eyes at her.

But Dina stood up and strolled over from the couch. "I'll have to help him drink it."

The sisters locked gazes.

"Because his hands tremble too much to hold the cup," Dina added.

With great restraint, Martha poured the hot water into the teapot.

Samuel remembered his shock at discovering the two women were related—and his embarrassment that he hadn't realized it.

They looked alike—Gypsies, both of them, short with dark hair and eyes, and of a similar age.

But so many things had pointed away from their kinship. Most significantly, Dina had a gift; that meant she had been discarded as an infant. Normally that meant there was no family, no relatives to care.

The two women watched the pot as it steeped.

Martha poured a cup for Irving.

While Martha watched, Dina sauntered to Irving's side and helped him sip.

Samuel thought—and no one had spoken of it, so he wasn't sure—that Martha was the eldest, that they'd both been abandoned when Dina was a baby, and Martha had rescued her sister. But somehow Dina had turned to evil, to the Others. Perhaps Martha resented the fact that she had done the right thing, and her reward had been . . . no gift.

Family relations . . . they were always tangled. Sisters told different truths, and who knew which was right?

When the tension in the room was thick enough to taste, Caleb asked, "Irving, what can *you* tell us about the safety-deposit box?"

"Don't know what's there. Important secret held by"—Irving lifted his hand, struggled until he was able to lift three fingers—"only three people at any time."

"Not you?" Aaron asked.

"No."

"Do you know who they are? Or were?"

"Everyone I knew is gone." Irving's eyes fluttered as if he were keeping secrets.

"The story I heard was that the contents are greater than all the riches in the world," John said.

"Yes." Irving waved a hand at Martha. "Answer."

"Martha knows?" Aaron asked.

She smiled tightly. "Not all of us have gifts, but we do have our uses."

"I never thought any differently." Aaron stared at her until she acknowledged him with a gruff nod.

She passed the plate of cheeses, then the fresh-baked breads. "I believe it's true that the contents are valuable. The bank has always had instructions to make sure the box was protected by the most modern safeguards available and to change those safeguards at will, notifying only those people who are the keepers. But in addition, there is magic that secures the contents." She gazed at Samuel. "You are lucky you didn't open the safety-deposit box and then try to open the case. I believe that would have been the last thing you did."

Isabelle's hand tightened on Samuel's.

"Could I steal it?" Aaron was their cat burglar, the man who could turn into mist, slip into any hidden place, and retrieve any treasure.

"I don't believe that's a good idea," Martha said. "The magic doesn't care what form you take. It attaches to your soul and sends it elsewhere."

"How come everything is so hard?" Charisma asked plaintively.

Samuel knew what she meant. The tension, the frustration, the pure difficulties thrown at them at every turn—it made him want to break things.

"When I was a teen, I worked out with a personal trainer," Isabelle said.

Everyone looked at her as if she'd lost her mind.

But Samuel knew her; she had a point to make.

Isabelle continued. "I worked out three times a week with her, and then three times a week by myself, and then once a week, I'd take a day and sulk because I still didn't look like Angelina Jolie."

Charisma gurgled with laughter.

Isabelle smiled back at her. "The longer I worked, the stronger I got, and you know what my reward was?"

Caleb grinned. He knew.

John looked like he knew, too. "No, tell us."

"I had to lift stronger weights. I had to work out longer. The better I got at working out, the harder it got."

"Is that what's happening here? We bust our asses every day fighting evil, learning the ropes, and every time we succeed, the next challenge is harder? Is that fair?" Samuel's voice rose.

"I don't know about fair." Isabelle sounded cool as always. "But it beats having all the hardest stuff at the beginning, when we would have gotten our asses kicked."

They laughed, all of them, the Chosen and their mates, Irving and Dina. Even Martha.

Samuel stared at them in chagrin.

His friends. His crazy friends.

He looked down at the hand he had intertwined with Isabelle's.

She . . . was so much more than a friend.

"Missed you," Irving said. "Good to be home."

A quiet knock sounded on the door.

John opened it, and stepped back to allow Amanda in the room.

In the imperious tones of a dictator, she said, "Mr. Shea is exhausted and needs his rest."

"No!" Irving struggled to speak.

"Whatever you need to say, it can wait until you've had some sleep." Putting her hand on him, she leaned over and looked into his eyes. "Sleep."

He took a long breath, nodded, and closed his eyes.

For all intents and purposes, he seemed to slip instantly into slumber.

Like an anxious bumblebee, McKenna hovered in the doorway. "Is the exhaustion because of his move home today?"

Amanda looked at him. Looked at them all, and her young face was as stern as any elderly schoolteacher's. "It's a miracle he's alive at all, and that his mental capacities remain intact. His body is mending itself, but very slowly, and he can't do—will never be able to do—what he did before. In addition, he needs physical therapy."

"So he can walk again?" Jacqueline asked.

"So his joints don't freeze. He's in constant pain from his hip and shoulder replacement, and the fall down the stairs impaired not his thought processes, but his speech. The mere act of putting words together exhausts him. If you *must* consult with him, plan on short sessions, and clear it with me first. I will do my best to assist you, but my first responsibility is to Mr. Shea and his health, not to you." Amanda took his wheelchair and pushed him from the room.

"I guess she told us," Charisma said.

"She's right," Martha said.

"Yes." John stepped into the center of their circle. "We have to be careful with Irving. It seemed as if we would have him forever, but we know that's not true. We've got to take care of him. We've got to keep him as long as we can. Because without his knowledge, we're groping in the dark."

Chapter 39

———⊰❈⊱———

Dina followed Irving and his nurse out of the library. She watched them get into the newly installed elevator, watched the door close.

Swiftly, before anyone could catch her, she grabbed her jacket and headed for the door.

Irving had his nurse.

He was surrounded by his Chosen.

He was going to be okay.

And she was outta here.

She made it all the way through the foyer before Martha clutched her arm and asked, "Where are you going?"

"Out to smoke." Dina jerked herself free.

"You're running away." Judgmental as always—and right.

"What if I am?" Dina said. "What do you care?"

"I care because Irving cares. After what you did to him—"

"After what he did to me!" Dina pointed to her nose. "This is his fault."

"If you hadn't gone running back to the Others—"

"If I hadn't gone running back to the Others, they would have caught up with me anyway."

"If you hadn't joined them in the first place, you wouldn't be in trouble for breaking your vows to them."

They always picked up just where they left off, fought the same fight, hated each other in the same way.

"That's true." Dina looked her sister in the eye. "I could have been like you, part of the Gypsy Travel Agency and a female who was never as important as the males. Remember the men who always imagined themselves to be better than anyone else, and never mind that I had a gift and the most important thing any of those jackasses possessed was a dick?"

"The sixties were difficult," Martha allowed.

"And the seventies and the eighties and the nineties. At least with the Others, the organization wasn't run by men for men about men. People like me with gifts of power were honored for our contributions."

"That's no excuse for turning to evil."

"Maybe I'm just evil. Maybe it runs in the family." Dina stepped forward until she was standing on Martha's toes. "Have you ever thought of that? That our mother and father were evil for abandoning me, for leaving you to find me and keep me and raise me? Have you ever thought that evil is bred into our bones, and there's no escaping our destiny?"

"No!"

Dina was glad to see her sister back away. She'd been thinking about her parents her whole life; now she had taken her sister's oh-so-perfect nose and rubbed it into the pile of crap that had been their early days. "Maybe that first time when Irving tossed me out on the street, I could have run away and hidden myself well enough to live." She sneered. "We're about to find out."

Martha recovered her superiority. Of course. She always did. "I knew it. You are running away."

"You know, I can't make you happy no matter what I do. You don't want me to stay, but you bitch at me because I'm leaving." Dina lost her temper. "What do you expect me to do? By now, the Others know I've been caring for Irving, and I like these Chosen kids, but they can't protect me from . . . *him*."

"You're going back to *him*." Martha's dark eyes, so much like Dina's own, snapped with rage.

"No, I'm not."

"Why should I believe you? You've already switched sides twice."

"Right. You don't trust me. I don't trust you, either." Dina had a strength gained from the realities of a life marred by evil and challenged by love, a strength Martha had never had to draw on. "But I'd like to think that since you're my sister and you practically raised me, you won't call the Others as soon as I set foot out the door."

"No. I won't do that."

"For Irving's sake."

"Yes. For Irving's sake."

"Take care of him. For my sake." Dina slipped out the door. Stopping, she looked back toward the mansion.

Irving occupied her whole heart, but that stupid boy occupied her mind.

Samuel. While half a world apart, she'd been in his mind, communicating so smoothly. While he was in the Swiss bank, she'd heard his every thought clearly, as if he'd been speaking. And he heard her, too, and it hadn't taken the usual effort.

She thought . . . well, she suspected there might be a reason for their success, or at least a better reason than the fact that they were both reprobates.

She suspected they might have a blood connection between them.

They were, obviously, both Romany.

She couldn't linger here, so she started walking. Fast.

Samuel was facing challenges that in his cockiness he couldn't comprehend.

She ought to worry about herself and let him fall on his face on his own. But she recognized his arrogance, and she wanted to spare him a little of the agony that had broken her life.

So she sent him a message. *Be careful where you use your gift. There are traps that catch power like yours, and you can't trick the devil. Believe me. I know.*

She heard his bewildered response. *What?*

But she shut down the connection and hurried away.

*   *   *

Amanda settled Irving into his bed, brought the covers to his chin, and asked, "Mr. Shea, is there anything I can do to make you comfortable?"

Irving opened his eyes. "No. There is no comfort in purgatory."

Walking to the window, Amanda watched Dina hasten down the street, her hat pulled over her hair, her collar pulled close around her neck. "No. There isn't. We all go to hell in our own ways."

Chapter 40

───────◆◆◆───────

Samuel slid his arm around Isabelle's waist and, in a tone both cajoling and firm, said, "I imagine you want to talk now."

She shook her head. He was angry; she was embarrassed . . . a talk was most definitely not going to go well for her.

Samuel, being Samuel, paid no attention, and led her—dragged her—toward a door under the stairway. A door that led to the winter coat storage.

She set her heels. She did not need to be reminded of Frau Reidlinger's fur and what it felt like on her naked skin, and how he used it to brush her nipples, her belly, and how she had reciprocated.

Opening the door, he pushed her inside, followed her, and shut the door behind him. When he faced her, he looked pleasant.

This was Samuel. So she didn't trust pleasant.

"What a surprise when you weren't there to greet me after my rescue!" he said.

She would have sworn he was going to be furious that she had fled before he was rescued, but . . . he actually did look amiable. Genial. Friendly.

It was spooky. "I . . . thought it would be best if I returned right away to give a report to John and the team."

"So generous of you to take that burden off me." He took a long step toward her.

She backed up against the coats, hangers clanging.

She didn't mean to, but she was definitely cowering.

He kept talking, kept looking pleasant. "I am so glad to know the things we did together . . . you know, the things?"

She nodded.

"It's good that you realize it was only desperation and fear that made us act that way."

"Right."

"I would hate to think that we meant the things we said to each other."

Isabelle opened her mouth, but no words came out.

"My point is"—he grasped her upper arms and brought her close—"people who think they're going to die say things they don't mean. They do things they shouldn't. We did. Right?"

"Right. Exactly." She swallowed. His body was pressed tightly to hers.

"I fell back on my old feelings for you, and you fell back on your old feelings for me, and there we were, humping our brains out because we thought we were about to take the long dirt nap."

His body against hers . . . it felt nice. It felt right. Warm. Tough. Comforting. She wanted to lay her head on his shoulder, snuggle into his arms, listen to his heartbeat and his voice telling her everything was going to be all right.

But that wasn't what he was saying. And he was right. The way she felt about him was automatic, a knee-jerk reaction to being close to the guy who for five long days had been everything to her.

Well, longer than that, really, but she wasn't going to remember their first time together in the window seat, or those months after he returned from law school and they lived together and she had fallen more deeply in love with him than ever. Because that had ended in disaster. . . .

She swallowed again to clear her dry mouth, and said, "A natural occurrence, I'm sure, for us to do what we did—"

"Have sex?"

"Yes. That. It was a natural occurrence in those circumstances. We don't need to make a big deal about it. We've already proved twice that we couldn't have a relationship and maintain it."

His hands tightened, then relaxed. "The sex was good, though."

"Oh, my God. The sex was great!" *Oops*. She'd been a little too emphatic.

"We won't be doing it again."

The moment of silence that followed was profound.

Never again? Even to herself, her inner wail sounded pathetic.

"Not that I didn't thoroughly enjoy our time together," he assured her.

"Me, too."

"But we can't do these things together unless we're a couple." He'd shaved off that tough black beard and now he smelled like some kind of spicy European aftershave.

"I agree. It was a *'we're trapped in a claustrophobic place in Switzerland'* thing."

"Right. It was a Switzerland affair. A vacation fling with too much snow. A visit to the set of *The Bourne Ice Creamery.*"

A laugh caught her by surprise.

He grinned.

They had so much in common. . . .

"No need to tell anyone," he said.

"No, although . . . well, that's silly." What was she saying? Had she lost her mind? But she kept on talking, and she half laughed as if she were joking. "I'm so jet-lagged, I'm still on Switzerland's time."

"Me, too."

"Here in this claustrophobic little closet, it's almost like being back in the ski lodge. Facing death."

"That's what I was thinking."

They stared at each other, body-to-body, face-to-face.

She didn't know which one of them moved first,

but suddenly they were kissing, touching, making love. . . .

"That is the last time we'll ever do that," Isabelle said.

"Absolutely never again. My body clock will adjust soon." Samuel helped her button her shirt.

"Thank heavens we're the only ones who know what we did."

"Yeah. Thank heavens."

Charisma watched Isabelle and Samuel slip out of the coat closet. Turning to Genny, she said, "Did you say Samuel had Isabelle in him? 'Cause now, I think it's the other way around."

Chapter 41

Aleksandr Wilder stood on the street outside Irving's mansion and debated going in through the
kitchen and grabbing something to eat, or going in the
front door.

Making his decision, he headed up the front steps.

This was just easier. If he went through the kitchen,
Martha would nag him because he wasn't eating
enough, and frankly, lately he'd had trouble swallowing past the constriction in his throat.

He wasn't sick; he was just a little . . . conflicted.

At the top of the stairs, he looked back.

She stood at the corner, her blond hair blowing in
the breeze, and when she knew he was watching her,
she kissed her hand and threw it toward him, exuberant and joyful and the most wonderful woman he'd
ever met.

His throat tightened a little more.

He loved her so much.

And he was afraid, so afraid.

Lifting his burned, damaged hand, he saluted her. Turning back, he inserted his key in the lock and opened the massive front door.

The blast of laughter and talk almost drove him back onto the street. It sounded as if the Chosen Ones were having a spontaneous party, and he wasn't in the mood.

But they were in the library. If he were careful, he could sneak past. Because let's face it, if there was one thing a descendant of shape-shifters should be able to do, it was move quietly.

As he passed the door, the laughter quieted, and a loud, Russian-accented voice boomed out, "Then I stopped pretending to be infirm, took off running, and when the explosives packed on the wheelchair blew, it took out a bunch of Varinskis and burned the tails off the rest of them!"

More laughter. Boisterous applause.

Aleksandr stopped.

He'd heard that voice tell that story a hundred times.

He backed up and looked into the room.

There stood his grandfather, Konstantine Wilder, holding court in the middle of the crowd. Irving and his nurse, the Chosen and their mates—Konstantine was charming them, each and every one.

Of course.

Aleksandr didn't know for sure how old Konstantine was—*Konstantine* didn't know for sure how old

Konstantine was—but the family thought he was in his eighties, tall and broad, hale and hearty, with the cruel face of a Cossack, a head of iron gray hair, bright white teeth that flashed in an infectious smile, and a heart as broad as the Ukrainian steppes.

For the first time in weeks—months—Aleksandr broke into a spontaneous grin. "Grandpa!" He strode into the library, arms wide, and caught his grandfather in a bear hug, lifting him off his feet in an exuberant outburst.

Konstantine hugged him back, and as soon as he got his feet under him, he returned the favor. Radiating love and joy as bright the sun, he exclaimed, "My boy. My boy!"

They broke apart and pounded each other on the back, then hugged again before standing apart and looking at each other.

Aleksandr saw the moment dismay struck his grandfather, and he would have given anything to give the old man comfort.

"So," Konstantine said, "they starve you here in this New York City?"

Aleksandr searched for the best answer, the one that would help him explain the least. "I miss Grandma's cooking. What I wouldn't give for her cherry varenyky! The Russian restaurants make them here, but they don't hold a ruble to hers."

There. That was diplomatic enough.

Aleksandr looked around at his friends, at the Chosen Ones. "Varenyky are dumplings filled with all kinds of wonderful things. Sauerkraut, potatoes, sausage, cabbage . . . My favorite is the cherry varenyky served with sour cream." His eyes half closed. "They taste like heaven. Grandma always made them especially for me. . . ." He was hungry. For the first time in weeks, he was suddenly, sharply hungry.

A ripple of laughter went through the room. The Chosen Ones stepped back, and Aleksandr's gaze fell on the table set up in the corner with pickled mushrooms, chopped herring, rye bread, cheeses . . . and varenyky. Lots and lots of varenyky.

McKenna and Martha stood behind the table, serving spoons in hands, waiting to hand out the plates.

"Oh, Grandpa." Aleksandr walked toward the table. "This is a feast! How did you do it?"

"Eat. Eat!" Konstantine waved the Chosen Ones and Aleksandr toward the table, and as they loaded their plates, he talked. "Your mother and aunts and grandmother were cooking for days. Your father shipped it overnight, which cost too much." Konstantine frowned fiercely. "The shipping company are pirates and thieves!" He pinched Aleksandr's cheek, hard. "But for you, it was worth it."

Belatedly, Aleksandr realized he should be worried. "Why are you here? Is everyone all right?"

"Everyone is good! What, you think your old grandfather can't fly to this New York City by himself?"

"I've been here over four years and this is the first time you've visited me here." Aleksandr shoved a pickled mushroom into his mouth, followed by a curd varenyky.

"There is a first time for everything." Konstantine poured icy-cold vodka into little glasses and passed them out.

His nurse took the glass he presented to Irving.

Konstantine poured another.

"He can't drink," Amanda said.

Konstantine looked down his nose at her. "Who are you?"

"I'm his nurse," Amanda said. "With the combination of drugs in his system, he should not be imbibing alcohol."

"Nonsense!" Konstantine roundly dismissed her concerns. "When I was sick, ready to die and go to hell, the doctors forbade me my vodka. But I drank it and grew strong!"

"I thought it was breaking the deal with the devil that cured you, Grandpa," Aleksandr said.

"Vodka! And vodka will cure what ails Mr. Shea!" Again Konstantine presented Irving with a glass.

"What am I going to do?" Irving's speech had improved, become more precise as the days rolled along. "Die happy?"

"You're better," Amanda insisted. "I want you to continue that way."

"I will continue." Irving accepted the vodka. "Until I find Dina."

Aleksandr's gaze shifted to Samuel.

Samuel contemplated his vodka as if he were listening to some inner voice.

Ever since he'd been back from Switzerland, the

guy had had some weird vibes going on. Every time someone mentioned Dina, it was like he was listening to something in his head.

Then Samuel shot a glance at Isabelle.

Or, heck, what did Aleksandr know? Maybe he was not listening in his head. Maybe he was listening in his pants. But he sure had the hots for Isabelle.

"A toast!" Konstantine boomed.

Aleksandr lifted his glass.

Everyone lifted their glasses—everyone except Amanda.

Konstantine looked at her. Just looked at her.

She lifted her glass.

Konstantine continued. "To Irving Shea, long may he live and prosper and confound the enemies of the great good! *Za vas!*"

Aleksandr had long thought his grandfather spoke in exclamation points, and right now he approved.

Everyone drank, exclaimed, smiled. The women kissed Irving on the cheek, then, not surprisingly, kissed Konstantine on both cheeks.

Konstantine Wilder had always been a lady magnet—but his heart and soul belonged to his wife. To his Zorana.

Irving drank his vodka, then handed his glass to Amanda. "Let us all leave Konstantine and Aleksandr alone so they may have a reunion." Again his speech was stilted, but so much clearer than it had been.

"Can we take our plates?" Charisma asked.

She looked so pathetically eager, Aleksandr laughed.

"Ukrainians are hospitable people. Please. Take everything you wish!" It amused him to realize he sounded like Konstantine—loud, enthusiastic, with a faint Russian accent.

The room cleared slowly, with much stopping for a last helping of varenyky or pickled mushrooms.

But at last, McKenna closed the door on grandfather and grandson.

Aleksandr put down his plate, went to his grandfather, took his shoulders, and looked into his eyes. "Tell me the truth. Why are you here?"

Konstantine's strong face sagged with worry. "Your grandmother—she is having sinister dreams about you."

Aleksandr dropped his hands.

That wasn't what he expected. A disaster in the grapes or an illness. Not one of his grandmother's famous prophecies. Not about him. Not now. He didn't need her to know so much. "What kind of sinister dreams?"

"She dreams that you are alone in a dark place." Konstantine watched him anxiously. "Men come to you; they stab you with needles and poke you with electric wires, and in agony you transform into a beast, a monstrous thing of claws and fangs."

"I'm sorry she dreams that. There's no truth in it, I swear."

"She is very disturbed, so I promised I would come and see you and prove you are still our Aleksandr, our first and best grandson." Konstantine smiled, but his boisterous voice was a low rumble, and he watched Aleksandr from beneath lowered brows. "This is true, no? You are as you always were, unchanged and untouched?"

"I have never taken any other form." Then, driven by some belief that Konstantine would understand, Aleksandr said, "But sometimes I feel as if, if I tried hard enough, I could be like you and change into a wild wolf who runs free in the forest, strong and unbound, glorious in my freedom."

When Konstantine wrapped his elbow around Aleksandr's neck, held him in place, and slapped him hard on the cheek, Aleksandr could not have been more surprised. "No! No!" Konstantine said fiercely. "You cannot do this! Your father, your mother, your uncles and aunts, your grandmother and I risked our livelihoods, our lives, our souls to break the deal with the devil."

Aleksandr yanked himself out of his grandfather's grasp. His hands itched to return the slap, and only the knowledge that Konstantine was old and seasoned and deserving of respect stopped him. But nothing could stop the hot words that bubbled to his lips. "What has that to do with me? You always said you thought I would be a wolf. If I can grasp that destiny without dealing with the devil, what do you care?"

"Who are you talking to? Are they telling you that you do not need the devil to change? It is not true. Somehow, it all comes back to Lucifer, the fallen angel who rules hell and tempts each man according to his desires. And once you change, each change brings you euphoria, like drugs, like heroin, and all you want to do is change again. The slide down to hell is dark and dangerous and alluring, and that you desire such a thing—no!" Konstantine grabbed Aleksandr by the shoulders, held him still, leaned until his forehead touched Aleksandr's. "Listen to me, my grandson, no! Find a girl. Marry her. Breed babies and be satisfied to be what you are—a strong man, a good man. But merely a man."

Aleksandr stared into Konstantine's dark eyes.

He couldn't talk to him. Konstantine was caught in the memory of the old curse and the old story, and Aleksandr's mistake was in thinking Konstantine would comprehend his feelings, his desires.

This whole conversation proved *she* was right. She was right.

But Konstantine wasn't finished. "Come home, my boy. See your papa and your mama and your little brothers. Eat your grandmother's cooking and remember who you are."

"I signed a contract, Grandfather. Until my seven years are up, I'm one of the Chosen." Aleksandr posed the question that he knew would make his grandfather suffer. "Should I break my word and abandon my friends?"

He could see Konstantine struggle between his love for his grandson and his hard-won honor. At last he said, "No. You should not." He brightened. "But perhaps, hey, your grandmother and I could come here and stay. Zorana could cook for the Chosen Ones. I could help Mr. Shea, who is so old and weak. What do you think about that?"

"Grandpa, I appreciate the offer, but really, I'm fine." Konstantine could smell a lie a mile away, so Aleksandr searched for the best piece of truth to dangle before him. "I am dating a girl, and we're pretty serious."

But his grandfather wasn't so easily diverted from what he thought Aleksandr's role should be in life. "This girl—who is she? What is her name?"

"Her name is Iskra. I've tutored her in math for a couple of years. She's beautiful and smart." As Aleksandr remembered, his heart lifted. "She makes me happy."

"You bring her to meet me!"

"I'll do what I can, Grandpa, but she's an orphan. She had a pretty tough childhood, and she is shy of family. It took me months to convince her we could be involved and nothing bad would happen. She's just so tender and reserved, and I've had to coax her every inch of the way." Aleksandr knew he was wearing a doofy grin, but it happened whenever he thought about Iskra.

Or else he remembered some of the stuff she said, and he was stressed again.

"She should not be afraid of me!" Konstantine thumped his chest with his ham-size fist. "Who could be afraid of me?"

"I don't know, Grandpa." Aleksandr loved the old man so much, but never had he felt a stronger rift. "It's a mystery."

More quietly, Konstantine said, "I will be here for four days."

"Great! I can show you the city."

Konstantine would not be distracted. "You'll bring this girlfriend to me, yes? I will meet her so I can reassure your grandmother?"

"I will try. I really will try." But Aleksandr knew it would never happen.

Iskra had allowed Aleksandr to introduce her to no one on the Chosen Ones team. She was certainly not going to meet his grandfather.

He didn't want her to, because if what he suspected was true . . . Konstantine would tear her limb from limb.

Chapter 42

"Samuel, I'd like a word." Isabelle's breath brushed his ear.

"Of course, Isabelle. I've been wanting to talk to you, too." He glanced around the breakfast table.

No one was paying the least attention.

Charisma was reading something on her e-reader and chuckling.

Caleb held the newspaper in front of his face, turning the pages and grumbling.

Aaron was concentrating on his eggs—he'd been out late the night before, working a job, and needed fuel.

McKenna was picking up the coffee cups John and Genny had left behind.

"There's no rush, Samuel," Isabelle said. "When you've got a minute, I'll be working at the computer station in the study."

Samuel watched her walk out. She was wearing a

pink dress, casual and flirty, not too short—she didn't wear too short—and her butt looked great.

As soon as she was gone, Caleb lowered his paper. "Aaron, what did you get Rosamund for Valentine's Day?"

"I found a letter signed by Mark Twain and managed to buy it before the owner put it up on eBay," Aaron said. "It cost a fortune, but you know Rosamund. She wouldn't know what to do with jewelry."

Charisma didn't even look up. "Good one."

"Thank you." Aaron looked smug.

"Crap." Caleb ran his hand over his short hair. "All I have for Jacqueline is a box of those chocolates she likes so much—I'm pretty sure I got the right ones—but last year I took her back to Napa Valley for a long weekend."

"That was a good one, too," Charisma said.

"Do you think the chocolates are enough?" Caleb asked.

Charisma snorted.

Caleb threw down the paper. "Fine. What would you suggest?"

Charisma looked up. "She's a seer. Take her somewhere she's not likely to have a vision."

Caleb stared with panicked eyes.

In an exaggerated, patient tone, Charisma said, "There's a great show off-Broadway she's been hinting about for three months. It's a comedy."

"You are the best, Charisma." Caleb reached into his briefcase and pulled out a netbook.

"It's booked," she said. "There are no seats."

"I've got connections." Eyes narrowed, Caleb went to work.

Samuel grinned. "You guys are so pussy-whipped."

"Yeah. So you're not getting anybody anything for Valentine's Day?" Caleb asked.

"Not taking anybody dancing or out for dinner?" Aaron asked.

"Nope." Samuel put down his fork, folded his napkin, stood up, and strolled out.

Behind him, he heard Charisma say, "There goes the world's biggest fool."

He wasn't worried. Isabelle's wealth and background meant she had every possession she could ever desire. No need to gild that lily.

But he could give her the one thing she couldn't get anywhere else. . . .

The computer station in the study was nothing but a small utilitarian desk and desk chair tucked into a cramped six-foot-wide nook set in the wall. Pocket doors discreetly hid the monitor and the usual stacks of papers from view.

The doors were open now, and Isabelle was online, looking at train schedules, when Samuel slid his arms around her and kissed her neck.

"Samuel. We've been back two weeks. We can hardly say we're still on Swiss time." But she didn't push him away.

"I've got a stubborn internal clock."

"You've got a stubborn something." Reaching behind her, she stroked his cheek.

Encouraged, he stepped in as tightly as he could; he pulled the doors closed.

She turned to him, incredulous. "Have you lost your mind? There's no room in here!"

"I love a challenge."

"No, really. I need to talk to you."

"I need to talk to you, too." He smiled at her, remembering their days in the ski lodge—and the nights—remembering how she ran from all the things they'd said to each other, knowing it was time to put an end to this farce of not being together.

Her stern expression relaxed, and she smiled in return.

"Later." He pushed the chair back—the door was only a foot away, so it wasn't easy—turned it, and pulled her up into his arms.

"We can't manage this," she said again.

He slid his hands under her skirt and up her legs. He cupped her butt and realized—"You're not wearing any panties."

She plucked at the button on his shirt and watched her hand. "I thought we might have, um, one more farewell, um . . ."

His libido, already edgy, came roaring to life.

"But not here!"

"We are so doing it here." He shoved papers aside, lifted her onto the desk, and stepped between her legs.

She was the woman he had always loved, and if he managed these next few minutes just right, she would be his forever.

"Okay. Here." Bracing her hands behind her, she tossed her head and smiled up at him, that seductive promise in her eyes.

And he lost it. He needed her. He needed her *now*. "I can't wait," he said.

She slid one bare foot up and down the back of his thigh. "I'm not asking you to."

He unzipped. Got the condom out of his pocket. Dropped his jeans, his underwear. Applied the condom in record time, then used his fingers to open her . . . and she was damp, ready.

He pulled her onto his cock, worked his way into her tight passage, and when he was in to the hilt, he slid his hands under her rear, picked her up, turned, and pressed her back against the wall beside the desk.

Her wide eyes stared into his, startled and aroused. "Samuel," she whispered.

"Sh," he said. "There's no lock on the door of the study."

"Oh, Samuel," she said in dismay.

He didn't give her time to recover, to think of caution. Bracing himself, he drove into her, over and over, sheathing himself, pulling out, making her feel every inch, every twist and shift.

She clutched him with her arms, with her legs, held helpless by the position, forced to take whatever he gave her. She was slick inside, warmly clasping and releasing. Biting her lip to muffle her moans, she clawed at him, wild with passion.

His balls drew up, ready to finish, but he held himself back.

He didn't want this to end. Not so soon. Every time with her was like the first time. Every time was the best time.

Yet inevitably, his speed increased, the friction increased—and she was climaxing, spasming in his arms, her pleasure as violent as his.

He couldn't hold back anymore. He pressed her against the wall, coming so hard he could do no more than rock against her, small, violent motions that made her climax again . . . still.

Gathering handfuls of his T-shirt, she pressed her head to his chest, whimpering, and when at last he could thrust again, and she came again, she sank her teeth into his chest.

He placed her on the desk.

She was gasping.

He was gasping. "I adore you," he said.

She laughed, breathless. "Tell me that someday when you're not inside me."

Gently he drew out. "I adore you."

She laughed again, a little unsteadily. "I adore you, too."

Stepping away, he discarded the condom, pulled up his pants, got himself together.

Suddenly shy, she didn't watch him, but he observed her as she tidied herself, changing from the primitive lover into the self-possessed lady. It was, as always, an amazing transformation, and he thought Aleksandr's shape-shifting relatives had nothing on her.

Now . . . "I wanted to talk to you." He helped her off the desk—it was an excuse to touch her—and into her seat. "Do you realize we didn't use a condom that last night in the locker room? It felt so good, and we thought we were goners."

"In retrospect, that was foolish." With a faint smile, she pleated her hem. "But at the time, it seemed like the right thing to do."

"The thing is, I want to say—if you're pregnant, we'll get married."

She stopped pleating. Stopped smiling. "Will we?"

"I don't know if you've thought about it, but you definitely could be expecting a baby, and better than anyone, we both know that a child needs both its parents. We love each other, so marriage is the natural solution."

"Solution? To this problem?"

Something was wrong with the way she phrased that, but he was so anxious to reassure her, he couldn't quite put his finger on it. "I'll arrange everything for the legal ceremony. I realize Las Vegas isn't the most romantic situation, but that would do. If you want, I'll even go through with a big wedding for your mother's sake."

She sat stiffly, her head turned away from him, her fingers clutching her skirt. "So we're getting married for the baby's sake, and you're willing to go through with a big wedding for my mother's sake."

Now he understood, and he added what she needed to hear. "For your sake, too! I know you, Isabelle, and it's not as if having a child out of wedlock is any great shakes anymore, but you wouldn't like it."

She smiled flatly. "I am glad to hear I had some small influence on your decision." She stood. "Now it's my turn to talk. Samuel, sit down."

He had expected more reaction from her. Or a different reaction from her. Joy. Appreciation. Relief. Something. "What's wrong?"

She pointed to the chair.

He sat.

"First—I already know for sure. I am not pregnant."

"You're not? Do you think there's something wrong with one of us?"

She stared at him as if he were speaking Mandarin. Then she nodded. "I definitely think there's something wrong with you. But it's got nothing to do with your sexual organs. Unless we consider your brain a sexual organ, in which case, I'm afraid it's been deprived of blood too many times in the last weeks." Her voice seemed to be getting louder. "But not to worry—it's not going to happen again." Her voice was definitely louder. "If I had my way, you wouldn't even have any sexual organs, which would make Darwin happy, I'm sure."

Catching her hand, he kissed her palm comfortingly. "This is because you're not pregnant, isn't it? You're upset because you're not pregnant, but, darling, I want to marry you anyway."

He never even saw her fist coming, but she must have swung hard, because she slammed the side of his head with her knuckles.

He dropped her other hand. "Holy shit, what did you do that for?"

"You figure it out." She shoved the pocket door back so hard, it bounced halfway closed again, and stormed out.

Rubbing his head, he followed her out into the foyer. "What?"

She was putting on her coat. Pulling on her hat.

McKenna had been dusting his prized sixteenth-century Ming vase. Now his feather duster slowed, and he unabashedly watched as Samuel strode toward Isabelle.

"What did I say?" Samuel demanded.

"I wish we had never met at that party after you finished law school." Her voice sounded as if she'd swallowed ground glass.

"We didn't *meet*. I came on purpose to find you."

"Was it revenge for leaving you?"

He laughed roughly. "You don't know the answer to that? No, it was for lust. I wasn't finished with you yet."

She shot him one last, scorching glance and headed toward the door.

"You could at least tell me what you're mad about," he yelled.

McKenna managed to get to the door first. He opened it for her.

She smiled sweetly at him. "Thank you, McKenna." She walked out onto the top step. Said, "If you don't mind . . ." Removing the butler's hand from the door handle, she took the huge, heavy, solid wood door and slammed it as hard as she could.

McKenna glared at Samuel.

"I didn't do anything!" Samuel turned in a circle, hands outstretched, telling the world he wasn't at fault.

Charisma ran by, coat in hand, and rammed him in the back with a straight-arm push. "The world's *biggest* fool," she repeated.

McKenna hustled back to the door, opened it.

Charisma raced out, yelling, "Isabelle! Wait up!"

McKenna shut the door. Glared at Samuel again. And started toward the kitchen.

Samuel stood there. Just stood there. He didn't know what to do.

He'd thought they were making progress, but Isabelle had hit him. Smacked him right across the head with the full strength of her arm behind it. He had a knot on his head!

Walking into the library, he poured himself a stiff drink. Turning, he found himself facing two pairs of eyes.

Caleb. And Aaron.

"Pussy-whipped?" Caleb asked Aaron.

"Oh, yeah. He is so whipped," Aaron agreed.

They knew. They knew Samuel and Isabelle had been getting it on, and now they were laughing.

Samuel gave in, flopped down in an easy chair, and said, "I'm sorry. You're right. What do I do now?"

Charisma caught up with Isabelle at the corner, and as the two women turned toward Fifth Avenue, a black sedan pulled out of the alley and followed.

Chapter 43

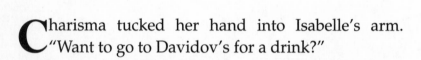

Charisma tucked her hand into Isabelle's arm. "Want to go to Davidov's for a drink?"

"In the morning?" Humiliatingly, Isabelle's laugh broke in the middle. "No."

"Sometimes it doesn't matter what time it is; you have to believe it's five o'clock somewhere." Charisma bumped her lightly.

"No." Isabelle's inescapable manners forced her to add, "Thank you."

"So where are we going?"

"To Saks. I need a new dress for tonight's party." Isabelle didn't look at Charisma. She didn't want her to see the tears that pressed at the back of her eyes.

But of course Charisma knew. She was a difficult person to hide anything from; she and her stones always seemed to know what was going on.

"There's a party tonight?" Charisma asked.

"At my mother's. Her annual Valentine's Day party. She gives it every year."

"Thus the annual part."

Isabelle whipped her head around and glared.

Charisma got the unspoken message. "Yeah, that was unnecessary."

They turned onto Fifth Avenue.

"Want to get a cab?" Charisma started to raise her arm.

"No." Isabelle picked up her pace. "I want to walk."

"But it's a long way to Saks and . . . I want to walk, too. It's a great day for it." By which Charisma meant snow had started to drift down, a few flakes at a time, and a raw, brisk wind was blowing.

It didn't matter. Nothing could cool Isabelle's hot cheeks.

"I guess Samuel isn't taking you to the party?" Charisma asked.

"I didn't ask."

"Why would you have to? If it's an annual event, he knows it's happening. He should have asked you."

"I thought that, too. But he didn't. So I was going to be a modern woman. And ask him. Luckily for me"—Isabelle's fists clenched—"he was a jerk first, so I don't have to put up with him tonight."

"Samuel was a jerk? This is a change *how*?"

"Shut up, Charisma." They walked on in silence until Isabelle said, "I'm sorry. This isn't your fault. It's mine. I got involved with Samuel again."

"Oh." The one word hung on the frosty air.

"I guess we were obvious?"

Charisma coughed to cover her smile. "We, the rest of us, noticed you two had come back from Switzerland and spent a lot of time talking in closets and whatnot."

"You'd think I'd know better."

"Because you two were involved before?"

Isabelle had never discussed Samuel with anyone. Now she admitted, "Twice. We were involved twice before."

"Wow." Charisma's green eyes rounded with surprise. "I mean, we all suspected once. But twice!"

"Obviously, I never learn." That was the bitterest pill to swallow. Isabelle had done it to herself. Again. "Did I really need to see again that he is without honor or morals or kindness and has not a civilized bone in his body?"

"I agree with you about him not being civilized, and he is way too blunt, kind of crude, and he can really be offensive. And honestly, the man cannot figure out how to change a roll of toilet paper." That had been a bone of contention between Samuel and Charisma the whole time they'd known each other. "But I've known him for almost three years now, and I can't complain about his morals; he seems pretty grounded. I've seen him be really kind to the kids we rescue, and frankly, I'd trust him with my life."

Isabelle could hardly contain her irritation. "Whose side are you on?"

"Yours! Really! I simply thought there were more realistic reasons to complain about Samuel. . . ." Charisma's voice trailed off. She pointed into one of the small stores that lined Fifth Avenue. "I love that hat, and my ears are freezing. Do you mind if we go in?"

Isabelle did mind. She wanted to walk fast enough and far enough to escape her own thoughts. But Charisma was her friend, she had come after her, and she didn't deserve to lose an ear for her kindness. "Of course not."

They ducked inside, and Charisma said, "You might find something you like!"

Isabelle looked around the shop, lined with studded leather jackets, jeweled dog collars (for humans), and boots covered with chains and zippers. "Not today."

Charisma tried on half a dozen knit caps before settling on one that looked like a Halloween fright wig. She bought matching gloves that made her hands look like the Wolf Man's, and out they went onto the street again.

The snow had picked up. Charisma tried to catch flakes on her tongue before asking, "What did Samuel say this time?"

So in his exact words, Isabelle told her.

She was able to use his exact words because they were burned like acid into her brain.

"Samuel actually said that?" Charisma pursed her lips.

"He is an . . . an asshole. A . . . a fucking—"

Charisma put her hand over Isabelle's mouth. "Don't even try. Swearing is organically foreign to you."

Isabelle pushed Charisma's hand away. "I need to practice."

"If you've lived with and loved Samuel twice and haven't learned, it's never going to happen."

Isabelle sighed. She supposed Charisma was right.

"We've known Samuel was an asshole for years. But what you told me he said . . . it was kind of sweet."

Isabelle stopped midstride. "I beg your pardon?"

People walked around them, grumbling.

"No, really. Think about it. He says everything wrong all the time, so you have to put this through a Samuel filter, which is clogged with heaven knows what kind of disgusting gunk, but when you clean it up a little bit, he was declaring he wants to take care of you no matter what the circumstances."

"You are absolutely insane."

"Really." Charisma seemed very certain. "Think about it."

"No. I want to think about something else." They stopped on the street corner and waited for the light. "Like the party tonight. Do you know what I'm going to get? I'm going to get the tightest, reddest, sluttiest dress you've ever seen, and I will make Samuel sorry he didn't ask me out."

"If he's not taking you, how will he know?"

Isabelle smirked. "Honey, in the right circumstances, I'm someone the paparazzi would love to stalk."

"Man." Charisma blinked at her. "I never realized it, but you can be scary."

"Yes. And listen—"

Without warning, Charisma slammed into Isabelle, knocking her to the concrete behind a parked car. "Stone!"

"What the—" Isabelle half rose.

Charisma pushed her down again.

Shots sounded.

People screamed.

Tires squealed.

Charisma yanked Isabelle to her feet. "Okay?"

"Good." Isabelle's knees were skinned and her wrist was swollen. Hurt like the dickens, but when bullets were flying, that was minor damage—and she healed quickly. It was *the* benefit of her job.

The two stayed low, running, keeping the parked cars between them and the street. When they'd covered a block, they ducked inside a store and stood, white faced and shaking.

The store owner hustled forward, as pale as they were. "Did you hear the gunshots? My sister's shop is there, and she texted me. She says it's a gang-related violence. Here! On Fifth Ave!"

"We definitely heard the shots," Charisma said. "We were out there."

"Was anyone hurt?" Isabelle asked.

"Six guys from a rival gang, but no one seriously. A couple limped away. The rest are stretched out on the street. Cops and ambulances are everywhere." She waved her phone. "Here, my sister took a picture!"

Isabelle and Charisma exchanged glances, sighed, and relaxed.

The bullets hadn't been meant for them. Which they knew, because the Others didn't work that way, but it was good to be certain.

The shop owner looked worried. "You look a little shaken up. Could I get you something? Tea? Champagne?"

Isabelle looked around, recognized the clothes, realized she was in a small exclusive dress shop. "Aren't these Asiah Miller's designs?"

The owner's eyes lit up. "You know her?"

"I wear her."

"This was lucky." Charisma put her arm around Isabelle. "She needs a dress. Cocktail length. Red. Tight. Slutty. Have you got one?"

"Yes. Wait here. I'll be right back." The owner disappeared into the back.

As soon as she disappeared, Isabelle asked Charisma, "How did you *know* the shooting was about to occur?"

"I hear the stones sing. It turns out that in the right circumstances, bullets are stones, too."

Three hours later, Samuel walked into Irving's mansion carrying a bouquet of flowers and a box from a jewelry boutique. He started up the stairs.

From the library, Charisma shouted, "She's not here."

He backed up, headed in to meet her.

Charisma was lounging in the recliner in front of the fire, e-reader in hand. And she was smiling at him, the kind of shit-eating grin he had hated to see from a rival lawyer, much less from Isabelle's friend.

"Where is she?"

"She's in Boston, at her mother's, getting ready for the Valentine's Day party."

"Valentine's Day party."

"Yeah. You know—the one you didn't invite her to?"

"I didn't know she wanted to go."

Charisma sat up straight and gave him the evil eye. "What a crappy excuse."

Even he had to admit it was.

He glanced at his watch. "I can catch the train and be there in five hours." He threw Charisma the flowers and started out the door.

In a taunting tone, Charisma said, "Give me the jewelry and I'll tell you the rest."

Turning back, he paced toward her, leaned down, his hands on the arms of the chair. "I picked out the jewelry for *her*."

"In that case . . ." She mocked him with her smile.

"What's the rest?"

"She's bringing a date."

Chapter 44

———⋙⋘———

Isabelle stood at the head of the stairs, her hand on Senator Noah Noble's arm, and surveyed the ballroom of Patricia Mason's fabulous Valentine's Day party. Flowers filled the marble vases that hung on the marble columns that lined the marble floor of the ballroom. Waiters circulated with silver trays full of champagne and hors d'oeuvres, while at one end of the long room, a band played twentieth-century tunes. Guests stood in clusters along the edge, waiting for that moment when the alcohol swept away their inhibitions so they could go out and dance.

It was the event of the season. Always had been, always would be.

And Isabelle wanted nothing more than to return to New York and tell Samuel . . . well, tell him something. That he was a jerk, mostly. That even if she had been pregnant, she wouldn't have needed him. That assuming she wanted him to marry her was insulting and demeaning.

If only Charisma hadn't defended him. What was it she said? *When you clean it up a little bit, he was saying he wants to take care of you no matter what the circumstances.*

Isabelle had thought about it. She was still angry.

But every time she really started to work herself into a lather, Noah spoke . . . and spoke. "The legislation I introduced for the month of February proclaimed the fourteenth not only Valentine's Day, but also the day we appreciate the sawmills of America."

Turning her head slowly, she stared at him in patent disbelief.

He didn't notice. "It's a good balance—romance leveled against the raw materials and solid workmanship of America."

With impeccable logic, she asked, "Doesn't the lumber industry ship most of its raw materials overseas to be processed, leaving thousands of sawmill workers out of jobs?"

"We celebrate the history and the glory of the great American forests. . . ."

As he droned on, she thought, *When I was engaged to him, he wasn't this dull, was he? He's worse than he used to be, isn't he?*

"Darling, you came!" Patricia Mason came out of the crowd to kiss Isabelle's cheek, then stepped back and scrutinized her dress. "That is quite the gown."

"Thank you, Mother." Isabelle's dress was not only crimson velvet; it was also tight, sequined and short, and bared one shoulder. Even Noah, who during their engagement had been impressively uninterested in sleeping with her, had done a double take and straightened his tie.

"You didn't let me know ahead of time that you'd be here," Patricia said.

"I wouldn't miss this for the world." Feeling guilty because she knew good and well she would have missed the party if Samuel had said the right things, asked in the right way, Isabelle said, "It is the best party of the whole year."

"Thank you! And you came with Noah." Patricia's approval slid around them like a satin ribbon, tying them together. "Isn't that nice? Your father will be so pleased."

My father doesn't care at all whom I date. But you do. But Isabelle smiled and nodded. "It looks as if Boston turned out tonight."

"It is a good mix. Even Samuel came, although his father simply does not handle that boy well." Patricia shook her head.

"Samuel? Samuel who?"

"Samuel, dear. The butler's son."

"Wow." Noah sounded awed. "He brought Allysen Cadell."

Isabelle followed his gaze and saw Samuel, in a suit that shouted Armani and a black cashmere sweater, standing next to the most gloriously beautiful model of the decade, laughing at something she said.

Isabelle literally saw red. *"That fucking bastard."*

"Isabelle! I am shocked!" Patricia *was* shocked, eyes wide, hand to her mouth.

"I don't know that we ought to be discussing his antecedents in those tones," Noah rebuked. "After all, it's not as if he can help being born without the benefit of his parents' wedlock."

"Maybe not, but even Charisma would have to admit I said that just right." Isabelle felt a bitter satisfaction about that. "Come on, Noah. We have some mingling to do."

Samuel watched Isabelle work the room like a pro. She shook hands, kissed cheeks, flirted with elderly men, and complimented ladies. And she looked absolutely right doing it. She was so accomplished. So beautiful. And that dress . . . he was torn between wanting to cover her up or strip it off.

His plan to make her jealous had better work, or she'd find herself facing a desperate, horny man.

"Who is that in the red dress?" Allysen asked.

"Hm?" Samuel pretended he'd only a minute ago noticed Isabelle. "Oh. That's Isabelle Mason, the Masons' daughter."

"She doesn't look anything like them."

"She's adopted," he said briefly.

"She's gorgeous! If she were a little taller, she would be a top-drawer model. She has that magnetism that attracts every eye. That radiance." In heels, Allysen was his height, willowy-thin, and gorgeous, with startling green eyes that glowed in her dark face. She was pleasant, too, athletic, good at poker, and not worried about chipping her nails.

He liked Allysen. "As do you."

"Thank you." But she wasn't paying him any heed. "In fact, I know a photographer who's desperate to find the next new face. I might suggest her to him."

Isabelle? Posing for the camera? She'd never do it.

But what did he know? He had never imagined she would wear a dress that showed off her ripped shoulders, revealed her legs almost all the way up to her ass, and wrapped her tiny waist like an embrace.

He did not want her modeling. "She's got a job," he said.

"Not very many women would keep a nine-to-five in preference to modeling." Allysen smiled at him. "It's perceived as glamorous, you know."

"I do."

"Who's she with?"

"That's Noah Noble, or as I call him, Senator Slick Hair."

Allysen laughed out loud. "He could use a little less mousse. But he's good-looking, and he's the senator from . . . ?"

"New York."

"Ooh. Powerful. Always an aphrodisiac. Are they involved?"

"Who?"

"Isabelle and Noah!" Allysen joggled his arm. "Pay attention!"

"They used to be engaged. He dropped her like a hot potato to marry someone more appropriate"— actually, his wife hadn't been more appropriate, and

Samuel had never figured out why he'd done it—"and now they're divorced."

"Isabelle must really like him if she's willing to date him after that."

"I don't know." Did Isabelle like Noble? He supposed she did. Samuel thought the guy was a complete yawn, but she'd been engaged to him, and she could have chosen anyone. Now they were together again.

Samuel thought it was to make him jealous. After all, that was what he was doing with Allysen.

But what happened if Senator Slick Hair romanced Isabelle? Would she rebound into his arms?

Glancing up, he saw that Isabelle and Noah were getting close.

Samuel couldn't fake civility. Not now. Turning to Allysen, he asked, "Would you like to dance?"

Suspiciously, she asked, "Are you good at it or are you going to step all over my feet?"

"I'm very good at it. And at dancing."

It was a stupid joke, but she chuckled anyway. "In that case, let's dance."

He swung her onto the floor, deftly avoiding Isabelle and the senator, and when the music ended, he managed to put them on the far end, away from Isabelle, but still in plain sight.

Bring a date, would she?

Two could play that game.

He played like a pro, flaunting himself and the beautiful model, being witty, clever, dedicated to Allysen's

every desire while never letting her know she was
being shamelessly used. . . .

Then Isabelle disappeared. Her and Senator Slick
Hair.

As soon as Samuel realized they were gone, he
stopped right in the middle of the floor. Stopped dancing, stopped talking, stopped smiling.

"What's the matter?" Allysen asked.

"Huh?" He scanned the ballroom.

"They headed out that door." Allysen pointed toward the Masons' art gallery.

"Who?"

"The two people who have you tied in knots. Isabelle Mason and the cute senator."

For the first time that night, Allysen had his total
attention.

She smiled. "Oh, Samuel. She's gorgeous, and I
didn't get to the top of the modeling business by being
dumb."

"Right." He walked Allysen toward the edge of the
dance floor, and felt like the jerk Isabelle told him he
was. "I'm sorry. This was crappy of me."

"It's okay. I've had a great time, and I'm pretty sure
when you leave me here alone to chase after your girlfriend, I'll find someone to take your place."

He looked around.

Men eyed Allysen as if she were a parrot in a flock
of blackbirds.

"You don't mind?" he asked.

She waved him off. "Go on, or you might catch them

kissing, and I'd hate to hear you've gone to prison for killing a US senator."

As he turned away, she was smiling at Gruene Cole, the second-best dancer here.

Samuel walked swiftly through the crowd, attention fixed on the entrance to the art gallery . . . which was lit only dimly.

Oh, sure. Mrs. Mason wanted to discourage her guests from touring the house without her, so she had lowered the lights.

Didn't she know *someone* was going to get the bright idea to slip in there for a quickie? *Someone* like her daughter?

He walked faster. He stepped inside. Heard voices at the far end of the thirty-foot gallery. A woman's laughter. Isabelle's laughter.

He reached for the light switch, ready to raise the lights on this little assignation.

Then Noah shouted, "Watch out!" . . . right before something big and unwieldy crashed to the marble floor.

Chapter 45

S amuel ran.

He found Isabelle kneeling by an unconscious Senator Noble, surrounded by the debris of a broken marble bust and the pedestal on which it rested.

She was fine. Thank God, she was fine.

Glancing up, she saw him. "Samuel! I'm so glad it's you. Keep the rest of the guests away. I've got to fix him."

Noble's open eyes had rolled back into his head, his forehead was sliced open, and his elbow was twisted at an odd angle.

Isabelle had a drop of blood on her cheek, that was all, and Samuel thought perhaps it was Noble's.

"I'll head them off," Samuel said, and strode back toward the entrance.

He met his father coming in.

"We need to keep everyone out of the gallery."

"What did you do?" Darren tried to look beyond him, into the dim reaches of the gallery.

"Right. It's got to be my fault." But for the first time in his life, Samuel recognized that what his father thought of him didn't matter. Darren always believed the worst of Samuel because it was easier than dealing with his own failure as a father. In fact . . . when it came to relationships, Samuel's level of maturity far outstripped Darren's. *Whew.* Something to remember in his future dealings with Isabelle.

Coolly, Samuel told him, "A marble bust somehow fell and hurt Noble. Isabelle is working her magic, so unless you want—"

"I'll handle it." Darren might not have been much of a parent, but he was ever the efficient butler. Swinging back toward the ballroom, he met the initial rush of guests brought by the sound of the crash. "A small accident," he called. He herded them back to the ballroom and shut the doors.

When Samuel reached Isabelle's side, the senator was already stirring.

"What happened?" Noble asked groggily.

"I bumped into one of my mother's art pieces and apparently it wasn't anchored as it should have been." Isabelle helped him sit up.

Samuel looked at the scattered remains of the massive marble bust, looked at the curtained cubbyhole that had protected it, and realized there was no way Mrs. Mason would have so abjectly neglected the safety of her art object. No way Isabelle could have bumped the heavy thing and moved it.

He glanced at the stairway that led upstairs, at the door that led out to the gardens, then at her. "Did you see anything?"

She shook her head. "Not now, Samuel."

Noble glanced up, saw him. "Hey, old man, been meaning to come over all evening and say hello. Isabelle and I were never in the vicinity, that's all." Ever the politician, he offered his hand.

Samuel shook it. "Let me help you up."

"Whoa. Yes, I must have hit the floor a little harder than I realized." Noble leaned heavily on Samuel's arm and got to his feet, then looked around at the mess. "It's a miracle someone wasn't hurt worse."

"A miracle," Isabelle agreed.

"Last thing I remember was admiring you in that dress. . . ." Noble leered.

Samuel let go of his arm.

Noble staggered a little, but kept his feet. "And then bam! The whole pedestal was headed right toward us."

"Shocking," Isabelle said. "I'll speak to Mother about getting a curator in here to make sure the other pieces are more securely placed. Samuel, can you stay with Noah? I want to speak to Darren about the staff he's hired for the party."

Samuel weighed the situation.

She wouldn't be alone.

And Noble *shouldn't* be alone.

Samuel nodded at her.

She hurried toward the ballroom, slipped out, and shut the door behind her, leaving Samuel with the senator.

Noble watched her leave, then heaved a sigh. "That is one fine-looking woman."

Samuel wanted to throw him out the window. Instead he asked, "Can I get you a drink?"

"That would be great. Whisky and tonic, if you can find it."

A discreet table had been set up for Mrs. Mason and the guests she intended to treat to a gallery tour later, and Samuel poured for Noble. His hand hovered over a glass for himself; then he grabbed a bottle of water.

It looked as if he was going to need his wits about him tonight.

"I can't believe I dumped Isabelle for my ex." Noble accepted the drink. "Isabelle's gorgeous. She's a jewel on any man's arm. She knows the right people, always says the right thing, is a fabulous hostess. She's everything a man in my position could want. But you want to know the truth?"

"You dumped her because she has a gift?" Samuel savagely twisted the cap off his water.

"A gift?" Noble looked puzzled, then nodded. "I guess you could call it that. A gift for making my cock shrivel. The woman is famous throughout the whole East Coast. Listen, man, if you're interested, fair warning—she's as frigid as the great frozen North."

Samuel paused, the bottle of water halfway to his mouth.

The senator was still babbling. "I tried. I mean, I really tried to get it on with her. She was willing in a 'sure, you can do it, just don't mess up my hair' sort of way. But honest to God, I couldn't make the little soldier perform. It was like . . . as soon as he got close to that woman's cunt, he got frostbite and turned away."

"Really." Visions flashed through Samuel's mind.

Isabelle kneeling before him, kissing his dick.

Isabelle in her gold silk dress, her legs wrapped around his shoulders, demanding more.

Isabelle riding him, her eyes shining, her cheeks flushed with glory.

Isabelle in his arms, pressed against the wall, climaxing as he hushed her.

Noble said, "I take it you haven't given her a try, or you'd know."

Samuel waggled his head noncommittally.

"While we were engaged, I kept going to the call girls to prove the problem wasn't mine, but that's dangerous for a man in my position." Noble puffed out his chest. "The press loves that kind of scandal. So I figured, '*Dump Isabelle* and get someone who has blood in her veins instead of ice chunks.' The marriage didn't work out, and Mrs. Mason wanted me to try with her darling daughter again, but I swear to God, that time she spent with you buried under that avalanche must have really frozen her solid, because she won't even let me kiss her cheek."

"Not much of a date, hm?"

"No, and now this happened." Noble waved a hand at the scattered pieces of marble.

"What *did* happen?"

"I really don't know. We were looking at a bust of Napoleon done by some famous nineteenth-century French sculptor, and when we turned away, the whole pedestal slammed toward us. Toward Isabelle, really."

Samuel's teeth clenched.

"I thought she was a goner, so I shoved her as hard as I could."

Samuel viewed the senator in a new light. "You're a brave man."

Noble shrugged and winced. "Anyone would have done the same."

Not true. Most people thought of themselves first. The fact that Noble didn't did a lot to dispel Samuel's need to murder him. "How's the injury?"

"There was this blast of pain, I hit the ground so hard I bounced, and it occurred to me . . . well, I wondered if I was going to wake up dead." His eyes narrowed as he thought. "I must have passed out, because the next thing I know, Isabelle's rubbing my shoulder and it's better all the time." He looked at Samuel in puzzlement. "I guess I didn't get hurt as bad as I thought I had."

"Guess not." Noble didn't know about Isabelle's gift. She'd never told him. She was going to marry him, and *she never told him.*

"I suppose I can find someone to pet my fevered

brow." Noble rubbed his head, then his shoulder. "But it's not going to be Isabelle, I can tell you that."

Samuel thought fast. "Listen, you've got my sympathy on the bad-date thing. I don't suppose you'd consider a switch?"

"A switch?" Noble cautiously looked up from his drink.

"You can take my date off my hands and I'll take Isabelle off yours."

"You would give me your date?" Noble's voice rose. *"You'd give me Allysen Cadell?"*

Samuel played dumb. "You don't like her?"

"I like her . . . a lot. A lot. She's gorgeous and she looks . . ."

"Easy?"

"Well. Yes."

"She's not. She's smart, she's witty, and she likes to dance. Although"—Samuel remembered Allysen's earlier comment—"she does like power."

"I've got power." Noble sounded deeply satisfied.

"Isabelle and I have to go back to work tonight and I don't have time to take Allysen home." Samuel slapped him on the shoulder hard enough to make him whimper. "Consider it a mutual favor."

"No," Noble said fervently, "I owe you."

"No, I owe *you*." For saving Isabelle. And for telling Samuel that she never put out for another man like she did for him. He smiled, the kind of smile that, if Isabelle saw it, would make her flee in fear. She was going to be so sorry he found this out. "I'll tell you what. Go find Allysen; tell her I was called away and I asked you to escort her home. Then it's all up to you."

"All right, man." Noble shook Samuel's hand once. Twice. "You're stuck with Isabelle. Try not to get frostbite!"

"I'll be careful." He watched the senator walk away, open the doors, and slide like an oil slick into the ballroom.

He turned to face the shadows by the stairway and noticed Isabelle lurking there. She must have come down only a moment ago; he didn't know how much she'd heard.

She stepped into the light. "So now you know."

She'd heard enough, then. It was on the tip of his tongue to say, *You're frigid with every man except me. In fact, I may be the only guy you've ever slept with.*

But she spoke first. "Someone tried to kill me here— and this is the second time today."

He forgot all about the senator's revelation and focused on Isabelle's face. "The second time? Today?"

"Charisma and I were caught in the cross fire of a gang shooting on Fifth Avenue. But the bullet almost got me."

"Today?" His brain snapped to the obvious conclusion . . . about two weeks too late. "The avalanche was set to take *you* out?"

"When you add it to the fact that the flight that took off for Amsterdam a few minutes after mine blew up in midair, and I'm pretty sure it was because this guy put a bomb in what he thought was my bag . . . yes."

"It's you." The realization hit him like a blow between the eyes. "Someone's trying to kill you."

"Yes, Samuel. Yes!" she said impatiently. "Have you got it now?"

"You?" He stared at her, graceful, elegant, poised, and tried to wrap his mind around the fact that someone hated her enough to kill her.

She looked hurt and bewildered. "*Why* would someone put out a contract on me?"

He gave the obvious answer. "You *are* one of the Chosen Ones."

"I flatter myself that I am the least likely of the group to have enemies!"

"Point taken. If someone, anyone, the Others, were targeting the Chosen, why not me? Everyone hates lawyers."

"Don't be ridiculous, Samuel. Everyone doesn't hate *all* lawyers. They just hate you." She sounded a little too fervent for his taste.

But keeping Aaron's advice in mind—and Caleb's, and Charisma's—he didn't challenge her. Instead he took her hand and tugged her toward the exit. "Come on. I know someone who might have the answer."

Chapter 46

———⊰❖⊱———

"Mathis sleeps so much better since you helped him in Switzerland." The corridors were dim in the Moreaus' Washington DC home as Madame Moreau, dressed in a robe and nightgown, led Samuel and Isabelle toward the boy's room. "Before he was kidnapped, the illness, the pain, the demons kept him awake half the night."

Samuel figured the kidnapping must have given the kid enough nightmares to last him a lifetime.

But no.

"Now . . . he sleeps!" Madame Moreau smiled at Isabelle, tears in her eyes. "Wait until you see him. He looks so much better. Thank you for curing my boy."

"I am so sorry, but I promise you, I didn't cure him, madame." Isabelle smiled sorrowfully. "The disease is still with him, a part of him."

"But somehow, you chased it into a corner and made it cower. Even if you gave him only a little more time, it is quality time." Madame Moreau held open the bedroom door. "Wait here. I'll wake him. He'll be so happy to see you."

After Samuel had made his phone call to Ambassador Moreau, they had flown down to DC in the Masons' private jet, been driven to the Moreaus' home, and now they waited while Madame Moreau used a low, sweet, singsong voice to wake her son.

He replied sleepily.

A light went on, and she called them inside.

They walked in—and Samuel was astonished to see Madame Moreau's report was true. In the space of two weeks, Mathis had gained weight, grown taller, and, most important, he looked stronger, like a boy and not a wraith.

His eyes lit up at the sight of them, and to Samuel's surprise, Mathis said, "*Monsieur* Faa, I was hoping I would see you again so I could thank you for the rescue. I told Mama I want to be like you when I grow up."

"Like Samuel? How's that?" Isabelle sounded droll.

"A hero! He wasn't afraid to come into that house and rescue me."

Samuel grinned and ruffled the boy's hair. "But you'd already shot your guard."

"Yes, but you didn't know that." Mathis stared at him worshipfully. "And you were so good about making sure we were safe before you would call in the woman."

Isabelle raised her eyebrows. "I've never been the woman before."

"I assure you, you have." Samuel held her gaze for a long moment. "Mathis, we have questions we think only you can answer. Things have been happening to Isabelle, bad things, and we think they have something to do with your kidnapping. We want you to think back—did you hear your guards talking about anything? About their plans for you and for us? About why they were doing what they were doing?"

Mathis shook his head. "I can't remember most of the evening. I don't know why."

Isabelle softly sighed, then hastily said, "You were in shock. Pain and horror will do that to a person—block their memories, change their thoughts."

Samuel, too, contained his disappointment. He had been so sure this would work. Yet it wasn't Mathis's fault. "That's okay, buddy," he assured him. "We'll get it figured out."

But Mathis was a smart kid. "You wanted to know or you wouldn't have come to wake me up. I can't remember, but I can show you what happened."

Samuel and Isabelle exchanged glances, then looked inquiringly at Madame Moreau.

She seated herself in the chair beside the bed, curled her feet under her, and said, "Watch."

Mathis lifted his hand and waved it slowly toward the center of the room.

There, in the emptiness, a screen formed.

No, not a screen. A vision, like a movie, transparent yet as real as life.

They saw the room in the Swiss castle where Mathis

had been kept prisoner. They saw it as if they sat there in Mathis's bed. Two men stood in the doorway, frozen in midgesture.

One was the big-bellied man whom Samuel had last seen dead on the floor. The other, smaller, slighter, Samuel didn't recognize.

Mathis waved his hand again—and it was as if the movie started. Both men shifted their feet, moved their hands—and spoke.

"He's not going to live long enough for us to collect the ransom." The big man spoke English with an accent—French or maybe Cajun.

"He will." The smaller man smiled evilly. He had a gold-toothed smile, a sixties haircut, and a voice like a New Jersey gravel pit. "You forget, the Chosen is coming to heal him."

"Then what? Will we get the ransom?"

"You've got ransom on the brain. We're not doing it for the money. We're doing it for the contract."

"A contract that makes no sense. Why not just take her out cleanly with a bullet to the heart?"

A good question, Samuel thought.

With exaggerated patience, the short one said, "The contract specifies that the woman be killed in a way that seems natural. So we've got the kid as bait. She comes to save his lousy little life—and if you ask me, it's not worth saving. . . ."

Isabelle stirred.

Samuel calmed her with his hand on her arm.

The short guy continued. "Then she's swept away

with the avalanche. Afterward, *if* we get the ransom and split it, that's a bonus."

"I still don't know why we can't just kill her."

"Because Winstead is a pussy, that's why—"

Now Samuel straightened, and Isabelle patted him.

Still the short one talked: ". . . scared to death the Chosen Ones will find out he's behind it and take him out. The contract says we play it this way, so play it this way we do. Do you really want to explain to the boss your way is better than his?"

The big guy shivered and shook his head.

"Okay, then. I'm leaving to set the charges."

"What about me?"

"You stay and watch the kid."

"What about when the Chosen show up?"

"Get the hell out. What are you, afraid to stay with a little kid? It's not like he can hurt you." The short guy shoved him toward the chair in the door of the bedroom. "Now go on. We'll pick you up later." He walked down the hall and out of sight.

"Okay." The big guy started to sit down, then stood, stepped into the corridor, and yelled, "Pick me up where?"

Samuel heard Mathis laughing, but it wasn't the Mathis that was here with them. It was the Mathis from that day in the past. They couldn't see him. It was as if he were behind the camera.

"Are you laughing at me, you little shithole?" The big guy started toward the bed. Then, "Where did you get that?" He looked down at his empty holster.

A gunshot sounded, loud and almost in their ears.

Surprised, the big guy looked down at the blood blossoming on his chest.

And he fell over, dead.

The vision faded.

In the here and now, Madame Moreau clutched her robe over her heart and gave a sob. "So close. It was so close. Mathis, where did you get the pistol?"

"I stole it from him when he carried me in." Mathis fell back on the pillows, looking tired and dismayed. "Was my life really not worth saving?" he asked.

"You have a very interesting gift, young man." Samuel tucked the blanket around him. "And that helped us very much."

Isabelle smiled at him. "If not for you, we wouldn't have known all this incredibly useful information. So in my opinion, your life is valuable indeed."

Mathis reached for her hand.

She gave it to him.

He kissed her fingers with all the elegance and charm of any Frenchman. "I am glad to help . . . but I fear you are the woman they wanted to kill. Isn't that right?"

"That's right," Isabelle told him.

"Do not worry, *mademoiselle*," Mathis said with assurance. "Samuel will save you from harm."

Chapter 47

That settled it.

"Is it possible for me to speak with the ambassador?" Samuel asked Madame Moreau.

"Indeed it is." Going to the door, she gestured to the servant waiting outside. "Please take Mr. Faa to Monsieur Moreau in his office."

"Good night, Mathis, and thank you for your help. It has been most valuable." Samuel shook Mathis's hand, then leaned down and kissed the top of his head. "I'll see you again soon, I'm sure." He followed the servant down the corridor, down the stairs, and waited while he knocked, then opened the door. When Samuel was inside, the door was closed behind him.

"Samuel!" Moreau stood up from his desk, came around, and shook Samuel's hand. "I'm glad you had time to speak with me. What can I do for you?"

"I have a problem." Samuel seated himself where Moreau indicated and accepted a cigar. He did no more than tap it on his knee, but it kept his hands busy when what he wanted to do was . . . kill somebody. "Actually, several problems, and I remembered your promise to do us a favor if you could."

"I owe you a thousand favors, you and Miss Mason, for what you've done for my son. So if it is in my power . . ."

"Someone"—Samuel scowled as he remembered the name Mathis had revealed—"has put out a contract on Isabelle."

"On *Isabelle*?" Moreau's eyebrows rose all the way to his nonexistent hairline.

"I know who took out the contract on her. When it came to finding a name, your son has been most helpful."

"He will have been pleased to be of help. He speaks of you both fondly and often."

"He's a good kid, and because of him, I look forward to showing the son of a bitch who would harm Isabelle exactly what a mistake he's made."

Samuel must have sounded fiercer than he realized, because Moreau scooted back a little. "I would suppose you do."

"But it isn't clear which organization he hired. I don't know who to go to see the contract overridden."

Moreau clicked his teeth together as if he imprisoned words at the back of his throat.

"Monsieur, is it possible that you have the connections to find out what I need to know?" A delicate question with no easy way to ask it.

"Perhaps. My connections are mostly European, but there is always gossip, and as we all know, gossip is frequently . . . truth." Seating himself behind his desk, Moreau started typing.

Samuel watched him, and all the while, he cursed himself for his own ego that imagined the assassination attempt in Switzerland had been on him, cursed himself on the shortsightedness that led him to imagine the assassins would stop when they realized he had successfully retrieved the bank accounts in Switzerland. "Also . . ."

Moreau looked up inquiringly.

"There's a safety-deposit box in one of the Swiss banks that belongs to the organization I work for."

Moreau shifted suddenly, awkwardly.

Samuel pretended he hadn't noticed. "Due to a series of unfortunate circumstances, the directions on how to open that safety-deposit box have been lost and the contents are trapped within. I was wondering if you had any connections with the Swiss banking authorities that would help us discover the combination that would open the box. The contents are very precious to us."

"Out of idle curiosity, do you know what's in the box?"

No, but I'm not sure that you don't. "I haven't a clue." Who was Moreau? Not merely the French ambassador to the US. But certainly someone with more knowledge than Samuel had previously suspected.

"Yet you think you need those contents?"

Samuel weighed his answer. "You know your son has a gift?"

Moreau gestured noncommittally.

"You know Isabelle has a gift, also?"

Again the gesture.

"Those who are gifted in different ways"—Samuel could also gesture noncommittally—"tell me that the contents should be in our possession. Whatever is inside the bank will soon be required outside. Disaster has already befallen us with the explosion of our headquarters."

"Yes, I know."

"We fear the beginning of the end." Remembering Jacqueline's vision, Rosamund's revelations, Samuel didn't feel as if he were overstating the matter.

Moreau treated Samuel's pronouncement with appropriate solemnity. "I will see what I can do. There are rules and safeguards, but—" An alert sounded on Moreau's computer, interrupting him. He stared. His ruddy complexion paled. He said, "This contract on Isabelle—it was made with the Others."

"The Others?" Samuel's knee-jerk reaction was disbelief. "They don't do contract killings."

"They do what they are told to do. Do you know that their leader, Osgood, controls the corruption on the East Coast? That includes prostitution, drugs, graft—"

"And assassination."

"Assassination is a good moneymaker, especially with politics being such big business here."

"Of course it is."

"The problem—Osgood is bound by his word. Once he has made a vow, he cannot fail to keep it, or the eternal rules have been violated."

Moreau's knowledge confirmed all Samuel's suspicions about him. Somehow, Moreau *knew* things. Someday Samuel intended to come back and see what he could learn, but for now . . . "What happens if Osgood breaks his vow?"

"He loses everything, and in recent months, he has acquired much—more wealth, power, publicity. Osgood was a wicked man, and invited Lucifer into his soul. That's been done before. But never have I heard of such a creature becoming so influential." Moreau frowned. "It is as if it was the perfect joining."

Samuel filed that information away in his mind.

"So—the payment for Isabelle's murder has been given. The deal has been made. There is no canceling this contract." Moreau looked drawn and tired as he made his pronouncement. "The Others will never stop . . . until Isabelle is dead."

Chapter 48

The ambassador's private jet was smaller than the Masons', but the appointments were more luxurious, and more important, it was fast, the fastest Learjet in the air.

Samuel needed that, needed to be able to drop Isabelle at her parents' home in Boston, then go take care of matters before the night was over.

The flight was forty minutes.

But she didn't wait until they were off the ground before she pounded him with questions. "Did you talk to Moreau?"

"I did."

"Did he know anything about the firm that creep Winstead hired to kill me?"

"He was surprised to hear a contract had been put out on you." Not a lie, but she had no reason to think Samuel was withholding information.

"That makes two of us." Leaning back in her seat,

she closed her eyes wearily and was quiet while the engines revved up and the jet taxied down the runway.

Their ascent into airspace was smooth. Below, lights dotted the coastline.

Samuel used the time to look up an address on his phone, and text a message to John Powell. He figured he'd hear back from John soon enough.

When the jet had reached cruising altitude, she opened her eyes again. "When I signed up for the Chosen Ones, this wasn't what I expected. The Gypsy Travel Agency was full of people selected especially for their competence and enthusiasm."

"I know." He remembered what it was like when he'd arrived at the Gypsy Travel Agency for his interview. There had been people everywhere, carrying ancient texts, handheld computers, walking briskly, walking slowly, wearing Birkenstocks, wearing Armani, speaking in Latin and English and God knew what other languages.

Isabelle rambled on. "When I went into that building, I discovered I wasn't the only physical empath. Not that it's a common gift, but while I was there, I met two others. They told me about my duties, that I would ride along with the Chosen Ones and heal people as necessary, but they assured me that for the most part, I wouldn't have to worry about expending my life force. Neither of them had ever faced life-threatening injuries. Neither of them had ever had to face the moral dilemma of having to retreat from someone who was dying. They said it had happened in the past, but not anymore. The worst I would experience was the occasional broken bone, and they both seemed to think *that* was a big deal. I'm pretty sure they were telling the truth, too, and that neither one of them had to cure a seer from devil-induced smoke inhalation."

Samuel remembered that time; Jacqueline had almost died from the smoke, Isabelle had almost died helping her . . . and when he had seen Isabelle *in extremis*, he hurt as if he were the empath. Actually, that was his common reaction to seeing Isabelle in pain: He always wanted to do whoever hurt her a violence— even himself.

Opening the bar, he poured a drink—Scotch and Drambuie, no rocks—and handed it to her.

She took a sip, coughed. But she didn't continue to drink. She was bewildered; she wanted to talk. "When I signed up for my stint with the Chosen Ones, Zusane was there to handle the weird stuff like visions and prophecy, and that was good, because what did I know about seeing the past and the future? Even now, what do I know about it? Nothing. I don't understand prophecy at all."

"Nor do I."

"Nor does Jacqueline, I think." Isabelle took a swallow and put down the glass. "But what I'm trying to say is—when I signed on with the Chosen Ones, I wasn't worried about getting killed. It never crossed my mind. The main thing I was worried about was having to spend time with *you*."

"I can imagine." When he signed up, it had been

because the directors of the Gypsy Travel Agency had blackmailed him. But discovering Isabelle would be on his team had been the beginning of his acquiescence. He loved her; he wanted her. Here was another chance to have her.

"The sheer number of people involved in the organization made me think I wouldn't see you too often."

"Didn't turn out that way, did it?" She was an innocent; she had never been safe from him.

"Then all those people were gone, blown up by the Others. To think of so much vitality, enthusiasm, knowledge lost . . . even more than two and a half years later, it doesn't seem possible."

"No." Samuel was glad he had barely joined the Gypsy Travel Agency at the time of the explosion; to have personally known those people would have been a crushing blow. He knew Irving still grieved, and when the anniversary of the explosion rolled around, Martha always disappeared. She would return the next day, heavy-eyed and still a little drunk, and go back to work without a word.

"Those first months when we were the only Chosen . . . they were so difficult. Caleb was training us to fight. We were rescuing children. I was healing horrible injuries and trying to be the leader of the group when I knew so little of what our missions should be and what procedures we should follow. Worse, I was with you all the time. Nothing was like I thought it was going to be. Nothing. But through all that, I never imagined I would anger someone so

much that he would take out a contract to kill me."
She sounded incredulous. Hurt.

Samuel handed her the drink again. The next few minutes would go easier if she wasn't thinking too clearly.

"I know Todd Winstead," she said. "I've known him for years. And I guess from what Mathis showed us, he's the one who—"

"He's the one."

She took a good swallow. Coughed again. Croaked, "Why?"

"Because you saved his grandmother from death." Samuel couldn't stand that expression on Isabelle's face, the one that looked like her belief in the goodness of mankind had at this minute shattered. "Look. Todd Winstead is a worm. You know that."

"Yes, but—"

"He tried to kill his own grandmother, a lady who has been nothing but good to him, and all because she has money and he's too feeble to go out and get his own. Then he tried to kill you for saving her." Samuel snorted. "He didn't even have the guts to try to kill either one of you himself. He's afraid of getting his ass kicked."

"He should be," Isabelle said evilly.

"Let me freshen your drink." Samuel added more Scotch, more Drambuie.

"No, it's too strong."

Samuel added ice and handed it back to her.

She took a sip, swirled the glass to melt the ice, took another sip. "Better."

Okay. She had a little anesthesia in her. Now was the time to start breaking the ties that bound them. In a voice rough with contempt, he said, "When I signed up for the Gypsy Travel Agency, I wondered if we'd see much of each other, too. It didn't seem likely, which was good, since with our past, I knew contact could be dangerous."

She chortled. "Yes."

"Turns out I was right. Here we are, right back where we were—what? Five or six years ago when we separated the second time. We've had sex, we've fought, and we've discovered all over again we're incompatible."

Isabelle's glass slipped out of her fingers.

He caught it and placed it in her cup holder. "We can't do all this again. Not and work together."

"W-well," Isabelle stammered. "Caleb and Jacqueline are involved and they work together. So are John and Genny. And Aaron and Rosamund."

"They're not on the team together. Only one of each couple is Chosen."

"Yes, but—"

He didn't give her a chance to talk. "I mean, look at us! Sex one minute, violence the next. I've still got a lump on my head where you hit me today."

"I'm sorry about that. Charisma explained that you were trying to say you'd take care of me no matter what the circumstances." Isabelle smiled at him ruefully.

Oh, no. No smiles. No conciliation. "Which goes to show you Charisma doesn't know as much as she thinks she does."

Isabelle flinched as if he'd slapped her.

"We simply don't have much in common. That second time we were together, we were living together, we were happy, and you left me because of one little incident that didn't add up to anything."

"What are you talking about? Wait. Are you talking about Benedikta Vos? Are you dismissing what you did to her—and me—as 'one little incident'?"

"What would you call it?"

"You dare . . ." Isabelle twisted to face him. "I was working with that woman. What I knew about her and where she was hiding was confidential. You had no right—"

"Look. Benedikta Vos came to me because her husband was powerful, corrupt, and he beat the crap out of her. She had the goods on him, she knew I would prosecute him to the full extent of the law, and with her testimony, *I* knew I could put him away for a thousand years." It was the kind of case Samuel had reveled in, because the good guys were going to win and the woman was going to get away to a better life.

"She had the right to change her mind about testifying!" Isabelle said hotly.

Good. He was getting to her. "No, she didn't. He was hurting people and she could stop him."

"He abused her, and she was afraid he would kill her."

"Like if he ever caught up with her, he wasn't going to kill her anyway? Once I put him in prison, he couldn't catch up with her and she was safe." His logic was impeccable, now and then. "I needed that information and I got it."

"You used your mind control on me and I didn't even realize I had told you where she was!"

That had been his mistake. His sin. He had known it when he did it, but in his arrogance, he had believed she would understand.

It hadn't happened that way, and he had been left without the one woman he loved.

Now he drove her away using the same sword, and he knew that when he was finished they would both be bleeding.

"Once I talked to her, convinced her I would keep her safe—which I would like to point out that I *did*—she was willing to get on the stand, and we took him down." The plane was rapidly descending. Thank God, this was almost over. "With her help, I was able to do a lot of good."

"You mind-raped me," Isabelle said quietly.

"Very dramatic. But think on this—the end does justify the means, and you need to face the facts."

"The fact that I can't trust you not to do it again?"

"For the same results, I would do it again."

The plane touched down. Before they had come to a halt, she was out of her seat.

Isabelle wasn't a rule breaker. If the pilot told her to sit, she sat. So her flouting of that immutable rule of flying told Samuel he had succeeded. "What are you doing?" he asked. Like he didn't know.

"Getting as far away from you as I can. After all, I

might know something you're curious about and you would feel justified in controlling my mind to discover it."

"Like . . . ?"

As they cornered, she hung on to the opposite seat and looked down at him. "Like the fact that I do love you. And at the same time, I feel total contempt for you."

He shrugged. "I told you. We're incompatible. Better to find out now than after we've done something stupid, like gotten married."

"When you're right, you're right." She walked to the front of the plane.

The pilot shut down the engines, came back, and opened the door.

She walked down the stairs without a backward glance.

Samuel uncoiled himself from the seat.

Looking sympathetic and embarrassed, the pilot met his eyes. "Ambassador Moreau said to take you wherever you wanted."

"Stay ready; I may need you again tonight." Samuel followed Isabelle through the airport at a discreet distance, keeping her in sight, observing the crowd around her, and he didn't relax until she got into her parents' limo. Running to the waiting taxis, he grabbed the first one in line and told the driver, "Follow that car."

At her parents' house, he watched her go to the door, saw his father answer it, usher her inside, and close the door behind her.

Only then was Samuel satisfied.

He'd back Mrs. Mason against any assassin.

Meeting the driver's eyes in the rearview mirror, he gave him an address. "I'm going to visit a friend."

"At this hour?" The driver peeled off the curb. "Must be a good friend."

"Yeah. He and I—we're going to have a talk."

Chapter 49

———❦———

Ever since he'd heard that Samuel Faa and Isabelle Mason had escaped the avalanche, Todd Winstead had been hearing noises in his Boston apartment. Creaking floorboards. Scratching in the walls. Tapping at the windows. No matter how many times he had contractors and exterminators in, the noises continued until the doorman suggested maybe the sounds were nothing more than the rattling in Todd's head.

Todd had made sure the doorman was fired.

But he'd also stopped complaining out loud. He couldn't afford to get kicked out of this apartment building. It was old, it was run-down, but it was prestigious, and with what he made working for his grandmother, this was the best he could do.

Now he lay in bed, covers up to his chin, eyes open, staring at the ceiling over his bed.

It was the middle of the night. His night-light was on. His security system was blinking green. Yet something had woken him, and it took him a few minutes to figure out what.

The noises had stopped—and for some reason, that bothered him. He couldn't help but wonder if something bigger, something more dangerous had frightened away the rats, the cockroaches . . . the gremlins.

This was his grandmother's fault. If the old woman had drowned in her car like she was supposed to, he'd be living in her penthouse apartment instead of this fourth-floor shithole, listening to weird noises and feeling as if he were seven years old again and afraid of the monster under the bed.

The creepy thing was—he was no longer sure there *wasn't* a monster under the bed. When his grandmother was still sick from the plunge in the Atlantic, she'd babbled on about Isabelle Mason and how she had healing hands.

Todd believed Isabelle had pulled his grandmother from the ocean and given her CPR and thoroughly screwed up his plans. But he hadn't believed the woo-woo stuff.

In frustration and rage, he'd put out the contract on Isabelle, figuring to get her out of the way and then take care of Granny himself . . . but the assassins he'd met made him believe in woo-woo. And not good woo-woo, either. They were scary in a way that made him want to call it all off.

But it was far too late for that.

Finally he couldn't stand the silence anymore. Throwing back the covers, he locked his bedroom door, checked the locks on the windows in the bathroom and the bedroom, pulled the drapes so tight not a speck of light could escape and nothing floating outside on bat wings could look in. When he was satisfied nothing could come in, he got back in bed and pulled up the covers, and, in his first act of daring in two weeks, he turned out the light.

And froze as a deep, cold, angry man's voice said, "Now we're closed in nice and tight . . . just the two of us."

Chapter 50

———— ❖ ————

Isabelle walked into her parents' house, past a stiff and worried Darren, sat down on the bench in the entryway, put her face in her hands—and sobbed.

She heard Darren's footsteps hurrying away, up the stairs.

Samuel. Samuel.

She had never felt so betrayed. So broken.

She should have known better.

Hadn't she done this before with him? Sure, they loved each other . . . or at least, she loved him. But five years ago, they'd been living together, loving each other, but she had known even then that they were very different people.

She had been working at an abused women's shelter.

He'd been a lawyer making a name for himself.

And when she'd held information he wanted, he took it from her.

She would never forget the moment she realized

what he had done . . . and what she had done. All un-knowing, she had betrayed a woman whose very life had been nothing but abuse and betrayals. Isabelle had despised herself, and despised Samuel.

And when she reproached him, he claimed not to comprehend her distress.

So she had left him. Left him forever, because how could she live with a man who couldn't understand that he could not take what he wanted from her? A man whose morality saw no reason for regret?

Three years later, through the auspices of the Gypsy Travel Agency, she'd been flung into his company.

She'd resisted the desire to be with him again.

He'd helped by being a jerk.

Then the forced proximity in the ski lodge had changed everything, and here she was, crying again over Samuel Faa when she should know better.

"Honey?" Her mother's voice. Her mother's hand on her shoulder.

Isabelle took a breath and looked up.

Patricia Mason stood there, clutching her robe, frowning, gnawing her lip.

How many times had Isabelle seen her polished, cosmopolitan mother flustered, anxious, searching for the right words to comfort her?

So seldom.

How many times had it been because of Samuel?

Every time.

Isabelle forced herself to her feet and faced her mother. "I, ah, I just . . ." She tried to hang on to her dignity, but emotions roiled to the surface, scraping away her composure. "Oh, Mother. What am I going to do?" To her horror, she burst into tears again.

"Isabelle." Patricia put her arm around her daughter, led her to the office, and shut the door. "Tell me what happened, honey."

Crises like this were the only times Isabelle's mother called her an endearment.

Isabelle cried harder and, between sobs, told her mother the whole story.

In a hard, angry voice Isabelle had never heard from her before, Patricia said, "This is what you get for signing that contract with the Chosen Ones."

Isabelle took a long breath, got control of her anguish, and pulled Kleenex out of the tissue holder. "Mother, I had no choice."

"What do you mean, you had no choice?" Patricia paced across her office, flinging her hands in the air.

Isabelle noted that although it was three o'clock in the morning, her mother wore diamonds big enough to weigh down her hands.

"Are you saying they blackmailed you?" Patricia asked. "Because if that's the case, I know some good lawyers who will get you released from your obligation."

"No, I'm saying I was taught to do the right thing, and giving of my gift to help people is the right thing." Isabelle stared at her mother meaningfully. "Do you know who taught me that, *Mother*?"

Patricia breathed hard, lifted her chin, and admitted, "I did."

"I signed with the Chosen Ones because you told me I had an obligation to make the world a better place." As Isabelle spoke, she realized the ugly truth.

Samuel or not, she had to return to her duties with the Chosen Ones.

"I only wish he hadn't . . ." Isabelle shook her head. "But why wish something that can never be? Samuel is Samuel, and as you said once, he's a charming, deceitful beast."

"Yes, I know I said that, and I believe it, mostly." Patricia stopped pacing. "Yet after he was rescued from the avalanche, he seemed so dedicated to the two of you being together. I thought for sure . . ."

"He's Samuel. He's always a disappointment." Years ago Isabelle had sworn she would never cry about him again. "In the plane, he reminded me what he'd done wrong. He still doesn't regret betraying me. And he said it was a good thing we'd found out we were incompatible before we did anything stupid, like getting married."

Her mother stared at her, head slanted to the side, face puzzled. "I don't understand. I don't like Samuel, but I saw him in Switzerland. Right or wrong, good match or bad, he would marry you in a minute."

Isabelle wiped the tears off her face, took a few deep breaths, got ready to argue, and realized . . . Patricia was right.

Samuel had instigated a fight with her. He'd said all that purposely—to make her angry.

The question was . . . why? Why, when she'd scarcely

discovered that she was the target of an assassination attempt, would he try to get rid of her?

What is he planning?

"Oh, my God." Isabelle stood up, arms tight against her sides, fists clenched.

"What?"

"That skunk. He manipulated me."

"It sounds as if he did." Patricia leaned toward her daughter, brow furrowed. "Darling, what do you intend to do?"

Chapter 51

Winter nights were long and cold, and at five o'clock in the morning on the Boston docks, dawn was three hours away. The city lights shone up on the cloud cover, providing a dingy light as Samuel walked toward the warehouse on dock thirty-seven A.

Nothing moved. Anywhere. But he knew they were inside. According to Todd Winstead, the Others' contract team was stationed here.

Samuel believed him.

But then, Samuel hadn't played fair.

Todd admitted to a lot of stuff, including trying to kill his grandmother and getting so pissed at his failure that he hired assassins to kill Isabelle. He blamed her, of course, for making him do it. If she hadn't interfered, she wouldn't be on the list for a short life span.

A single industrial-size light hung over a narrow, dirty, banged-up metal door.

Samuel stood outside and listened closely.

It sounded like a poker game was in session. Sounded like someone was losing and taking it badly.

The most important thing Todd had admitted was that, yeah, once the contract was taken out, it couldn't be rescinded.

So Samuel had no choice. John Powell had texted that he should wait for backup. Yet two attempts in one day convinced Samuel the Others were getting desperate. He wasn't going to take the risk that their next attempt would succeed. He had to cancel the contract his way, and he had to do it now.

With one hand flat on the door, he pushed it open and called, "I've been told this is the place to come to pay for a contract."

All sound ceased.

Had they not set a watch?

Sloppy.

He backed away from the building into the open air. The boards beneath his feet were damp; the air he breathed was also damp, full of the scents of Boston Harbor, and he listened to the slosh of the tide as the waves splashed beneath the dock.

Men slipped from some unseen entrance and gathered in the shadows just outside the light cast by the flickering fluorescent lamp, a half dozen in a semicircle around him. The players were in place.

He stood relaxed, his hands visible and loose at his sides.

Finally, the least of the assassins, the one most easily

expendable, stepped out into the open. "You want to put out a contract?"

"You do them?"

"For a price."

"First I want to know I'm in the right place. Some people in this town say they can take care of my job for less than you charge."

"But we're the only ones who really deal. Anyone else who says they do, you should let me know. I'll take care of them." The little guy swaggered forward.

He was five-five, a hundred and thirty pounds, looked like he'd been doing drugs since he was twelve. He had a gold-toothed smile, a sixties haircut, a voice like a New Jersey gravel pit.

Samuel recognized him. He'd seen him earlier in Mathis's vision. He'd been in that room in Switzerland.

So Samuel was definitely in the right place.

Too bad the little shrimp held a pistol pointed right at Samuel's gut.

Samuel lifted his hands over his head. "I'm not the one I want killed."

"I get that. I have to know you're serious about the contract. That you're not a reporter."

"Or a cop?"

Shrimp's nostrils flared as if scenting something rotten. "Not a problem. The cops down here are ours."

"Good to know."

"But did you bring money?" Shrimp's breath puffed

white in the cold air, and two of the onlookers betrayed their posts every time they exhaled.

"I'd be a fool to bring money *here*." Samuel waved his raised hand around at the warehouses. "All I've got is a recommendation from a friend of mine."

"Who?"

"Todd Winstead. He said he had hired you."

"What a weenie he is." Shrimp's voice was full of contempt.

"See? We can do business. We already agree on something."

Shrimp laughed.

Samuel laughed with him. "But also, Winstead said you were the best."

"Best or not, we've taken over this business. You want someone killed? You deal with us." Shrimp wasn't saying too much.

He wasn't saying what Samuel needed to know. "Tell me who you work for." Samuel sent out a feeler, pressed on the little guy's mind.

No resistance there. Shrimp didn't have much of a brain left. "We work for the Others," he said.

A voice spoke from the shadows. "Shut up, man."

"I've heard of the Others." Samuel lashed out with his mind, blasting not the little guy, but the voice of caution behind him.

The man in the shadows grunted in pain, stumbled, and plunged backward into the water.

Shrimp turned and looked. "What happened?"

Samuel didn't give him time to find out. "Who do the Others work for?"

Shrimp said, "What do you care? You want somebody dead."

Samuel pressed on the little guy's brain.

"Osgood. They work for Osgood." Shrimp gained control, realized he'd been indiscreet, and added, "But he's given us a free hand down here. We're the ones you need to talk to."

"Right." Samuel saw movement in the shadows. He reached out, found the mind there, and broke it.

Another splash.

"What the hell . . . ?" Shrimp looked at Samuel. "You got people out there? Taking our guys out? Are you *challenging* us?"

"*You* ought to know whether I have guys out there. Surely you have a guard posted?" Samuel shoved at Shrimp's mind.

Shrimp stumbled backward, dropped his pistol. Looked up furiously. "Yeah, we do."

A pole slammed Samuel in the back of the neck.

A woman's voice said, "Take that, asshole."

He fell to his knees, shook his head, tried to send out a blast.

She whipped the pole around, aimed at his ribs.

Grabbing the end, he rolled backward and yanked it out of her hands.

He swung, aimed the pole for her—and she vanished.

Men stalked out of the shadows, holding guns, holding knives, and one of them laughed.

The woman was gifted. One of the Others.

He swung wide, hoping to catch her, and by chance caught her behind the knees.

She stumbled out of her concealment, fell to the dock.

Samuel smashed her on the back, knocking her flat, then used the pole to vault toward Shrimp.

Shrimp scrabbled around for the pistol, got it just in time—and shot.

The bullet struck Samuel in midair. In the hip. Hit the joint and broke it. Hurt like nothing he'd ever felt in his life.

He landed. The leg collapsed.

The second bullet missed, punched through the dock, sprayed splinters everywhere.

No time for mind control.

Samuel wielded the pole like a lance, rammed it into Shrimp's gut. The gun hit the ground, went off.

Shrimp shrieked.

The three assassins rushed Samuel.

Still on the ground, Samuel swiveled on his good hip, punched the pole up underneath one guy's crotch.

That guy screamed, too.

The fight was getting noisy.

One attacker projected so much excitement, he was easy to find. Samuel blasted him with a thought.

He went down.

Samuel pulled his pistol. For one fleeting second, he felt a rise of triumph.

Isabelle will be safe.

With his mind, he groped for the remaining uninjured assassin—

The guy shot him.

The bullet slammed through his shoulder, cracked his shoulder blade. He couldn't feel the pistol. No—he couldn't feel his hand. The pain was agonizing.

But it didn't matter. He was bleeding to death.

He tried to gather his mind control, send out a blast.

The Other stumbled backward, then picked up the pole and smashed him on the side of the head.

He lost consciousness for a second. Came back to pain, anguish, and piercing regret.

No second chance to save Isabelle.

He'd failed.

Her life was in the hands of John and the Chosen Ones now. Perhaps they could do what he could not.

Through the buzzing in his ears, he heard a voice. Opened his eyes. Saw the vultures gathering.

The Other had blood smeared across her face.

One guy was holding his 'nads.

Shrimp was awash in blood, and his face looked funny. The gunshot had torn his ear off.

"You look like shit," Samuel said.

Shrimp kicked him in the hip.

Samuel screamed.

The guy with the gun lifted it, pointed it.

The Other pushed the barrel aside. "No. That's too easy." Picking up her heel, she stomped it into his face.

A pack of vultures?

No, they were hyenas, and they all wanted a piece of his flesh.

Chapter 52

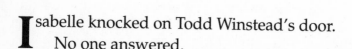

Isabelle knocked on Todd Winstead's door.

No one answered.

Like she cared. Pulling the pick from her pocket, she went to work and was inside in thirty seconds.

The place was a mess—a shattered lamp, a broken coffee table, blood. . . . "So Samuel has been here," she said with satisfaction.

She was on the right trail.

There were two doors leading out of the small living room, both of them shut. The first was the bedroom, also trashed. The second was the tiny, darkened bathroom with nowhere to hide except in the tub behind the shower curtain. A stupid place to hide . . . and there she found Todd, pasty with fear, holding a vase over his head.

She stepped back. "Auditioning for a role as the Statue of Liberty?" she asked.

He lowered the vase, breathing hard.

He had a black eye, a split lip, a broken tooth.

Seeing his battered face, she felt briefly sorry for him.

"You!" he said. "You've ruined my life."

Good to be finished with compassion.

"Samuel's been here. He questioned you. Where did you send him?" she asked.

He stepped out of the tub, put the vase in the sink. Looked in the mirror and dabbed at his face. "To hell, I hope."

"For your sake, you had better hope not."

"What are you going to do?" He looked her up and down insultingly, at her dark, formfitting catsuit. "I may not be a gorilla like your boyfriend, but I can still defend myself against a woman." He pushed past her.

"I'm a healer. If we made a deal, I could fix your face as good as new. You realize that, right?"

He halted in midstride. Hopeful, he turned toward her.

Catching his hand, she twisted his arm behind his back, and savagely slammed his face to the floor. Pulling her pistol from the holster strapped to her shoulder, she pointed it at his head. "But I won't. I want you to suffer." She felt his pain and exulted in it. "Now— tell me what I want to know."

The clouds were clearing. The sun was a hint in the eastern sky. The retreating tide sucked at the pilings.

Isabelle ran the last half mile to dock thirty-seven A, keeping to the shadows, pistol in her hand. She turned the corner toward the warehouse. Paused and scrutinized.

The area looked empty. No movement.

It sounded empty. No voices.

As she watched, the automatic light over the door flickered off.

But she'd spotted a dark cloth sack discarded against the building. Moving softly, swiftly, as Caleb had taught them, she loped forward, drawn by the sack, which was long and man-shaped, and the dark stain beneath it . . .

As she approached, it moved. That wasn't a hand, was it? A hand covered with blood?

It wasn't Samuel's hand, was it?

Whispering, "No. No. Samuel, no," she ran the last few feet with no care for the danger. She dropped to her knees beside him.

His nose was broken. His left cheek was concave. Blood trickled from his mouth, from the wounds on his shoulder and his hip. He gurgled when he breathed, as if he had a punctured lung.

She held one hand over his heart.

The beat was slowing.

He was dying.

No.

"Samuel." She touched his cheek.

His eyes opened. His hand flashed up, caught her wrist. He looked at her, just looked at her. He smiled. "Beautiful . . . to see you . . . one last time." He slurred

CHAINS OF FIRE   357

his words, struggled for breath. "Love you." His hand fell as if he were too weak to hold it up.

"The assassins did this?" She wanted to kill them. "Where are they?"

"Gone. To report. Change locations. For the moment . . . you're safe."

She placed the pistol on the dock close to her side. With her other hand she reached for him.

He flailed, pushed her away. "No. Don't touch. Can't survive this."

He was right. She couldn't survive these gunshot wounds, the injuries from the beating those savages had given him.

She would have to let him go.

Because . . . she didn't want to die.

She loved her life. She loved the winter sunshine, New York, great clothes, Jimmy Choo heels, her parents, her friends. She'd loved being part of the Chosen Ones, of a higher cause. She loved knowing she could help people who were hurt. She had always taken that responsibility seriously, and when injuries had been too severe, she had been careful not to sacrifice herself and her gift. The decision had never been easy, yet she had always been sure she was doing the right thing.

No one would blame her if she said it was God's will and let Samuel go.

No one would blame her . . . except her.

Because she would know the real reason she let him die.

Sitting there at the very beginning of day, she faced her greatest fear.

She was afraid to suffer like this.

But this was Samuel. He was here, in this condition, because of her.

She had always wondered if he really loved her.

Well. Here was her answer. Knowing full well the possible consequences, he had come to this place to save her. He had been willing to sacrifice himself for her.

Could she do any less? She loved him.

Very gently, she pushed the damp strands of his hair off his forehead. "I'm not going to survive anyway. I talked to Todd." Todd hadn't enjoyed their conversation. She had put her fight training to use, and for the first time in her life, she had enjoyed inflicting pain on another person. "These assassins—they won't stop until I'm dead."

"Tell John. Run away. Hide. Get a new identity." Samuel had to stop to breathe again. "Stay safe. For me. Promise."

She could do that. Her parents had money. She could leave the Chosen Ones, have surgery, change her looks, spend her life in hiding and be safe.

"Promise," he mumbled. He was losing his grip on consciousness.

Today one of them had to die.

"Shh. Go to sleep." Decision made, she put her hand over his eyes. "I'll take care of everything." As he slipped into a coma, she added, "When you wake, my darling, remember—I don't want to live in a world without you, but you must live for both of us. Be strong. Be honorable. Love with all your heart. Laugh with all your soul. And fight the good fight, just as you did today."

Chapter 53

The early-morning sun on his eyelids woke him, and Samuel frowned.

The bed was hard. He was stiff. And damp. Something smelled like blood. *What the . . . ?*

Abruptly, memory flooded his mind.

He opened his eyes.

He was here, at the warehouse where he'd tracked the assassins. He'd lost the fight. He'd been dying. Then . . . "Isabelle!"

He sat up. And saw her. Isabelle, stretched out beside him, shot in the shoulder and hip, battered, bleeding, wheezing with the broken ribs and punctured lung that had only recently been his. "Isabelle." Her name was a sorrowful breath on his lips.

Yet she heard him. She opened her eyes . . . and they were bloodshot, cloudy with pain. Her powers had healed him, but at a dire cost.

Pressing his palm to her unshattered cheek, he said,

"Don't leave me. Please. Heal yourself. You have to heal yourself."

"Too much. Must go. Pain . . . so much." She closed her eyes again, struggling for breath. Opened them. "*You* know. Want to go."

Yes. He knew. When pain grew overwhelming, death was a gift.

Her lips and fingernails were blue. Her breathing was labored. Death was coming swiftly.

"Hold me," she whispered.

Leaning down, he put his arms on either side of her, holding himself away, desperately afraid to damage her more.

"No," she said. "Really hold me."

"I'll hurt you."

She laughed soundlessly. "No. Doesn't hurt . . . now."

He hurt. As he gathered her into his arms, the pain in his heart threatened to destroy him.

This was Isabelle. She had been his first friend, his first lover, his only beloved. He could feel her breathing fail, her skin grow cool, her muscles grow lax. As inevitably as the tide, life was stealing away from her. . . .

She observed him, scrutinized him so intently he knew she wanted his face to be her last sight on this earth.

So for her, he smiled, nodded, said, "I have loved you every day I've known you, and no matter where you go, I will always love you."

Her lips moved without sound. "Love . . . you."

As he watched and grieved, her ruined lungs took

their last breath. Her heart gave its last beat. The soul slipped out of her eyes.

He should want to weep.

Instead, he roared, "No!"

No, he wouldn't allow this to happen. Not to her. Not to Isabelle.

He hugged her to his chest, rocked back and forth, tried desperately to do what she had done for so many others—for him—and give her all the days of her life lived in health and happiness. Inside him, a part of her was still alive, and he took what she had taught him— how to heal—and pushed it at her.

Her heart gave a single beat.

He lifted his head, overwhelmed by sudden hope.

But that was all. A single beat.

And she was gone again.

Healing wasn't his gift. He couldn't do this.

But Isabelle had given of herself to others, too, so many others.

They weren't here. They didn't know she needed them.

Yet . . . yet if they knew . . . they would help her. He knew they would.

Holding her tightly, he stood and, not knowing where he was going, what he was doing, he staggered toward the water. Lifting her body toward the rising sun, he shouted out loud—and in his mind—"Listen! Everybody! Listen! Isabelle helped you when you needed her. Now she needs your help. Find her inside yourself and heal! *Help Isabelle! Heal Isabelle!*"

*   *   *

Mathis Moreau woke. Eyes wide, he stared around his room.

In his mind, he heard Samuel's voice.

Help Isabelle! Heal Isabelle!

Throwing back his covers, he rushed to the window. In the flood of sunlight, he closed his eyes and sought Isabelle inside himself . . . and he gave back.

Jacqueline D'Angelo stood in the light shining in her window. She slid smoothly from cobra to downward dog, the yoga as natural as breathing to her. She inhaled into the posture, slid back to stretch her spine, brought her arms above her head—and froze in her salute to the sun.

It wasn't a vision, not really, yet she heard Samuel's voice.

Help Isabelle! Heal Isabelle!

Going to the window, she took a long, deep breath, sought Isabelle within herself . . . and gave back.

Lady Winstead cursed the old age that interrupted her sleep and woke her as soon as the sun came up over the horizon. She sat in her breakfast room, sipping her tea and nibbling at a croissant when she heard someone. . . .

That handsome young man Samuel called her.

Help Isabelle! Heal Isabelle!

Isabelle needed her.

Pushing her chair back, she used her cane to stand;

then with the usual morning stiffness, she hobbled to the window.

Looking out at the wash of sunlight, she gave back.

Patricia Mason sat wrapped in her robe, staring at the rising sun and mentally urging Isabelle to call her. Reassure her. Tell her she'd found Samuel and told him off and was coming home.

Isabelle hadn't been the child of her body, but she had always been the child of her heart: the kindest, the smartest, the most loving . . .

The first time Patricia had seen Isabelle heal something, it had been the family German shepherd. The animal had run into the street. A car had winged it. The dog limped back, yelping, in anguish. And three-year-old Isabelle had taken the injury into herself and made the dog better.

Patricia had never heard of such a thing, but she did her research and discovered all the information about abandoned children and why they had been given gifts.

But that wasn't what Patricia wanted for her little girl.

Magic? Fighting evil? Patricia discouraged her daughter, pointed her at charitable organizations, gave her different outlets for her gentle intentions. She thought she had sent her in a different direction.

Then came the day Patricia suffered an ectopic pregnancy. She would have bled to death, but thirteen-year-old Isabelle saved her.

On that day, Patricia really understood that it wasn't

social suicide for Isabelle to heal people. This gift was worse than that. It could kill her. Patricia's focus changed from what was nice, what was proper, to a much more commanding directive.

No matter what happened, she would save her Isabelle from impending death.

But she hadn't been able to change what she had taught Isabelle. Isabelle believed in helping people, and although she was a good, obedient daughter who tried to make Patricia happy, when push came to shove, she did what she thought was right. That included joining the Chosen Ones. And loving Samuel Faa.

If only Isabelle would call . . .

Then Patricia heard Samuel.

Help Isabelle! Heal Isabelle!

Patricia found herself on her feet.

Isabelle was hurt. Her baby was hurt.

She ran to the window, pushed the curtains as wide as she could.

Deep inside, her body remembered the shift that occurred when Isabelle healed her.

And she gave back.

Samuel held Isabelle's lifeless body up toward the sun, held it until his arms trembled and his legs collapsed. Pulling her in close to him, he held her against his chest and once again tried to push his life force into her.

Nothing happened. No matter how much he pleaded, demanded, wanted, *needed* her to come to life . . . nothing happened.

Dry eyed, he cried. Deep, wrenching sobs that tore at his lungs and sent his muscles into spasms.

She was dead. She was gone. She was beyond his reach, and until the day of his own death, he would never see her again.

And she had sacrificed herself for him.

The Chosen Ones had a myth that deliberate sacrifice compensated for many sins. But what sins had Isabelle committed? She didn't deserve this fate.

He had been the one who sinned. He had wanted to be the sacrifice.

"Take me." He closed his eyes, bent his head over Isabelle's broken body. "Bring her back and take me."

Long moments passed . . . and someone touched his cheek.

Isabelle whispered, "I'm here."

Chapter 54

S amuel froze.

Had he imagined that voice, that touch?

He opened his eyes.

Isabelle lay in his arms, watching him, her face battered, but wearing a crooked smile. "What did you *do*?"

"I . . . I asked for help." He gazed at her, entranced at the sight of Isabelle, always a miracle, but now . . . a miracle in his arms.

She was alive.

Or maybe he was dead.

He looked around.

No. He was still sitting on dock thirty-seven A. The smell was rotting wood and salt water. He saw the sun on the water, the grubby warehouse, the dirty metal door. And in his arms, he felt warmth returning to Isabelle's body. With each breath, her chest rose and fell, and before his eyes, her wounds were healing, leaving her unmarked and with a healthy glow.

"Thank you," she said. "You brought me back to life."

"Me? No." He laughed a little. "I'm no miracle worker. I think . . . it's a case of what goes around comes around. Only this time, it was the good stuff." Leaning over her, he wrapped himself around her, trying to absorb her into his skin, his heart. "What you received was just what you deserved—the best, the kindest, the most generous parts of your soul were given to others, and they gave back to you."

She wrapped one arm around his neck, hugging him in a wild desperation. "Samuel, what happened, happened because of you. You were the lightning rod."

"I hope so." He wanted to laugh. He wanted to cry. He wanted to be worthy of Isabelle. "I hope so."

A man's voice called from the end of the dock. "Samuel!"

Samuel jumped in alarm.

The assassins. The Others. Osgood. This place wasn't safe.

No place was safe. Not for Isabelle.

Even before he looked up, he reached for the pistol.

Big and strong and worried, John Powell stood there, gesturing wildly. "Come on. Come on! We've got to get out of here. Look!" He pointed at the warehouse.

Wisps of smoke were leaking out from around the battered metal door. One yellow flame licked through the wall near the metal roof. Smoke . . . Samuel could smell it, and beneath his knees, he felt a vibration in the wood that signaled a shift on the dock.

As Samuel watched, fire blasted through the warehouse, consuming the old, damp, rotten wood in one greedy gulp. Fire roared toward them, eating the dock from under their feet.

No. The assassins weren't going to kill Isabelle with a fire.

They weren't going to kill her at all.

He knew what to do now. If he acted fast enough, he could protect her.

Isabelle took her gun from him.

Samuel picked her up. He raced toward John, flames licking at his heels. "Have you got a car?" he shouted, and ran toward the street.

"A cab." John fell in behind him. "It's waiting."

"Good man." Samuel glanced at Isabelle, at the gunshot wounds that were not totally healed, at the blood on her clothes.

She was a miracle. She was a lady. She should be eating caviar off silver plates. She should be relaxing on silk sheets.

She should not be running from a fire set to dispose of his body, or holding a gun and scanning the vicinity for enemies. She should most certainly not have to worry about Osgood's scumbags hungering for her blood.

They reached the street.

John sprinted to the cab, held the door open as Samuel, still holding his precious burden, slipped inside.

John followed.

"Richardson Airfield," Samuel told the cabbie. "I pay for speed. We've got a plane to catch."

Isabelle sat between the two men, rubbing her upper arms with her hands.

"Are you cold?" Samuel asked. Did she have a chill? A premonition? An injury?

She put her hands in her lap. "I'm fine."

John waited until the cab had hit the main road and accelerated into traffic. "Where are we going?"

Haunted by a new, desperate torment, Samuel said, "New York City, as fast as we can."

The landing in New York was smooth. Irving's 1952 classic Rolls-Royce Silver Wraith limousine with dark-tinted windows waited on the tarmac. Samuel made sure that he and John served as a shield as Isabelle, now almost completely healed, ran toward it.

As they reached the Rolls, the door opened.

The men shoved Isabelle inside and followed.

Samuel was desperate. He was worried. He was dirty and tired and had stared death in the face. Now the one thing he wanted was to get this over with. They *needed* to get this over with, and as soon as possible.

For Isabelle.

As soon as the door closed, McKenna drove away at a stately rate.

Caleb was there with Jacqueline, Aaron with Rosamund, and John Powell sat alone, his pale blue eyes cool and intense.

The interior was lavish, leather, chrome and exotic woods polished to a luxurious gleam.

"Can you make him hurry?" Samuel gestured toward McKenna in exasperation.

Everyone stared at him as if he were speaking Greek.

All except Rosamund, who *did* speak Greek, and she said, "I haven't really paid a lot of attention, but I don't believe McKenna knows how to hurry."

"It's all right, Samuel." Isabelle put her hand on his. "The limo is bulletproof."

"It's *not* all right. We've got to get there as quickly as possible." Samuel would have gotten out and pushed if he thought it would help. "Are all the Chosen on their way?"

"In different cars. And on the subway. I thought it would be best if we arrived separately." Caleb spoke to Samuel, but his gaze ceaselessly scanned the traffic around them.

Jacqueline bit her lip. "This is so dangerous. My skin is crawling."

Leaning forward, Isabelle patted her hand. "You don't have to go in if you don't want to."

"Yes, I do. Samuel's plan is sound and right. This is something we need to do together." Jacqueline turned her hand over, caught Isabelle's and squeezed, and smiled at her friend. "For you."

In the airplane restroom, Isabelle had washed her hands and face. She had been in there for such a long time, Samuel had been convinced she'd fainted or worse, and been ready to charge in to help her. But she

had come out, smiling mysteriously, and still wearing the black catsuit, torn and stiff with blood.

His blood. Her blood.

Soap and warm water had done wonders for Samuel, too, but his Armani suit had been blasted by two gunshots, and so much blood had soaked his cashmere sweater he smelled like the goat that had donated the wool.

A good look for a corporate meeting.

Actually, considering the circumstances, maybe it was.

"Aleksandr's behind us in a cab." Caleb watched the cab zoom past.

"Now he's ahead of us." Leaning back in his seat, Aaron grinned at Samuel.

Samuel tried to grin back. He really did. But it felt like a grimace.

Isabelle rubbed her upper arms.

He whipped his head around to stare at her. "What's wrong?"

"Nothing, Samuel. I'm fine."

"That's not the first time you've done that. Rubbed your arms."

"They itch. That's all. If that is the least of our worries, we're a happy little group." Her voice grew soothing. "Don't worry. I truly am well, you saved me, and together we can do what must be done."

"Yes." She thought she knew him so well, yet she didn't comprehend the breadth and depth of the conflict that raged within him.

None of the Chosen Ones did. They thought he was vulgar, obnoxious, irritating. They had no idea he used those traits to hide his true character from them . . . and from himself. They had no idea he was weak, easily tempted . . . tainted.

Traffic was impossible, start and stop, cars crammed together, door handle–to–door handle. In other words, typical Manhattan. The lanes slowed even more as they approached Times Square.

Yet for all their stately speed, Samuel's heart pounded as if he were running. Turning his head to look at Isabelle, the miracle beside him, he said passionately, "Once we get this taken care of, I never want you to heal anyone ever again."

Isabelle was quiet. Finally, she said, "We'll talk about that later."

He took a breath to argue.

"Crap!" Caleb thumped his head on the back of his seat.

"What?" Samuel looked around in alarm.

"Charisma is riding her bicycle," Caleb said.

Samuel craned his neck, saw Charisma spin past. "That girl is such a pain in the ass. Ever since she saw the special on New York City messengers, she's been riding that blasted thing all over town. Doesn't she realize how important this is?"

"I think she does." Isabelle's rebuke was clear in her tone.

"In this traffic, she's going to get there sooner than we are," Jacqueline said.

Samuel exchanged glances with the other guys.

Women. They always stuck together.

"Where's Genny?" Rosamund asked.

John glanced at his phone. He smiled the way he always did when he talked about Genny. "She texts that her cab is there, circling the block."

"Then we're all in place." Samuel took a breath as they passed Times Square and headed for SoHo, to the site of the blast that demolished the Gypsy Travel Agency and everything it stood for.

As they reached their destination, Isabelle slid her arm around his shoulders and hugged him. "It's okay, Samuel. This will work."

"If we keep you alive long enough to get you to the meeting," he replied vehemently. Then he shivered in a fear that had nothing to do with his anxiety for her, and everything to do with his own weakness and the secret knowledge that Darren and Patricia were right—he wasn't good enough for Isabelle.

In fact, he wasn't a good man at all.

"I'm alive." Isabelle peered out the window, up at the behemoth rising on the same spot where the Gypsy Travel Agency had had its headquarters. "But I never thought that to stay that way, I'd have to enter the Osgood Building to confront the devil himself."

Chapter 55

⬦

The Chosen Ones merged on the sidewalk across from the construction site. Genny had the cab drop her at the curb. Charisma hurried up, pushing her bike toward McKenna, who took it and put it in the trunk. Aleksandr loped over from the corner. They stood abreast, soldiers facing the field of battle, and looked up. And up.

The Osgood Building was thirty stories and growing. The bottom twenty-five floors were closed in, windowless, gray, and dull.

Yet above them, the largest crane in the history of New York lifted steel beams into place. Metalworkers, yellow hard hats in place, rode the elevators to the top floor, where the framework sketched the outline of the structure to come. Welders sparked and the rhythmic blasts of riveters created acoustic bedlam.

On the ground, front loaders roared, delivering material from one spot to another, and like some bizarre trim on a dirt cake, a dozen blue Porta Potties lined the perimeter of chain-link fence.

Office workers scurried through the pitted, filthy site in plywood tunnels built to protect them from dropped tools or, more ominously, the wall frames that were giving form to the offices.

"Is that legal," Genny asked, "to have the building open at the same time it's being constructed?"

"No." Aleksandr, Caleb, and Jacqueline spoke at the same time.

John added, "But Osgood gets what Osgood wants."

"His power is growing," Jacqueline said.

Samuel didn't know if she was having a vision or simply stating the obvious fact.

John assumed the leadership mantle he wore so effortlessly. "All right, we're going in. McKenna, stay close. Park, or circle the block. We may need you and we know we can depend on you to be there in a minute."

"Yes, sir, you can." McKenna's brogue was strong and steady.

"McKenna, don't forget—drive carefully for my bike's sake." Charisma smiled prettily.

"As opposed to the way I drive when it's merely you I'm transporting." McKenna glared in Celtic exasperation. Returning to the Rolls, he opened the door and said, "I think I speak for Mr. Shea and Martha when I say . . . this is as brave an act as any Chosen have ever done, and it has been a privilege to work with all of you." Getting in, he closed the door and drove away.

The Chosen Ones exchanged glances.

"Some people might think that sounded like farewell," Charisma said.

"Just in case we weren't scared enough," Aleksandr said.

"We would have to be fools not to be scared." Isabelle spoke in a low voice, reminding them of what they already knew. "For years, Osgood has been the vague, shadowy power behind every corrupt operation on the East Coast from Florida to Maine. His was the name whispered in the night, the man no one ever saw, a myth to scare children, and now"—she gestured up at the building slicing like a razor blade into the blue winter sky—"he's no longer anonymous. He has so much power, he feels indestructible."

"Personally, I'm terrified," Samuel said.

A ripple of nervous laughter went through the group.

They thought he was joking to lighten the mood.

He was not.

"Stick together." John pinned them, one by one, his gaze a slap of cool good sense. "Be strong. Be swift— we want to get in and out before the sun sets. Stay close to Isabelle."

"I'm fine, John," she assured him. Assured them. She clasped Samuel's hand, reminding him of the battle he had steadfastly fought and so far won . . . reminding him why he fought that battle.

"We intend that you should stay fine," John answered. "Please don't forget—stick together."

"You said *'stick together'* twice," Rosamund pointed out.

"That's the important one. We are the Chosen Ones. When we are shoulder-to-shoulder, we're invincible. But we're only as strong as our weakest link." John's gaze lingered on Samuel.

John had come back to the Chosen through an anguished, torturous path. He must suspect the truth about Samuel.

Samuel looked him in the eyes, put his hand on Isabelle's shoulder. "I have my reason to remain as one with the Chosen."

John was worried. All too obviously, he was worried. But he nodded, then started across the street.

With Isabelle in the middle, protected by their bodies, the Chosen Ones followed.

The gate into the construction site was their first hurdle. The guard didn't want to let them in without proper ID.

Using a little mind control, Samuel convinced him they had proper ID.

They joined the other office workers in the tunnels, who eyed them oddly.

But nothing was said. In fact, the office workers didn't speak to the Chosen Ones or one another.

It was quiet. It was grim.

"This is spooky." The atmosphere must have been weighing on Aleksandr, for he spoke with a tense conviction that caught Samuel's attention.

Samuel gave him a sharp look.

The kid was still too thin, and his eyes were haunted.

Again Samuel resolved to have a talk with him . . . as soon as this was over. As soon as Isabelle was safe from assassination.

Isabelle . . . She moved easily, the signs of her ordeal diminishing every moment. But she examined Osgood's people as if their existence made her uneasy.

Samuel put his hand on her waist. Leaning close, he said, "I'm not going to let them get you."

"I know, Samuel." She wore her faith in him serenely.

She understood him so well. She thought she had seen the worst of him.

But she didn't understand the test he now faced. Why would she? She had never faced the frustrations of his life. She had never hungered for *more*, hungered for . . . everything.

Genny stopped, stared at the plywood-covered entrance, at the construction sign scrawled in black Magic Marker that proclaimed this the Osgood Building. "This is so obviously unfinished, I feel sorry for the staff."

Samuel and Aaron opened the glass doors sheathed in plywood. "We'll worry about them another time," Samuel said. "For now, let's get this done as quickly as possible."

Charisma stepped through to the lobby.

He heard her gasp.

Crap! What now?

Aleksandr rushed in close on her heels. He stopped. "Wow. Cool."

Jacqueline bumped into him. "I didn't expect this," she said.

"Who would?" Caleb pushed them inside.

Isabelle walked through the door.

Genny and John trailed after. "You have to be kidding," John said.

Rosamund said, "How exciting!"

Samuel exchanged glances with Aaron, and they walked in, letting the doors close behind them.

The lobby was nothing like Samuel expected.

It was lavish, stylish, complete in every way, from the elegant milk-white marble columns that grew treelike out of the ice-white marble floor, to the gold-embellished chandeliers that sparkled with crystal splendor, to the polished white stone benches that lined the walls.

No way it should be here. Not yet. For how could this have been built and decorated so quickly and without interference? Osgood used the slipshod exterior to disguise his masterpiece, to hide this demonstration of power over city inspectors, politicians, laws, artists . . . and time itself.

The splendor and the glory made Samuel's mouth water.

But he ignored his envy and walked to the guard at the elevators. "Tell Osgood we're here."

"Do you have an appointment, sir?" The guard— Elvin, according to his name badge—watched him coldly.

"Tell Osgood the Chosen Ones are here to speak with him." Samuel kept his gaze firmly on the guard, wordlessly commanding him.

The guard didn't move.

John took his place at Samuel's side. "Osgood will want to know that we're here. Are you going to tell him you turned us away?"

"I would not—if I believed you were the Chosen Ones," Elvin said, his scorn both biting and obvious.

John laughed, leaned across the podium, and opened his frosty blue eyes wide. "I could crush you like a bug."

He wasn't using his considerable power, yet Elvin shook as if he'd been exposed to an icy wind. His hand slipped down to the holster at his belt. Cautiously, he stepped back, fingering the safety on his pistol as he pushed the button for the elevators. He got in, pushed another button, and as the doors closed, he kept his gaze fixed on them.

"I guess you don't call up to Osgood's office," Genny said wryly.

The Chosen and their mates spread across the lobby.

Rosamund found her way to the centerpiece, a dark granite plaque and a mural in stone three feet high, running the length of the lobby. With the lack of caution that characterized her when she studied, she walked along it, scrutinizing each panel, her brow furrowed with fascination.

Aaron followed close at her side, watching her unwary back, protecting her.

Clearly the mural told a story in pictures, although Samuel didn't have the urge or the curiosity to look. He was busy watching Isabelle as she rubbed her arms, up and down, up and down.

What is wrong with her arms?

Charisma sat on one of the benches, her hands beside her and flat on the stone. Lifting one hand, she placed it on the column, smoothing the marble as if communicating with the stone.

Aleksandr stood apart, hands in his pockets, head down.

Again Samuel looked around the amazing, luxurious lobby. He scrutinized Osgood's staff as they walked back and forth, got into and out of elevators—although never the one the guard had used—looked at clipboards and computers. "They remind me of something," he said.

At once Isabelle said, "This is the flip side of the Gypsy Travel Agency."

"The flip side . . ." Samuel muttered.

She was right. He had seen people like this before, exuberant, interested, at the Gypsy Travel Agency.

Now he was here, in some ghastly negative of that organization. These people, these office workers, were special, knowledgeable, passionate. They spoke dead languages, carried ancient manuscripts, looked interested in their jobs.

Osgood had superimposed his own order on the site where the Chosen Ones had fallen.

Once again, Samuel's flesh crept in horror . . . and in fascination.

He had to be careful here. So careful.

Here there was no hiding from himself. Here he would face his true nature.

Would he have the strength he needed to deny it?

Genny observed the workers. "They carry in them the seeds of their own downfall."

John put his arm around his wife's waist. "What do you mean?"

"Can't you see it?" Genny leaned against him as if needing the comfort of closeness.

"I can," Isabelle said. "These people . . . they're the antiquities experts. They're the dead-language graduates. They're artists and writers. They were unemployed."

"Or asking customers if they wanted fries with that," Genny said. "The economy's in a downturn, and out of the clear blue sky, they got a great job offer for fabulous wages doing what they love. It seems too good to be true. They realize there are discrepancies, things that are odd, like working in a building while it's under construction, but they'd be fools not to grab any employment, much less a cushy job like this."

"Most of them haven't got a clue what they have gotten themselves into." Isabelle's eyes filled with tears. "They can never escape."

Charisma rolled her bracelets up and down her arms, pressing the stones too hard and leaving marks on her skin. "That's right, Isabelle, but how did you know?"

"I can feel the pull of a wounded earth, of a thousand souls waiting to be broken and damned. I want to heal them all." Isabelle kneaded her upper arms as if they ached. "And I know I can't."

Samuel looked at her. To the casual eye, she looked normal, healed completely, but what she was saying . . . that was new. That was different. She had returned to the land of the living as the same being, but she was changed, and he could see the frailty in her.

She worried him. He must save her, and yet . . . would he have the strength?

She didn't know about him. She didn't know—and if she had realized the truth, she would never have rescued him from death.

Jacqueline shivered. "I feel a vision pulling at me, and I know I shouldn't give in, for I fear I would never find my way out."

"Be careful, Samuel," Isabelle warned. "Don't use your mind control again."

"Yeah, because"—he remembered the message Dina had thrust into his mind weeks ago—"there are traps to catch power like mine."

Dina . . . Was she still alive somewhere? Had she escaped Osgood's vengeance?

Samuel hoped so. She might be one of the Others and wicked as any witch, but her bone-deep love had kept Irving alive, and Irving's search for her had motivated him through hours of agonizing physical therapy. The old man wanted to do more than survive—he wanted to find Dina, and for that, he needed to be mobile, articulate, and alert.

Samuel waved John close, spoke softly. "No matter what happens, no one should use their gift here."

"Great," John said.

Samuel understood the sarcasm. For what if this venture went awry? They carried no weapons, only their wits and their gifts.

The elevator opened. The guard stepped out. He pointed at Isabelle. "Only you."

Samuel stepped up to stand with her. "She doesn't go without me."

"Only you," the guard repeated to Isabelle.

Isabelle laughed, a chime of merriment that dismissed the guard's authority. "We've proved ourselves to be foolhardy enough to face Osgood on his own ground. Is he afraid of us *here*?"

The guard hesitated. Put his finger to his ear as if listening—but he wore no earpiece. Yet he nodded as if to some inner counsel. "All right." He pointed at Samuel. "You can go up, too." He held the elevator doors open.

Isabelle stepped inside. Samuel followed.

The elevator doors shut, and the elevator rose.

At least, Samuel thought it rose. He didn't experience the sensation of motion. The interior was utterly silent. No Muzak, no mechanical noises, no ding of the bell as they passed floors. If they passed floors. They could have been standing still, as far as Samuel could tell.

He looked at Isabelle and lifted his eyebrows.

She whispered, *"Indiana Jones and the Cone of Silence."*

He laughed softly and took her hand. "Are you frightened?"

"Yes."

"I am, too." He thought of the white marble lobby, the gold embellishments, the beauty and the power it all demonstrated. "This place holds a fatal attraction for me."

Chapter 56

"*What?*" Isabelle's head whipped around. She stared at Samuel in consternation.

Without warning, the doors opened.

He pressed her hand in support.

They stepped out into a large, empty, dimly lit office.

But not quite empty; in the corner was a gray steel desk.

They walked toward it.

A green-shaded desk light shone on the surface. In the chair sat a man: scrawny, unimpressive, his eyes a dark glitter in an unilluminated face. They could clearly see his pen, a platinum Montblanc, and his hands as he signed documents, one after another, and those hands were thin-skinned, liver-spotted, with the raised veins and swollen joints of an elderly man.

They reached the desk.

The hands stopped signing. The man looked up.

"Mr. Osgood?" Samuel asked.

"That's right." His voice was gentle, with a vague Southern drawl.

Isabelle positioned herself directly in front of him. "How disconcerting to realize such a soft-spoken, frail-looking gentleman bears so much evil within him."

Samuel swallowed a gasp. He hadn't expected that Isabelle would go on the attack.

Apparently Osgood was surprised, too, for his hands stilled. He blinked, and again Samuel saw the dark glint of his eyes. "It's a gift, Miss Mason." He smiled, but that smile held no comfort, no warmth, no humanity. Osgood's smile was a cruelty, a hint of the torment in store.

A piece of art had been sculpted into the wall, an amazing likeness of two men and one woman struggling in a death agony, fighting to escape from the wall that had trapped them in place. It was a sample of hell aptly demonstrated by an artist whose skill surpassed talent.

Disturbed, intent on finishing their business as soon as possible, Samuel stared into Osgood's shadowed face. "A contract was taken out by Todd Winstead on Miss Mason with your corporation. The contract was fulfilled."

"And yet she stands before me." The smooth voice was politely incredulous.

"This morning she died," Samuel said.

"As we know through our theology, death is, of course, not the end, but I find that someone who has recently left this life doesn't, er, breathe and speak and move. Miss Mason's clothing appears to have taken more damage than she has." Osgood's head turned toward Samuel. "As have yours. So you'll pardon me if I don't believe—"

Isabelle leaned across the desk and placed her hand on his.

The physical interruption made Osgood freeze.

Samuel wanted to yank her hand away. *What is she doing?*

Osgood's eyes flared, no longer dark, but blue and hot as coals. "You cannot heal me, Miss Mason."

"No, I can't." Her voice pitied him. "But you can feel the truth, can't you? You have powers far greater than mine. I am alive, yet this morning I was dead. The contract has been fulfilled."

"Yes." His voice ground with irritation and malice. "I can feel that."

"You're bound by eternal rules not of your making. So call off your dogs."

"It's done." As if her touch burned him, Osgood pulled his hand out from under hers. "You will have no more trouble with assassins from my organization."

"From any organization," she insisted.

Yes, Isabelle knew enough to carefully examine Osgood's promise and close the loophole there.

"How can I guarantee that?" Osgood asked.

"Your assassins gave me to know that your organization did not allow for competition in their territory," Samuel told him.

Osgood glanced at the wall. "Of course they did. Very well." He wearily waved that fragile-looking hand. "I'll let it be known that I would take it ill should you suffer an injury from an assassin."

Samuel started to insist on more assurances.

But Osgood said, "No. That is as far as I am forced to go. Miss Mason might, after all, sustain an injury or lose her life in the ridiculously wild activities the Chosen Ones believe necessary to justify their existence."

Isabelle widened her eyes. "We don't know what you mean."

Osgood snorted softly.

For the first time since she had returned to him, miraculously alive again, Samuel could breathe again. *This* was what he had come for. With Osgood's capitulation, Samuel's mission was complete.

Isabelle was safe.

But Osgood wasn't finished with them yet. The blue flames faded from his eyes, but in a voice rich with malice, he said, "Mr. Faa, I see you are in good health."

"Very good health, thank you."

"My employees reported to me that they'd killed you. I was displeased." Osgood gestured toward the wall, toward the horrific sculpture.

In a flash, Samuel realized why the faces looked so real.

He'd last seen them, alive and vicious, on dock thirty-seven A. The Other, the man with the pistol and deadly aim, and Shrimp, frozen in his last agony . . . or was the agony ongoing?

This wasn't art. This was torture.

"Mr. Faa, I have long watched you with interest." Osgood leaned back in his chair, his face deep in shadow, and played with his pen, a hypnotizing motion. "There's a place for you in my organization. As lead counsel to my law team, you would make great contributions to our development. Rather than the pitiful existence you now live, chasing after lost children and comforting broken old men . . ."

He let the sentence dangle, but Isabelle heard the unspoken words: *Broken old men like Irving Shea.*

Why was Samuel letting him get away with such an insult to the elderly gentleman who had been so good to them?

Osgood continued. "You, Mr. Faa, could have wealth beyond your imaginings, the authority of life and death over thousands, the freedom to use your gift as you wished whenever you wished."

Isabelle was mesmerized by the pen, spinning slowly around and around in the light shining on the desk, and by the power Osgood projected.

"Mr. Faa, that proposition is appealing to you, is it not?" Osgood asked.

When Samuel didn't answer, alarm gave her the strength to turn away from Osgood and look at Samuel.

He stood motionless, watching the pen with a fierce intensity.

And she remembered what he had said in the elevator. *This place holds a fatal attraction for me.*

Of course. As a child, Samuel had been beaten down

time and again—by the circumstances of his birth, by the woman who raised him, by Darren, even by Patricia, working in defense of her daughter. All his life, Samuel had craved power, and in that pursuit he had been clawing his way to the top of the legal profession.

Then the Chosen Ones had happened. Forced to join, he'd been one of seven, struggling against impossible odds, without influence or income of his own.

This place holds a fatal attraction for me.

She wanted to reach out to him, to tell him no.

But she couldn't move, couldn't speak.

Because Osgood had somehow used his powers to leave her unable to move, to speak?

Or because she knew this was a decision Samuel had to make on his own?

"I signed a contract with the Chosen Ones." Samuel's voice sounded far away, as if he had sunk inside himself far beyond her reach.

"Mr. Faa, I comprehend your concerns and admire your integrity. You think of your vow to the Chosen Ones, the contract you signed." Osgood sounded as if he were Samuel's best friend, and still he turned the pen around and around. "But you didn't want to sign that contract. The Gypsy Travel Agency board of directors blackmailed you. You're a lawyer. You know a contract entered into under duress would never stand up in court. And why should it? It's not legally binding."

"I've always known that." Still Samuel used that quiet, subdued voice.

"You signed that contract because you would have

gone to prison if you hadn't. At the time, you truly had no choice, and I'm appalled that an organization that touted itself as the bastion of goodness and defender of the weak would stoop to such behavior." Osgood sounded indignant on Samuel's behalf.

"It was the cause of their downfall," Samuel said.

"Exactly! Yet now, the Gypsy Travel Agency is gone. The proof of your influence on that witness—which, let us remember, you performed in the pursuit of goodness and justice—is gone." Osgood lifted one hand to toss the image of the Gypsy Travel Agency away. The other hand spun the pen in slow, constant motion.

"It is gone," Samuel agreed.

Now Isabelle knew what to say. "The Gypsy Travel Agency was not a faceless *thing*. It was an organization filled with people, and they're gone, Osgood, because you killed them."

Beside her, Samuel stirred.

Osgood turned on her and snapped, "That was never proved."

Had she broken the spell he had cast over Samuel? *Could* she? "So you deny you caused the explosion that destroyed the Gypsy Travel Agency, with its repository of knowledge, ancient texts, and artifacts? You deny killing hundreds of people in your pursuit of dominance?"

"Please, Osgood, let me answer for you." Samuel looked at her, his eyes as black and shiny as obsidian, and in a tone she'd never heard from him before, in the tone of a ruthless, immoral lawyer, he said, "Look at Osgood.

He's old, he's thin, he's feeble. He's a businessman. To accuse him of anything else is mere supposition."

"Samuel!" She held out her hand to him.

He stepped away. "Let Osgood finish."

Her heart pounded in dismay.

"Mr. Faa, you've just proved my theory correct. You would make an excellent counselor for my organization. And the power you would wield! You would be second only to me in strength, in authority, in influence. You would be my face to the world. You would own New York City. You would direct every operation already in place, expand into new territory. Men would cower at the sound of your voice." Pale, quiescent, Osgood coiled in his chair like a huge python whose prey was willingly walking into his maw. "And women . . . ah, women. I feel your desires. I understand them. No one understands better than me. You love women. Pretty women, young women."

Osgood's gloating gaze touched Isabelle.

Repulsed, she stepped back.

"Think of the women who would come to you, beg you for favors, offer you anything, adore you, please you in every way you could ever imagine. . . . You would be a god, long-lived, vigorous, commanding the loyalty of all you touched." Osgood allowed his voice to trail off, waiting for his words to work their magic.

Isabelle wanted time to go backward. She wanted never to have come here. She would rather spend her life in hiding from Osgood's assassins than to face . . . this.

This isn't worth it. Having my life back isn't worth it if I leave Samuel behind.

I can't *leave Samuel behind.*

"Mr. Faa"—Osgood's pen spun—"let me say a final word to dismiss any lingering doubts you might have. The Chosen Ones and the Others are simply flip sides of the coin. Members have been defecting in both directions for time immemorial."

At last Samuel stirred. He smiled, that toothy lawyer-shark smile Isabelle despised. He looked up from the pen, into Osgood's eyes. "You're very persuasive. You say all the right words, push all the right buttons. I do long for power and glory. There's not a doubt in my mind that I could run New York City better than it is run now. I do love women, all women, everything about them."

Samuel's words made Isabelle sick. He was succumbing to temptation.

What could she do? She had to stop him.

Somehow, she had to make him realize that this was a betrayal of all that he was, all he had pledged himself to be.

He took Isabelle's hands. "But only one woman holds my heart. If I took your offer, Osgood, I couldn't have Isabelle, and without her, what good would wealth and power do me?"

Isabelle's head buzzed. She took a good, deep breath, the first she had taken since Osgood had addressed Samuel. And her eyes cleared.

She should never have doubted him.

Samuel had made the right decision.

He was hers.

The pen stopped. The voice froze. "Touching, Mr. Faa. Very touching." The voice warmed and enticed once more. "For you, I could possibly bend the rules and influence Miss Mason to stay at your side."

Isabelle stilled in terror. She had thought Samuel was Osgood's prey. Now she realized that if Samuel failed this test, she would be the one who vanished.

She should never have worried.

Samuel lifted her hand to his mouth and kissed it, and smiled at her. "If she were influenced to stay with me, she would not be Isabelle. I only want her if she wants me."

"Samuel . . ." she whispered, her eyes filling with tears.

"You must be very proud of yourself, Miss Mason." Osgood's gaze sliced over her.

"No." She squeezed the fingers that held hers, and cleared her throat. "I'm proud of Samuel."

Osgood stood. "Very well. If our business is concluded, I'll walk you back down to the lobby. I'm sure your friends are anxious about you."

"Yes," Samuel said. "It's time to leave."

"Before you're further tempted by my offer?" Osgood asked.

"No." Samuel gave a jaw-cracking yawn. "Before I fall asleep right here. Remember, I was up all night fighting assassins."

"And Miss Mason was healing your wounds. Quite the miracle workers you two are." As Osgood moved into the room, they could see him clearly, a frail elderly man with a receding hairline, a receding chin, and brown eyes that to Isabelle seemed unremarkable— until he turned them on her, and she shivered. Walking around his desk to a door hidden in the wall, he opened it and gestured them inside. "If you're up for a little exercise, we'll walk down."

At first, Isabelle didn't understand why they took the winding spiral staircase. Then, as they descended, she saw them. Faces, like the faces in his office, struggling against the white marble, dying in agony, trying to escape . . .

The walls in this building were cemeteries.

And Osgood wanted them to see.

Chapter 57

———◆———

Osgood opened a narrow door set in a hidden panel in the wall of the lobby. "Here you are, Miss Mason, Mr. Faa. I hope we meet again one day under different circumstances."

"Very different circumstances." Isabelle offered her hand, wanting to touch him once more, to feel what she had felt before.

She knew that information was important.

He ignored her gesture—because he didn't want her to know him better? He turned his head as if listening to something, then walked out of the stairwell and into the corridor.

Samuel and Isabelle exchanged glances, and followed.

As they stepped into the lobby, Isabelle saw the Chosen Ones gathered around the long plaque that decorated the lobby, and from the midst of the group, she heard Rosamund's voice loud and clear.

"In the mural," she said, "in these two panels, we see Lucifer's expulsion from heaven, his fall toward earth, and how his angel wings peeled away during his fiery descent."

The group murmured and shuffled forward, their gazes fixed on another panel, looking for all the world like a group of tourists spellbound by their guide.

Rosamund continued. "Here we see how he completed his descent to hell and set himself up as lord of the wicked."

The group murmured and shuffled again.

"Most interesting of all, because this is a part of the tale I've never heard before, here Lucifer exults as he entombs the final surviving feather from his angel wings in the building's foundation." Rosamund's voice rose questioningly. "It looks like this building. Is that right, Wendy?"

A strange woman's voice answered her. "Yes, it's this building. See? Here Lucifer—who, by the way, looks *incredibly* like our boss—clearly believes that the wing makes the building invincible. Which, according to my research, it should!"

Who was this Wendy? One of Osgood's corporate librarians? One of his researchers?

Isabelle glanced at Osgood. He stood frozen, listening without emotion or any apparent flicker of interest.

She knew that wasn't true.

Whoever the woman was, she was giving information freely, without thought to the consequences.

Or perhaps she was so like Rosamund, she never imagined that consequences for providing knowledge could even exist.

The group moved again to allow everyone a good look at the carvings, and for the first time Isabelle saw the stranger. Although Wendy was an older female with bobbed gray hair, she bore a marked similarity to Rosamund in her boundless enthusiasm and her knowledge of the arcane.

"According to *my* research"—Rosamund's eyes snapped with excitement—"and that research is confined to only one source—"

Wendy's eyes narrowed. "A good source?"

Rosamund nodded. "So far, I've been unable to document the texts back any further than the late 1950s, but I'm following a lead into the ancient Abyssinian texts—"

"Darling." Aaron placed his hand on Rosamund's shoulder to recall her to the subject. "You can talk with your new librarian friend about sources and research trails *later*. Right now, we're all hanging on your words. What is it that you think you know?"

She flashed him a warm smile, then turned to her audience. "According to my source, there were *two* feathers that were torn from Lucifer's wings as he fell in flames into hell. If this is true, and one went into the foundation of this building, then what can the Chosen Ones do should they find and retrieve the second one?"

"That is absolutely fabulous information," Wendy

said in excitement. "Because there's another source—again undocumented—that says that whoever possesses angel feathers and faith should be able to—"

Apparently Samuel decided they'd said enough, for he called, "Isn't anybody going to pat us on the back for our success?"

As one, the Chosen Ones turned. En masse, they swept toward Samuel and Isabelle.

Charisma and Jacqueline hugged her. Rosamund jumped up and down and clapped her hands. Aaron hugged her, then pounded Samuel on the back. Caleb pounded Samuel on the back. Genny hugged him and laughed delightedly.

As the Chosen Ones surged around them, Isabelle glanced toward the spot where Osgood had stood.

He had vanished.

She saw the door to the stairway close. She breathed a long sigh of relief.

She was so happy to see him go.

Wendy stood watching in puzzlement. "What did you think would happen up there? You act as if your life were in jeopardy."

The Chosen Ones exchanged glances.

"What?" Wendy looked from one to another. "Mr. Osgood is a very learned and erudite man. His knowledge of ancient writings is unique in the business world!"

"He is most definitely unique." Isabelle rubbed her arms again.

Rosamund turned to Wendy. "Would you like to go

with us? To our headquarters? We could use another researcher!"

"No! Why would I do that?" Osgood's staff member was clearly befuddled by Rosamund's invitation. "This employment is by far the best I've ever had. There are few positions for librarians with my expertise. Most people think what I do is unimportant."

"It's not. What you know will save the world—or destroy it." Blunt as always, Rosamund said, "Come with us. It's not safe to stay here."

"Are you mad?" Wendy gestured at the vast lobby, the gold and marble and crystal. "Who did you say you were?"

"Don't you get it? We're the Chosen Ones," Rosamund said. "Well, not me, exactly, but my husband and these other people—"

"Come on, darling." Aaron urged her away. In a low voice, he said, "You can't save her."

Rosamund looked around, realized the Chosen were moving toward the door, and called, "It's been good speaking with you, Wendy. Good luck to you. . . . If you change your mind . . ."

"Of course." Wendy backed away. "Good luck with your search for the second . . . feather. . . ." She looked around, suddenly nervous, wiped her damp hands on her pants. "I'll go back to work now."

"That poor woman," Isabelle said in a low voice.

Samuel wrapped his arm around her waist and swept her toward the door. "Yes. That poor woman. But she has made her choice." He lowered his voice.

"Now let's get out of here. Osgood will keep his word, but when you stand in a hornet's nest, sooner or later you're going to be stung."

Once outside, John pulled out his phone and called McKenna.

When they reached the street, the Rolls was waiting. They climbed inside, all of them, and as Aaron was shutting the door, McKenna pulled away from the curb.

"Take the long way around, McKenna," John instructed. "We have business to conduct." He sat on one side of the car and scrutinized the neighborhood and the traffic.

Aaron sat at the rear and did the same.

Caleb, always on alert, observed everything around them as they left SoHo.

Isabelle drew a sigh of relief. They were safe. At last, they were safe.

Turning on her, Samuel took her shoulders and shook her. "Woman! What did you think you were doing in there?"

Chapter 58

Isabelle blinked in astonishment and offense. "I beg your pardon?"

"You touched Osgood. You snapped at Osgood. The man holds the devil in his soul, and you faced off with him without a lick of sense!" Samuel was shouting at her.

He was *shouting* at her.

She pointed a finger into his face and shouted back. "Are you trying to insinuate that I didn't know what I was facing? Have you not noticed what we do on a regular basis? I know the evil that exists in the world. I confront it every day. But I don't choose to look only at that. I choose to remember the bravery I see around me and emulate it."

"I don't want you to do that!"

"Samuel, you're an idiot," Aaron murmured.

"Don't you talk to me that way, Samuel Faa. It's not about what you want. It's about our mission and what we, all of us"—she gestured around the car—"choose to accomplish. I did what I had to do. I wanted to get out of there with the contract finished, and for that he needed to touch me to know I had died."

Samuel started to speak.

She talked over the top of him. "Furthermore, I was not going to leave you behind. Ever. So it's a good thing you decided to come with me, because I would have hated to have to add to my offenses by knocking you out and dragging you downstairs!"

McKenna listened to the delighted laughter as his passengers urged Isabelle on. Glancing in the rearview mirror at the high fives, Irving's man-of-all-trades asked, "Who would have thought the seven inexperienced Chosen I picked up off this very street almost three years ago would have ever been able to face Lucifer himself?"

Samuel looked around at the odd group of people he had come to think of as family. "It's a miracle," he said dryly.

Isabelle kissed him. And kissed him again.

"All right. That's true. I haven't the right to deny you your work." He leaned close and looked into her eyes. "But listen to me. Don't ever frighten me like that again. Don't challenge the devil on his own turf. My heart can't take the stress—and I can't live without you."

She was startled to see tears in his eyes. Cupping his face in her hands, she said, "Oh, Samuel. I love you so much. I promise to be at your side . . . always."

"You'll marry me." It wasn't a question.

"I will," she said.

As she went in for another kiss, Charisma stuck her hand between their faces. "None of that! Not yet! Tell us what happened."

Isabelle relaxed back against the seat and, as New York City glided by at a stately pace, she let Samuel tell the story, and smiled at him when he emphasized the way she dealt with Osgood and forgot to mention Osgood's offer to him, and how he refused temptation.

"So you two are together, in love forever." Aleksandr leaned forward, rubbing his palms together nervously. "You both faced your greatest fear and conquered it. Has the prophecy worked as it should? Were your talents enhanced? Did you get your marks?"

The interior of the car grew quiet. All eyes fixed on Samuel and Isabelle.

Samuel gestured for Isabelle to go first.

"Usually when I touch someone who needs healing, I feel their wounds, their pain. I touched Osgood—and I felt his soul like a living thing." She looked at her hand, surprised that the skin had not scorched. "Osgood the man has always been dark, treacherous, exulting in vice, lies and deception, endlessly seeking power, and he found what he wanted when he invited the devil to share his body, to do evil works through him. It was the perfect melding of man and demon, and now the two beings are so intertwined . . . Lucifer is like a cancer, sending tendrils into Osgood's soul, corrupting an already black and wicked creature." She looked around at her friends, reluctant to impart the bad news, but knowing it must be done. "Always in the past, the being that worked the devil's will on earth was human, and could be destroyed. Frankly, at this point, I don't know that Osgood *can* be killed."

"I'd like to give it a try," Caleb said.

"You think Osgood's body has been made immortal by Lucifer's attachment to him?" Remembering those faces frozen forever in the walls of the Osgood Building, Samuel felt fear like a lump in his stomach.

"I'm giving you my impression, and the gift is new to me. I could be wrong," Isabelle said.

"Genny?" John turned to his wife, who, although she was not Chosen, saw their gifts with a special vision.

"I've always perceived Isabelle's gift in her touch. But now it clings to her . . . for lack of a better word, her aura." Genny studied Isabelle. "It's greater, more inclusive. Before, she healed with her hands. Now she sees with them, too."

Isabelle nodded. "Yes! That's what it feels like. Later, Osgood was so reluctant to shake my hand—he was hiding something because he knew I could *feel* him."

"Before he left us, you tried to touch him. I can't *believe* you tried to touch him." Samuel's voice rose again.

Isabelle turned to him. "Do you have something to say?"

He took several deep breaths. "Yes. You said you'll marry me?"

"I will."

"Will you forgive me, too?"

"For yelling at me about Osgood?"

"For using my mind control on you. For forcing you to tell Benedikta Vos's location, for not knowing how betrayed you would feel, for thinking that the ends justify the means."

"Oh." She dropped her gaze and some of that billowing elation faded. "That."

"It was wrong."

"Do you really mean it?" When he would have reassured her, she waved him to silence. "I mean, do you understand in your heart that manipulating me was wrong?"

"I am not naturally a good man. I am wicked to the core of my soul." Obviously, he really believed that. "But I do learn, and after I was through being resentful that you had left me for no good reason, I wondered why I loved a woman who was so unreasonable . . . and that made me remember that you weren't unreasonable. Which made me think you at least believed you had left for a just cause."

She lifted her eyebrows. "Believed?"

"That hurt me. And I hated it. But I didn't want to ask myself if *I* thought your reasons were just. I was afraid to face that realization, so I put that off as long as I could. But you didn't come back. And I was miserable." He flushed. "So I asked myself how I would react if someone had taken over my mind for whatever reason and—"

A ripple of laughter slipped through the car.

Samuel broke off.

Isabelle glared around at her friends. "This is important! Would you mind at least pretending you're not listening?"

A few coughs. Gazes averted. The only sound the humming motor and muted street noise.

She focused on Samuel. "Go on."

To her surprise, he set his chin and kept talking. "I hated the idea of someone doing something so high-handed, so superior, so lacking in respect for me as a person. I treated you like a foolish child. I insulted you at the very base of your being. Mind you, I still think you were wrong—"

She lifted her eyebrows.

Caleb groaned softly.

"But *when we're married*"—Samuel emphasized the phrase—"that will happen all the time."

John made an *airplane-crashing-to-the-ground* noise.

Isabelle glared at their audience again.

Eyes averted again.

She asked, "What will you do when you *think* I'm wrong?"

"I'll try to convince you that I'm right . . . with my words."

"Score!" Charisma pumped her hand, then ducked her head and pretended to be examining her bracelets.

Isabelle was so pleased, she wanted to cry. She wanted to dance. She wanted to make love with him until the world melted away and only Samuel and Isabelle were left.

He got it. He truly got it.

Taking his hands, she asked, "Do you really think you're wicked?"

"Every day, I fight the temptation to use my mind control to get what I want—and I want everything. So yeah, I'm wicked."

"I want everything, too, so I guess I'm wicked along with you." She slid her hands up his arms to his shoulders and smiled into his face. "Besides, do you really think a reasonable woman like me would love a wicked man like you?"

He smiled right back. "I don't think you can resist me."

Genny groaned.

"He was doing so well," McKenna called back conversationally.

"Sooner or later, Samuel is going to revert to being Samuel," Jacqueline said.

Isabelle didn't care what they said or did. She laughed softly and kissed his lips. "No, I never could resist you, Samuel Faa. And I trust you with my heart *and* my mind, forever and always."

Always quick to follow up an advantage, he asked, "When will you marry me?"

Carefully she untangled herself from him. Taking a fiendish delight, she answered, "When my mother has arranged the wedding."

He slammed his head against the back of the seat. "No!"

Charisma clasped her hands. "Oh, boy!"

"A real wedding will be good for the group." Aaron didn't mind. He liked dressing up like James Bond.

"Heh, heh." Caleb smirked at Samuel. "You're stuck now."

"You know *you'll* have to wear a tux," Jacqueline said.

"Ha!" Samuel looked at his male friends. "You'll all have to wear tuxes. I intend to make sure of it."

"It'll give Irving something to look forward to," Isabelle said. "So suck it up, all of you. Especially you, Samuel. You deserve every bit of torture my mother can devise."

"I thought you loved me," he said.

Okay, he was whining.

"If I didn't love you, I'd marry Senator Noble."

"If you married him, you'd never get laid again."

"That's the other reason I'm not marrying Senator Noble." She flirted with her eyes. "I like sex . . . with you."

McKenna coughed reprovingly. The car swerved.

Outside, horns blared and a cabdriver beside them rolled down his window and shouted.

"Right." John ruthlessly brought them back on track. Turning to Rosamund, he said, "If you would, please, research this turn of events, find out if it's possible that Osgood has become—or could become—immortal."

"Of course." Rosamund loved to research, but she didn't look happy now. She huddled against Aaron as if the winter's chill had seeped into the car.

"I'll try to encourage a vision," Jacqueline said.

"Any information you can get from a vision or from your mother would be appreciated," John said.

Aleksandr turned to Isabelle. "So you have had your gift enhanced in a *really* scary way."

"Yeah, thanks for putting it like that," Isabelle said.

Driven by some need, he said, "You didn't have a mark. Did you get one?"

"Two." Once again, she put her hands protectively to her upper arms.

"Really?" Obviously intrigued, Samuel faced her. "What are they?"

"It's weird. You know that symbol of the medical profession? The rod with the two snakes twined around it?"

"That's the caduceus," Rosamund, ever the librarian's librarian, told her. "Actually, the rod of Asclepius is the true symbol of the medical profession—it has only one snake—but the two have been confused since the fifteenth century . . . " Rosamund looked around at the glazed eyes and trailed off. "No one cares, do they?"

"I'm *fascinated*," Aaron teased her.

She pinched him, and her smile promised retribution . . . later.

"Isabelle, your marks?" Samuel prompted.

She told him, "Around each arm between my elbow and my shoulder, like decorative cuffs in glorious Technicolor, the serpents coil . . . and their eyes glitter."

"Really?" Samuel sounded more than interested. He

sounded . . . aroused, and his gaze lingered on her cat-suit. "I can't wait to see."

"They're beautiful," she said.

"And appropriate for your gift. Isn't the symmetry of the universe amazing?" Charisma sounded as pleased as if she'd directed matters herself.

Samuel got a funny expression on his face. "Isabelle, your mother is going to be mortified that everyone thinks her daughter got tattoos."

Isabelle smiled smugly. "I thought of that."

"She'll blame me," Samuel added.

"I thought of that, too."

They laughed together.

As if some anxiety tugged at him, Aleksandr glanced out the window at the New York streets, then interrupted their amusement. "You got what was promised to you, then, Isabelle. What about you, Samuel?"

"I saved her," Samuel said simply. "That's enough for me."

"But we all hope that's a onetime thing," Aleksandr said. "So the prophecy didn't work for *you?*"

Isabelle looked sharply at the young man. He seemed almost pleased at the idea.

"There's more," Samuel admitted. "I developed my gift, the mind-control thing, in my teens, and it's pretty powerful. But I've never been able to communicate with my thoughts." He rubbed the back of his neck as if it ached. "Yet now, I can."

"Early this morning, I heard your voice call me to

help Isabelle," Jacqueline said. "And instinctively, I knew what to do."

"I heard you, too," Genny said. "You called me to give back. And I did."

"Now I know that if I open myself to another mind, we can communicate." He sent his thought to Isabelle. *Can't we?*

She jumped. She stared at him. *Yes?*

He relaxed against the seat. "It's as easy as falling off a log."

"Wow." Isabelle rubbed her head. "That was weird."

"But not painful or anything, right?" Samuel asked.

"Just weird," she assured him.

"Okay, so you're talking to Isabelle," Aleksandr said impatiently. "But you guys are in love, so that probably gives you a connection. Can you talk to anyone else?"

"Yes," Samuel said. "Dina."

The name dropped like fragile glass into their midst, and exploded.

"You can communicate with Dina?" All John's attention was fixed on Samuel. "How do you know that?"

Samuel flashed him an annoyed glance.

"Okay, that was stupid," John admitted. "She's a mind speaker and she can communicate with you. Are you sure you can send back to her?"

"I can and I do, because she has answered me. Not recently. Since she left, she's been blocking me. But she's out there somewhere."

"She's alive?" Jacqueline asked.

"Oh, yes." Samuel was sure of that. "More interesting, in my opinion, is that it's a new development for her, too, to be able to hear someone's thoughts."

Charisma went, "Ooh," so she understood.

Rosamund said, "So you're saying that what has occurred with Dina is related to the Mayan prophecy that I translated, but I didn't translate the whole thing, because I broke the stone tablet over the bad guy's head—"

"I totally approved," Aaron said, "since the bad guy had been trying to kill me."

"Seemed a waste of a good stone tablet," Samuel said.

Aaron shot him an obscene gesture.

"The prophecy I read concerns only the Chosen, or so I thought," Rosamund said. "Intriguing. Is Dina one of the Chosen, or are the Others somehow part of the prophecy?"

"All seven Chosen must succeed before the next cycle of the Chosen or we lose our gifts and the Others are triumphant, able to wreak their havoc unopposed. Think of it! In less than three years, five of us have found true love and enhanced our gifts." Charisma bumped Aleksandr's arm. "We've got a little more than four years to get our kudos. Think we can do it?"

"Sure." But he didn't meet her gaze, didn't meet anyone's gaze, and he returned to the subject that held a firm grip on his attention. "Samuel, what about your mark? Did you get one?"

"I've always had one. Marks on my scalp that looked like fingerprints. My fingerprints." Samuel put his hand to the back of his head. He gave a tug. Just as it had in his adolescence when he received his mark, his dark hair came out in handfuls.

Isabelle gasped.

Aaron said, "Whoa, man."

McKenna glanced in the mirror. "Good heavens!" he said.

Samuel turned his head and showed them the bare places that extended from the previous marks—the fingerprints—down to the back of his neck. "It's no longer merely my fingerprints, right? It's the whole palm print now. My palm print?" He held up his hand so they could compare.

"That's it." Rosamund sounded as if she couldn't wait to research his mark.

"That is awesome," Aleksandr said.

Isabelle lightly touched Samuel's bare scalp. "After we give our report to Irving, I'll take you upstairs and shave the rest of your head. I love your hair"—she stroked his head—"but I want to fully see your mark. I'm sure it's magnificent!"

In a falsetto voice, Caleb crooned, "Oh, Samuel. You're so strong and brave."

Jacqueline jabbed her elbow in his gut.

Caleb doubled over.

"Pussy. Whipped," Samuel said to him.

"It's catching." Caleb recovered so suddenly, Jacqueline couldn't escape when he grabbed at her.

She snickered while he kissed her.

"You are not getting horizontal on my lap," John said sternly. "So knock it off."

Caleb and Jacqueline sat up, still smiling.

"My interest is still piqued by that building and the mural and the feathers," Rosamund said.

"Of course it is, honey." Aaron put his arm around her shoulders and grinned at her in delight.

"No, listen. It's the building, the mural, the story, the feathers." She waved her hands at them. "Don't you see?"

"No," Samuel said baldly. He never understood half of Rosamund's babbling.

"Come on, Samuel. You're being simpleminded. It's the prophecy. *My* prophecy." Jacqueline smiled triumphantly.

"The prophecy. Of course!" Caleb quoted, "'*Some must find that which is lost forever. For rising on the ashes of the Gypsy Travel Agency is a new power in a new building. Unless—*'"

Jacqueline's voice joined his.

"'*Unless this hope takes wing'*"—they both emphasized "*wing*"—"'*this power and this building will grow to reach the stars, and cast its shadow over the whole earth, and evil will rule.*"

"See? When you put the pieces together, it's easy," Rosamund said.

"I don't think it's exactly easy." John was a stickler for detail. "We don't know the location of the second feather, and the first one is entombed in concrete under that building."

"The concrete has not contained the feather Osgood entombed beneath the building," Charisma said. "It's working its way down through the concrete to the earth."

Samuel remembered the way Charisma had been feeling up the marble columns. Now he knew why. And he took the next logical leap. "But you're wrong, John. We *do* know where both feathers are, and that's a start."

Isabelle followed his thought and looked at him, wide-eyed, startled, worshipful. "Of course. That's brilliant. The second feather. That's what's in the Swiss safety-deposit box!"

Chapter 59

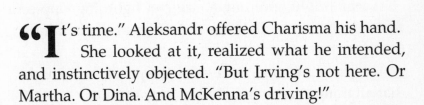

"**I**t's time." Aleksandr offered Charisma his hand.

She looked at it, realized what he intended, and instinctively objected. "But Irving's not here. Or Martha. Or Dina. And McKenna's driving!"

"Mr. Shea, Martha, Dina, and I are assistants to the Chosen Ones and their mates," McKenna sternly rebuked and, at the same time, reassured. "If it is time, then you do what you must."

"*It's time,*" Aleksandr repeated.

Charisma quieted, observed the youth she had known for almost three years, trying to see what was different about him. She hadn't been paying attention, but now that she was, he felt . . . older, the last vestiges of his youth vanquished by . . . by anxiety. Or resentment. Or emotions she had never imagined this openfaced, pleasant, well-balanced guy could experience.

"All right," she said uncertainly. She rolled her bracelets up and down her arms, trying to read her stones, to catch some hint of the discontent that plagued him. "We can always do it again later when everybody's with us."

She put one hand in Aleksandr's, another in Samuel's. Samuel took Rosamund's. Rosamund took Aaron's. And so on around the line until the Chosen and their mates were linked.

John lifted his hands, and Genny's and Jacqueline's at the same time. "Here's to you two. We are so glad you've come together at last."

Hands tightened.

Warm, bright, and hot, a sizzle of lightning rippled through the circle, lighting their nerves, their minds, their hearts.

The sensation was, as always, the proof they sought that all things had transpired as they should.

Everyone irresistibly laughed.

"Approval from above!" Aaron turned to Rosamund and kissed her.

John kissed Genny.

Caleb kissed Jacqueline.

Samuel kissed Isabelle. And kissed her. And kissed her.

Aleksandr looked at Charisma. He didn't reach for her to share a kiss; he merely shrugged.

So she shrugged in return.

Samuel and Isabelle were still crushed in each other's arms, and it was getting pretty intense.

"Hey, you two." Charisma jostled them.

Samuel cradled Isabelle to his chest. "When we get

back to the mansion, I don't care what kind of crisis occurs. I don't care if Jacqueline predicts the Cubs will win the pennant. I don't care if Davidov decides to hold a Tupperware party and invite every vampire and elf he knows. I'm taking this woman upstairs and we're going to have sex. Not in the window seat. Not in a tent. Not on a desk. In a *bed!*"

The Chosen Ones laughed.

Looking into Isabelle's eyes, he said, "I would rather be miserable with you than happy without you—but we can do better than that."

"I love you," she said. "I saw you today in Osgood's office while he dangled your deepest desires before you, and now I know . . . I can trust you. With my heart, with my soul, with my life. You make me laugh, you make me cry, but always, always you have loved me."

"This time it will be happily ever after," Samuel vowed.

Charisma had never seen anything so sweet as Isabelle dabbing at her eyes with a handkerchief—leave it to Isabelle to have a handkerchief stashed in a catsuit—while Samuel smiled all doofy at her.

Digging an elbow into his side, she murmured, "You bought her jewelry."

He glared at her meaningfully. "I will give it to her later. When we're *alone.*"

"Ah, you guys." Charisma dug her elbow into his side again. "You make me believe in fairy tales."

"Yeah. Fairy tales." Aleksandr slapped the back of

McKenna's seat. "Hey, wait! Pull over! I've got an appointment at the courthouse."

"What kind of appointment?" Aaron asked.

"I'm going to get married." He glanced at his watch. "And I'm late!"

Everyone in the car laughed.

Everyone except him . . . and Charisma.

Opening the door, he jumped in the direction of the curb.

Charisma turned and watched as he hurried toward the courthouse, toward a girl standing at the top of the stairs by the pillars, her blond hair blowing in the breeze, a welcoming smile on her face.

She was gorgeous.

Again Charisma ran her bracelets up and down her arm.

She didn't understand why, or even how, but her feel for Aleksandr was changing, twisting, fading. She couldn't reach him through the stones; she couldn't hear the earth sing his name.

She faced forward.

In all of her senses, the Aleksandr Wilder she had known faded from existence.

Read on for an excerpt of

New York Times bestseller Christina Dodd's

sparkling new historical romance

TAKEN BY THE PRINCE

Coming from Signet Select in April 2011.

England, 1837

"So, Grimsborough, this is your little bastard."

Eleven-year-old Saber stood on the thick rug in the middle of the big English room in the big English manor. He glowered at the tall, elegant older woman with the sneering mouth and the pale yellow hair. She stood in front of tall shelves filled with more books than he had ever imagined, and she dared to insult him. In his native tongue, he said, "In Moricadia, I kill people who call me names."

"What?" The woman frowned, angry and alarmed. "Grimsborough, what did he say?"

The shadowy figure behind the wide polished desk did not look up from his writing.

Five brightly dressed girls, ages five to twelve, stood lined up by the fireplace, and one of them, the skinny one in the middle, said in awestricken tones, "He's so dirty."

"And skinny," said another.

Saber shifted his attention to them. *Soft, silly English children.*

They stared at him as if he were a trained dancing bear, and when he scowled, the littlest's eyes filled with tears; she popped her thumb into her mouth and slid behind her sisters' skirts.

"Look, he's tired." The oldest spoke with authority. "He's swaying on his feet."

Then, in unison, the four biggest girls smiled at him. Kindly, sweetly, as if nothing ugly or brutal had ever touched their lives.

Saber hated them. He hated the lady, hated the tutors assembled to meet him, hated the uniformed servants standing at attention, hated them all. Most of all, he hated the evil man in charge, the man behind the desk, the one he knew must be the English viscount . . . and his father.

Again in his native tongue, Saber spat, "Stupid English wenches."

"What did he say?" Again the sneering English lady looked between Saber and the viscount. "What did he mean?"

For the first time, the man spoke. "Bring him to me."

Two of the man's absurdly dressed servants grabbed Saber's arms and propelled him around the desk to face the man.

Grimsborough gestured the candelabra closer, and when the light played across his face, Saber thought he looked like the older woman. Not in his features, which were sharp and strong, but in his attitude: in the aristocratic lift of his chin and contemptuous curve of his mouth.

The English lady drew in a sharp breath. Because although Saber didn't realize it, he and Grimsborough looked alike, also.

Grimsborough examined the skinny, filthy, tired child as if he were a bug to be squashed beneath his shoe. Then he reached out a pale, long-fingered hand and slapped Saber across the face with his open palm.

The sound of flesh against flesh echoed like a gunshot.

At the impact, Saber fell sideways.

One of the girls gasped. One whimpered.

The woman smiled in satisfaction.

And cheek stinging, Saber lunged for Grimsborough.

The servants caught him, dragged him backward.

The viscount waved him forward again.

The servants didn't let go of his arms this time.

Grimsborough brought his narrow patrician nose so close it almost touched Saber's, and his soft, deep, menacing tone raised prickles of fear up the back of Saber's spine. "Listen to me, lad. You are nothing. Nothing. My bastard by a foreigner, and if I had had another son, your filthy feet would have never sullied the floors of my home. But God in His infinite wisdom has blessed me with nothing from this marriage but *daughters*." He glanced at the girls, so colorfully clothed, so sweet in their innocence, and he despised them with his gaze.

"Five *daughters*. So you will live here until you're fit to be sent to school. And never again will you speak of your betters in that insolent manner."

Saber shook his head, shrugged, and gestured helplessly.

"Don't pretend with me, lad. Your mother spoke English. So do you."

Saber didn't quite have the guts to swear at Grimsborough, but he spoke Moricadian when he said, "English is for the ignorant."

Again Saber didn't see the blow coming, but the impact of Grimsborough's palm against his cheek snapped his head sideways so hard his neck cracked and his ear rang.

"Never let me hear you speak that barbaric tongue again." Grimsborough's voice never rose.

Saber lifted his chin. "I hate you," he said in clear, plain English.

"I hate you, *sir*," Grimsborough said with chilling precision.

Saber loathed him with his gaze.

"Say it." Grimsborough's frigid eyes held nothing: no spark, no interest . . . no soul.

Saber glanced toward the elegant, sneering woman. She stood terrified, looking at her husband the way a mouse looked at a snake.

Saber glanced at the girls. Four of them stood with their heads down. One, the middle girl, stood with her hands clasped at her skinny chest, was staring at him, and when their eyes met, her lips moved in appeal. "Please."

He looked back at Grimsborough. This man who was his father scared him—and he wasn't afraid of anything. But he couldn't give in. Not quite. Straightening his shoulders, he said, "I hate you, *sir*, but my grandfather told me I had to come to this damp, cold island and learn everything I could in your savage schools about mathematics and languages and statesmanship so I could go back to Moricadia and free my people from cruel oppression."

The oldest girl stepped forward as if he interested her. "If you want to free your people, shouldn't you learn how to fight?"

He swung a contemptuous glare on her. "I already know how to fight."

"You'll need an army. Do you know how to lead an army?" She looked him right in the eyes, not at all impressed with his bravado.

"I know how to lead," he retorted. Then grudgingly he added, "But I will have to learn military tactics."

"Then we are in accord in one thing: You will cease to be a little beast and become a civilized gentleman." Grimsborough gestured to the servants. "Take him away. Clean him. Give him over to the tutors and tell them to use any means necessary to teach him what he needs to know. I will see him here in six months. Please note: I expect an improvement, or I will be unhappy."

Saber felt the little shiver that raced through the room at the idea of incurring Grimsborough's displeasure.

Picking up his quill, Grimsborough turned back to

his desk and his papers, and ignored the servants, his wife, his daughters, and Saber.

"We will begin with a bath," Lady Grimsborough said decisively.

At the mere idea of this woman seeing his naked body, Saber struggled, lunging against the grips of the servants.

The second-to-oldest girl, a pale, soft, silly thing dressed in pink and ruffles, begged, "Mama, he's so skinny. Please, can we feed him first?"

"Do you not have a nose? Can you not smell him?" Lady Grimsborough waved her lace handkerchief before her face.

Saber had learned to fight in a hard school, and he swung on one servant's arm, knocked the feet out from beneath the other, broke free, and raced toward the door.

The head servant, the one who was dressed in black and wore white gloves, tackled him around the knees. The two footmen leaped on top of his back, crushing him into the flowered carpet.

His father's unemotional voice intoned, "A few good canings are in order. Thompson, I trust you'll handle the matter."

The man in black and white helped haul Saber to his feet, then dusted his white gloves. "Yes, my lord. Immediately, my lord."

"Clearly, the little bastard will survive without a meal for a few more hours." Lady Grimsborough eyed Saber as if he were a plucked chicken ready for the pot.

Grimsborough's cold, clear, emotionless voice intoned, "As of now, his name is Raul. Raul Lawrence."

Clearly dismayed, Lady Grimsborough asked, "Lawrence? Surely you don't intend to—"

"Adopt him? Indeed I do. He is Raul Lawrence, son of Viscount Grimsborough, and he is to become an English gentleman. Wife, please ensure that everyone in the household realizes how quickly he or she will incur my displeasure should the boy be given the wrong name or title."

Once again that shiver rattled the room. These people—the wife, the daughters, the servants—were afraid of their master.

Saber had left a land where he roamed free, and landed in a hellish nightmare of hunger, pain, cold, and fear.

And his father was the devil himself.